SAVAGE

DAN SOULE

5 FREE BOOKS

NIGHT TERRORS

SWEET DREAMS AREN'T MADE OF THESE. If you love spine chilling horror, full of monsters and great characters, then Dan Soule's two anthologies of short fiction are the perfect introduction to one of the new talents in horror. Not only that but you also get three of the all time classics to keep you up at night.

Check out what some of the top editors of short horror fiction say about Dan. Paul Guernesy of The Ghost Story, said: "Dan is a cinematic writer... he steadily builds the mood of his narrative from a whisper of uneasiness to a crescendo of full-blown cosmic horror."

While Caitlin Marceau, editor Sanitarium Magazine commented, 'His stories aren't just guaranteed to scare you, they're guaranteed to devastate you.'

Join the growing horde of insomniacs who've said goodbye to sleep and hello to NIGHT TERRORS. Free from www.dansoule.com.

For Phil.
The best uncle a boy could hope to have.

MEMENTO MORI

"By the pricking of my thumbs,
Something wicked this way comes."
— **William Shakespeare,** *Macbeth*

1

FLOTSAM

DAWN WAS STILL a distant shore for all those souls cast adrift on the night. If Annie could keep walking, keep moving, keep on hustling, she would make it through and wash up on her sofa, a fix ebbing in her bloodstream. Then all those thoughts would be kept battened down, along with the ghosts of memories which made them—for a little while longer at least.

A fix—God! Gotta get a fix. Just one more to see her through the night.

No point asking God, you silly bint. God don't live in hell. Got to get it yourself.

No money, though.

Wanna fix, gotta turn a trick. But who wants to screw a smackhead?

Annie had that itch, flushing hot and cold at the same time. How was that even bloody possible? But it always was. She felt like crap. Clammy as a pig's arse. Maybe too rough. A pale and pasty skeleton in high heels clipping down the streets of Whitechapel.

With no knickers on, she fixed the hem of her miniskirt. No need to give away the goods, such as they were, and there was definitely no point in getting arrested for indecent exposure. A night drying out in a cell was a sentence to the whip hand of withdrawal.

Perk yourself up, girl. One thing is for sure: there is always a John with an itch just as big in his trousers. So big they'll go with a skank like you. Always have, haven't they? He don't need to be Prince Charming on a white stallion. Cheese breath with a pony would do. Twenty-five nicker for a blowie. Cock and hen for a bag of brown would still leave fifteen for Henry Grime.

The pimp always took the lion's share.

Law of the jungle, innit?

It wouldn't be much of a haul for a night's work. Long gone were the times when Annie could pull in a monkey for a late shift on the kerb, and give her pimp those five-hundred pounds in tens and twenties, palmed off in a kebab shop doorway. She'd walk away with a ton if she was lucky. Just enough luck to make a living while her figure lasted.

Heroin had put paid to that, eating her away with each needle and every pull on the foil, exhaling the dragon's breath to fall into that warm blanket for the soul. Swaddled in the nether, detached from pain, where the world didn't disappear, it just didn't matter. Nothing mattered.

Until it wore off.

'Alright, darlin'?' Annie crowed at a man in a raincoat across the street, who she'd caught looking at her. He turned away horrified and hurried to join friends who poked fun at him.

'Screw you, you limp dicked wanker!'

Annie scratched the skin on her arms and then rubbed them, scanning the streets for another likely punter. There wasn't much time left. The clubs had already turned everyone out, and it was pushing three in the morning. She had to get something, or it was a ring-encrusted fist from Henry Grime on top of the torture of withdrawal for Annie.

The main roads, with their mix of Victorian yellow and red brick tenements, felt too exposed and busy for her kind of punter tonight. With a plan forming, Annie crossed the road, throwing up two fingers at a cabbie who blared his horn at her.

'Tosser!' she called back without looking.

Her ankle wobbled as she mounted the pavement, and her heel broke. 'Bollocks!' Annie staggered to a payphone nearby and took off her shoes. They were cheap, their red high-gloss shine now dull and scratched. She tossed them into the phone box and fixed her lipstick in the dirty glass door and froze.

A dog was reflected in the door. It stood staring at her. Annie didn't like dogs at the best of times, and for good reason, but this wasn't some stray mutt. It was enormous, black and sleek, with long, pointed ears and an even longer snout. It stood stone still, its gaze fixed on her.

Annie's heart galloped in her skinny chest. *Don't start hyperventilating, you silly cow!* But the terror of the old memory had gripped her. She turned like she had done as a little girl in the flat on the fourteenth floor of a tower block long since demolished. Her one-armed dolly lay on the stained carpet in front of the TV, while the programme sang that Mr Spoon was off to Button Moon. It wasn't her home. Annie had been off-loaded on a family friend while her mother worked her second job. The friend had gone out on an errand and left Annie in the living room. They had a dog kept locked in the kitchen whenever Annie was around, but the door to the kitchen lay open, and Manson the Rottweiler-Pit Bull cross was growling in the opening.

Ever since, Annie had worn long sleeves. They didn't just cover up track marks. The gouges of Manson's teeth were scored into her skin forever. Her shoulder had been weak and prone to dislocation ever since the dog rag-dolled little Annie, all while her one-armed toy gazed blankly as her best friend screamed.

All grown up now, Annie backed away from the dog. The pavement was hard under her bare feet. The dog didn't move; it watched like Manson had done—until he didn't.

Don't run, Annie told herself. Her eyes darted around the streets looking for other people. Now her plan to go somewhere quieter wasn't looking so great, but heading back towards the livelier heart of Whitechapel meant going towards the dog. Instead, she crossed back over the road. Someone was bound to be around soon.

With a slow turn of its head, the dog watched her go, its short, black hair shining in the streetlights.

Annie quickened her pace, crossed the entrance to a dark alley full of rubbish bins, and glanced behind. The dog wasn't there. She slowed and put a hand to her heart.

'You silly bint. It was a dog, was all,' she told herself. *You ever seen a dog that big, though?* Annie buried that thought as quickly as she could; she wished she had a score ready to go.

'Right, girl, you've still got work to do. One hand job, ten quid. You can get that, and we'll worry about Henry Grime tomorrow.'

Annie turned back around and crossed the entrance to the alley once more. As she did she was nearly knocked off her feet, but a strong pair of hands caught hold of her. She squawked in protest and shock, with visions of Manson, the hellhound of her nightmares. He was bounding out of the darkness to finish the job he'd started thirty-four years ago. Then, she was lifted effortlessly and placed on her feet. Manson vanished. Annie looked up into a pair of dark eyes, set in a long and handsome face. The man smiled.

'What you think you're doing? Could have killed me.' She would have sworn, but Annie, old streetwise Annie, saw that the possibility of turning a trick had fallen straight into her lap. Perhaps she could get away with rolling this guy over without even having to put a hand in his trousers, or her mouth somewhere else.

'You wouldn't be able to help out a poor girl with her taxi fare, would you? I broke me shoes, and some bugger nicked me purse in the *Good Samaritan*. Ironic that, innit?' Annie tugged at her top as if she was cold and gave her best demure smile, hiding her fag-stained teeth.

The man returned the smile and gave an ambiguous tilt of his head.

'I'll do anything,' Annie offered, feigning shy eyes, and touched the man's arm.

He was alright looking, this one. A bit oddly dressed, but he had a handlebar moustache that was quite fetching. Those hipster wankers usually dressed like they were either tramps or living in the wrong century. This one was the latter breed of tosspot. He even had a bowler hat to go with his brown, checkered waistcoat, and a bow tie, of all things. Annie had seen a gold chain of his pocket watch too; a side plan to pick his pocket was already forming. She could pawn the timepiece tomorrow, have enough for Henry Grime—*the cruel bastard* —and some left over.

The man put a hand on top of hers and turned towards the alley. 'Gosh! Your hands are freezing. I'll have to warm them up a bit for you.' He patted her hand gently. There was the risk he was Old Bill, but Annie didn't think so. Pigs always wanted to bring up money to get you on solicitation. Plus, they never dressed so dapperly. He clearly knew this pantomime and how to play his part.

They strolled by a pair of large, dumpster-style bins for the businesses either side of the alley. A dark little corner, hidden from the eyes of the world. Annie felt a small thrill of excitement. She'd need him close and distracted to get that watch.

'That taxi fare, I reckon fifty would do it. It's a long way home, but I'll let you take me all the way, love.'

The light from the end of the alley glowed like the fires from a distant shore. They stopped, and Annie stepped in something wet and slimy, but she wasn't about to break character. That would risk scaring him off.

He faced her, looking down into the eyes of a little girl playing with her dolly.

'You don't say much, do you, darling?'

He smiled.

Annie smiled back, gazing into those black eyes. The corners of her mouth faltered. Her heart raced. There was something about those eyes. Johns had beaten Annie before. It was an occupational hazard. There was a look in violent men's eyes she'd come to recognise and know. This was different. Not human. Manson had that look. An empty void, detached from all other emotions.

Except hate.

Annie could see Manson stood at the kitchen door, his lips pulling back over his gums, exposing rows of pointed teeth. Saliva dripped from his muzzle, and a growl rumbled in his powerful chest like thunder from a coming storm out at sea.

Annie would have screamed. She would have wailed into the night like a child being rag-dolled by a monster. But she couldn't. Her mouth opened to try, but a gash in her throat from left to right opened even wider than her jaw, and only blood came out of her throat.

There was more pain, much more. There was blood too, so much blood. It was the end of Annie, but other things were only just beginning.

2

PAPERBOY

DYLAN SAVAGE'S five a.m. alarm clock marked the changing of the guard between two worlds. He dragged himself out of bed, like he had to every morning, and lifted his bike from the hall while his mum slept. At the front door, he turned the light on and off, flashing once, twice, three times. Because the lift was out of order again, he trudged down twelve flights of stairs, counting each step. Twelve to each mid-landing; twenty-four per storey; two hundred and eighty-eight to the ground. Within their numbers were patterns, division and multiplication. They were always the same. Regular, consistent, reliable.

Mr Chatterjee's shop was across from the Renfield tower block that squatted on the edge of the invisible border between Whitechapel and Spitalfields, in the East End of London. A lifeless bing-bong of the electronic bell announced Dylan's entrance.

'Extra papers for you today. Gallows Court, Botham Street, and Victoria Close.' Mr Chatterjee made no mention of extra money. 'Chop, chop, Dylan. People want papers with their breakfast.'

Dylan hauled the heavy satchel over his head, his heart already racing. Gallows Court and Botham Street both ventured into territory any boy from Renfield Tower knew was out of bounds. Eyes watched those streets, but maybe it was early enough to go unseen.

With his hood up, Dylan pushed off, hoping the chain wouldn't come off and the brakes wouldn't fail. He pumped the pedals, squinting against the blade of sun slicing around the side of the tower block. Long shadows staggered across the road, like vagrant giants listing towards their favourite doorways to sleep off the night before. The satchel bit into Dylan's shoulder. The extra papers weren't the worst of it, because they weren't the only thing Dylan had no choice in delivering.

He pushed a soap star's adultery, along with countless deaths in a refugee camp and the sacking of a Premiership football manager, through a couple of doors. Further down the street, a young man, wearing a body warmer over a hooded sweatshirt, crossed the road and leaned against a bus shelter.

Dylan stood on his pedals and looked behind before swerving over the road, the frame of his bike groaning. The man at the bus stop flicked his thumb over the screen of his phone without looking up. As the bike drew near, the man put the phone away, stuffing both hands into his pockets.

Dylan squeezed the brakes and nothing happened. He dropped back quickly to his seat and jammed his heels into the road. The front tyre hit the kerb, jolting him from his perch, and the crossbar hit him in the balls as the satchel spun from his side and pulled him off balance. He came to a clattering halt, and the young man with his hands in his pockets hopped out of the way.

'Nice one, knob head.'

'Sorry,' Dylan said, trying not to grimace at the pain in his crotch. 'The brakes failed.'

'Get a new bike, then.'

'Can't afford it.'

The young man raised an eyebrow, as though Dylan had said something stupid. He shook off the situation and leaned against the bus stop again, looking at his phone as he checked the street out of the corner of his eye.

'Say something to me, make like we're having a conversation.'

'Like what?'

'Anything, you prick, or it'll look suspicious.' The young man put his hands into the pockets of his body warmer again.

Dylan fumbled. 'Nice weather.'

The man sucked his teeth disapprovingly, pulling a hand from his pocket and offering his fist. Dylan bumped it with his own. As they leaned in to touch shoulders in a half-hug, the man opened his hand, and Dylan took the packet containing even smaller bags of powder and pills. The sleight of hand was complete as the man walked away, and Dylan slipped the packet into his satchel. That was it, until the end of his round when Dylan would slide the packet into the middle of the last paper for delivery on his route and post it through the letterbox.

The rest of Dylan's round went as normal until he approached the Duppy Crew's territory, which started at the broken white line running down the middle of the south side road of Gallows Court. Gallows Court ringed an open patch of grass, sprinkled with graffitied benches and a vandalised playpark at the north end. Five-storey, nineteen-sixties apartment blocks surrounded the green. Their brutalist vision of a better London built out of the rubble of the Blitz had long since degenerated into a grubby cataract.

Dylan came to a stop using his heels. A road cleaner trundled along, its circular brushes shovelling the detritus from the concrete into its insatiable maw, like a bottom feeding monster cleaning up after the higher life forms of the underworld slumbered in their caves. The next paper was for number twenty-five, one of the new ones on his round. The south side of Gallows Court was the only side with a parade of shops. They were built around the same time as the apartment blocks but only three storeys high, with shops underneath and accommodation on top.

Dylan counted up from twenty, hit twenty-four, and then jumped to twenty-six and stopped. He tried again and the same thing happened, so he checked the number on the paper. Twenty-five and then the customer's surname, Vieil. The paper was a copy of *The Times*, which was unusual for Dylan's round. He delivered red top tabloids, weekly glossy doses of gossip, and the occasional pornographic magazine covered in a plastic modesty bag, for people too old to understand how to get unlimited free pornography on their phone.

He was hanging around for too long, and Dylan started to feel eyes on him. The road cleaner hummed in the distance. A door slammed from somewhere over the other side of the park. Dylan looked at the number on the paper, fixing it in his mind. It had to be there. Mr Chatterjee would dock his wages if he missed one. When Dylan looked up, he found the nail bar at number twenty-three, scanned to the charity shop at twenty-four and then moved slowly to the fried chicken bar at... Dylan moved back.

There was a three-storey, red brick house between the fried chicken bar and the charity shop. He had walked and ridden down the safe side of Gallows Court countless times but never noticed the old house. It was boarded up, with plants growing from the gutters and cracks between the bricks. Up a short flight of stone steps, paint flaked from the black front door which bore a rusted number twenty-five. The house was utterly out of place, more akin to the Victorian terraces and tenements that still stood in the heart of Whitechapel, most of which were now bars and restaurants. They serviced tourists and the constant diasporic turnover of people that moved through the city like blood through veins, constantly recycled and renewed but always there.

Dylan hurried over the street. His chain slipped halfway across. With a hasty backpedal, he saved the chain, caught the tension, and hopped over the kerb to the rusted iron railings. Folding the paper in thirds, Dylan stood before the rotting house. There didn't appear to be any signs of life. Perhaps Mr Chatterjee was mistaken, but the paper clearly had the house number at the top.

Something about number 25 Gallows Court made Dylan nervous. He wanted to run, and yet his feet wouldn't move away. One, two, three, four, five, six, seven. Dylan touched his thumb to the tip of each of his fingers, down and back again. Then he repeated it. Seven, it was a good number. A prime. It had a square root of 2.645751. The next prime was eleven. The previous prime was five. Seven had its exact place. It was always the same. You knew where you were with seven.

Dylan's thumb kept tapping up and down the tips of his fingers until he'd done it seven times. Seven sevens are forty-nine, always have been, always will be. The ritual was complete. There was no going back.

Dylan mounted the first step. The world around him, the omnipresent background hum and clank of the city, fell away. By the second step, his heart pounded in his ears—gugung... gugung... gugung. A gutter creaked overhead. At the top of the stairs, the plants twisting from the crevices whispered inaudibly in a breeze fetid with damp and mould. Scales of paint arched their brittle backs, peeling themselves from the sleeping dragon's back.

The newspaper was crumpling in Dylan's grip, and he quickly flattened it out. *It's just a house, that's all. Post the paper and get moving.* But he was paralysed on that top step, unable to move his feet and, worse, his fingers.

One. The word distorted and echoed in his mind. *Two.* The mental sound of the number bounced back in on itself. *Three.* Dylan ignored the contortions of fear. He knew how to do that. *Four.* The numbers came clearer now, quickly following each other and rooting him. *Seven.* Dylan could move.

Stop being stupid, he told himself and slid his fingers in the brass letterbox. It was stiff with age, and Dylan had to force it up. His fingers tingled; he told himself there were no monsters about to pull off his hand. He pushed the newspaper through until it slapped on the floor inside.

Dylan turned his back on number twenty-five. It was over. The place was merely a creepy old house. It was probably a mistake anyway. What Dylan needed to do was get the hell out of Gallows Court and then Botham Street as quickly as possible. This new problem occupied his thoughts as he readied to descend the stairs. As such, Dylan was distracted when the door behind him shook with the force of an enormous dog clattering against it from inside. Missing his first footing, Dylan tumbled down the steps, landing in a heap on the pavement as the dog barked ferociously and jumped at the door again.

Dylan hauled himself up, leaping on his bike, and pedalled until the barks were no more. Unfortunately for Dylan, the worst of his paper round wasn't yet over.

3

ECHOES

Detective Sergeant Kenny Stokes pulled on a pair of blue latex gloves to complete the fetching forensics ensemble of white, disposable coveralls and boot coverings. He looked back down the street towards the phone box and closed his eyes to concentrate.

'Tosser!' Kenny mouthed. His index and middle fingers on his right hand twitched briefly into a V. The clip of high heels. People horsing around faded into the distance. A sharp pain in Kenny's ankle, like he'd gone over on it, and yet he stood stone still. 'Bollocks!' he whispered, and then it started to come fast. There was a flash of something red—the shoes maybe—and a pang of fear. It tasted old and familiar; a mouldering damp spotting the walls black. Kenny glimpsed a gold pocket watch and desired to take it, but it quickly evaporated. There was nothing else he could glean; the echoes, or whatever they were, had dissipated.

The uniformed officer at the entrance to the alley was giving Kenny an odd look while holding up the police tape. Kenny ducked under and trod carefully into the heart of the crime scene. He could feel it already, although "feel" didn't quite capture the visceral and personal nature of the experience. The tastes and smells, fragments of sounds like a bad line on a telephone, and worst, the echoes of emotions from both sides. They were much stronger here and recent,

13

so recent the impression retained a pure and bitter acidity that practically sizzled.

Kenny's gift was equally a curse, but it shot him up the ranks. Everyone else knew Kenny's gut feelings tended to pan out. No one questioned the results. He'd never got lazy with it, though. Like forensics, it was a tool that pointed him in the right direction, saved time by narrowing an investigation's focus. Then the evidence would follow. There were downsides too, of course, so *many* downsides.

Kenny closed his eyes again and breathed in slowly, tuning out the background echoes of London's emotional past, which was akin to trying to turn the volume down on an orchestra tuning itself. He could never get rid of it entirely. It was always there, making his nights restless with fitful sleep, but he could dampen it with concentration.

Kenny focused. His skin itched, and he felt a powerful craving. There was nothing clear at the head of the alley. Walking slowly, he checked the ground and walls. The alley was overlooked by bricked up windows, and the end was blocked with the back of another building. There was no CCTV in the alley, just the bins serving the businesses facing the main street. There was a good chance something was picked up by a camera out on the road, but the alley was a dead end in more ways than one.

The body was found by the deputy-manager of the artisan sandwich shop which flanked the alley. She'd nipped out for a fag after getting the bread in the oven. That was at five-fifteen. It was six-thirty now. Forensics were on their way, and the uniformed patrol officers had cordoned off the alley and the main street for fifty yards either side of the crime scene. A pair of red shoes, possibly the victim's, had already been discovered in a phone box by the observant uniformed bobby who'd held the tape up for Kenny.

Reaching the bins, Kenny halted. A bare foot stuck out. Its sole was filthy, which probably explained the red shoes. One of the heels had been broken. She likely threw them off to walk more easily. Kenny remembered the pain in his ankle. She was walking away from the busy pubs, clubs, and fast food takeaways looking for something. A fix? A taxi? A boyfriend? A punter? That last idea stood out in bold in his mind. There was no evidence yet that she, whomever she was, was a working girl, but time would tell.

A step closer and the edge of a small crimson lake came into view. The memory of a book rose up from the depths of his subconscious. It was the lake in hell from Clive Barker's *The Scarlet Gospels*. Misha had got him it at Christmas, knowing his love for horror novels. He'd read them at night when he couldn't sleep. He read a lot. Harry D'Amour's motley crew of characters had to cross the lake to reach Lucifer's cathedral. Crossing lakes in hell was never an easy thing.

Kenny checked the ground at his feet for clues. There was nothing for the naked eye. He moved another step closer, and a bloodstained hand lay on the cobblestones. This was like pulling off a Band-Aid slowly, ripping the hairs out individually by the roots. Kenny winced. The emotional reverberation of the murder suddenly squealed like feedback from a PA system at a gig. He put a finger in one ear, listening, feeling. These things couldn't be rushed. But the deputy-manager's splatter of vomit signalled it was time for the big reveal.

'You don't say much, do you, love?' Kenny whispered. She had a cockney accent, not the new pan-urban accent the children of the internet had developed. She was older, then, late thirties or more.

Kenny saw a smile. No, not a smile. *A dog? Teeth? No—no, that's not right.*

As a murder squad detective, Kenny had seen plenty of dead bodies. His trepidation, however, came from more than a caution not to disturb the forensic integrity of the scene. In part, it was that the deputy-manager dry heaved when he asked what she saw. She'd had nothing left to bring up but bile. Her face was as grey and clammy as discarded fish skin at Billingsgate Market. Her eyes reflected the nightmare of what she'd seen. There was something else too.

He took the final step. The feedback peaked into a piercing psychic scream. In a second, he took in the scene, his teeth clenching, fighting the urge to look away. He breathed in short, fast breaths through his nose. The need to open his mouth made Kenny bring his sleeve to his face. Better to try and mute the smell than take in a mouthful and taste it. He looked away briefly before forcing his gaze back to the mutilated body. The whistling feedback continued screaming in his head.

A woman. Hair dyed blonde, her roots a darker brunette with greys appearing. A wide-eyed stare was fixed on her upturned face. Kenny had seen something of that terror in the deputy-manager. Fear was a contagious thing.

There were several deep cuts to her face, committed ante or peri-mortem. Kenny couldn't make out any defensive wounds to her arms, but one was bent under her body. Her legs were splayed, and her garments had been cut up the middle to expose her torso. The killer had wanted access. It wasn't only about killing her. The gory cavity, flayed opened from her sternum to her anus, presented Kenny with a confusing tangle of viscera, some of which had been pulled out and placed on her right shoulder. He'd have to wait for the autopsy and crime scene photographs to tell him specifics.

Kenny saw a one-armed dolly in his mind, accompanied by a childlike feeling of helpless terror, as though the bottom had fallen out of his stomach and he would fall forever because there was no one there to catch him. The image didn't tally with the scene. It was older, like a psychic fingerprint, maybe of the victim, maybe the killer.

The massive wound in the body initially distracted Kenny from what he now realised was probably the killing blow. A deep lacera-tion ran across her throat. The perpetrator would have been covered in blood as her heart pumped out the last of her life through her neck. Kenny doubted she would have known anything about what happened after that. Or was that hope rather than doubt?

It was hope. He felt the burning of exposed nerve endings in his stomach and the tugging as the dirty strip of London sky overhead was swallowed by a massive dog lunging and closing its jaws over the light of her life.

'He gets no points for originality.'

Kenny gave a start. 'Christ, Roj! You're a ninja?'

Detective Constable Rojish Dabral smiled sheepishly. 'Sorry, boss. It's the new parent soft-shoe shuffle. You were miles away. I got here as quick as I could. Baby was up all night again.'

'Don't worry about it. What were you saying?' Kenny tipped his head towards the victim's body.

'I said, it's not very original, is it?'

Kenny knitted his eyebrows together and scanned the scene for what he was missing. There was something familiar about it, but what was it? 'You're going to have to help me out, Roj.'

'Looks like whoever did it is a big time Jack the Ripper groupie.'

4

ENEMY TERRITORY

THERE WAS PROBABLY nothing left of that newspaper except shreds of slobber-drenched confetti. Still, Dylan had done his job. It wasn't his fault the psycho living in that squat on Gallows Court kept a rabid monster. He wouldn't be the first thug with an over-muscled dog, kept hungry and beaten mean as hell.

Botham Street was nearly done with. Four more papers in his bag after that. The last of which must include his special delivery or Henry Grime would beat the living piss out of Dylan, or worse, his mum. At least the last paper was back on safer territory, in the Blud's turf.

Dylan mounted up and kicked down on the pedal. The chain slipped off, and the bike free wheeled until Dylan put his feet down cursing. He crouched to inspect the problem. Oil coated his fingers as the chain refused to take the gear's teeth. Mr Chatterjee would kill him if the customers complained about having dirty paw prints all over their newspapers. With a crank on the pedal, like he was starting a biplane, the chain took the gear and was closely followed by a shout.

'Oi! You lost, blud?'

They were running across the street, three of them with their hoods up—around the same age as Dylan. *Three, a prime number. The next prime is five.* There was no lower prime. They were only divisible by one and themselves. Three flashes of the lightswitch. Ready, steady, you can go, Dylan. Go. Go. Go.

A bottle of coke flew over Dylan's head, spraying him with brown liquid as he pumped the pedals. They were already giving up on their chase as Dylan pulled away, smirking in relief.

The chain came off and so did Dylan's smirk. He looked behind with desperate hope they had turned away and hadn't seen. But as he backpedaled trying to catch the chain, one of the boys pointed, and all three of them started to sprint. Dylan did the calculation of how long he needed to fix the problem and concluded the sum by throwing the bike down the pavement to create a pathetic obstacle, and he ran.

'That's it. Run, blud. We're gonna ghost you,' one of the boys shouted after hurdling Dylan's bike.

Botham Street was a long road of terraced houses, with few chances to cut out. Few but not zero. Dylan spotted the entrance to an alley, turned hard right and cut over the road. A car screeched to stop inches from him. Dylan paled but didn't have time to wonder at the close shave with death, as the Reaper appeared to have a second cut-throat razor meant for Dylan in the shape of three hooded youths from the Duppy Crew. He darted into the alley, bouncing off one side to the other.

The boys were closing. Dylan hit the back wall and pulled himself up onto the top. The satchel hung down around his neck. The first boy got to him and grabbed Dylan's leg. Dylan kicked free, and the boy seized the delivery bag, nearly hauling Dylan off the wall, but he slipped free. The other two boys were catching up, and Dylan jumped down into a garden.

A pair of arms and a hooded head appeared over the top of the wall, and Dylan didn't wait. The papers were lost. The drugs were lost. Better not make it three with his life too.

As Dylan hit the fence on the other side of the garden, only two hoods followed. Three, only divisible by itself and one. Dylan was the one, and they had split up. They'd try and cut him off at Coffin Street.

Dylan took three more fences, pulling away. He'd always been fast with numbers and fast on his feet. In the next garden, a geriatric Jamaican lady was hanging up her washing. She squawked when Dylan whipped through her sheets and into her back door. A small dog barked at him in the galley kitchen, yapping at his heels through the front room and stood barking at the front door as Dylan kept running.

A bus headed towards him, and a supermarket delivery truck rolled the other direction. Dylan cut between them as the two boys emerged from the house. The old lady beat at them with a floral patterned cushion. They looked for Dylan along the row of shops on the other side of the street, but he had vanished like their crew's name, Duppy, a ghost.

Dylan held his breath. He heard them talking. One even walked down the alley. The footsteps stopped next to the commercial refuse bins. The lid opened and closed, and the boys left. Dylan waited fully fifteen minutes before he climbed out of the bin, covered in waste food and God knows what else.

He stunk and something slimy trickled between his shoulder blades. No bike, no papers, and no drugs. *At least you're alive*, he thought. *Until Henry Grime catches up with you.* Dylan checked his watch and sighed. On top of everything, he was going to be late for school if he didn't hurry.

5

INDEBTED

DYLAN RAN ALL the way back, only relaxing when he got on home turf and counted every step back up the twelve flights to his flat. He opened the door, sweaty and rank with rubbish, and clicked the light switch on and off three times. A shower was a necessity, though it would make him even later for school. His best friend Samuel had probably been and gone, so he'd face detention by himself. Maybe it wouldn't be too bad? Detention would give him some more time. *Stay of execution, more like.*

'All right, bruv?'

Dylan's blood ran cold.

Henry Grime was sitting on the sofa in the living room, reclining with his legs splayed, arms draped along the seat's back and behind the head of a scared looking boy in his school uniform, clutching a rolled up comic book. Dylan only nodded in response to the question.

Henry Grime ran his tongue over gold teeth, took a spliff from his inside pocket and sparked it up. Through a plume of thick, pungent smoke he said, 'Something you want to tell me?' And he picked a flake of tobacco from the tip of his tongue and flicked it away.

News travelled faster than Dylan could run. Eyes fixed on the floor at his feet, Dylan shrugged and mumbled, 'I got jumped by Duppies.'

Grime pulled slowly on the joint. His cheeks hollowed skeletally as the weed flared red hot. He looked Dylan up and down, and then he took in the schoolboy on the sofa and blew the smoke over Samuel, making him cough. 'Speak up, little bruv. I can't hear you.'

Dylan cleared his throat and shifted nervously. 'Mr Chatterjee added extra roads to my paper round. I had to go onto their patch.'

'And?' Grime prompted.

'They took my bike and...' Dylan didn't want to say it, and with a hand behind his leg, he counted fingertips.

Henry Grime rose from the sofa and pinched off the hot embers at the tip of the spliff, grinding them between his thumb and index finger. 'And what, little bruv?' Henry stood over Dylan glaring down.

'And they took the delivery,' Dylan whispered.

Henry Grime cuffed Dylan's neck hard and grabbed hold, pulling him close. 'I must be going deaf, little bruv. I thought I heard you say you lost my gear.'

Dylan cried out as the vice of Henry Grime's hand tightened.

Samuel got up. 'Leave him alone.'

Grime ignored him, as Dylan shrank in on himself.

'Did you put up a fight?' Grime snarled.

'There was three of them. I ran. Please, it hurts.'

'This ain't pain, Little Dee. This is a lesson. Are you learning?'

'Yes,' Dylan cried.

Grime's gold teeth flashed. 'What you learning, little man?'

'It hurts, please.' Dylan collapsed to his knees. Frozen to the spot, Samuel wrung the comic book between his fists.

'Nah, Dee. That ain't it. You gotta fight back or the world is going to eat you alive.' Grime let Dylan go. Dylan fell to the floor, and Samuel went to him, but Dylan shrugged him off.

'You owe me, Little Dee, big time. Understand? Good. Get up. Look at me, bruv. Look me in the eye like a bad man.'

Henry Grime sucked his teeth in disapproval. 'You carry a shank? No? Seems you're marked, Little Dee. Best take this one.' Henry Grime handed Dylan a switchblade. 'Call it a loan.' He walked to the hall and paused in the doorway. 'Loans gotta be paid back. Remember that. Oh, and get a shower. You stink, bruv.'

The front door slammed behind Grime, and his shadow passed across the living room curtains.

Dylan stared at the knife in his hand. It had a weight beyond its size, a kind of dark magnetism that pulled and pushed at the same time.

'What you going to do with it?' Samuel said.

'Dunno.'

'We should tell my mum.'

'Are you mental? She hates me.'

Samuel looked hurt. 'She doesn't hate you. She's just a bit intense, you know? She sees what's going on around here.'

Dylan shook his head. 'I need a shower. You should go without me. No point us both being late.'

Dylan went to his room and hid the knife in his sock drawer. He checked his mum. She was a crumpled lump of bedclothes. An almost empty bottle of vodka sat on the bedside table, with a scattering of pills around its base. A used condom drooped over the side of a waste bin. Dylan closed her bedroom door quietly and went to the bathroom.

He pulled the light on by the string dangling from the ceiling. Three times the room flashed in and out of existence before it was okay to proceed. Dylan peeled off his clothes and turned on the shower. Only a weak trickle came out, and after a minute it remained cold. He got under it anyway, attempting to get wet and wash away the morning, but try as he might, it wasn't possible. He gave up and towelled himself off, shivering on the bath mat, and sprayed himself with deodorant until he coughed on the sweet miasma clouding the tiny room.

When he emerged from his bedroom fixing the tie of his school uniform, Samuel was waiting for him in the hall.

'I thought I said leave me.'

Samuel had a face as round as his belly and dark brown eyes that creased into slits when he smiled, like now. 'I never get detention. It might be fun.'

Dylan opened the front door. 'Your mum is going to hate me even more.'

'Just ask her to forgive you. She has to.' Samuel patted his friend on the back, the slight Nigerian accent of his parents colouring his otherwise London accent.

'That's hilarious.' Dylan fought the urge to touch the lightswitch and closed the door behind them.

They walked along the balcony running in front of the flats. The sun was up, but dirty drifts of clouds were blotting it out. Below, people moved around like ants.

At the top of the stairs, Samuel stopped. Dylan halted a few steps down, pausing his mental count, and looked at his friend. 'What's up?'

'What you going to do?' Samuel said, his bright face now gazing down like a serious chubby seraphim.

'About what?'

'Come on, Dylan. The knife, the drugs, Henry Grime.'

Thoughts darted through Dylan's mind. 'I don't know. What can I do?'

'What about your mum?'

The look on Dylan's face said it all.

'Okay, maybe not your mum. I still think my mum would help, or what about a teacher?'

'I ain't a snitch.'

'That's not snitching. It's not fair. You never asked to deal drugs.'

'Shut up, bruv, or someone will hear you. And what's fair got to do with anything?' There was bitterness in his voice, as Dylan turned back to the stairwell. 'No one can help me. Grime said it: I've got to stick up for myself.'

Dylan wasn't in the mood for listening. He disappeared around the turn in the stairwell, and Samuel hurried after him.

'But you're just a kid.'

6

ALIBI

DETECTIVE SERGEANT KENNY STOKES took a sip of tepid coffee and winced. The mug had gone cold as he sat at his desk clicking between web pages. With a few targeted internet searches, and a look at the police file still available online, he caught himself up with the particulars of the 1888 Whitechapel Ripper murders, focusing on the so called "canonical five" victims: Mary Ann Nichols, Annie Chapman, Elizabeth Stride, Catherine Eddowes, and Mary Jane Kelly. Kenny scribbled notes on his pocketbook as he scrolled through the macabre details.

He discovered there were in fact eleven murders between 3rd April 1888 to 13th February 1891 that fell under the umbrella of the police investigation. However, the canonical five were considered the most likely to be linked and committed by a single unidentified male perpetrator between 31st August and 9th November 1888.

What separated these five victims from the others was the modus operandi of the killer. Deep cuts to the throats, facial lacerations, and the removal and deliberate arrangement of internal organs. This element had led some to draw the conclusion that Jack the Ripper, so named after a probable hoax letter from an enterprising journalist, had anatomical knowledge either of a surgeon or a butcher.

Kenny could see the logic of grouping the canonical five together.

The murders prior and after the five involved stabbing but not abdominal mutilations and organ removal. The first victim, Mary Ann Nichols, worked as a domestic servant and prostitute. She was still warm when two men found her in the entrance to a stable in Buck's Row, since renamed as Durward Street. One of the men thought she may even have been still alive. She had cuts to either side of her face, just like Annie. Kenny scribbled the similarities in his notebook.

And just like Annie from the present day, the first victim, Mary Ann Nichols, also had her throat cut back to the vertebral column. However, it wasn't possible to tell if Annie's vagina had been stabbed like Mary's because there was nothing of it left to find. This made Annie much closer to the second victim and her namesake, Annie Chapman, and the fourth and fifth victims, Catherine Eddowes and Mary Jane Kelly. All these poor women had parts or all of their uterus removed, along with kidneys, or, in the case of Mary Jane Kelly, her heart. All the women were made to "wear" their internal organs: the killer arranged their entrails over their shoulders. Mary Jane Kelly's murder took place in a more secluded location, and the display was far more elaborate, the mutilation even more gruesome.

The third victim, Elizabeth Stride, was the only one of the five that didn't fit the modus operandi entirely. However, her throat had been cut in the same manner. Her murder occuring less than three-quarters of an hour before Catherine Eddowes and led most to believe the Ripper had been interrupted and forced to find another victim to satiate his need. Kenny tended to agree with this.

So what did it all mean? Kenny rubbed his eyes and clicked back to the crime scene photos of Annie. Roj was right. It looked alarmingly similar to the contemporary police drawing of Catherine Eddowes' body. A picture that was widely available on the internet. The possibility of a copycat was on the table. Was it a one-off? For now, yes. But motive? Now there was a question. That was *always* the question, even if the answer was often as familiar as jealousy. First move was to check the spouse, boyfriend or sexual partners, along with the family. The thing was, Annie Drew—her ID was in her purse recovered at the scene—didn't have any family. Another tragic story.

A long charge sheet listing possession, affray, resisting arrest, shoplifting and numerous arrests for solicitation going back well over two decades. Kenny's hunch had been right: she was a working girl.

Without close family, they'd moved on to the next best thing. Annie was too far gone to be an escort, holed up in an Airbnb for a pop-up brothel-cum-webcam studio. She was an old-fashioned street walker. A monkey with an organ grinder. The euphemism was apt, if in poor taste.

As if on cue, Detective Dabral appeared at the double doors of their open plan office. 'Boss, the organ grinder is here to see you.'

Kenny locked his computer terminal and grabbed a file on his desk, wondering if that phrase had bounced out of the ether from Roj or if it was one of life's miniscule synchronicities. A random pattern in the chaos. Perhaps there was no difference.

HENRY GRIME LOOKED DISMISSIVELY at the two police officers across from him in the interview suite, saying something only when his surprisingly expensive solicitor leaned in to mutter in his ear. This mostly consisted of 'no comment' or simple 'yes/nos' confirming basic information such as address and name.

'Could you tell us your whereabouts last night between the hours of two and four in the morning?' Roj asked.

The solicitor leaned in. Henry sniffed. 'Home.'

The solicitor got there before Roj or Kenny could follow up. 'My client will happily supply a list of witnesses to corroborate his alibi.'

'A list? You weren't asleep then?' Kenny asked.

'Detective, my client has attended this interview willingly. He is fully cooperating with whatever your investigation is. But I must insist that you get to the point and inform my client what exactly it is you want help with.'

'At this time, we're not at—' Roj stopped as Kenny picked up the file.

Grime was hiding something, but Kenny didn't need his gift to know that. 'Do you own a dog?'

Roj struggled to suppress his look of surprise.

'Really, Detective, does this pertain to the matter at hand?' The solicitor raised an eyebrow.

Kenny gave a small shrug. 'We can ask around and find out.'

'Nah, I don't have a dog. Now can we get on with this?' Henry Grime said, folding his arms.

Strange, but he's telling the truth, Kenny thought and spun the folder around to face Grime and opened it.

'Detective Sergeant Stokes, I must protest.'

'Why?' Roj said.

'Do you recognise her?' Kenny tapped the gruesome photograph, in all its high definition glory.

Grime swallowed and the muscles in his jaw rippled before he looked calmly into Kenny's eyes. 'Not much to recognise, is there?'

Kenny felt no flicker of recognition at the photos. Grime didn't do it. 'It's Annie Drew.'

Grime's nostrils flared, and he looked back to the photograph.

'Our information leads us to believe you knew this woman.' Roj said.

The solicitor whispered in Grime's ear again, to which Grime cast an annoyed glance. 'I knew Annie. She's an old smackhead and prozzie in our Ends.'

'You know a lot of addicts and prostitutes?' Roj asked.

Grime sneered. 'I live in Whitechapel. What do you think?'

Kenny leaned forward on an elbow. 'I think you've done time for dealing heroin and cocaine, and you have several charges for affray and assault, one of which involved Annie Drew on the 10th December 2018.'

'My client finished serving his sentence more than six years ago and is now a law-abiding citizen. No conviction or penalty ever resulted from any charges of affray or assault, which, in addition to this interview, is starting to look more and more like police harassment,' the solicitor said. Kenny noted the clipped private school accent.

'Harassment?' Kenny mused. 'We're just trying to rule your client out of a murder investigation. It appears he knew the victim. You've already told us he has an alibi, and we'll confirm that. Therefore, any information you can give us, Henry, will help us catch whoever did this.'

Roj gave an extra prod at the suspect. 'Do you think it is worth making a call to vice, boss? I heard there's a turf war going on between the Blud and the Duppy Crews.'

'This interview is over.' The solicitor began putting his notepad and pen away. 'My client will answer no more questions at this time, unless you intend to caution him? Well? No? I thought not. Mr Grime, shall we?' The solicitor stood and gestured for Henry to go first.

Henry got up and had a final look at the picture on the desk before sauntering out of the interview suite with his lawyer in tow.

Roj turned off the tape recorder. 'What do you think?'

Kenny closed the folder and spun it back towards himself. 'I think he's telling the truth. Let's get moving on the alibi and start going through the CCTV from the street beyond the alley.'

The two detectives got up to leave, and at the door Roj said, 'Boss, what was that thing about a dog? Did you hear something from forensics?'

Huge jaws, frothing with drool, snapped in Kenny's mind followed by the image of a one-arm dolly. 'Nah, I was just messing with him. Throwing a curveball. It's nothing.'

7

PI

PAROLE from the school day loomed tantalisingly close. The class were restless for the bell, fidgeting in their seats, surreptitiously putting away pens and pencils.

'No tidying away until the bell. You know the rules,' Misha Stokes said sternly, but not without kindness.

The tidying desisted.

'And Michael Groves, you'll have to wait until after our class to talk to Bobby Smith. Now, I've your papers from last week's test to give back to you.'

A unified groan went up.

'I know. What possible use could mathematics be in a world full of computers and unfathomable amounts of data?' Misha said, walking up and down the lines of desks, handing back the students' papers.

'And remember, if you are disappointed with your mark, it is not a failure. What is it?'

A feeble response came from a few of them. 'Data.'

'What? I can't hear you, class 9b. What is it?'

'Data.' Most of them managed a droning chorus.

'That's right. And what do we do with data?' Misha said in an impersonation of the world's most affable drill sergeant.

'Learn from it,' they said, with the tiniest note of enthusiasm.

'Good job,' Misha said in the ear of Kylie Johnston, a shy girl with acne and a squint sat in the middle of the class. To the whole room she said, 'That's right. There are no failures in our class. What are they?'

'Opportunities.' It wasn't a Baptist revival or *Henry V*'s St Crispin's Day's speech, but in the bubble of her class, Misha carefully fanned the dying embers of confidence in every child. They believed, if only for fifty minutes, that they could do better, that they could be better. She saw those tender flames in the eyes of every pupil struggling to pass. It was what she taught for. They believed, and where they believed in themselves there was hope, and where there was hope there was a child prepared to try tomorrow, no matter what the obstacles.

'Dylan Savage, wake up,' a voice boomed from the front of the class. Dylan woke up with a start, and all the flames guttered and dimmed as if an ill wind had gusted through their sanctuary.

Head of year nine, Mr Bestwick, glowered at Dylan before sharing the look with the rest of the class.

She could have kneed him right in the balls; instead, Misha modelled the appropriate behaviour for her charges. 'Mr Bestwick, it is always a pleasure to see you. However, my class and I are not finished with our test results.'

'I shouldn't think it matters,' Mr Bestwick retorted.

'It matters a great deal to me that they understand their marks.' Misha continued down the rows of tables handing out the rest of the papers and stood in front of her desk. 'Right, class 9b—'

'If it matters so much, why was Dylan Savage asleep?' Mr Bestwick fixed eyes on Dylan.

I don't know, you malevolent prick. Maybe the poor boy is exhausted because he hasn't eaten, or his mother, who we have never met and is known to social work as a prostitute, had clients around all night. 'Dylan wasn't sleeping,' Misha said matter-of-factly. A couple of boys at the back tittered at the obvious lie, which Misha silenced with a flick of her eyes in their direction.

'No? What was he doing, then?'

31

'Dylan, as you might not remember, is a talented mathematician. While I handed back test results, in which he received another A star, I set him a challenge.'

Mr Bestwick looked suspicious. 'What challenge?'

'I asked Dylan to calculate pi to as many decimal places as he could. Dylan, if you please.' Misha nodded to the uncomfortable-looking boy.

Dylan felt the whole class staring at him, along with Mr Bestwick's glare. He cleared his throat and looked at his desk. 'Three point one, four, one, five, nine, two, six, five, three...' Dylan paused for a moment, looking to the left, and went on, 'five, eight, nine, seven, nine—'

'Fine. Very good, boy,' Mr Bestwick said, unable to disguise his annoyance.

The bell rang. The class didn't move until Misha unclasped her hands and raised her palms up to her chest, giving them permission to leave. Chairs scraped. The children broke into raucous conversation and rushed out of the classroom, filing around Mr Bestwick, who ignored them. Misha had a smile and a kind word for each of them.

'Dylan Savage and Samuel Adekugbe, wait for me in the hall,' Mr Bestwick told them as they tried to pass unnoticed around the back of Mrs Stokes' desk. 'You've detention, in case you'd forgotten.' He followed them to the door, adding, 'I'd expected more from you, Samuel.'

Misha had wanted to talk to Dylan after class. He'd looked more and more tired recently. Falling asleep today wasn't a surprise. It was hard enough to break down the barriers with some of her pupils without Alan Bestwick trampling all over their self-worth.

'Dylan,' she called out.

Dylan and Mr Bestwick stopped. Bestwick rolled his eyes.

'Dylan, I want to have a chat tomorrow about taking the GCSE early. You've a special gift.'

'Thank you, Mrs Stokes. School is over,' Bestwick cut in. 'They are my problem for the next hour. You two get moving. You're tidying the gym store.'

As the boys moved off, Misha added so they could hear, 'Oh, they're no problem.'

'There we'll have to agree to disagree.'

'Yes, I think we will.'

Bestwick was about to leave but seemed to get pulled back into the doorway. 'You're wasting your time with them, you know that?'

'Is that so?' Misha inclined her head as if she was listening to one of her class.

'At best, we're educating cleaners, fast food servers, and teenage mums.'

Misha gave an indulging smile. 'And there was me thinking we were teaching children.'

Bestwick gave a cold snort. 'Very good. You know what I mean. We're not social workers, and we're definitely not miracle workers.'

'We're not prison guards either.'

'It won't hurt for them to get used to it.'

'Like you said, we'll have to agree to disagree.' Misha turned her back on him and began tidying her classroom, trying hard not to show just how much she wanted to kick Alan Bestwick in the nuts.

8

SPIDER'S WEB

MOANS, sometimes mournful whimpers, sometimes aggressive and guttural grunts, along with an incessant creaking seeped through the walls and dripped poisonously into Dylan's ears. The haunting would stop intermittently to be followed by indecipherable voices, the opening and closing of the flat's front door, and the ringing of a telephone. Then the coital lament would start over, until his mother had made enough to satisfy Henry Grime.

Dylan turned on his side and covered his ears with a pillow to stare at the mould on his wall. He was so tired and struggled to think about something else. Anything else. He might have wished more carefully. It was an invitation for his other problems to scramble over each other in a war for his attention, while his mother's blighted cradle rocked, and rocked, and rocked.

The image of the knife in his sock drawer loomed out of the darkness behind Dylan's eyelids. 'Loans gotta be paid back. Remember that,' Henry Grime's voice intoned. The Duppy Crew chased Dylan on his paper round. 'That's it. Run, blud. We're gonna ghost you.' The reassuringly terrible weight of the knife weighed in his hand. 'You owe me, Little Dee, big time. Understand?' The vice-like grip on the back of Dylan's neck transmuted into the strange house at 25 Gallows

Court. A savage dog barked behind the black, psoriatic door. Like a dragon king, Henry Grime sat in a cloud of cannabis smoke. In that fog, the weeds and saplings growing from the crevices of number 25 Gallows Court whispered. *What were they saying?* An old Jamaican lady shouted as Dylan ran through drying sheets. A flash of gold teeth. 'What you learning, little man?' Dylan collapsed to his knees. 'It hurts, please.' His crouched form became red-hot embers snuffed out between Henry Grime's fingers. 'Nah, Dee. That ain't it. You gotta fight back or the world is going to eat you alive.' Savage and angry, the dog growled, and the door to the rotting house creaked ajar. Mr Bestwick's angry face loomed large. 'Dylan Savage, wake up.'

Dylan surfaced from the deep fathoms of the dream world with a gasp. The flat was silent but for a siren calling out in the wilds of London. Dylan swung his legs over the side of the bed, rubbed sleep from his eyes and opened his sock drawer. The switchblade's steel hilt and pins were cold, and the polished wood of its handle was seductively smooth.

Green neon digits cast an eerie halo around the alarm clock. Ten minutes to five. Dylan dressed, pulling up his hood, and slid the switchblade into the front pocket of his tracksuit bottoms. The hall light flashed on and off three times, and Dylan quietly closed the door behind him so as not to wake his mother. He waited for a moment, clinging to the handle and resting his forehead on the door.

He liked to think if she woke, she'd make him stay at home and they'd go out for breakfast to a greasy spoon. They'd have strong cups of tea with two sugars and plates piled high with a full English breakfast of fried eggs, bacon, beans, sausages and toast. She'd wipe the ketchup from his chin and ask about school. Stuffed to the brim, they'd catch the District Line to Monument, then change and ride the Central Line to Oxford Circus. The rest of the day would be spent window shopping in the crowds on Oxford Street and end with an ice cream while they fed the ducks in Regents Park with a couple of slices of bread they'd saved from their breakfast by wrapping them in paper napkins. But something more than Henry Grime had a hold on Dylan's mum. Manacled in a dungeon of pills and vodka, she was deaf and blind to anything beyond that prison. Dylan knew that, and so he walked away.

A heavy drizzle fell like static through the white glow of the streetlights. Dylan shuffled across the concourse of uneven paving slabs between the Renfield Tower and the squat concrete tenement opposite, being careful not to step on the cracks. Mr Chatterjee's shop glowed in the gloom.

Bing-bong, and the door slammed shut from its overly aggressive automatic mechanism.

Mr Chatterjee harrumphed on seeing Dylan. 'You're early.'

'It'll take me longer without my bike, Mr Chatterjee.'

The shop keeper's head wobbled from side-to-side in a gesture Dylan never understood. 'Last chance today, Dylan. I don't want any made-up excuses this time. *All* the papers must be delivered. I've docked yesterday's missing papers from your wages, plus the cost of the bag.'

'Yes, Mr Chatterjee.'

The pot-bellied shopkeeper's small moustache twitched. Perhaps he expected Dylan to give up. Perhaps he didn't realise the greater forces compelling Dylan to keep the job. Either way, he showed no other emotion and lowered his eyes back to the stack of papers in front of him and went on marking them up with his biro. 'Your papers will be ready in two minutes.'

Dylan waited with his hands in his pockets. The knife seemed to throb with menace. Why did he bring it? *You know why*, he thought. And the prospect of using it immediately sucked all the spit from his mouth and made his hands and legs heavy.

The bead curtain at the back of the shop rattled, and Anila, Mr Chatterjee's daughter, appeared. She was in the year below Dylan, with rich, dark skin and long, black hair that shined like silk. When she saw Dylan, she smiled shyly and turned down her eyes. Dylan did the same, feeling a reddening blush burn on his cheeks.

Mr Chatterjee grunted and stuffed Dylan's papers into a new hi-vis satchel and snapped, 'Well, get going. You haven't got all day. And remember, this is your last chance.'

Chagrined, Dylan fled the shop with his heavy load.

Never the same twice, Dylan had received a text message telling him the new hand-off point. At the bottom of the concourse, a couple appeared from a dark doorway. They walked arm in arm. Under a streetlight they stopped and began to French kiss. The girl wrapped a leg around the young man's thigh, riding up her skirt, while he groped at her buttocks. When they broke off, they passed a vandalised, pebble-dashed bin, cracked and chipped like an old coffee cup. It was seemingly forgotten by the council, with rubbish overflowing onto the ground. The man dropped a packet into the bin. Dylan waited for them to disappear into the guts of Renfield Tower before retrieving the drugs from the rubbish.

Soon, Dylan was panting. He jogged to make up time now that he was on foot. He couldn't be sure that being earlier would make any difference, but it was all he had. Most of the tabloids carried front page stories about reality TV show stars, alongside ads for online gambling sites and contests to win a better life by having that life scripted into a reality TV show. Dylan would deliver all the opioids in his bag like a good boy.

There was a rhythm of numbers in running, footfalls synchronising with breathing in and out. It came with an ache in his muscles and a stab in the side. That pain made the numbers visceral and alive with every breath and every stride. As he ran, all his problems dissolved into the background, subsumed by the embodied pain of counting: one, two, three, in; one, two, three, out. Without knowing it, he found himself running onto Gallows Court.

Chest heaving, Dylan came to a stop and bent over to catch his breath. The park was deserted. He'd made good time, and the sun was still not up. Between the drizzle and his sweat, he was now wet through, and on the black cusp of morning, steam rose from his head and shoulders. The coast looked clear. No Duppies haunted doorways or loitered by the bus stop.

Number 25 Gallows Court sat in darkness between the security lights of the fried chicken and charity shops. Its door looked to be a black maw, and its many windows the eyes of a spider, filled with death and predation. From over the road, the giant spider whispered something Dylan couldn't make out. The threads were invisible, and yet the forces in Dylan's world led him towards the centre of its web.

Dylan pulled *The Times* from his bag and folded it in thirds. Another quick reconnoitre, and with the sweat already beginning to chill on his flesh, Dylan ran across the street.

Apprehension made Dylan pause and take a deep breath, girding himself for the dog's rabid attack at the door once more. He had started to take his first stride through the iron gate when the shout came.

'Oi! Thought we told you—'

Whipping his head around, Dylan saw them too late, and as he had fallen down the steps yesterday, this morning he fell up them, sprawling flat and narrowly missed smashing his teeth on the top step. Sound changed. The shouts of the Duppy Crew were pulled away like the yelps of a puppy plunged into a bucket of water.

Dylan rolled over onto his backside, hoping for somewhere to flee, but realised he was trapped. With the door to his back, the only other choice was the troughs in front of the basement level to the house, but they lurked in the darkness below after a jump over rusted *fleur-de-lis* spiked railings. Likely, he'd break a leg and be stranded in the shadows with the rats and jetsam bags of dogshit.

The same three boys from the Duppy Crew came to a halt at the gate to number twenty-five. Dylan got to his feet and reached for the knife in his pocket. As his fingers closed around the switchblade, the boys on the street became confused. Their heads swivelled this way and that in search of Dylan. The one who'd stolen his satchel yesterday, a lanky boy with a feathery tash and sallow skin, pushed the pigeon-toed fat one. They were shouting, but their voices were the same as the muffled tones of his mother's punters handing over money and saying goodbye in the hall.

The tall one began to pace up and down. Shouts of, 'Where did he go?' and 'He can't just disappear, bruv,' were barely audible. One rattled the shutter in front of the fried chicken shop and peered through the grille.

Dylan watched in disbelief. He was right in front of them, but they couldn't see him. If he waved his arms or shouted an insult,

Dylan had the feeling whatever spell this was would be broken. Therefore, without a word, he let them move off, pushing and snapping at each other.

And yet the curiosiness of Dylan's morning wasn't over. *The Times* needed delivering, and his round needed finishing, but as Dylan aimed the folded paper at the brass letterbox, the front door of number 25 Gallows Court creaked ajar.

9

GALLOWS COURT

WHISPERS CALLED at the margins of perception, a seductive tide pulling at the shores of Dylan's mind in a rhythmic, hypnotic encouragement to plunge into the unknown.

Yesssh, yesssh, yesssh, the whispers breathed.

Unsure, Dylan opted for the letterbox, but the door swung farther away from the paper clutched in his hands. A musty waft of mouldering decay kissed his face. This was the point at which he should have run. He would have, but for the fact his legs would not move and nor would his hands. Dylan wanted, no, he *needed* to count his fingertip taps to root himself to a predictable pattern in his control and break the unknown's psychedelic of fear. But, like an addict with the best of intentions, Dylan's limbs betrayed him.

One hand clutched the paper while, against his will, the other pushed the door. Flakes of paint crumbled at his touch. The door moaned and, heart thumping and racing, Dylan felt himself drawn over the threshold. It was like stepping into a dream in which he was observing his actions but was unable to influence the dream as it unfolded before him.

Yeeessssh, the tide of whispers encouraged.

Narrow and long, the corridor was shrouded with the curtain of night. A threadbare and moth-eaten carpet runner plunged away from Dylan's feet into the bowels of the house. It was probably once plush and red, but in the dark and smothered with dust, it was as brown as an old scab. Wallpaper split at the seams in puckered wounds and shed from the walls in flayed coils. Pictures lined the walls in once ornate frames, their subjects invisible beneath centuries of grime. A staircase lay at the end of the corridor, which was punctured with more blackened portals on either side. Dylan noticed the paw prints in the dust and willed himself to turn around. The beast which made them had paws as big as Dylan's hands. But try as he might, Dylan could not retreat. This was no dream; it was much worse.

There came a cough, dry and crackling.

'Come in, young man. You have brought my paper, I see.'

The voice was weak and old, but it sounded clearly in Dylan's ears.

'Come, come. I won't bite.'

Dylan's feet began to move. In slow steps, he advanced down the corridor. The floorboards were brittle and weak underfoot. He expected them to give way and find his leg sunk into the basement where unseen things would claw at his flesh. But they held.

A dead rat lay in the dust, with its back in an extreme arch, as if it had been snapped in the middle, leaving its mouth frozen in an agonising grimace. A thread from a spider's web irritated his face, and, try as he might, he could not bring his hands up to brush it away. Resistance was impossible, but resist he did, trying to call on his fingers to move. Anxiety smothered his breathing. The whispers turned into an excited rustle. Dylan thought of the knife in his pocket and pivoted all his energies to it. If only he could reach it. The bad dream would not allow it.

An amused titter came from an open door to the left, which Dylan approached with slow, gelatinous steps. A faint glow emanated from the door. The newspaper trembled in his grip. Dylan's feet turned him toward the threshold. He wanted to close his eyes but, like the rest of his body, they were not his to command.

'*Bonjour*, young man. Do come in.'

Dylan's body obeyed, approaching a man who appeared impossibly old. He was more of a wizened husk, shrivelled and thin, wrapped in a dark purple robe that hung like loose flesh from his bones. A few white hairs sprouted from a bald head, covered with liver spots. Thin, bony fingers, with nails so long they had begun to curl in on themselves, poked from baggy sleeves and rested on the arms of the winged chair before the fire. Flames danced in the old man's pale grey eyes, which glinted either side of a sharp nose.

Beside him, an enormous black dog sat at heel, with long, pointed ears and an equally long snout, and eyes black as obsidian mirrors. Baring its teeth, it growled so deeply the floor vibrated and china ornaments rattled on the mantle.

'Tais-toi, mon Anoup.'

The massive hound quieted at its master's words, with a plaintive lick of his chops. 'Do not mind him. He is surly, but you are not to his taste.' The old man smirked, but Dylan didn't get the joke.

'Sit, sit,' the old man said beseechingly, offering a footstool before him. Dylan did as he was told, still breathing heavily through his nose in the effort to resist, eyes darting around for a way to escape. When the old man leaned forward to take the newspaper, Dylan thought he might break. One moment, the newspaper was in Dylan's hands, the next, the old man sat with it unfolded on his lap. 'Thank you,' he said. The old man had the trace of an accent but not one Dylan could place. Hadn't the old man spoken French to the dog? But that didn't carry over to his English. Then, as if to confound him, the old man addressed the dog, who eyed Dylan with blank intensity.

'Aller chercher Monsieur Boucher.'

With grace that belied its size, the sleek, muscular giant trotted out of the room.

'Better?' the old man said to Dylan, as if the dog was the thing that had been bothering him. 'You can relax now.' With a merest gesture of the old man's gnarled hand, Dylan felt the sudden release of whatever had held him. However, he did not run. The giant dog had left by the door Dylan had entered. He might still be in the hall as he had been yesterday when it went berserk at the delivery of the newspaper. And then there was the matter of Dylan's apparent invisibility and the force which had brought him here, which seemed impossible. But here he was, sat in front of a man who looked like the Crypt Keeper in one of Samuel's horror comics.

'Where are my manners?' the old man went on. 'My name is *Châtelain du Vieil*, but Vieil will do. And you would be?' With what seemed like a great effort, Vieil lifted his wrinkled brow.

'Dylan Savage.' His name was a dry pebble in his mouth.

'Savage?' Vieil was amused. 'Ah! Mr Butcher, nice of you to join us. This is the young man who brings us our newspaper. His name is Dylan.'

Mr Butcher walked into the room with a rat in his hand and stood next to Vieil's chair. He wore a white shirt with a grandfather collar, silver sleeve braces, and a brown waistcoat. Over his lip hung a handlebar moustache. His face was long, and his eyes were glistening dark beads. He gave a curt nod to indicate he'd understood.

Vieil's pale eyes danced in the firelight. 'He is a man of few words, but you have your uses, don't you, Mr Butcher?' Mr Butcher's only response was to move his eyes to meet Vieil's before moving them back to Dylan.

'If we get him started, he'll never stop.' Vieil chuckled, showing perfect teeth, luminous as pearls behind cracked charcoal lips.

'To business. I can see you are a busy young man with things to do.' Vieil eyed the fluorescent satchel slung over Dylan's shoulder, and he smirked to himself. 'You deliver things, isn't that right, Dylan?' Dylan nodded and Vieil wheezed, taking a large breath. 'You have brought me invaluable information about the outside world. I have been away for some time, you see? Mr Butcher arranged the delivery, but even that was rather beyond his normal duties. And as you can see, he is not much for badinage.'

Dylan could feel Mr Butcher's eyes burning through him, and the bones of the rat in his hand cracked.

'Oh, don't mind him,' Vieil said, as if reading Dylan's mind. 'His bite is worse than his bark. Where was I?'

'D-d-deliveries,' Dylan stammered. *Why are you helping him, you muppet? What the hell is happening?* Again, he had that feeling that he couldn't have stopped himself.

'Hmm? Quite so. London, it seems, has changed a great deal since last I walked its streets. And yet,' Vieil's eyes again fell upon Dylan's satchel, 'other things remain as they always were.' The old man tapped the paper. 'This tells me very little of the London right outside my door. For example, those boys have chased you two days in a row.'

Dylan opened his mouth ready to deflect with a lie. Vieil cut him off, dismissing the need for Dylan to speak with a meagre wave of his clawed fingers. 'You need not lie, Dylan.' The old man's eyes had a cold intensity that held Dylan's attention and made his heart pound against his ribcage. 'All that I ask is that you visit with me a while and bring me information and things from the outside world, and for that I will help you.' Vieil pointed a bony finger at Dylan. 'If you are ever in need of sanctuary, call on this house.'

Dylan's throat was dry and hoarse. 'Thanks,' he croaked. But his mind raced. *This place is weird. I've got to get out of here. The old guy is mental, and his boyfriend is a psycho, and he wants me to drop in, so they can what? But what was going on outside with the Duppy Crew?*

Vieil guffawed and then hacked into his sleeve, still enjoying the joke through the fit of coughing. 'He has you pegged, Mr Butcher.'

'You think you can read my mind?'

Vieil wiped a tear from his eyes with a shaking hand. 'See, Mr Butcher? He has spirit. Most people wear their feelings on the outside, Dylan. If you know how to read them, they spill their guts for you. Isn't that right, Mr Butcher?'

Mr Butcher just stared at Dylan.

Vieil went on, 'I don't need to be a psychic to know you are hiding from those boys out there, or that something else even worse compelled you to come back a second time. Just as I can tell you carry a knife in your pocket and there is something in your bag other than yesterday's news. My guess would be illicit narcotics. Ah! And there it is. The merest flicker in your eyes, extra blinks, the racing of your pulse flushing your swarthy complexion.'

'If you're not a psychic, why did the Duppy Crew, I mean, those boys, not see me?' Dylan's curiosity made him bolder. The house and these men were beyond strange, but they had ample time to attack him and hadn't. In fact, they, or at least the house, had kind of saved him. And this old guy, Vieil, there was something about him, something... Dylan couldn't put his finger on it, but he was drawn to him, both figuratively and literally.

Weak and small, Vieil reclined in his mouldering, winged chair and regarded Dylan with a satisfied smile. 'That is a good question. The weak-minded are easily misled. Have you ever observed people seeing only what they want to see?'

Dylan thought of Mr Bestwick only seeing the bad, and Henry Grime only seeing what he could use Dylan for, and his mother, and it broke his heart to admit this, who didn't seem to see Dylan at all. He nodded.

'It is a bagatelle; fools deceive themselves. They rarely need help in the matter.' Vieil's eyes drooped. Mr Butcher sniffed, flaring his nostrils, and shifted his gaze from Dylan to the wooden boards nailed over the windows. They were covered with long, velvet curtains, dirty with dust.

'Hmm?' Vieil inclined his head drowsily to Mr Butcher. 'I know. Forgive me, Dylan. I am still regaining my strength and must sleep. We'll talk again soon. Call whenever you need.' He could hardly keep his eyes open.

Mr Butcher dropped the dead rat and stooped to scoop up the old man in his muscular arms, as if Vieil weighed nothing, and carried him from the room.

The fire had petered out to little more than orange embers. The room was cold again, and Dylan shivered in his wet clothes, noticing the first hints of dawn in the bluish light seeping through the cracks of the boarded-up windows. With the realisation that time and the outside world was moving on and he had to catch up with it, Dylan left the strange house on Gallows Court, remembering Vieil never answered his question.

Within moments of closing the door behind him, he was more concerned with avoiding enemy gang members, posting newspapers, and moving Henry Grime's shipments around their territory. By the evening, the whole visit with the old man and his mute attendant would seem like a vague dream, washed away by the troubles of his day.

Dreams, however, especially bad dreams, have a way of recurring.

10

DARK INTENTIONS

MISHA STOKES WAS KILLING time sitting at the kitchen counter of their two-bedroom flat in Spitalfields. She ran a pen over the regulations on submitting a child early for the GCSE in maths, highlighting key points. It wasn't a complicated or unheard of thing to do. A little more unusual for a thirteen-year-old, still two years off from the exam, and even more atypical for him to be from Whitechapel. The form wasn't the problem, though. Alan Bestwick was. Misha doubted he would allow Dylan to sit the exam. He'd probably cite the boy's attendance, which, to be fair, was bad, and yet he never fell behind. How could he? He was already miles ahead of the next best student in the entire school, regardless of age group. Imagine what he could achieve if he was in a safe home and applied himself?

She was chewing the end of her pen, pondering what to do, when keys slid into the front door. Kenny came in, mobile phone held in his mouth, and dumped his bag and coat in the hall.

'Hey, love,' he mumbled through the phone.

Misha tidied away the conundrum that was Dylan Savage into a file, hopped off the kitchen stool, and padded to the hall barefoot. 'Don't speak with your mouth full.'

'Hmm, what?' Kenny said distractedly, having fished the phone from his mouth and read something on its glowing screen.

'Doesn't matter,' Misha said, leaning against the door frame. 'Hard day at work?'

He continued to read, concentrating. 'No more than usual.'

'I thought you'd be home earlier tonight?'

Kenny stopped reading. Misha could tell he knew something was up.

'This is good,' she teased. 'What has the great detective forgotten?'

Kenny put down his phone and paid more attention. He looked at her leaning against the door frame in her red dress, hair and makeup done. Misha enjoyed the brief flash of horror in his eyes that he might have forgotten an anniversary or a birthday. She knew he'd pick up from her tone that she wasn't angry. When they were alone, and she had him all to herself, it was as if Kenny could sometimes read her mind. Sometimes. The poor boy was still struggling until... And there it was.

Realisation dawned on Kenny. 'It's a Tuesday.'

'It is indeed.' Misha's lip gloss sparkled.

'It's the second Tuesday in the month.'

'Mmm, is that so?' she said coquettishly.

'And you've checked you're ovulating?'

Misha rolled her eyes and slunk over to Kenny, taking him by the tie. 'You sure know how to make a girl feel sexy.'

'What? Sorry... I mean...' Kenny stammered, but Misha was grinning and already pulling him to the bedroom. He followed her ample curves swaying in the close-fitting red dress, hurrying to pull off his suit jacket as he did, and kicked the door closed behind them.

In the dark of the bedroom, everything became about touch. Misha let out a long sigh. Without the distractions of the world, it really was like Kenny could read her mind. They blended into each other as if they were one body, one mind, a single animal enraptured with itself.

This time it would work. She could feel it; there was something in the air. After tonight, everything would be different.

THE NIGHT'S work had already begun for Dylan's mother. Phones rang; the door opened and closed to let men in and out.

Dylan was starting to wish he'd agreed to go out with Samuel and his mother, but the church wasn't his thing. A bunch of God-botherers with their amens and hallelujahs, Bible-bashing passersby about heaven, was usually a hard pass for him. Not that Samuel was like that. He never mentioned God. He was just a good laugh, always saw the best in people and always had Dylan's back ever since primary school. The thick Nigerian accent Samuel had turned up with had eroded away completely over the years. Their relationship was sealed on that first day by a boy named Jason Little, who was anything but, who had stolen Dylan's lunch. Samuel shared his food, and it was so spicy Dylan had to drink from the tap. Samuel's round face creased into laughter, but it wasn't mean, and both boys ended up in hysterics and friends ever since.

Banging at the front door made Dylan look up from the maths textbook Mrs Stokes had given him. It was her old A Level textbook, a bit out of date, she said, but Dylan was to look through it and see what he could and couldn't understand. Bits of it were challenging, but he could more than handle it. They were just a puzzle with rules about how they worked. Once you figured that out, everything slotted into place. It was satisfying, and more than that, it was comforting. He was looking through the trigonometry formula list when a second round of banging came at his own bedroom door.

Dylan opened the door ajar, and Henry Grime looked down at him.

'Time to make a down payment, Little Dee.'

Dylan added up his choices, and the sum amounted to zero. He nodded and retreated into his room to get his trainers. Henry Grime pushed the door wide, his shape backlit from the harsh light of the hall.

'Don't forget what I gave you yesterday. I'll be out here.' Grime shut the door.

When Dylan emerged, Grime wasn't in the hall, but a man with a blotchy face and hair wet from the rain was. He wore a long coat, and Dylan didn't like the way the man looked him up and down. It was like he was hungry. His eyes darted between Dylan and Dylan's bedroom door.

'You live here too?' the man asked.

Dylan said nothing, but he stuffed his hands into the pocket of his body warmer and curled his fingers around the knife.

The man leered, showing yellow teeth between plump, rubbery lips too big for his face. 'Donna your mum? Didn't know you were here too. You dumb or something?' He moved closer.

Dylan could smell the stink of old sweat and booze off him but stood his ground and moved his thumb onto the small latch of the switchblade. The man leaned down, his foul breath hot on Dylan's face.

'Is it extra for you?' A worm of a tongue squirmed wetly across his lips.

'What the fuck's going on here, then?' Henry Grime had appeared in the hall from the living room, stuffing a roll of money into his jeans pocket.

Rubbery lips man stiffened. 'Nothing. We were just having a chat.'

'You ain't paying for the rabbit and pork, dickhead. So piss off in the other room like a good boy.'

The predator had turned to prey and scurried into the living room.

'You ready, Little Dee?' Henry Grime opened the front door, indicating for Dylan to go first.

No, I'm not, Dylan thought. Henry Grime stood in front of the lightswitch. 'Yeah, sure,' he lied.

A NIGHT STANDING in the cold and probably the rain was something Samuel actually looked forward to, even if it was seasoned with the spice of apprehension. It was a night spent at his mother's side at the soup kitchen, handing out a warm meal to whomever came along. Reverend Adekugbe had continued her mission after they fled to England from religious persecution in northern Nigeria. Persecution that had taken Samuel's father from this world. She shook hands

49

warmly with the waifs and strays of East London, greeting each with the kindness of a prodigal child finally returned, even if it was only for ten minutes on a rainy English street in the dead of night. His mother seemed to effervesce an even greater aura of kindliness on these nights.

Samuel had once asked his mother why she was so happy as the rain beaded on the tips of their noses. Reverend Adekugbe had hugged him and trumpeted in that hearty laugh of hers. 'We do God's work, and there is no better work to do, eh?'

Samuel had found that easy to accept standing next to a woman who beamed at a homeless person in almost the same way she did at her own son, even if it was through one good eye. The other eye was a glaucous mist of white and grey, a visible scar of persecution. Samuel only wished that Dylan would have agreed to come with them. He worried about his friend and thought the soup kitchen was the kind of sanctuary Dylan needed.

Tonight, they had walked to the park in the middle of Gallows Court. They'd set up their trestle tables and laid out their flasks and food. Soon they would come, the lost souls of the city, and with hot tea, warm soup, and fellowship maybe the woes of the world could be kept at bay, at least for one evening.

This wasn't one of their usual spots, however. Typically, they'd be near a parade of shops on Commercial Road, Leman Street, or Whitechapel Road. This was in the heart of an estate. The bottom end of Gallows Court had shops, but their pop-up soup kitchen was on the other end of the rundown park surrounded by council flats.

As they finished their preparations, Samuel thought he saw a crack in his mother's gusto. She stared at something across the park. Her eyes narrowed in the same manner as when she saw through a lie Samuel was telling. Funny how she could see through him so sharply with just one eye. In fact, Samuel had a suspicion it was the blind one which saw the lies. Across the park, Samuel couldn't see exactly what his mother was looking at. There might have been some boys running towards the road at the far end of the park. It was hard to tell over that distance and in the gathering darkness. But then the look was gone, and Reverend Adekugbe tore through the plastic wrapper on a stack of paper coffee cups and ruffled her son's hair.

The day was dying. All that was left of the sun was a bleeding ligature of light tangled in the rooftops. Then they appeared, gathering for the day's wake, turning up hoods and pulling down their caps, scuttling from the nooks and crevices of the estate, boys on BMX bikes, teenagers in packs, and men with dark intentions.

THEY WALKED FROM RENFIELD TOWER, picking up more of the Blud Crew as they went. A distant nod or the touch of a baseball cap indicated their fealty. The whole way, Dylan's head swam. He felt like a drowning man with no shore in sight. How long could he tread water before the ocean swallowed him or one of the creatures from its depths pulled him beneath the waves? They moved as a nebulous shoal, undulating from point to point, a bus stop here, a streetlight there, until finally they arrived at their destination.

They dispersed across Gallows Court at the border between Blud and Duppy territory. Cars drove along the street in front of the shops. A house in the black space between streetlights looked out over the park. Dylan's limbs were heavy with adrenaline. Treading water would not be enough tonight.

'Hang back here, Little Dee.' Henry Grime jerked his head, and Dylan followed him to an overhang covering the entrance to some of the flats. It smelt of urine and was littered with fag ends. 'You know where we are?'

Dylan did.

'Good. I know I was hard on you,' Henry Grime said and grabbed Dylan around the neck again, but this time it wasn't so rough. He drew him close, forehead to forehead.

'I've a soft spot for you, little man. I know you owe me for the gear, but you showed me the Duppies were pushing at the edges of our territory. That ain't right, bruv. Can't let that stand. You're my boy, and this is your chance to pay me back, make us square. You feel me, fam?'

'How?' Dylan croaked.

'You gotta shank a Duppy, bruv. Here's the plan. You stick one of them, do it good and do it quick. Get one on the edge of our territory and then leg it back up here. You ghost one of them for me, and you'll be a bad man. All grown up, bruv, a proper Blud Crew. You don't want to let me down again. I told you debts gotta be paid, and someone's gotta get cut to pay this one. It's them or you, Little Dee. Now, put your head up like a bad man. That's it.'

Henry Grime nodded in approval, massaging Dylan's neck, and pushed him out into the rain.

With blood rushing in his ears and tears boiling in his eyes, Dylan crossed the park. The knife had grown warm in his sweaty grip, like a living thing with its own will. This was the last thing he wanted to do, but a familiar feeling passed through him, like he was in a dream observing himself but unable to choose a different course of action. Except it wasn't a dream, was it? It was a nightmare, and he was sleep-walking towards something from which there was no coming back.

He stopped under a sycamore tree. It bore the scars of initials cut into its bark and a short epigraph, informing any dog that wished to piss on the tree that 'JT luvs dik'. Three Duppies sat with their backs to Dylan on a park bench. They were only twenty feet over the invisible border, but it was a clear encroachment into Blud's territory. The park was out of bounds for Duppies, everyone knew that. They were Spitalfields boys. This was Whitechapel's Ends. But cross that road, and the script flipped.

A man came up to the boys, a ratty-looking skeleton with dirty clothes. An addict needing a score, the rat fidgeted until the exchange was done with a palm-off in a half-hug. He scurried off to find whatever oblivion they had sold him. They were dealing, and Dylan was the patsy to score first blood in this turf war.

The knife was in Dylan's hand, but Henry Grime was in his head. *It's them or you, Little Dee.* Dylan left the shadows under the tree, crossing the wet grass. His breathing was fast and ragged, and his hands shook. The three boys were coming closer and closer with each step, not knowing what was stalking them from behind. Which one would he do? It didn't matter. The one in the middle. Maybe he could stab him in the shoulder. Would that be enough for Henry Grime? 'You stick one of them, do it good and do it quick.' No, it wouldn't. Where, then? The neck? The head? Under the ribs? Oh shit! Too late. Now or never.

Dylan pulled the knife from his pocket. He pressed the button on the top of the handle, and the switchblade snapped open with a solid click. The boy on the right of the bench got up to act out a story he was telling and turned to face his friends. The huge grin on his face fell immediately when he clocked Dylan and the five-inch blade in his hand. It was the fat boy with pigeon toes who'd chased him. The other boys swivelled on the bench, and sure enough, it was the rest of the Duppy trinity who patrolled this part of Dylan's paper round.

'Get him,' the lanky one with a tash shouted before he vaulted the bench.

For a moment Dylan stood glued to the spot. The knife slipped from his hand as three more knives appeared from their pockets. Dylan turned to head back up the park to his crew, but the lanky one cut right, heading him off. Dylan slipped on the slick ground. He tripped onto his knees, put a hand down, and managed to find his feet again, his trainers sliding spasmodically under him. With that fall, even the fat one had managed to catch up and cut off his escape. The third one was right behind him, a sneer smeared on his pale face. The skinny boy beelined for Dylan, who veered out of the park and onto the main road.

A car slammed brakes and narrowly missed hitting Dylan, who fell on his backside in the middle of the road. Another car beeped its horn angrily at the stopped vehicle, and they both drove away. Dylan darted for the pavement.

On the other side, Fat Duppy and the third one, a curly redhead with a front tooth missing, had cut Dylan off. Coming directly across the road was the lanky, pale-faced boy, who'd even stopped to let a taxi drive by. Knife in hand, he came for Dylan. They had him, in the dark between the fried chicken and charity shops, where their three blades could slide over and over into Dylan, and either way, his debt would be paid.

Dylan looked left and right and back to the lanky boy who grinned darkly.

'Nowhere to run, blud.'

The Duppy Crew smelled blood, until Dylan stepped back between the wrought iron railings of number 25 Gallows Court and, like a ghost, vanished.

11

LEVIATHAN

THE MAGIC TRICK had worked again. Dylan was invisible standing on the steps before the black door while the whispers hissed with excitement in his ears.

Yesssh, yesssh, yesssh.

A throbbing power quickened Dylan's heart and raised the hairs on the back of his neck. A powerful thing was rising behind him, a leviathan dripping with aphotic night as it climbed out of the shadowy depths of slumber. He'd stepped from one dream into another, but in this one he wasn't a passive passenger of fate.

Yessshh, yessshh. The black house pulsed, and Dylan felt the intoxicating power course through his veins. He wasn't afraid anymore.

Surprise and anger mixed together in the faces of the three boys from the Duppy Crew. Their hungry blades had been denied the opportunity to feed, and they paced back and forth, with the volume of their shouts inexplicably turned down.

'What the fuck, bruv! Where is he?' the lanky one shouted in the face of the ginger boy.

'He's Houdini or sommit, innit?'

'Cool down, blud,' the fat one said, prying them apart. 'He's got to be about here. He was right there. What about the chicken bar?'

The boys appeared struck by the obviousness of this. The charity shop was closed, and therefore, it was the only possible explanation. The fact that the fat one had been standing in front of the door to the chicken bar was easily sacrificed for the sake of a rational explanation.

'I'm here, you wankers,' Dylan said from the top step.

Yeessshh.

The three boys turned in shock at the sudden appearance of Dylan before them on the steps of a house they'd failed to notice, but shock quickly turned back into bloodlust.

'What you say, blud?' The lanky one pointed with his knife.

'You deaf as well as stupid?' Dylan said and pushed open the black door and ran inside.

Yeeessshhh.

The three Duppies followed, bounding up the steps. The fat one blundered against the rotting door, which slammed shut behind them.

Dylan knew the logic of this dream before it happened, as though he surfed on its crest. He ran along the corridor and into the front room, knowing that Vieil would be sitting in his moth-eaten chair before a roaring fire.

He came to a juddering halt next to the old man, and only then did the absurdity of what he had just done become apparent. Vieil was as frail and desiccated as before, nothing more than an ancient man Death could take at any moment. And Dylan, the fool, had fooled himself and ran into a dead-end, bringing Death with him. The old man would stand little chance against three young brawlers with knives. Perhaps Mr Butcher was here or the enormous dog? One look told Dylan they were not.

The Duppies almost ran past the door to the lounge. The ginger one caught hold of the door frame and skidded in the dust, calling to the other two. They filed in and fanned out, cutting off any hope of escape, and the fire blazed in their eyes.

'Leave us alone. He's just an old man, and you were in our Ends,' Dylan blurted out, that sense of exuberant power having evaporated. The only hope he had left was a chance at mercy, even if it was only for the old man. But hope and mercy didn't live in this house.

The three boys advanced.

Dylan looked around for anything he could use when he spotted a poker for the fire, but before he could make a lunge for it, the old man spoke.

'Stop.' The word was uttered with the same frail, scratching voice Vieil had used with Dylan before, but its commanding force hurt Dylan's ears, though it wasn't meant for him. The three boys winced and froze, unable to move.

The dreamlike visit of yesterday, which Dylan had brushed aside, came rushing back. The compulsion to come to this room and sit before Vieil. The inability to move his body of his own free will. His hyper-awareness of every sensation at the time, but the way it quickly became a forgotten dream once he left, like the house itself.

'Mr Vieil, I'm sorry. I didn't know what to do and—'

'Vieil will do; I am not a mister, and you did as I asked, Dylan. I said to call whenever you needed and to bring me things of the outside world, and for that, this house would provide you sanctuary. I believe we have both made good on our deal.'

The three boys had not moved a muscle. Only their eyes darted around the room, betraying their incomprehension and growing anger and—*yeesshh*—fear.

Mr Butcher appeared in the door behind the boys. He was dressed as dapperly as the last time.

'*Nous avons des invités pour le dîner, Anoup,*' Vieil said to his attendant, blocking the exit. Mr Butcher said nothing. He only tilted his head to briefly look at the three living statues in their parlour.

'W-what's going on?' Dylan said, edging away from Vieil's chair. He could feel that huge, dark presence again and knew this time it had only been behind him as a matter of convenience.

'Come to me, Dimitri,' Vieil said, and the pale, lanky boy took an unsteady step forward, as if he was fighting an internal battle with everything he had, and it wasn't enough.

Moving in front of the boarded-up windows, Dylan began the rapid taps of thumb to fingers, one to seven and over again, as the fear in the room rose.

The fat boy with pigeon toes wet himself. The dark patch spread out from his crotch and down his left leg.

'Ah!' Vieil sighed knowingly. 'Some of the piglets always piss themselves before the slaughtermen.'

Mr Butcher guffawed, opening his mouth wide and rocking back his head, but no sound came out.

The lanky boy was at Vieil's feet as Dylan reached the far wall and bumped into a piano. It rang tunelessly, while Dylan frantically tapped a thumb to his fingers to no effect. Nothing was regular. Nothing was in his control.

'Kneel,' Vieil commanded, and the lanky boy dropped to his knees.

Vieil ran a bony hand through the boy's hair. A tuft snagged in the old man's curling nails, and Vieil pulled it free, tearing a clump from the roots. All the boy managed to do was utter a pitiful whimper from his throat.

Dylan had made it to the door, but Mr Butcher's muscular form blocked the way. The man laughed and laughed with noiseless mirth. Dylan looked back at the unfolding nightmare. The crest of the dream had broken all around him, and now he floundered in the churning eddies of Vieil's power.

The old man tilted the boy's head to one side and caught Dylan's eye as he did. 'Thank you for this, Dylan,' the old man said, then his pearl white teeth transformed, growing sharp and long, crowding out of his mouth as irregular, piercing fangs. From their tips dripped a milky liquid. Vieil opened wide, his jaws seemingly projecting forward. Dylan closed his eyes. But in the dark he was only left with the sound of Vieil's feeding, a sucking and gulping mewl. He opened his eyes only to find a getaway and caught a glimpse of the boy, awareness still in his eyes but dimming beneath heavy lids.

Dylan scrabbled at the laughing Mr Butcher, who would not move. 'Let me out, let me out, let me out,' Dylan screamed.

'The trick, Dylan, is to not let the heart stop beating.' Vieil spoke with a slurred ecstasy as he tore open the boy's shirt.

Unable to stop himself, Dylan glanced back as he pushed ineffectually at Mr Butcher. With blood covering his face, Vieil sat astride the boy, Dimitri. He looked down at his food, a pulse pumping weakly from its neck. Placing the fingers of both hands at the edges of the boy's ribcage, the old man's fingers danced with a pianist's exactitude as they searched for the right chord. Dylan tore himself away, whimpering as he struggled to dig himself out of the hole he found himself in, but it only seemed to grow deeper. There came a sickening crunch, and the mewling began again.

Mr Butcher bent double in hysterics, and Dylan slipped through the gap, tumbling into the hall amid the dust and peeling wallpaper. He flung open the front door and sprinted from the house, with the whispers hissing in his ears, like one of his mother's clients groaning through the walls of their flat.

Yessh.

Yessshh.

Yesssshhh.

12

BAD MAN

DYLAN DIDN'T STOP. He didn't go back to the house or the park. He ran along the pavement, jumping over the homeless sprawled in doorways and swerving between people staggering outside pubs and takeaways. Every obstacle prevented any respite found in rhythm, where he could lose himself in the certainties of a pattern.

Tears streamed down his cheeks, air burned his lungs, and fire seared the muscles in Dylan's legs, until he hit the stairwell in Renfield Tower. There, gasping, crying, with a head still spinning full of the silent laughter of Mr Butcher and the suckling mewls of Vieil, he threw up all over his trainers, retching over and over, purging hot vomit until there was nothing left but raw guilt.

Counting the stairs back home didn't help. Three clicks of the hall light were nothing more than the lighthouse of childish superstition blinking an ineffectual warning. Curling into a ball, Dylan hid under his duvet, pulling the covers over his ears.

His mother's bed squeaked, and strange men grunted and moaned. Dylan put his fists to his ears to block it all out. *Yesshh*, the whispers purred. He saw Vieil sitting back, blood dripping from his chin, ivory fangs crowding from his mouth. In the lanky Duppy's paralysed face, his eyes glistened with fear. The images replayed on an eternal cycle as the sky turned unseen above the light-polluted sky of London.

Dylan's alarm sounded, and he ignored it. The green neon numbers changed in a predictable order that was now a lie, mocking him with excruciating and slow regularity, until finally, the sun banished the night. Rising higher, it brought Samuel knocking at the flat's door. He tried four times and looked through the letterbox before giving up. As the sun reached noon, even Dylan's mother came tapping gently at his door.

'Dylan, you still here, darlin'?' He didn't answer, and she didn't check again.

Soon, the police would come knocking, and part of him wished they would drag him away to Borstal and lock him up with the other delinquents. At least he'd be away from here. The guilt would go with him, though. Dylan would carry the weight of those dead boys with him forever. It was already pulling him under. He'd led them to their deaths and had a hand in it as sure as if he'd ripped out their throats himself.

But with the guilt there was fear as well. Who was Vieil? What was he? Not an old man. *You know what he is.* But how could that be? They weren't real. *What aren't real? Go on, say it!* Dylan shook his head, burrowing into his mattress. He could see the cloudy drops of venom beaded at the tips of Vieil's fangs. *So many fangs, not just two. So? What else bites open necks and drinks blood?*

'No!' Dylan cried into his bedclothes.

He wanted to tell Samuel. He'd always told him everything. But this? Would he lose Samuel as well, either because he'd think Dylan was mad or because of what he was a part of? Dylan already knew he wouldn't tell him, not because he thought Samuel wouldn't believe him or think that he was mad. Worse, Samuel *would* believe him and he'd want to help, and Dylan wasn't going to risk Samuel getting involved. His best friend wasn't going to end up like those Duppies, or worse, like him. No, whatever the cost, Vieil mustn't get the chance to do to Samuel whatever he had done to Dylan. What was that? He had played Dylan, drawing him in, and at the end Dylan had thought he was the one in control leading those boys to their deaths. Was that part of the- the-

Go on, say it.

Was that part of the vampire's power? What was it called? His glamour.

Suddenly, Dylan was struck with an idea, a crazy and dangerous idea, but it was maybe his only way out of this. The sun was still up. Now he had given himself permission to acknowledge what Vieil really was, everything he'd read in comic books and seen in movies about vampires played in his head. He wasn't about to go and try to stake him in the heart. For one thing, he didn't have a wooden stake or know how to easily get one in the time left before sundown. He'd wasted too much of the day freaking out. But sunlight, that was his window of opportunity, and the fact that no one else seemed able to see the house. All he needed was something flammable. Petrol would be great, but who would sell that to a thirteen-year-old? His mum was bound to have bottles of vodka she'd be drinking throughout the day. His chances of getting it without her noticing was another wrinkle to be avoided. He needed something certain. White spirit, paint cleaner, even perfume, anything flammable, that's all he needed, along with some rags and matches. Mr Chatterjee had all those things in his shop.

'Crap!' Dylan said, sitting up on the edge of his bed. He didn't turn up for his paper round this morning and was bound to be fired. There was a slight pang at the realisation that he wouldn't see Anila in the morning, or maybe ever again once the police turned up.

Okay, think. Mr Chatterjee's isn't the only shop in Whitechapel. You can do this. Burn Vieil and Mr Butcher out before sundown. It's perfect. No one will be able to see you do it. They'll either burn inside or run into the sun and that will finish them off. What about Mr Butcher, though? Is he a vampire? And the dog? They would be guarding Vieil. What about the busi-nesses on either side?

Dylan scrunched up his eyes and ground all the questions between his gritted teeth. They were muddying the waters. This was the only answer. He knew it. Burn the vampire. End it now.

He jumped out of bed still in yesterday's clothes. There wasn't

time to change. The sun was already hovering above the rooftops. Twelve pounds was all he could scrape together. He stuffed it into his pocket and grabbed two old T-shirts for rags to soak, stuffing them in his school bag. There was the possibility of cadging another tenner from his mother, but she might slow him down and ask questions about what it was for. Besides, Henry Grime had probably taken it all, and what was left was for her dealer, who also happened to be Henry Grime. No, it would have to be enough.

Dylan sneaked out of his room and crept to the front door. He looked at the lightswitch, brushing away the childish habit, and was about to carefully unlock the snib on the front door when it opened.

Henry Grime stood on the walkway outside. *Even thinking of the Devil seems to make him appear these days.* He looked Dylan up and down with an approving nod. At first, Dylan didn't even notice the new BMX bike leaning against Grime's legs.

'Little Dee. Not so little anymore, eh, fam? What's up, bruv? You look like you've seen a ghost. But of course you did. Gonna have to call you Ghostbusters.' Henry Grime shook his head in a mix of disbelief and pride. 'Gotta say, didn't think you had it in you. Thought you'd tag one of them at best and run back to us.' He glanced up and down the walkway. 'Best not talk about it here. You gonna let me in or what?'

Dylan stood aside.

'This is for you, Dee. You earned it.' He gave him the BMX. 'Well, what do you say, little man?'

'Thanks.' Dylan was still trying to catch up and figure a way to get out.

Henry Grime took him by the back of the neck. 'You is dark, blud. All three of them, dead and floating in the Thames. Where'd you take 'em?'

'I-I-' Dylan didn't know what to say.

'I get it. First one is always tough. We all make out we are hard men. I don't care how hard you are, taking a life is cold. Hurts right here.' Grime put his fist to his heart. 'Doing three, shit must have got out of hand. Am I right?'

Eyes cast down, Dylan nodded.

'You did good. Putting them in the river was a good move. Looks like a boat propeller chopped them into pieces. You throw the shank away as well?'

'Yeah,' Dylan said, voice cracking.

'Top boy. This is cause for a celebration. You're a bad man now, Little Dee.' Grime put his arm around Dylan's shoulders and led him to the living room.

'I was going—' Dylan looked back at the front door.

'You ain't going nowhere. You're my fab now, blud, and we're having a party right here.' Spread out on the sofa, Grime lit a joint and puffed it to life in clouds of smoke before handing it to Dylan who stood dumbfounded in the middle of the floor. 'Go on, you've earned it.'

Dylan took the joint, and his mum came out of the kitchen with a glass in one hand and a cigarette in the other. Donna Savage's long, black hair was tied back in a ponytail, and she wore a sweatshirt with "New York" written across the chest and matching bottoms sagging from her bony hips. She was still pretty, with high cheekbones and green eyes, and she looked even prettier with the smile on her face. 'What's he earned?'

Henry Grime gave Dylan a conspiratorial wink as he pulled on the joint and started to cough. Grime laughed and, standing up, took the joint back. 'Dee's been doing a good job for me.' He opened his arms, and Donna obediently came over. 'Things have been going well, and I'm feeling like Little Dee and my girl need a night off to let their hair down.' He put his other arm around Dylan.

'Good boy, Dylan,' Donna said, a little wanly, cradling her glass to her chest.

Henry Grime showed his gold teeth. With his arm around Dylan's neck, he put the joint back in the boy's mouth. 'Well then, let's get this party started.'

MEMENTO MORI

"I wander thro' each charter'd street,
Near where the charter'd Thames does flow.
And mark in every face I meet
Marks of weakness, marks of woe."
— **William Blake**, *London*

13

JETSAM

TWO POLICE DIVERS surfaced from the depths further upstream and signalled. A police dinghy sped out to them across the Thames, throwing up white foam. DS Kenny Stokes watched them manhandle a weighty object from the water. Behind Kenny was a litany of death. So far, two dismembered and decapitated torsos, two arms, and one leg had been discovered tangled in the moorings around the boats at the Metropolitan Marine Policing Unit, just south of Whitechapel at Wapping. The initial torso was discovered at first light when the morning shift rolled onto their private dock.

The call had reached Kenny while he was still asleep, and he and DC Rojish Dabral had spent the entire day on the riverbank watching as piece after piece was brought on land and laid out on plastic sheets inside a white forensics tent.

The two divers descended back beneath the surface, and the boat swerved away to shore. Crowds of onlookers beyond the police cordon, and on the south bank of the Thames opposite, filmed with their phones. The MET had all but shut down river traffic for the day, inadvertently drawing more attention to themselves, while they carried out the slow underwater investigation, hindered by the murkiness of the Thames.

'You reckon they've found another body?' Roj said.

'We'll see soon enough.' Kenny edged to the waterside. His gut already told him it was a third victim. But that wasn't the worst of it.

It was the strangest thing. Kenny could swear he heard the same growl and saw that same flash of canine teeth he felt at Annie Drew's murder scene. That was strange because in Kenny's experience those echoes were always tied to the place of murder. They didn't follow the bodies around. He didn't know why; that's just the way it was. These remains must have washed downstream, and it was unlikely they were murdered and dismembered on the riverbank for all to see, or CCTV to pick up. The murder site would be elsewhere, perhaps miles away, and yet, the remains still carried the trace of their deaths. The growl was low and menacing. Maybe he was mistaken. It was faint, after all. A trick of the memory perhaps?

The boat pulled up, and the sack was handed to forensics officers who carefully took it into the white tent. Kenny and Roj ducked inside. They stayed at the edge, out of the way. Professor Naomi Peevers, the pathologist from the Royal College, arrived two hours ago to consult. She was a short, round woman with red-rimmed spectacles, wrapped in white coveralls, and only briefly acknowledged that Kenny was there before turning her attention back to the sack.

'Sarg, something's been bugging me all morning about this,' Roj said.

'You mean more than the dismembered and decapitated bodies?' Kenny was focused on the forensics officers and Professor Peevers as they explored the sack.

'Ha, right, yeah. No, I mean it's not funny ha-ha, but funny coincidence.'

That got Kenny's attention. Coppers aren't fans of coincidences. In their experience, ninety-nine times out of a hundred, coincidences result in enough paperwork to cause a DVT. 'Go on,' Kenny said with trepidation.

'Well, you know how Annie Drew's murder looks too much like a Ripper copycat?' Roj kept his voice down so that no one else would hear. This little fact was not something Kenny wanted broadcasting. The last thing they needed was to add a ton of manure to the crap the tabloids and social media spread anyway.

'I'm not going to like this, am I?' Kenny said.

'Probably not, but you know I was onto the Ripper thing because of the sightseeing tours I did when we moved down here?'

'Are we getting to a point, Roj?'

Professor Peevers gently peeled down the sack, and there was that growl again.

'Sorry, Sarg. The thing is, on that Ripper tour, the guide mentioned another set of murders that overlapped with the Whitechapel cases. I double-checked it on my phone there now. They were called the Thames Torso Murders.'

Kenny turned to Roj. 'You're shitting me?'

'I shit you not, Sarg.'

That's when Professor Peevers sidled up to the two detectives with a sombre look in her eyes. 'I'm afraid that is a third torso, decapitated and dismembered in precisely the same manner as the other two. Are you alright, Kenny? You look like you've seen a ghost.'

14

ADVOCATE

Toby Thatcher—sadly, no relation—stood staring at the instructions on his phone, feeling jolly well hot and bothered *and* underappreciated. This task was not only entirely beneath him but bloody well ridiculous. He'd been sent all over London like a common bicycle courier and ended up in the East End looking for an address that didn't exist. A knife could be plunged into his back at any moment by some hooded ne'er-do-well on a moped. Then his family would have to endure the ignominy of their Winchester and Oxbridge educated son becoming a mere statistic in the long lament of this country's inner city fecklessness.

He was Patroclus before Apollo's bow, because Achilles was too busy working on his golf swing to storm the walls of Troy himself. Okay, daddy had made a few calls to get Toby into *Freshfields Bruckhaus Deringer*, one of London's oldest and most prestigious law firms, but was he really nothing more than an errand boy? It seemed so. He had a 2:2 in PPE from Pembroke College Oxford and finished in the top half of his class on Nottingham University's law conversion degree. Finding number 25 Gallows Court should be like doing a vocational course at a comprehensive school, for God's sake.

"Take six strides from the manhole in front of number 24 Gallows Court and stop. Turn to face the buildings on your left and picture a black door in your mind," the message read. Toby groaned in exasperation.

'It isn't damn well here,' he said out loud. He'd already asked in the charity shop. They looked at him as if he was mad—*him*! Try next door they said, as if he was a simpleton, but that was number twenty-six, and the spotty oik serving fried chicken sent Toby back in the direction of the charity shop. With no other ideas of what to do, and on strict instructions from a senior partner, no less, to make the delivery, Toby located the manhole in front of number twenty-four. He lined himself up with it like a first year about to be whipped with a towel after rugby practice and strode forth.

Six paces later, he stopped and turned to face the buildings. Before him was... a charity shop and a fried chicken emporium with dubious hygiene standards. Toby made a disgusted sound and looked at his phone, "and picture a black door in your mind," he read out loud, shouldering heroic levels of incredulity. An image of a black door popped involuntarily into his head, and as he lowered the phone, he nearly fell over.

What was going on? How had he missed it? It was right there: a Victorian, mid-terrace townhouse. A few weeds sprouted here and there. The door could do with a lick of paint, and they needed to get the boards off the windows, but it wasn't half-bad. Shabby chic, and it had a strange kind of allure to it. Magnetic, in fact. Odd that it should be the only building of its type among these modernist carbuncles.

'Well, Tobes ol' boy, let's get this over and done with.' The sun was westering below the rooftops, and he didn't fancy hanging around after dark. He didn't fancy hanging around in daylight for that matter, so Toby girded himself like Odysseus before the cave of Polyphemus and mounted the steps. However, before he could knock on the door, it opened ajar. A tall, muscular man with a handlebar moustache, wearing a brown bowler hat, white grandfather shirt, and brown checkered waistcoat answered the door.

'Good afternoon, sir. Are you...' Toby checked the phone for the unusual name. '*Châtelain du Vieil*?' He spoke with a polished French accent honed on the slopes of Courchevel every Easter ski season.

With an expressionless face, the man eyed Toby from head to toe. Without saying a word, he opened the door and stood aside.

As Toby entered the darkened hallway, he thought he heard the man whispering. 'Sorry. I didn't catch that.' Toby said, but the man's face was like stone as he slammed the door behind them.

The man pointed down the hall, and for reasons Toby couldn't quite fathom, he swallowed the lump which had grown in his throat. 'Right, yes, of course,' he said, not knowing what he was agreeing to. Yet he had the image in his mind's eye of a crackling fire burning in the parlour, and he somehow knew it was just down the corridor on the right. His mouth was dry as he approached the entrance. The hall was musty with faded wallpaper, a pale reflection of its former opulence. That lump stretched Toby's throat, and dread had grown as suddenly as the revelation of a cancer diagnosis at an annual check-up.

'Do come in, Master Thatcher,' Toby heard, before the slow turn into the parlour. One hand on the mantel, the other behind his back, a middle-aged man stood gazing into the fire, wrapped in a scarlet dressing gown. His hair was a salty grey, slicked back from an aquiline face bejewelled with grey eyes filled with flames.

Toby's legs moved as if they weren't his own, compelling him into the room. 'I—' Toby cleared his throat, the lump choking him along with an overwhelming urge to cry. He fought it down, and he tried again. 'I've brought what you requested...' The sentence gave him some of his usual bravado back. 'It isn't our typical service, but I have everything requested as per the instructions. Most odd, though, the age of the note. I have it with me also.'

'You talk a lot for one so insignificant,' the man at the fire said. He'd uttered it so softly, as if only speaking to himself, but it rang like a judge's gavel in Toby's head, and he shut his mouth, feeling exactly as he did when his parents abandoned him at boarding school aged eight. It was a memory long forgotten, but now it blistered afresh in his mind, weeping with childish emotions.

The man swept from the fire, seeming to glide from one place to another in an instant. He looked down on Toby, his grey eyes finding the trainee lawyer undeserving of any expression.

'Sit down, Master Thatcher. No, not on the floor. The stool will do.' The man was somehow already enthroned in the winged chair. Toby fumbled his way onto the stool before the man.

'*Châtelain du Vieil?*' Toby offered the old letter, inked with copperplate handwriting and yellow with age.

'*Oui, c'est moi,*' Vieil said with a smear of amusement on his lips. 'But *Châtelain* will be enough for you.'

'I b-brought the suits you requested.' Toby offered up his arm with a black suit bag draped over it. The muscular man from the front door appeared at his shoulder and relieved Toby of the suits. 'We had it made at *Ede and Ravenscroft* as per your great grandfather's instructions. It was a stroke of luck they still had your grandfather's measurements on file.'

'Luck?' Vieil tilted his head.

'Yes, a hundred and thirty years later. It's incredible they hadn't gone out of business. I also have the cash withdrawal from your investments.'

Toby offered Vieil a large, brown envelope packed with crisp banknotes. Vieil looked at the package with casual disregard and made no attempt to take it. Toby remained with his arm outstretched like a beggar proffering a pewter mug. Finally, Vieil waved a hand, and the attendant in the bowler hat took the money. Toby didn't put his arm down. He couldn't and his shoulder started to ache.

Amusement creased on Vieil's face again. 'What else?'

Toby stared at his outstretched arm as he stuttered, 'W-w-we thought th-this would be more useful to you than your l-l-ledgers.' He fished inside the carry case slung over his shoulder, struggling to one-handedly unzip the bag. Eventually, he produced a laptop, holding it up along with his other arm. Vieil raised an eyebrow.

Toby's shoulder now felt a stabbing pain, but he still could not lower it. The *Châtelain* said nothing. 'I-i-it's a laptop computer. It contains all the information and more. I also have instructions from the partners in the firm on how to use it. They said to tell you it has everything you n-need to know and more. Also, it has a means to contact them encrypted on it.'

Sweat wet Toby's brow as the pain in his arm caused him to grit his teeth. He so wanted to put it down, but feared if he did something terrible would happen. What? He didn't know. In his mind, he started to sing a nursery rhyme he used to say to himself on those lonely nights without his mummy and daddy at boarding school. *Sing a song of sixpence, a pocket full of...*

'Do shut up, Tobias. That can't help you, you tiresome boy,' Vieil said in that ever-so-quiet manner that roared in Toby's head.

'S-s-sorry.' A tear rolled down Toby's cheek.

'Sorry? Isn't it time to grow up? So mummy and daddy sent you away because you were an annoyance, and there's the fact you made your mother semi-incontinent after your bulbous head tore her birth canal to pieces. You have to learn to live with the disappointment you festered into. You may well find comfort in condescension from the happenstance of your privilege. Deep down you know you didn't earn it, any of it. You squandered opportunity and matured into the embodiment of mediocrity, only to wash up at my door as an over-priced errand boy, still suckling on the withered teat of his parents' fortune.'

'I'm s-so s-sorry,' Toby cried, tears dripping down his face. All his confidence had been peeled away, torn from him on the walk into this room until he was left with only the bleached bone of his emotional core, which, to his surprise, was a frightened child, eight years old, wetting the bed in a shared dormitory. A warmth grew in Toby's crotch as his bladder released, soaking the stool.

'Yes, you've said that.' Vieil looked away to the boarded-up windows, with the heavy curtains pulled across. 'Can you hear that, the city? I've been away so long, but its pulse throbs louder than ever.' Vieil closed his eyes, his nostrils flaring as he breathed deeply. When he opened them again, they fell on Toby. 'Why are you still here? I have things to do, a city to reacquaint myself with. Do see yourself out.'

Vieil stood with a sudden speed and Toby flinched, but when he looked back again, he was alone, sat in a puddle of his own urine. Embarrassed, he shuffled from the room with his head down. Tears dripped from the tip of his nose. The door slammed behind him. The streetlights were on, making the night sky a muddy brown. His wet trousers stuck to him coldly, and he felt utterly ashamed and wanted nothing more than to get home and hide.

With shaking hands, he used an app to call for a cab. On the steps of number 25 Gallows Court, the world around him moved along as if he didn't exist, as if he didn't matter at all, and in that moment, Toby was struck with a revelation of his true insignificance. The white mini-cab pulled up on the pavement across the road. Toby left the steps of the old house. A barrage of noise assaulted him as he looked left and right to cross the road and get away from here. With a space in traffic, Toby cut into the road between two parked cars. He reached the broken white line in the middle of the busy road and forged on, hoping the cabbie wouldn't notice he'd pissed his pants until he got out. That was when he heard his mother calling.

'Toby!' he heard through the traffic noise and stopped in the road, turning back toward the old house. It was his mummy, standing on the pavement. What a wonderful coincidence. But when he noticed her face, she was frowning and shaking her head. Toby wished the world would swallow him up so that he didn't have to see the confirmation of his mother's disappointment. And in a way, it did.

Eyewitnesses said the London bus sounded its horn. There was a screech of brakes that left long, black stains on the tarmac, but Toby didn't seem to hear any of it. The double-decker bus hit him hard, and Toby Thatcher—sadly, no relation—died painfully in an ambulance twenty minutes later.

15

PARTY TIME

THE ROOM WAS DROWNING in a smog of cannabis and tobacco smoke, and the sweet bottle of electric blue alcohol in Dylan's hand wasn't helping. He was adrift, swooning on the chop of booze, weed, and all his troubles. He watched from his anointed spot next to Henry Grime on the sofa as people partied in front of him. It was a small holiday from the nighttime work of the Blud Crew, a festival in celebration of Dylan, and it seemed a preparation for a war that he had sparked with the Duppy Crew and which everyone appeared excited for. All night the Blud Crew had talked about it, how the Duppies had asked for it, coming onto their territory. They'd had it coming for a long time. It was *they* who really started it. But, as the chat went, it was the Blud Crew who would finish it. Dylan couldn't believe it: things just kept going from bad to worse.

All night they had patted him on the back, called his name, thrown him looks of admiration, disbelief and, yes occasionally, wariness at the boy who'd dispatched three other young men his age in such a gruesome fashion. All that was bad enough, but paled compared to the other thing he'd become aware of: the whispers. They followed him from Gallows Court. They weren't always perceptible, but when they were, there was a tug in his gut—a not so subtle pull toward the black door.

Worst still, the side effects of the cannabis and alcohol had taken Dylan's protective numbers away from him. He felt them slip between his fingers uncounted, dissolving before his mind's eye. Dylan took another swig of the sweet liquor hoping, even though it had not worked so far, that it would dampen the churning thoughts. The phone buzzed in his pocket.

"Are you alright dude?" Samuel liked using "dude" in texts. Dylan didn't know anyone else their age who used the word. Even now, it brought the tiniest quirk to Dylan's face. Sometimes Samuel was old beyond his years, and yet in other ways, he was naive. He thought everything would be alright. He thought he was going to grow up to be a lawyer or a fighter pilot or the Prime Minister or, more passionately, a comic book writer. Dylan loved that about Samuel, but he also knew the truth. People like him didn't get to be people like that, and no amount of dreaming was going to make any difference.

As bass notes pounded out of the speakers in the living room, Dylan put his phone to sleep without answering. Not that he didn't want to tell his friend everything, but since last night, a great crack had opened up in their world, and Dylan could feel it pulling them apart. The continental plates between child and adulthood had seismically sheared apart with them on opposite sides of the divide. Dylan so wanted to leap over the gap back into the world of comic books and homework, of farting silently on the back of the bus, of passing notes in class, and stealing away to their hideout on the weekends. Maybe he could get back if he could do what needed to be done at Gallows Court? He suspected even that would make returning even harder. Why, he couldn't say, other than a vague and oppressive notion that monsters are never so easily slain. Impossible as a dream of getting out of Whitechapel.

'Little Dee, you look like you're gonna top yourself. Cheer the fuck up.' Henry Grime was sat with Donna Savage on one lap and another younger girl, named Chantel, on the other. The flat was packed with people from the Blud Crew and their girlfriends. They came from all over their Ends. Dylan knew many of them by name only, except now they treated him like one of their own. In a corner, a wannabe DJ called Meathead, on account of his thickly muscled but squat body, hunched over a set of decks while Tracks and Custard MCed, spitting bars on a mic. They were terrible, but they were also Henry Grime's closest lieutenants in the Blud Crew, so no one complained.

The music was so loud Henry Grime had to shout. 'Chantel, go put a smile on his face.'

A bottle of Russian mule and fag in her hands, Chantel hopped off Henry's lap and took Dylan by the hand, stubbing out the cigarette in an ashtray as they left the room.

Henry Grime flicked his hand, snapping his fingers together. 'Alrigh', my man, you get on dat ting.'

The king having spoken, everyone in earshot whooped in approval. Donna forced a smile and took a larger swig of her straight vodka. Tracks and Custard had noticed, and so Tracks slipped into a Jamaican accent and shouted through the PA, 'Big up, Little Dee.' Custard added, 'Duppy killa.' And the crowd whooped as Meathead pushed a button producing a sound effect explosion.

The catcalls followed them into the hall, and Chantel said, 'Where's your room, big man?'

Dylan could feel his heart beating like the bass from Meathead's speakers. 'There.' Feeling anything but the big man, he pointed to the white door with a D on it, a childish remnant of presents from Christmas past.

Chantel smiled gently at Dylan and pulled him to the bedroom. She closed the door behind them, before Dylan could turn on the light, and pushed him against the wall. Soft hands caressed his face. Chantel's warm breath brushed his lips, followed closely by the wetness of her mouth. Mostly because he didn't know what else to do, Dylan kissed her back. As she pressed her body into his, she tasted of cigarettes and sweet alcohol and she smelt of men's body spray. It was a trick he knew his mother used so that her clients didn't go home to their wives smelling of women's perfume.

Chantel's hand started to stray from Dylan's face, sliding over his chest. It wasn't that Chantel wasn't pretty. She was, in that way teenage boys find most things with lumps and curves attractive, even more so if they take an interest in them. She had light brown hair and dark brown eyes, small breasts pushed up in a padded bra, and hips that curved a little away from a slim waist. And even though she was nineteen, there were girls in Dylan's year at school that looked just as old with the right makeup and clothes. But Dylan's head tumbled with all his problems as her hand unzipped the fly on his jeans, and the whisper in his head grew louder.

Yesshh! And he could have sworn it tittered.

Dylan scrunched his eyes tight shut to block out the black door of number 25 Gallows Court opening. The dark corridor stretched out forever, but now the carpet was a lush red, red as blood, and gold leaf glistened in the frames of the paintings. Fool's gold.

Dylan moaned when Chantel released him from his boxer shorts and her soft fingers wrapped around him. Anila's shy face came to mind along with a familiar longing. Then the image was sullied. Vieil was arching back, sat astride the lanky Duppy boy, whose glassy eyes reflected only terror, and Mr Butcher laughed noiselessly.

Chantel had moved her mouth to Dylan's ear and bit gently at its lobe, sending electricity to every nerve ending in his body. He shrank away, sliding down the wall and staggering in the dark to his bed, embarrassed, aroused, and afraid all at once.

'What's the matter?' Chantel said.

He bumped into the desk, something fell over, and he groped to find a familiar object to orientate by. The glow of his alarm clock reached him, and he found the bed, slumping onto it, and attempted to cover his privates. 'Nothing. Sorry,' he apologised.

'Don't you like me?' She was coming across the bedroom towards him.

'No. I mean, yes. It's not that?'

She was standing in front of him. Her fingers stroked the top of his head, but the seduction was gone. This was tender. She sat down next to Dylan and put an arm around his shoulders.

'Is it your first time?'

'Yeah, I mean, I can't.'

'Sure you can, darlin'. It's easy. I'll show you how.'

Yesshh, the whisper encouraged.

'Please, no, go away.' Dylan shuffled up the bed but hit the desk with his knees.

'Okay, babe. Shush now. It's alright. You don't need to be afraid.'

Yessshhh, the whisper grew more excited.

Dylan started to cry, curling in on himself.

'Hey, babe. It's okay. There now, don't cry.' Chantel drew Dylan's head to her shoulder, and he let her. 'Grime will be angry if I don't make you happy. You know what he's like. He'd be mad if you turned down his favour. You know what I mean, sweetie?'

Dylan sniffed and nodded into her shoulder.

Chantel's hand was inside his jeans again, moving up and down as Dylan wept. After a minute or so of effort she said, 'Let's try something else,' and she slid off the bed to kneel between Dylan's legs. She tugged down his jeans and boxer shorts, but before she lowered her head, she looked up into Dylan's anguished face, tears streaking down his cheeks.

'Please don't,' he said.

Two small creases made a V between her eyebrows. For a moment Dylan thought she was going to explode like his mum did when she thought a client was wasting her time. Chantel didn't do that. Instead, she squeezed his two thighs in her birdlike hands and rose up on her knees in front of him. 'Come here,' she said, wrapping her arms around Dylan. She planted a kiss on the side of his head and spoke softly. 'We'll just make out you are a stud. It'll go with your new bad boy image, hey?'

This set Dylan off again, shaking with sobs.

'Hey, hey, it's alright,' she said, and then corrected herself, 'except it isn't, is it?'

'What do you mean?' Dylan grizzled.

Chantel stroked the back of his head. 'You tell me, darlin'. But I imagine killing three people, even if it is because you had to, is just the sort of thing to make anyone cry, anyone with half a soul, that is. I can't think what that must be like with everyone making out you're a hero.'

Dylan made a plaintive moan in agreement.

'Thought so. Here, let's tuck you back in.' Chantel helped Dylan with his trousers. 'Tell you what, why don't we lie here for a while?' She hopped on the bed and pulled Dylan back onto the pillow and lay down next to him on her side, with a hand resting on his chest. 'There, that's nice, innit? I haven't had a good cuddle in forever.'

The party pounded at the walls of the bedroom, while they lay with the lights off. Dylan's chest rose and fell, occasionally shaking with the aftershock of raw emotion as he brought himself back under control. The whispers from Gallows Court had quieted too, and his head was clearing.

Finally, Chantel said in a hushed voice, 'What do you want to be when you grow up?'

Dylan kept looking at the ceiling. 'Dunno. I've never thought about it.'

Chantel poked him playfully under the ribs. 'Liar!'

'Hey!' Dylan protested and turned to face her hiding his ticklishness.

'That's better. You've got a nice smile. Don't think I've ever seen it before. Now, answer my question. What do you want to be when you grow up?'

'You'll laugh.'

'Sweetheart, I'm a prozzie. On a good day, I take my clothes off for strangers on the internet. I ain't gonna judge.'

'I want to be an accountant.'

Chantel giggled and snatched her hand to her mouth as if trying to catch the laugh before it escaped.

But Dylan was smiling too. She had the sweetest laugh, like birdsong. 'You said you wouldn't laugh.'

'You gotta be quicker than that in Whitechapel, sweetie. I said I wouldn't judge. But seriously, accountant? Out of all the jobs in the world, how'd you come up with the most boring?'

She was teasing him, and he knew it. 'It's the only thing I'm any good at.'

'What is?'

'Numbers, maths.'

'Really?' She sounded shocked.

'Yeah, really. Like, ask me a sum, a really hard one.'

'Alright.' Chantel came up on her elbow to look down on him. 'What's four hundred and seventeen, times by thirteen, divided by seven and a half.'

After a couple of seconds Dylan replied, 'Seven hundred and twenty-two point eight.'

'Wait a minute. Are you pullin' my chain? How am I supposed to know if that's right?'

'Check it on your phone.'

Chantel got her phone from the back pocket of her skinny jeans. 'What did I say?'

Dylan repeated the sum for her.

'And what did you say the answer was?'

'Seven hundred and twenty-two point eight.'

Chantel's mouth dropped open. 'Fuck me! You're friggin' Einstein. Does your mum know about this?'

'Nah,' Dylan could feel himself blushing and was glad it was dark.

'Do it again!' Chantel said, giving him a sum of seventeen times thirteen, times twenty-three, divided by nine and a half, and times by six.

She typed it into her phone and had barely finished when Dylan said, 'Three thousand, two hundred and ten point three, one, five, seven—'

'Bugger me!' Chantel flopped back on the bed wide-eyed to look up at the ceiling with him. 'Accountant? I think you should dream bigger. What about computers, or you could work for NASA or summit, like a proper rocket scientist, sending people to Mars.'

'That's what my teacher says.'

'Who's that?'

'Mrs Stokes.'

'Oh, I never had her at school,' Chantel said wistfully. 'My friend Mindy did, though. Said she was amazing. Mindy even got a D in GCSE maths, which was enough to get into catering college. Gets up at four am every morning and bakes bread and shit in the college kitchen. She loves it.'

'That's not quite NASA,' Dylan said.

'If you knew Mindy, you'd know a D in GCSE maths was a God's honest miracle. I think she'd lose count of her fingers after the first hand. Just goes to show, dreams do come true for some people.'

'Some people,' Dylan repeated letting it hang in the air above them.

'Yeah, some people,' Chantel agreed a little sadly.

'Chantel.'

'Yeah?' she yawned.

'What do you dream of being?' Dylan turned his head to her

Her eyes met his, and in them he saw a vulnerable truth flickering. 'Now you're going to laugh,' Chantel said.

'No I won't, not ever.'

'A long distance lorry driver.'

Dylan's resolve nearly faltered, and his mouth quirked at the corners. Chantel's fingers pounced, tickling him under the ribs again. Dylan squirmed to protect himself. 'You cheeky sod, you said you wouldn't laugh.'

'I'm not laughing. I promise, but long distance lorry driver?'

'Freedom, innit? Driving all over the country, all over Europe even.' She gave a bigger yawn. 'I've only ever been out of London to go to Southend. Imagine all those places. Just me in my cab driving to the next delivery.'

'Why don't you do it?'

'Now you are gonna laugh. I can't even drive a car.'

'You could learn.'

Chantel turned on her side and curled into him, her eyes heavy. 'Nah. I got epilepsy. Can't ever have a license in case I have an episode behind the wheel. Still it comes in useful in my chosen career. Blokes think they're amazing if you have a fit mid-shag.' Her eyes were nearly closed.

'Don't do that,' Dylan said, watching her fall asleep.

'Do what, darlin'?'

'Make fun of yourself.'

Her eyes were closed now, but a small smile touched the corners of her mouth. 'You're lovely, you know that?'

She was asleep, and Dylan covered them both with a fleece blanket from the bottom of the bed. He watched her while she dreamed, wondering if she was on the open road leaving Whitechapel far behind. Maybe he was with her in a great big articulated lorry cadging a ride to the European Space Agency. It was a thought that managed to be painfully happy and sad at the same time, a kind of unsolvable equation that followed him into sleep.

16

HIEROGLYPHS

IT WAS one of those damp, autumnal nights Reverend Abigail Adekugbe had never quite learned to love in England. Crisp frosts, yes they were quite wonderful things. The warm days they called summer were pleasant too, if nothing compared to the heat of her homeland. The snow was quite possibly the best of all. It caught her off guard the first time, chilling her fingers and toes until they burnt with the cold. That was certainly a new experience. But once she learned to dress appropriately, snow had a wondrous beauty that transformed everything, filling the world with light, covering the dirt and grime, and putting smiles on the faces of adults and children alike. It was one of God's everyday miracles. But the damp, no, it made her feel older than her forty-five years and produced a grumbling ache in her bad knee and shoulder. It caused her scars to throb. It didn't matter how many jumpers, woolly hats, or waterproof coats she put on, the damp had a way of seeping into her bones and making her soul feel heavy.

'How come you're a priest here, then?' the homeless man asked. He had a ruddy and stubbled face marked with sores at the corners of his mouth.

Abigail handed the man a cheese roll to go with his cup of tea. 'This is where God sent me.' This statement had the benefit of both being true and likely to make the man move along. If it didn't, the conversation could go one of two ways. Time would tell which way that was. Abigail was firmly of the opinion that God continually presented people with different paths to choose.

The man sniffed and ran the back of his hand across his runny nose. 'Nah, I mean, why don't you do it in your own country? Aren't there druggies and tramps in need of a good Bible-bashing over there?' He took a swig of his tea and seemed to have grown in himself.

Oh well, Abigail thought, *he had to choose that path.* 'Sadly, yes there are. But things got too hot for me there. And I like the rain. No one does rain like England.' She beamed at the man, a smile of white teeth as brilliant as fresh snow.

The man grinned, his face mellowing. 'Ha! Ain't that the truth.' Someone shouted out the name Charlie, and the man with the sores around his mouth hailed one of his friends and wandered off.

It was then something caught Abigail's attention across the road. Cars and buses hurried in opposite directions, and two men walked casually through busy streets, people parting around them as they went, never bumping into them, never looking at them, as if they weren't there at all. Abigail fixed on them with her good eye. One wore a fine tailored suit under a long, Crombie overcoat. He wore his greying hair slicked back. The other man had a handlebar moustache, brown checkered suit, and a matching bowler hat. Abigail's shoulder gave a sudden twang, and the burns on her legs, back, and stomach prickled with cold fire.

Just before the two men went out of sight, the man with greying hair stopped. A pace later, the bowler hat man came to a halt. The two men looked across the road towards Abigail, who stood behind a trestle table of the pop-up soup kitchen. He paused only long enough for a small quirk to appear on his angular face, and then he turned on his heel, and the two men were immediately lost in the crowd.

THEY WALKED ON, invisible to the multitudes that flocked through the streets, even more numerous than the flying rats that crapped all over

Lord Nelson's Column. What a bore that man was. Mr Butcher inclined his head questioningly at Vieil.

'No, it was nothing to be concerned about. No, don't follow her. Besides, I thought you were hungry. *Non, je ne veux pas manger. Je suis plein.*'

Mr Butcher shrugged.

They passed Whitechapel tube station and Vieil paused. He turned and entered the station with his attendant at heel. He watched for a moment as Londoners swiped cards at turnstiles. A young couple entered the station hand-in-hand. They both had foldable plastic wallets already in their hands when something distracted them. They cut short their conversation and changed direction, coming to a stop in front of Vieil. They offered up the plastic wallets, and Vieil and Mr Butcher took them. Moments later the two gentlemen were gone, passing through the turnstiles. The young couple jumped, as if surprised to find themselves in the tube station. They got their bearings, smiling sheepishly, and ferreted in their pockets for the Oyster cards which weren't there.

The doors opened to the tube train. It was packed. Two over-weight men in puffer jackets, listening to music on their mobile phone loud enough for everyone to hear, suddenly stood up. Vieil and Mr Butcher sat in their seats. The fattest of the two men dropped his phone on the floor and stamped twice on it until the screen went dead and the music stopped. Vieil enjoyed the look of confusion and anger that spread across the two men's faces when they realised the phone was broken. They shot recriminations at each other. The other people on the tube, like one conscious organism becoming aware of the pathogen, moved away.

The two fat men began to push each other. One pulled a knife. Somebody screamed. A mother pulled the heads of her children into her midriff so that they would not see. The blade punched once, twice, three times into the fat man who had dropped the phone. On his face, anger turned to incomprehension and then to wordless panic. He dropped to his knees and reached out a beseeching hand to his friend, who stepped away to let him fall into a growing puddle of his own blood.

To a screech of brakes, the tube train came to a stop. The rest of the commuters looked on with quiet faces of wan horror. They did not notice the man in the expensive overcoat and tailored suit, with his bowler-hatted friend, stand and walk from the train. Screams and shouts of concern went up, and then the remaining fat man in a puffer jacket hurried from the train, sprinting past Vieil and Mr Butcher.

'It used to smell of horse shit, do you remember that?' Vieil said. 'Horse shit, coal and desperation. There's still plenty of the latter, but now it smells of... *Quel est le mot? Ah oui! Chimique.*'

When they reached the steps of the British Museum, Mr Butcher's eyes followed a young lady with red hair and a purple coat.

'Bientôt, mon amie. Humour me; I'm feeling nostalgic. Besides, there is so much more open this time. It was all opium houses, brothels, and gentlemen's clubs last time. And you know I don't care for brandy or cigars.'

They wandered the exhibitions until Vieil came across what he was looking for. He lingered briefly at the Rosetta Stone, resting in its glass mausoleum. Its Egyptian, Demotic, and ancient Greek scripts scurried across the stone to its chipped edges. Vieil quickly lost interest and moved on, finding four calcite canopic jars, used to store the internal organs of some long dead pharaoh or self-important courtier. One bore the head of a man with an Egyptian headdress, another the head of a baboon. The third was a beaked visage of an eagle, while the fourth was the jackal-headed god Anubis, with his long, pointed snout and equally long, pointed ears.

Mr Butcher rolled his eyes.

'Fine,' Vieil said with good humour, 'go and have your fun.'

Mr Butcher's face lightened. He seemed to sniff the air, and then in an instant he was gone.

Vieil sighed. *'Bonne chasse, Anoup.'*

He lingered at a set of hieroglyphs listing the lineages of pharaohs. A young woman with rings in her ears, nose, and eyebrows stopped next to Vieil and studied the English description beneath the display, before she scoffed and turned up her nose.

'Is something not to your taste?' Vieil asked.

The young woman clutched a hand to her chest. 'I didn't see you there.'

'My sincere apologies. Do you not like the exhibition?'

The young woman cast a withering look around the hall, lent her weight on her right hip, and opened a hand like a Roman senator about to make a proclamation. 'Talk about patriarchal, cultural appropriation. I mean, it's just the whole my dick's bigger than your dick, at the scale of empire.'

'Of whom are you speaking?'

'The British Empire of course. They stole this junk, didn't they?'

'They weren't the first. They won't be the last,' Vieil said, growing bored and turning his attention back to the hieroglyphs.

'You would say that, wouldn't you?' the young woman sniped.

Vieil lent closer to the glass but said, 'If you feel that strongly about it, you really should make people listen. Don't you think?'

The young woman's face hardened for a moment and then eyebrows rose as if experiencing her life's greatest epiphany and walked away.

Looking at the hieroglyphs and shaking his head, Vieil muttered, 'Self-aggrandising plagiarists.' He'd had quite enough of nostalgia for one night. The city had so much more to offer. When he reached the exit, he didn't look back at the young woman with facial piercings standing on top of the mezzanine balcony, shouting at the top of her lungs about patriarchy and self-sacrifice. Like a prophet, she opened her arms and plummeted head first into the polished stone floor beneath.

Panic churned behind him, and Vieil disappeared into the bustling throng of the London night.

17

RSPCA

IT HAD BEEN QUITE a night for Judy, rushing back and forth to the clinic with rescued animals. As soon as she saved one, there was another on the roster. Three stray cats. One pigeon with a broken wing, and one unfeasibly large, dead rat with a bloated belly full of maggots, which was less of a rescue and more of a public health issue. Still, it was her boots on the ground—if only it hadn't fallen to pieces as she shoved it into a black bin liner. She could still smell it now. Even Judy's stomach turned at that. Then there was a council flat with an industrial amount of cannabis growing in the attic under red lights, along with three illegal snakes, a baby alligator, and four species of bird-eating spiders in glass tanks. But the worst of all had been the last: a neglected greyhound, so thin it resembled a skeleton wearing rags of mangy fur, tattered with bloody sores. It was touch and go whether it would pull through. Judy was only mad the owner wasn't around so the police officers who'd called her in when they found the dog could have arrested the sicko straight away. The poor greyhound didn't even have the energy to lift its head off the floor. It gave a couple of pitiful wags. Its response to a world that had shown it only violence and neglect was to reflect love back at it.

That's why Judy adored dogs above all other animals, and that included humans. It was why she had four of her own, her babies, as she called them: a motley crew of strays she'd picked up over the years of her work as an animal welfare officer. Some dogs she just wouldn't leave to be put down or re-homed. She'd nurse them back to health, like Tink, her three-legged King Charles spaniel, William, her incontinent French poodle, Sharon, the neurotic border collie (when was a border collie *not* neurotic?). And the beating heart of their little family, Betty, a half blind Staffordshire bull terrier. They used to be called "nanny dogs" because they were so loyal and gentle. Not like the popular image of them as child-eating, pit-fighting beasts portrayed in the media.

Judy was on the first break she'd managed to snatch all night. She sat with a takeaway cup of coffee and a cheese sandwich past its sell-by date she'd picked up from the petrol station. She was now pulled up in an alley beside the concrete play area in Rope Walk Gardens, just up from the train tracks; she tried to enjoy her sandwich by thinking about her babies waiting for her at home and stretched out her legs in the footwell of the RSPCA van. There would be another call soon enough. But for now, she was content to wonder what was going on in their little doggy minds as they waited for her to return home.

Her mother was forever telling her she had let herself go in the last few years, and that she'd never get a man if she didn't watch her figure. Judy didn't care. She was happy with how she looked, and was firmly of the opinion that if, and it was a pretty big if as far as Judy was concerned, she was to find love, then that person would have to adore her for who she was, big bum, thunder thighs, and all. That's another reason dogs were better than humans. There wasn't a night Julie wasn't greeted by four wagging tails. Tink would try to jump up to lick her face, but due to only having three legs, he'd end up in a heap of excitement. William would stand with a pompous air, waiting to receive his scratch behind the ears. Sharon fetched a toy, only to doubt her initial choice and fetch another and then get herself in a fluster about which one she wanted Judy to throw. All the while Betty, with a big, beautiful, toothsome smile, sat beaming up at Judy like she was a combination of benevolent god, starlit celebrity, and soul-mate inexplicably returned from yet another heartachingly long odyssey. This, of course, could either have been an eight-hour shift at work or a five minute trip to the corner shop. It would have to be some special kind of man to compete with that love. Judy had often thought it might be better if he was half-dog, hopefully replacing the shitty parts of humanity, the parts that neglected their animals and treated them cruelly.

Judy stopped chewing her cheese sandwich and holstered her coffee cup in the circular holder beside the gear stick. She couldn't quite believe her eyes. A big dog, no, "big" didn't do it justice. An *enormous* dog, easily as large as an Irish Wolfhound, but black and sleek like a Doberman Pinscher, limped along the pavement down the road. Her heart immediately went out to it. Its forepaw was injured. Each time he tried to put weight on it, he lifted it away as if the pavement was red hot. Judy guessed there was perhaps an injury to its flank as well from how it carried itself, tense and laboured. Even injured, it was a truly magnificent beast, perhaps a thoroughbred, but Judy wasn't able to place it. She knew even the most obscure breeds, and all the fashionable crosses which had become so popular in recent years. There was something of a true Arabian Saluki about it, not the show dog versions found in the West, but true lion and game hunters. Yet no, that didn't capture its stature. The ears, for one, were all wrong. A Doberman analogue was closer. Perhaps it was a mongrel, but what accident of crossbreeding had produced such a massive, well muscled, and well-proportioned animal? Judy would love to know. But more than anything, she hated seeing an animal in distress. Her heart ached to think of that dog, no matter how magnificent it was, was right now lost, alone, and hurt.

The animal hobbled into the park. Judy tossed the half-eaten sandwich back into its plastic pyramid container and set it on the passenger seat, clearing her mouth with the dregs of a coffee. She tested a flashlight and moved to the back of the van to arm herself with the long pole hand snare and made sure she had tape to fashion a makeshift muzzle. However, if the dog showed any signs of aggression, given its size, Judy would retreat and call for help on her radio. Satisfied with a couple of clicks to test the flashlight, she set off, crossing to the wire fence surrounding the five-a-side football pitch.

Fingers laced through the wire, she shone her torch into the darkness. Two golden discs shone back from the enormous animal's face, before it turned away and slunk into the trees beside the toddler's play park, limping into the camouflage of dark.

Judy skirted the wire fence until she found a way through and trod across the wet grass. She swung her torch beam across the park, revealing glimpses of a place abandoned to the night. The place was eerily deserted, and Judy's nerves started to jangle. Not about the dog of course. It was the humans that worried Judy. Uniform, any uniform, helped provide a little protection to the wearer, but even that wouldn't put off the sickos and psychopaths. She knew that was more tabloid nonsense. Still, this was an empty park in the dead of night where personal demons and hard-wired genetic instincts filled in the blanks left by the absence of light.

A fox ran across open ground, stopped, saw Judy, and high-tailed it for cover. An owl hooted.

From the tracks nearby, a train made its rat-a-tat-tat progress. Judy crept closer to the small copse of trees from where the two golden discs shone. She panned the light there. Shadows lurched, causing an optical illusion of trees huddling together, trembling with fright. She took another step forward, and a twig snapped underfoot. Something black, possibly a tail, slunk out of the disc at the end of her torch beam.

Judy looked around before entering the copse. Water vapour was condensing into a fine haze, smothering the light from streetlamps warily edging the park. No cars drove down the nearby road. Judy looked back into the blackness under the trees.

'Here, boy,' she called gently.

There was a snort from somewhere outside the torch beam. Judy ventured further, under the boughs of a rhododendron.

'Have you got a sore paw, boy?' She aimed the torch towards the sound and found nothing.

A low growl, like a passing train, rumbled in the darkness to her right. *Maybe this wasn't such a good idea*, she thought. Then again, Judy knew dogs. They wore their hearts on their sleeves. The growl was a fear response, a warning. All she needed was to see it more clearly to make an assessment. If she wasn't able to placate him, she'd withdraw and call for another RSPCA unit. She had to find it first, and bit down on her growing unease.

'Where are you? You don't need to hide from me.' Another step deeper into the trees and Judy swung her torch the other way. The beam of light fell on a gargoyle squatting in the leaf litter, and Judy bit her lip. When the shadows settled, it turned out to be a rotting tree stump.

'I just want to see that you're okay.' Her hand trembled, clutching the torch.

Another twig broke, but this time it wasn't Judy. She didn't want to make any sudden movements and so slowly tracked her torch the other way until the light fell upon the beast. Despite all her training and familiarity with dangerous animals, Judy let out an involuntary whimper.

The hound was much bigger than she had expected. Impossibly large, in fact. Far bigger than an Irish Wolfhound. Its huge, shining eyes reflected the light of her torch beam back at her; they were two burning lamps in a tomb. She could feel its growl vibrating in her chest, and its lips peeled back to reveal its huge, yellow teeth dripping with thick strands of saliva.

Paralysed with fear, all Judy managed to do was drop the torch.

Its light snuffed out.

A STRANGLED CRY emanated from the small copse of trees next to the children's play park. Mist tangled in the shrubs and trees. A vixen stopped mid prowl and turned, pricking her ears at the sound. The noise could have been mistaken for the caw of a crow or the shriek of a feral cat. Only humans, afraid of the dark as they were, would make that mistake. The vixen, however, knew the difference. She smelt the scent of blood on the air and her mouth watered, but the scent of something much worse and far stronger came with it. Not a single morsel of that kill was for her. She and any animal with any sense of self-preservation would get as far away as possible and hide in the deepest burrow it could find. And that is what she did.

18

FLICKERING FLAME

HAMMERING on the inside of Dylan's skull woke him. Chantel lay exactly as she had fallen asleep, curled up under the fleece blanket. She looked peaceful, as if no trouble in the world had touched her. Dylan slipped out of the bed without disturbing her. There was no need to change; he still wore the same clothes from last night's party. As quietly as he could, he unzipped his school bag and took out the maths textbook Mrs Stokes lent him. He opened the bedroom door; Chantel didn't stir as he carefully closed it behind him. The flat stunk of stale booze and tobacco smoke. Stray bodies lay unconscious in chairs, one sprawled on the floor next to the DJ's speakers, another face-planted in spilt drinks and cigarette ash on the small dining table in the corner.

Dylan spotted what he was after. A half drunk bottle of white rum and another of vodka, almost full. He put them in his bag and, despite his care, they made the faintest clinking sound. Meathead the DJ was one of those asleep on the sofa. He opened half an eye, clocked Dylan, and went back to sleep with a grunt.

Dylan let out a breath and finished his thievery by taking a stray lighter.

His head needed a couple of paracetamol, a large drink of water, and a day in bed with the curtains closed. Instead, with the whispers of the night before silent, maybe asleep at last, Dylan touched the hall lightswitch for luck, completing a trinity of flashes before leaving his flat. For all he knew, it was for the last time. He counted each of the two hundred and eighty-eight steps down to the ground floor. On another day, in a previous life, he would have crossed over to Mr Chatterjee's shop for a job he no longer had, and a glimpse of Anila. Instead, he stopped by the broken bin sometimes used for drug pickups and found a dry newspaper beneath the layer of rubbish, damp with the previous night's dew. It would have been quicker if he had his bike, the new one from Henry Grime. He didn't want to risk waking everyone up trying to wheel it out of the flat. Even though he'd stuffed the newspaper between them, the bottles chinked in his backpack like bickering old ladies on a bus.

The early morning mist tangling around him, as he walked towards Gallows Court, Dylan repeated a fatalistic mantra to himself: whatever would happen would happen. But as he grew closer, he entertained the faint hope that the police would come for him. Blue lights flashing, a siren screaming out a warning, and a marked car would pull up beside Dylan. But the streets remained quiet.

Then there was the idea of turning around and curling up next to Chantel to sleep off his pounding head. It was a small wish, but one he knew couldn't come true. He thought about the Blud Crew, passed out in his flat; his mother's door had been closed, which meant she was entertaining someone last night, most probably Henry Grime. Either way he cut it, there were monsters in front and behind him. At least he had an idea about how to kill the one in front of him.

It was a strange thought, though: those three boys wanted to kill Dylan and probably would have done on the street right outside number twenty-five if he hadn't sought refuge like Vieil had told him he could. They would have left him to bleed to death in the street, and yet Dylan still felt the weight of their deaths on his shoulders. He wasn't like them, and he never would be, and so he dragged that burden all the way across the park to the black door.

The house had changed. It looked less dilapidated. The windows were still boarded up, but the wood was newer, the nails less rusted. The plants growing from between bricks and sprouting out of the guttering had been culled. The black paint of the door now shone, and only a few cracks blistered here and there; the railings were straight and sturdy and as black as the front door. Either side of the short flight of steps, the dark recesses of the basement level still loomed as menacing as ever, like empty eye sockets staring out of a bottomless pit.

Dylan took off his rucksack and unzipped it. His head throbbed as he looked left and right. Even this early, the occasional taxi and delivery truck tarried by. He couldn't be sure there wasn't CCTV on the road. He groped for the lighter at the bottom of the bag, took a deep breath, and stepped between the railings onto the first step of number 25 Gallows Court.

Immediately he realised he'd made a terrible mistake.

As soon as he disappeared from the street, it was as if his head was being scratched with pointed fangs from the inside. Whispers. He winced, putting a fist to his forehead, and moved as quickly as he could. Thinking was like wading against a current. He managed to take the first bottle of spirits and unscrewed the top with a shaking hand, and with a force of will placed it on the step. The ivy clinging to the walls rustled and crept. Dylan pulled several sheets from the newspaper, folded them over on each other, and twisted them around until they made a wick, stuffing it into the bottle. The ivy reached the edges of the door and slithered towards the steps. Turning the bottle upside down, Dylan wet the paper. Hard liquor dripped out. Because his mind couldn't seem to make his body do what he wanted it to, he held the bottle in one hand and the lighter in the other, staring at them dumbly for a moment as if each were two numbers that couldn't be added together. Somehow, he managed to get his thumb to strike the flint, but it seemed to have turned to stone. His bones creaked, and the muscles felt as though they might snap at any moment. The rough flint touched the pad of his thumb, and it felt as though it was in his own. Dylan focused, trying to force his thumb down to create a spark. His hands began to tremble but would not obey him.

The ivy slithered onto the stone landing in front of the black door. Groping to settle himself, Dylan hurriedly began to list the primes.

Two, three, five, seven.

Dylan felt the pressure of his thumb moving down against the flint.

Eleven, thirteen.

His hands moved together, bringing the wick of the bottle closer to the possible flame that would come from the lighter.

Seventeen, nineteen.

An orange spark flared and petered out. Muscles in his forearms corded with the effort. The ivy crawled to within inches of his feet. The rattlesnake whispers had grown to a churning maelstrom of noise.

Twenty-three, twenty-nine.

The door banged, and the enormous hound barked savagely from within. Each time it threw itself against the door, the whole house seemed to shake, rocking the world beneath Dylan's feet. The ivy licked at the tips of his toes.

Thirty-one.

As his thumb moved back onto the flint, his hands moved closer together. Suddenly, Dylan realised that if he struck the lighter and lit the Molotov cocktail he would be unable to throw it. An irresistible and dreadful idea rose in his mind. Once lit, he would drop the bottle at his feet, and the flammable liquid would ignite as it smashed on the stone step, spraying him with fire. He would be unable to move and be immolated, unseen from the outside world on the steps of number 25 Gallows Court.

It was as inevitable as sunset. His thumb struck the flint once more, and this time the gas ignited. The small, yellow flame flickered but didn't splutter out. Millimetre by millimetre, the flame drew closer to the newspaper. Its fiery kiss began to cause the edge of the paper to smoke black. In one of these agonising seconds, Dylan would be consumed by fire and pain and die alone in the slow movement of time.

'What are you doing, child?' The Reverend Adekugbe snatched the bottle of liquor from Dylan's hand.

The flame on the lighter snuffed out, but a light came back to Dylan's eyes. The whispers and the ivy retreated. 'I-I—'

'What have you got yourself mixed up in?' Reverend Adekugbe asked in a way that didn't expect an answer. She glared at the house as the black door shook again and the enraged dog barked. In profile to Dylan, her blind eye flicked this way and that.

'Come, away from this evil.' The Reverend took Dylan by the hand and pulled him back onto the pavement. Her hand was cold and oddly textured from the burn scars that stretched and folded there, like melted wax. They stopped at a bin, and the Reverend deposited the two bottles of spirits. Then she rounded on him, taking hold of both shoulders. 'You are never to go back to that house. It is a dangerous place. You would have died on that step playing with fire. Whatever you think you are fighting, it is not your battle, child. Now, let us get you home.'

They marched, not walked, all the way back to Renfield Tower. Holding the Reverend Adekugbe's hand, Dylan felt no need to count the steps on the way up to his flat. They swept through the front door, and Dylan heard her sniff sharply at what she saw, and then shouting began. Dylan felt sorry for Samuel if he was ever on the receiving end of her wrath. The Reverend kicked Meathead's foot. He woke with a perplexed look across his face. The Reverend bellowed and dragged the Blud Crew by their ears, like errant schoolboys in a Dickensian novel. 'Get out, get out.'

The slumped bodies jerked to life and scurried from the flat. Meathead squared up to the Reverend only for her to say, 'What is it, boy? You forget where you put your steroids? I know you and I know your mother. She'd be ashamed of you and what you do. Get out.' Meathead closed his mouth and followed the others. Dylan saw Chantel slip from his room, thankfully unseen by the Reverend.

Finally, Henry Grime appeared, wearing only tracksuit bottoms, yawning with one hand tucked in his waistband. Donna was behind him, wrapped in a dressing gown. Grime seemed amused. 'This ain't no church revival, Rev.'

The Reverend narrowed her eyes at Henry Grime. 'Wipe that smirk off your face, boy.'

Henry Grime's amusement waned; his gold teeth disappeared.

'You wanna be careful how you speak to people, Rev. I'm not sure God bothers his arse to save his lunatics in Whitechapel.'

The Reverend wasn't to be cowed. 'You don't scare me. I've seen far worse on this Earth than the likes of you.'

Henry sucked his teeth, and Donna tugged at his arm. 'Henry, we don't want no trouble,' she said.

'Shut up, bitch!' Henry spat back, shrugging her off. 'And what are you gonna do, you blind, interfering bint?' He stepped to the Reverend, invading her personal space, glaring down at her. She didn't appear intimidated. Her one good eye glared back with equal ferocity.

'Today, the police will do just fine.' She produced a phone and dialed 999.

'You want the boy's mum to go to prison? Don't think the police will be very happy to find these drugs lying about.'

'Why don't we find out?' the Reverend shot back as her thumb hit the call button, and she placed the phone to hear. 'See what they say.' Her voice was a confident singsong in her thick, Nigerian accent.

'Henry, please,' Donna said again, too afraid to touch him.

A small voice emanated from the phone in the Reverend's hand. 'Hello, 999 emergency services. How can I direct your call?'

Grime sneered and nodded. 'Whatever,' he said and sauntered out of the room.

The small voice from the phone repeated itself.

'I am so sorry, I rang the number by accident,' the Reverend said and turned off the call.

Donna stood with her eyes cast down to the carpet. The Reverend still held Dylan's hand. The silence hung heavily in the room, making Dylan shuffle from one foot to the other under its weight.

Henry Grime appeared in the doorway, having pulled on a T-shirt. He cast a withering, sideways glance into the room. 'Be seeing you laters.' The door slammed behind him.

The Reverend looked around the living room. Donna rubbed her arms and nervously tucked a strand of hair behind her ear.

'Right,' a smile broke across the Reverend's face, 'shall we make tea before or after we sort out this mess?'

19

OCCASIONAL APPARITIONS

THE MIST HUNG around like absent-minded ghosts who'd forgotten to dissipate with the rising sun. It draped itself in wispy rags across bushes, on random patches of grass, and in the corners of the concrete multi-sports pitch. Kenny looked inside the RSPCA van. A half-eaten cheese sandwich lay on the passenger seat. He could feel the texture of the stale bread and the bland rubbery cheese, seasoned with a touch of loneliness but nothing else.

'Locksmith is on his way,' Roj said. 'The victim never reported for the end of her shift. The vehicle is LoJacked for insurance and mileage monitoring. When she didn't answer her phone, they sent someone to check on the van. That was at 06:30 am. It's also when the dog walker found the body, or rather her dog did, and the RSPCA guy who was checking on the van heard the screams.'

Kenny didn't have a good feeling about this. There was something just out of reach. He knew it was there, in the corner of his eye, but he could not bring it into focus. He put the thought aside. Feeling washed out didn't help. Early calls were all he seemed to get right now. It didn't matter; he wasn't sleeping well anyway—when did he ever? Last night he and Misha made love again, trying their damndest to get her pregnant. Time was ticking, and she so wanted a baby. He did too, if it made her happy. That wasn't what he was supposed to say, so he didn't. It was the truth, though. Misha was like an unde-served miracle, and Kenny would do anything for her.

Normally, sex helped him sleep. With Misha, it was possible to get absorbed. There was only her, and the rest of the world melted away, replaced not with silence, but something more like a velvetine sigh. Last night, however, sleep was fleeting. A pain in his shoulder and the scream of a little girl woke him as a massive pair of jaws lurched from the dark, about to snap shut. Snoring a little, Misha remained sound asleep. Kenny left her to it.

He drank tea and read Hallie Rubenhold's *The Five*, trying to keep out the chatter of the dead —a perpetual whining and incoherent lament. The book was an interesting history-come-biography of the canonical five Jack the Ripper murders, and it made for much darker reading than his usual horror novels. Hours later, when his phone vibrated on the arm of the sofa, Kenny was almost grateful the day could begin. The message said they had discovered another body. And so here he and Roj were, on a pavement in Whitechapel, close to the train tracks.

In his black and white uniform, the RSPCA officer sat with his head in his hands on the back of an ambulance, while paramedics treated him and the dog walker for shock, draping them in foil blan-kets. Kenny looked over to the knot of trees beyond the wire fence that surrounded the multipurpose sports pitch, marked with a web of white lines for five-a-side football, tennis, and basketball. Patrol officers were cordoning off the entire park with police tape. Like with Annie Drew's murder, forensics were on their way, but Kenny and Roj were ready to go in their white coveralls. A handful of locals hung around at the margins, recording everything on their smartphones.

All the world's a show, thought Kenny. 'Guess we better talk to the RSPCA guy. You take point.'

The poor man's face fell when he saw the two police officers approaching. Cops were the thin blue line between order and chaos. Like occasional apparitions, they popped up to scare the criminals, hand out speeding fines, and break up fights. Otherwise, they melted into the background. Everyone knew they were there, but that didn't mean they wanted to see one coming towards them, in case all those assumptions about a safe life evaporated in their wake.

'Can we have a word?' Roj addressed the paramedic as much as the witness. She nodded and joined her colleague in the back of the ambulance to attend to the dog walker, who was in even worse shape. They'd give her more time before asking additional questions.

The RSPCA man was thinning on top and carried a little extra padding on his face and stomach. As he spoke, his hands shook. 'I already told the uniformed officer what happened.'

Roj gave him an understanding smile and took a seat on the back of the ambulance next to him. It was a nice strategy. Personal and informal, as though they were friends. This was something Kenny struggled with. He knew he came across as aloof, but Roj balanced him out—like Misha did in his personal life—though to be honest, not as attractive.

'Andy, isn't it? I'm Roj. You don't need to start from the beginning. We've got all the events. Tell me about Judy. What was she like?'

'Good at her job, almost to a fault,' Andy said.

'How do you mean?'

'You know, she was all about the animals. They came first. Crap!' Andy looked panicked. 'She's a whole menagerie at home. A pack of dogs—she loved dogs. She has birds and rabbits too. We'll need to go around and take care of them until...' Andy trailed off, realising that there wasn't an "until". Judy was never coming back for them.

'It's okay. We'll get that sorted,' Roj said kindly. 'So, Judy loved her work. What else? Any boyfriend, fiancée, girlfriend maybe?'

'Judy? Nah, like I said: she was all about the job. Quiet, sweet, caring. But, you know, a bit distant maybe. I got the impression she wasn't much interested in people.'

Kenny got the sense Andy held unrequited feelings for Judy. The taste of a sugared almond, one of the ones in a fancy Italian wrapper. He kept it close to his heart, as if he could give it to her when the moment was right.

Roj gave a wan smile. 'You can't think of anyone or any reason someone might want to hurt Judy?'

Andy's voice crackled with emotional static as tears misted in

Andy's eyes, and a single fat droplet rolled down his cheek. 'No. God, no!'

'That's okay. I know this is hard. One last thing. Can you think why she parked here, and why she might have gone into the park by herself late at night?'

That was two things, but Andy didn't seem to notice. He wiped his eyes with the back of his sleeve and rubbed a palm over his face, thinking. Then he shrugged. 'I don't know. Perhaps she was looking for a quiet place to have a break.' He paused, wiping his eyes again and sniffing. 'I looked at her jobs from last night, and she was run off her feet. Why she went into the park? She might have seen an injured animal and gone to check it out. I can't think of any other reason she'd be in a park in the middle of the night and end up...' Andy's voice tightened, strangling the words.

Roj stood and gave Andy's shoulder a solitary pat. 'You've been a big help. You really have. We might need to talk to you again, if that's alright?'

They left Andy to his misery and trudged over the wet grass towards the knot of trees to one side of the park. The walk yielded nothing but the background chatter of old London town, a mumble of unrequited sorrow from souls long dead, but the clump of trees was different.

The growl, there it was again, low and rumbling, like in the alley with Annie Drew and the three torsos pulled from the Thames. Predatory. Proprietorial. The dark of the previous night came then to Kenny, clotted with mist and sweetened with a desire to help. *Help what? The growl. A dog?* That made sense with the RSPCA, but not with the other murders.

Kenny and Roj stopped at the tape.

'There are a ton of footprints,' Roj said. 'Kids, dogs, their owners, teenagers, junkies, and rent boys could all be stomping through there at some point through the day or night.'

Kenny looked into the gloom, glimpsing sprays of blood painted onto some of the twisted branches of a rhododendron.

'Have you got a sore paw, boy?' Kenny mumbled, with the phantom weight of the woman's torch in his hand.

'What was that, Sarg?'

'Nothing, Roj. I was just wondering about the injured animal idea.'

Roj was inspecting the ground around the edge of the trees. 'Despite what Andy said, maybe she was a working girl, making a bit of money on the side. It's not as if colleagues know everything about each other. It would fit with Annie Drew, and the Ripper's original MO.'

There was an opportunity for a little banter here, for Kenny to ask what he didn't know about Roj. But he wasn't one for banter. 'Maybe, but that's a simplistic view of the Ripper's original victims.'

Roj straightened up from inspecting the footprints. 'How's that?'

'I've been reading up. They weren't only prostitutes, they also ran coffee houses, wrote ballads, worked in printing presses, which wasn't exactly the lowest status thing in Victorian times. Even today nurses pull tricks on the side to make ends meet, especially in London.'

'I meant nothing by it, Sarg.'

'I know you didn't. I'm only saying, I think we'd have too narrow a focus if we fixed on the prostitute angle. If he's a copycat, he's one with a deep knowledge of Ripper lore. I knew nothing about the torso murders until you mentioned them.'

Roj raised a hand in acknowledgment of the forensic team making their way across the grass in their coveralls. 'So, he's a big fan. We could look into some of the chat rooms, subreddits, Ripper websites, talk to authors to see if they've had any unusual correspondence, and check up on the tour guides. The one I had was more than a bit weird, had a cape and a silver topped cane, the full-Gothic-monty.'

'Sounds like a plan.'

They waited for the forensics team to secure the scene before they went in, stepping with care through the branches. *Where are you? You don't need to hide from me*, Kenny heard before the echos turned into an assault. It reverberated around the crime scene, trapped by the canopy and pinballed between the tree trunks.

Roj let out a quiet gasp at the bloody scene before them. 'Jesus!'

The growl had a thick, meaty timbre, almost like the V8 of a sports car, vibrating in Kenny's chest. Kenny realised he couldn't breathe. A twig snapped in his mind. There was a flash of a curved blade scything through the air. A hot wave flowed over Kenny's chest, and he realised, or rather Judy tried to comprehend, why blood was gushing down her chest. The need to breathe only increased the panic. Kenny brought a hand to his throat, mawing for air. The world pulsed in and out of a woozy focus. The blade slashed across her stomach. Kenny felt a terrible tug on the connective tissue in his belly as Judy's intestines spilled from the gaping wound in her abdomen. The dog's growl shook the world.

Kenny gasped for a lungful of air and found himself with one hand at his throat and the other clutching Roj's bicep. He was on his knees, falling into his partner.

'He's alright, it's fine,' Roj shouted to the forensics officer standing at the entrance to the copse, a camera in his hands. 'It's his asthma. Breathe, Sarg, breathe. That's it.'

Kenny reeled, trying to get his bearings. 'Pen,' he rasped, 'give me a pen.'

By the perplexed look on his face, Roj didn't understand. 'Sarg, it's okay, just breathe. It was pretty horrible.' He whispered it so no one else would hear.

'No!' Kenny's voice was hoarse. His throat seared with the sensation of every nerve ending exposed to the air. 'Pen—paper—now!' He swallowed back the blade in his throat.

Roj pulled open his coveralls and grabbed his notepad from his suit jacket. 'Here, boss.'

Kenny almost fumbled the small, black notebook and pen as he pulled it open. Roj looked on with worry and incomprehension, while Kenny sketched feverishly with an unsteady hand.

'There, that's it.' Kenny handed Roj his notepad and fell back on his arse and spat on the grass between his knees.

'That's what?' Roj's eyes flicked from the drawing to Kenny and back again.

'The murder weapon.'

'Boss, you were going blue in there. I think—'

Kenny clutched at Roj's forearm. 'It's the murder weapon. I saw it.'

The earnestness in Kenny's tone and face unsettled Roj. 'I didn't see any weapon in there. We were only in there for a minute, two max. And for half that time you were...'

Kenny shook his head and took a deep breath in through his nose and let it out slowly, the world was settling back on its axis. 'Not in there,' he whispered. 'In here.' With his index finger, Kenny tapped at his temple.

Roj opened his mouth but nothing came out. He reformulated. 'You mean...' he began, and seemed to have nowhere to go with whatever he was thinking. He looked down at the strange drawing. It resembled a stretched out question mark. 'I don't follow.'

Sat on the grass, with the images of the murder still rattling around his head, and his junior partner having just pulled him out of a situation that could have been altogether more embarrassing, Kenny decided something. But how to handle it without coming across as a lunatic, or freaking Roj out, was the question. It seemed the universe had decided the moment wasn't right yet, because like an immutable mathematical law of thermodynamics, a shitty situation can always get shittier.

A camera clicked. 'It must be bad if the police look like that. I guess my source was right. Would either of you officers like to comment on the rumours a Jack the Ripper copycat is bringing terror to the East End of London?' The journalist held out his phone to record their response.

20

COLD READING

THEY FILLED bin bags with beer cans, vodka bottles, and cigarette stubs, clearing away the debauchery of the previous evening. The Reverend Adekugbe made chit-chat as they worked, giving Dylan encouragement and saying bland things like, 'Ah, that's better'. When she swept a dusting of white powder, pills, and tobacco from the tabletop, she muttered a more hearty, 'Good riddance'. When they'd finished, Dylan made tea while the Reverend and his mother took bags to shoot for the communal bins. He was squeezing out a tea bag on the side of a mug just as they came back and added the milk. The tea billowed like a cloud, transmuting the dark brown liquid to a fleshy beige. He searched in cupboards but couldn't find any biscuits to serve so settled for adding two sugars to each mug and carried them through.

'Ah, there he is,' Reverend Adekugbe said in her sing-song voice. 'You know, Donna, my Samuel tells me Dylan is quite the mathematician. The best in the whole school.'

Dylan blushed and handed the adults their tea, but he loved that his mum was smiling at him, and her normally sad eyes glistened with warmth. 'Wow, Dyls! Is that so?'

The Reverend gave Dylan a wink with her bad eye, and then she became more somber. 'But I think Dylan has been getting caught up in things, things a young man shouldn't have to be involved with.'

Donna looked ashamed and hugged her mug of tea. Dylan didn't know whether the Reverend meant running drugs for Henry Grime, the strange house on Gallows Court, or maybe both. It didn't matter. An adult had finally stepped in and, as it turned out, he was glad it was Reverend Adekugbe rather than the police. She had always seemed so stern to him, striding with a purpose around the estate. Then again, she was a woman who could emit warmth and care as much as she could stare down Henry Grime or drag Dylan from the steps of a haunted house without flinching. He didn't know where she was going to take this now, but it was better than the path he had been on.

The Reverend took Donna's hand in hers. Dylan noticed again the burns stretching the skin there. 'I will phone the school to let them know he won't be in. Then I think we should have a talk. See if we can't sort all this out.' Her voice was like an upbeat military march, firm but alive with energy and direction. All that was missing was someone to twirl a baton.

Roj GOT BACK in the car and handed off a venti cappuccino and cinnamon swirl. 'No donut clichés for us, and I got us both an extra shot.'

'Baby still not sleeping through?' Kenny took the breakfast offerings.

'That and you look knackered, Sarg.'

'Cheers.' Kenny took a swig of coffee. He definitely needed the caffeine.

Roj peeled back the wrapper on a blueberry muffin. 'You're welcome. They pay us for the truth, don't they?'

'I suppose they do.'

Roj swallowed his mouthful. 'So,' he let the 'o' stretch out, 'I guess we better, you know, kinda, well—'

'Talk about the weird shit I just pulled at the crime scene?'

'Yep, that would be it, Sarg.'

'Guess you think I freaked out, panic attack, flashback from some buried trauma? That sort of thing?'

'The thought had crossed my mind. Then again, you've never done that before. And it's not as if Annie Drew was any better. In fact, the worst thing about the whole affair is that it was the *same*. Even that dickhead journalist knew what that meant. There could be some trauma in your life I don't know about. I've only known you eighteen months or so. Thing is, I can't see how that would lead you to drawing a suspected murder weapon.'

'It's not suspected.'

'Turn of phrase, boss. We don't actually have a weapon, and the thing is, I can't see from the evidence we've got how *you* got from there to here.' Like a flute player, Roj blew through the small hole in the take-away coffee cup lid, before chugging back a mouthful. He expressed no mirth, nor any incredulity, only the level questioning of a solid, capable detective, and, Kenny thought, the concern of a colleague, if not a friend. But that was one of Roj's skills, wasn't it?

Kenny inspected the cinnamon swirl. Its sticky icing coated his fingers. The swirl of dough resembled a coil of intestines. He dropped it back in the brown paper bag, having decided he wasn't that hungry. 'I owe you an explanation. It's just, I've never tried to explain this to anyone.'

'Wait a second, Sarg... Kenny. Before you say anything, this sounds like you're about to confess something, and as a mate as well as a copper, is this the right place and time to do that? Maybe you want a lawyer or a rep present?'

Kenny gave a tired laugh. 'It's sort of a confession, but nothing like that, Roj. Thanks, though.' The world outside the car moved on; people hurried about their day unaware of the murders, at least until that journalist, Dominic Priestley, published whatever salacious crap he wanted in the evening edition of the *Standard*. Kenny's inspector was going to be apoplectic. 'There's no way to put this without sounding completely mental.'

'Well, that bodes well,' Roj said, keeping things light.

'I might as well just say it.'

'Kinda seems like you're not just saying it, Sarg.'

Kenny nodded and sighed. 'Right, here goes. I—sense things. Things that ordinary people can't perceive. They're like, I don't know, echoes, I suppose, of things that have happened. Fragments mostly. Images, tastes, sensations, pieces of speech, memories, emotions, that sort of thing. So when I was at the murder scene, I—well I sort of relived the murder from the victim's point of view. That's how I saw the murder weapon.'

Roj sat quietly for a moment, eyebrows arched up. 'Yep, that wasn't what I was expecting. So, you're telling me you've got ESP? You're a clairvoyant? A telepath, that sort of thing?'

'Not a telepath. Empath maybe, a little. I'm not sure. But I suppose some kind of clairvoyant might be closer to the mark. It's not like you think.'

'Hmm! I'm kind of not thinking anything, Sarg. That stuff's not real. I mean, I know everyone goes on about your hunches, and you're above the curve on solved cases, but I put that down to solid policing and you're a clever bugger. But ESP? It's a bit much to swallow.'

'You believe in God, Roj?'

'Well, I go to temple nearly every week. It's not the same thing. It's about community, and the God stuff, that's for what comes after. The unknown. But how can we know? How can *you* know?'

'I don't. Maybe there is nothing after we die. I don't think people's souls linger on. That's not what I'm sensing—at least I don't think it is. All I know is that when people pass on they leave traces. In fact, they leave traces when they are alive. The stronger the emotion or the more violent the event, the bigger the echo. They fade over time but not always completely. The whole city is vibrating.' Kenny squeezed his eyes with his thumb and index finger. Like a distant schoolyard, the remnants of the city's past chattered on in his head, always needing to be kept at arm's length—until it couldn't be.

'Sorry, Sarg. I'm sure you believe it, but I don't buy it. You're probably very perceptive and can't put a rational explanation on the small clues you're picking up on.'

A homeless man with a dog paused on the pavement for his mongrel to take a dump. Kenny expected the man to walk on and leave the warm pile of excrement for a fellow Londoner to step in, but the homeless man—with his greasy hair and dirty army surplus jacket—confounded Kenny. He produced a small, plastic bag from his pocket, carefully picked up the dog's mess, and deposited it in the nearest bin. Then he gave the dog a treat from his pocket, patted him, and they went on their way. Kenny could feel the man's trauma, even from the car; it tasted like rusty metal, underneath the booze. It threaded through him, oxidised from a molten core of neglect and violence. The dog, on the other hand, produced a feeling in the man Kenny could only describe as "marshmallow", and he got a strong image of a little, white and tan puppy being handed over under a railway bridge. The white, fluffy mallow of the dog's love coated parts of the rusty iron branches.

Kenny rubbed his hands on his trousers, making up his mind. He wasn't completely sure about the idea. It could easily feel invasive. He'd never done it openly before, not like his mother used to do. 'Seeing is believing, right? Would you mind if I read you?'

Roj froze, his coffee cup to his lips, and looked sideways at Kenny. Then he swallowed and wiped his mouth. 'This is *definitely* not where I thought any of this was going.'

'Well? You up for it?'

Roj put his takeout coffee cup in the holder between them and shifted around in his chair. 'Yeah, okay, why not? I've an open mind.'

'You promise not to be weird with me after this?'

'Sarg, I already thought you were weird.' Roj gave a genial smile.

'Ha, very funny.' *Skills*, Kenny thought, *a defence turned into a tool, but why?*

'Don't you need to see my palms or hold an object of sentimental value?'

'I don't do circus tricks.'

Roj's smile faltered a little at Kenny's serious tone and the way he looked him up and down and then closed his eyes.

Four siblings, two are girls. He's the youngest. Love, lots of love. Mother. Homecooking. Spices. Onions and garlic frying in ghee on the stove. Brightly coloured sweets made of condensed milk and cut into unctuous squares. Small fingers pilfering treats. Laughter. Hugs. Father, warm, round belly. Generous. Gambler. *Something buried under the ashes of shame.* That was it. Kenny looked deeper and found the details of what he was looking for. *Helplessness like ammonia and damp clothes. Panic like salt water and falling.* Formative childhood memories could be persistent and dug in so that they couldn't be moved, and the individual has to grow themselves over them, as if the experiences were an ingrowing hair. Kenny opened his eyes.

'Are you sure you want me to do this? I had to find something I couldn't know.'

'Sarg, come on. I'm an open book.' Roj gave Kenny one of his warm grins, rather like his father's.

'When you were maybe six, three men came to your family home and beat your father at the bottom of the stairs while your mother and sisters screamed. You and your brother stayed at the top of the stairs, looking down through the banisters. You were supposed to be in bed. They took your TV, and you were angry at your dad because you couldn't watch your Pokemon and Ninja Turtle cartoons, and you wet the bed for several years after that. Later your parents sold the house, and you all had to move to Leicester to share a home with your father's brother. Your mum worked long hours as a cook for a takeaway to make ends meet and has a large burn on her forearm from an accident with the tandoor oven one night.' Kenny traced a finger diagonally on the back of his forearm from his wrist to his elbow.

Roj stared wide-eyed. He looked angry. Kenny sighed internally and was about to apologise when Roj spoke: 'Fuck me, Sarg! How did you? I mean, that's incredible. It's...' Roj couldn't finish the thought. He shut his mouth and puffed out his cheeks. They sat quietly for some time. Each time Roj put his coffee cup to his lips, he never quite managed to take a sip. He'd lower it again, and his eyes darted around the new realisations forming in his mind.

'What are you thinking?'

Roj came out of himself and furrowed his brow, looking out at the throng of life scuttling around the metropolis of London. He turned to Kenny, with the sides of his mouth quirking down. 'It must be terrible living with everyone else's trauma.'

Now it was Kenny who was surprised, and more than a little touched. His gift, his curse, was as old and familiar as any other part of him. He didn't keep a running tally of its costs, and his mother had always served as a demonstration of the ultimate arrears that might come due. All he said was, 'It has its moments.'

Roj got out his notebook and opened it to the page with Kenny's scrawl of the murder weapon. 'As you know things about me and I know things about you, I guess we better use this power of yours to our advantage.'

'I couldn't agree more.' Kenny started the car and allowed himself a smirk. What happens to a gentle little boy who witnesses bad men do bad things when there's no one to help? In some cases, he finds a way to turn his niceness into a weapon to catch the bad men.

A SILVER RANGE ROVER pulled up outside the workshop. Its wooden doors were painted green. A heavy chain and padlock, that'd once secured the door, hung loose and unlocked. But the locals knew better than to break into it. Built under the Victorian railway track, the brick arches provided spaces for businesses. In some parts of London, these had become gentrified emporiums, sporting everything from Jamaican restaurants, hair salons, and tech start-ups, but not in this part of the East End. Here, there was an old guy who fixed washing machines and fridge freezers. Another space was occupied by a car mechanic, which was really a front for a chop-shop turning out bent motors for nefarious uses. Several of the arches were used as both official and unofficial storage units. The one with the green door served another purpose.

A man in a Hugo Boss suit got out of the driver's seat of the Rover and walked around to the back. He had pallid skin, a jaw dark with stubble, and an overly muscled set of shoulders that ate into his neck. He opened the passenger door at the back of the vehicle, and a man equally as pallid, possibly in his mid-50s, stepped down onto the road in handmade shoes to go with his tailored suit. Pulling out a silver cigarette case from his inside pocket, the driver with no neck produced a lighter and lit the cigarette for the man, shielding the tip for him as he did so. Smoke puffed into the morning air as the man sucked on the cigarette, drawing in the trimmed black fur of his cheeks, like the flanks of a cat hidden in the grass.

The man with no neck closed and locked the Range Rover behind his boss, and they waited outside the green door while the boss man finished his cigarette. They stood impassively, not speaking to each other. No neck checked up and down the street with his hands folded in front of him. A wet snapping sound emanated from behind the green door, accompanied by grunts and cries of pain. Quite soon, the cries grew into weak groans and slurred pleas. In the end, even those stopped, and the wet snapping continued.

A war was about to start. It was something the boss had anticipated, anticipated because he'd played his part in provoking it, but the horrific dismembering of his nephew by one of the Blud Crew on behalf of The Company, had necessitated bringing things forward. The boss dropped his cigarette and ground it under his shoe, then he and his driver entered the brick arch with the green door.

The present occupant of the chair inside the empty vault, while now lifeless, had not been allowed to die until he had given the name of the one who had killed his nephew. It was a dank and bleak space, a dungeon as much as any other. On the drive over, the bearded gangster had received the message on his phone that the name had been obtained. The boss stood over the dead young man, whose face was an unrecognisable pulp. One of his men, wearing an apron splattered with blood, set down a hammer on a plastic sheet and picked up a power saw. While the battery was attached to the saw, the boss undid his fly and took out his penis. He grunted from the discomfort of his prostate and then urinated on the dead man. Once finished, he put himself away, zipped up, and told the man with the apron to continue. There was a body to dispose of, and then the arches required preparing for a special guest so that an example could be made...

21

SMALL PRINT

THE CHAIR next to Samuel was empty. Misha tried not to let it bother her, but Dylan's absences niggled at her throughout the morning's lesson. Things weren't as they should be in that boy's life, and it wasn't right that everyone seemed content for him to fall off the face of the Earth. She had to believe that it wasn't too late for him. If she could only get Dylan into school and focused on his gift, Misha was sure she could make him believe in himself, show him there was a bright future for him that didn't involve the crime and drugs and violence of the streets.

The bell rang, and the children waited to be dismissed. As they left, Misha called Samuel over.

'Is everything alright with Dylan?'

'I think so, miss. My mum said he wasn't feeling well.'

'Your mum?'

'Yeah, she was around at Dylan's this morning for some reason and told me to head on without him because he's sick or something.'

There was a note of surprise in Samuel's response, and Misha felt it too but was also heartened that the Reverend was getting herself involved with the family. She was a formidable woman in the community of Renfield Tower and the surrounding estate. She was also bright and warm, despite what she had fled in her home country.

Misha was always talking to her students about resilience, and perhaps there was a little more hope in Dylan's life now that the Reverend Adekugbe was involved.

Misha dismissed Samuel and was feeling decidedly better about things until Alan Bestwick sulked into her classroom, looking like a rat who'd discovered a nest of eggs. He held a piece of paper.

'Have you seen this morning's absences?' he crowed.

Misha leaned back in her chair as he came to a stop next to her desk and presented the paper. He'd gone to the care of circling Dylan's name.

'And?' Misha inclined her head and saw his eyes dart away from her cleavage.

He put the sheet of paper on her desk and tapped Dylan's name. 'Savage, he's absent again.'

'Sick, as I understand it. The boy is allowed to be ill.' Misha thought Alan was particularly clammy today and there was a coffee stain on his white shirt to the side of his crumpled tie.

'Ill? That's a likely story, but it is beside the point. This means he has exceeded the requisite days of absence mandated by the Qualifications and Curriculum Authority necessary in applications for early admittance to GCSE examinations.'

Jesus! Did he memorise that? Misha lost her cool. 'Oh, come on Alan, you know that's bollocks.'

Bestwick gave a haughty sniff. 'I told you, you can't save them. We're only at the end of autumn. There is a lot of the school year left to go, and he is already lagging behind.'

Misha unclenched her jaw and forced a curt smile. 'There is always next year.' It felt like conceding defeat, and it didn't help that it made Bestwick grin, showing off his two large front teeth.

'You keep telling yourself that. If next year is any different, it will be because he won't be here at all.' Alan Bestwick snatched up the absence list, allowing himself one last glance at Misha's chest.

'That would make you happy, wouldn't it, if he just disappeared.'

Bestwick stopped in the doorway and half-turned back to her. Dark delight flashed in his eyes. 'One less delinquent to waste our time on? Yes, I think that would add to the net happiness of the staff room.' And, like a rat stealing away with a raw egg, he scurried into the hall.

DYLAN HAD GONE to his room while the Reverend and his mother talked. He heard Donna weeping at one point and snuck out to check on her. Curled into the Reverend, she was sobbing on Abigail's shoulder, who hugged her and spoke softly into her ear. The Reverend saw Dylan and made a face that communicated that everything was okay, and Dylan slipped back into his room. It hurt to see his mother so upset, but there was another part of him that was glad. Not glad to see her suffering, but glad that maybe this meant that Donna would drink less and stop selling her body for Henry Grime to make money. He was glad that she might see him and be his mum again, a proper mum, like the Reverend.

The covers on his bed were still rumpled with a Chantel-shaped space from where she had thrown them back. He wondered what she was doing. Sleeping probably, saving up her energy for a night's work. That thought led him to the daydream about riding with her in a big rig to the European Space Agency for his new job, which led to Mrs Stokes' mathematics textbook. Negative and fractional indices caught his attention, and he was soon absorbed in the elegance of their solutions, filling in missing numerals and calculating their sum.

A knock came at Dylan's door, and he was almost surprised to find himself in his room. He opened the door, and the Reverend was putting on her coat. Puffy-eyed and hugging her arms, Donna stood in the hall with her.

'Dylan,' the Reverend said brightly, 'I have to go, but I'll be back.'

'Is everything okay?'

'Course it is, darlin',' Donna said. She looked tired and blotchy from crying, but she also stood a little taller.

'Yes,' the Reverend agreed and zipped up her coat. 'Why don't you make you and Dylan another cup of tea?' Donna gave the Reverend another hug and kissed Dylan on the cheek before she went to the kitchen. When Donna had gone, the Reverend's face hardened, and she took Dylan by the arms again, as she had at the steps at the house on Gallows Court. 'Now, mind my words. You are a good boy, and your mother is a good woman. Her problems are of this world, but *yours* are something else. I can help you both, I hope. I must go now to my church. We will talk about that house soon, and what is inside. Until we do, promise me you will not go near it, even if it calls to you. No matter what, do not answer that call. Do you understand? Good boy.' She placed a scarred hand to Dylan's cheek and then drew up and called through. 'Goodbye, Donna. I'll see you tomorrow.' Then more quietly to Dylan, 'Go, Be with your mother now.'

Once the Reverend left, Donna brought them mugs of tea and a plate of buttered toast. 'I'll go down to Mr Chatterjee's later and get some food in,' she said, tucking her feet up underneath her next to Dylan on the sofa.

'You're not working tonight?'

'Nah, I'll tell Henry I'm sick. Puking me guts out or something.'

'Will he believe you? What about tomorrow?'

'Maybe he will, maybe he won't, but we can't go on like this, sweetheart. I've not been a good mum, I know that. I wanna be better, for you and for me. I hope I can.'

Dylan put his head on his mum's shoulder, and she ran her fingers through his hair. More than anything in the world he wished her hope would come true. 'I love you, Mum.'

Donna's voice started to crack. 'I love you too, darlin'.'

Hope was such a small word. Whole religions were built on it. There was no hope in mathematics because it dealt in certainties. Hope was the shady small print no one read, like an insurance policy left in a draw that would pay out one day. Hope was the get out clause of addicts and daydreamers, and Dylan had read that small print before. Still, when hope was all that was on offer, it was best not to worry about the unpredictable fractals of the future and try to enjoy tea and toast with your mum.

22

BENT MATTERS

COMPETITION MAKES MEN. It exerts a force that either overwhelms the weak or makes them stronger. Like the bar Henry Grime pressed off his chest, grunting with the effort: if it was too light, his muscles wouldn't grow. Not only that, a heavy weight hanging above him at the limits of his strength required not just muscle but a mind strong enough to move that matter and bend it to his will. He grit gold teeth and arched his back for one final rep, screaming at the bar to defy gravity, and defy physics it did.

Meathead spotted Henry's set, standing at the top of the weights bench, helping to guide the bar onto the rack. Metal clattered against metal and, sweat dripping off his forehead, Henry Grime sat up.

'PB, fam. Nice work,' Meathead said, adding more iron plates for his own set. 'You alright, G? You seem pissed.'

'Why the fuck would I be pissed, blud?'

'Dunno, that weird-eyed, Bible-bashing bint maybe?'

'Yeah, dat and tings.' Henry saw Tracks hurry into the gym. Grime and his close crew used it as a base during the daytime. It didn't tie them to their apartments or expose them on the streets, and the constant traffic of people made it easier to come and go. Plus the business was one of the Company's many legitimate fronts used to launder their money. Of course, the gym, like the laundrette, barber's, and mobile phone repair shop were all legally in Henry's name. Other shell companies owned the buildings and leases, but that was all above Henry's pay grade, and he knew not to ask questions. He was a good soldier and had worked his way up the ranks by keeping his mouth shut and doing what he was told.

Meathead was settling onto the bench, and Henry was ready to spot him as Tracks reached the pair, nervously running his tongue over his braces as had become his habit since having them put in over a year ago. Who said crime didn't pay?

Henry hovered near the bar as Meathead unracked the weight, which bent with the iron disks loaded on either side. 'You got sommit to say, bruv?' Henry said, as Meathead lowered for his first rep.

'Yeah, yeah.' Tracks produced a piece of paper from his jeans while Meathead huffed through tight lips, completing his first press. 'Black Jag just pulled up by me on Batty Street. It was that stone cold guy, with the bags under his eyes.'

Grime took the paper and unfolded it. Meathead powered out another rep. All around the gym, weights clinked and treadmills whirred with the pounding rhythm of a futile factory. Henry sucked his teeth at the message.

'Everything alright?' Tracks sat down on a lat-pulldown machine opposite.

'People keep asking me that today.' Grime folded the paper in half and pocketed it. 'Get the crew together.'

'Cool, cool,' Tracks said, standing to leave and stopping. 'Why?'

Henry's face darkened. 'Don't fuckin' ask why. Just do it, fam. Tell 'em we're meeting at Little Dee's flat.'

Tracks' eyes darted around and he hesitated.

'What you waiting for?' Grime snarled.

Tracks gestured with his gaze to Meathead.

'Oh shit!' Henry moved quickly to help Meathead, who'd tried for his own personal best and ended up with the barbell crushing his chest as his face turned puce. Tracks left to carry out Henry's orders. Meathead sat up, his massive head still flushed red.

'Fuck man, what's the deal?'

'Don't be a pussy,' Henry told him. 'There'll be no room for any of that tonight.'

SAMUEL CAUGHT the bus from school. Most of the kids went to the top deck. He preferred to try and find a spot on the bottom, not right at the back, but somewhere just beyond the middle was best. It was as close to a blind spot as he could find to hide out. He was in luck, and there was a space available next to a man with thick glasses and greasy hair. Only after sitting down did he realise not all luck was good luck. The man was rank with stale body odour, tinged with the mustiness of clothes put away while still damp. Samuel rested his face on his fist and tried to use it as an air filter as he read his comic book, but the filter was worse than his luck. The comic was a copy from volume three of *The Walking Dead*, which he hid from his mother, suspecting she wouldn't approve. Sitting next to the greasy haired man, Samuel got a sense of what it might have been like to be in a world filled with the undead, constantly wishing for the ability to breathe through your eyeballs.

Usually, Dylan came with Samuel, but lately Dylan had been acting weird. Samuel knew why and felt bad for his friend. Maybe his mum could do something about it, though he was still surprised to find her at Dylan's flat that morning. She'd never been there before, and she'd been at the soup kitchen all night, or at least Samuel thought she had been. His mother had duties that took her out at all hours in the service of her flock.

Samuel had spent the evening at home, doing his school work and reading comics before bed under the watchful eye of Patricia and Eric Gorski, two of his mother's parishioners and, he supposed, her friends. Children had never been their blessing, they would say, even though they wanted them. Eric had taught Samuel how to play chess, and they would often have a game while Patricia watched her soap operas and hospital dramas, punctuated by making tea in the breaks and refilling a plate with biscuits. The church provided many other friends for their family, though none of them were Nigerian.

A picture of Samuel's father hung on the wall above the television. Samuel supposed he looked a bit like him, and his mother said he had inherited his father's heart, but Samuel had never met him; he'd died in Nigeria before they came to England. Samuel didn't know much about that time. It was something his mother didn't like to talk about. He only had flashes and fragments of memories.

The bus trundled through the streets. People filed on and off. Buses were always busy once the schools got out. London's system of school allocation sent children all over the city and not necessarily to the closest school. Samuel and Dylan, however, were both at Spitalfields Academy in the next borough over. It wasn't far from home, but as they'd gotten older, invisible lines had solidified into barriers they had to be wary of crossing. Hence why he tried to stay unnoticed.

Three boys who went to Cruikshank High got on the bus. Despite the different school, they were also born and raised in Renfield Tower. A lady with shopping bags stood in front of them in the aisle next to Samuel, giving him cover. The boys went upstairs, only to come back down unable to find any seats. They hung on the overhead rail infront of the shopping bag lady. The bus moved off jolting the passengers.

'It's on for tonight, big style,' the one Samuel knew was Chris Williams said.

'Duppies gonna get it, bruv,' that was Simon Roachford, but everyone called him Roach or sometimes Cockroach.

The third boy, an acne-afflicted redhead named Jonathan Potts, whose nickname was 'Bill' (derived from the elaborate word association of 'copper-pot' to 'copper' to 'Old Bill)', asked, 'Did you hear why?'

Samuel could tell the boys were being careful not to be too explicit.

Chris switched to a Jamaican accent. 'Duppies been blottin' where dem nah should.'

Roach hushed his voice, but Samuel could still make them out. 'Nah, bruv. I heard Isaac got lifted by dem on Botham Street, covering for Little Dee 'cos a dat big ting last night.'

Little Dee: Samuel's heart lurched. That was Dylan, he was sure of it. This was bad, and Dylan was caught up in whatever was going on between the Bluds and Duppies. The bus wasn't far from Renfield Tower, but it couldn't move fast enough, lurching between every bus shelter and staggering to a halt behind brake lights in the never-ending London traffic.

'Bet it's payback for that mad business.' Spotty Bill said the last word as "bidness" and made an action with his hand like cutting off his arm at the shoulder.

Roach nodded and Chris said, 'No doubt, blud, no doubt.'

Due to their blotting, aka drug dealing, duties on campus, Chris, Roach and Bill had immaculate attendance at school. They were one small part of the arterial network of the Blud Crew, all of which flowed to the heart of Renfield Tower; finally the bus was delivering them home with the hard jolt of a pacemaker.

Passengers filed off. The three boys were already walking onto the courtyard at the base of Renfield Tower as Samuel battled against the fresh load of commuters barging onto the bus.

He tried to phone Dylan, and when there was no answer, he sent a text. He should go up and warn him. They could go around to his flat. That made him think of his mother. She'd got herself involved. He'd go to her first. She'd probably be in the church hall. Whatever was going down would probably happen after dark.

A grubby eiderdown of clouds had suffocated the sun into a weak throb, dragging it towards a woozy twilight. Samuel broke into a run and didn't stop until he reached the church hall. It was little more than a disused community centre, three doors down from Chatterjee's *Cost Cutter* shop. When the council pulled its funding four years ago, Abigail Adekugbe and her parishioners scraped together everything they could, lobbied the Anglican Communion, and phoned the council's rents and leases department once every hour, every working day of the week for three months, until the property was theirs at a discounted rate. The Reverend Adekugbe was if not persuasive then tenacious, although poor Sherlie Childes, the council officer responsible for rents and leases in the boroughs of Whitechapel, Spitalfields, and Ratcliff, might have used less complimentary words.

Samuel burst into the church hall. Its glaring white striplights and magnolia walls shone like a magnesium flare into the failing light, and Samuel's eyes took a moment to adjust. Patricia Gorski stacked chairs at the side of the hall and gave a start, clutching the small gold crucifix hung around her neck.

Hands on knees, Samuel panted, 'Where's my mum?'

'Sammy, you gave me a fright. She had to go to the hospital. Gemma Dobson's boy, Phil—he—well he had an overdose. Gemma was distraught. She found him, well, you don't need to know about that.' Patricia went back to stacking chairs. 'I'll make you your tea tonight. We're having...'

The door to the hall closed on its automatic hinge, and Samuel was nowhere to be seen.

DYLAN CRIED OUT, 'Argh! No. Get off me. Please!' But Donna was relentless in her pursuit of him. The sofa just wasn't long enough, and Dylan was wedged in the corner, almost falling over the arm of the chair as he turned away all his muscles straining and barely able to breathe. 'Stop, please, no,' He gasped between fits of giggles, until finally, mercifully, Donna relented in tickling him. Flushed and sighing, they slumped into each other .

'I knew you were still ticklish,' Donna said, and made to go in for a second attack.

Dylan clamped his arms over his belly. 'No you don't,' he grinned. Dylan couldn't have imagined a more perfect day. A day drinking tea and watching daytime TV had proved better than his fantasy of Oxford Street and Regents Park.

She ruffled his wiry hair and leaned back to consider him more closely. 'You need a haircut. Let me get the clippers,' Donna said, getting up from the sofa. She returned a few minutes later with a square, padded hairdresser's bag.

'Come on, then, I'll smarten that mop up, make you look like Stormzy,' she said, taking Dylan by the hand and leading him to a dining chair.

Donna draped a towel over his shoulders and tucked it into the collar of his hoodie. Dylan felt as though he was seven years old again when Donna still cut his hair. She was already a working girl by then—Dylan couldn't remember a time that she wasn't, but he knew she had once worked at a barber's shop in Poplar. Her fingers teased his hair, and she looked at him like a sculptor assessing the clay for the shape hidden inside. Then she began to work.

The clippers buzzed, her fingers gently braced on his shoulder. She moved his head a fraction this way or that. Small tufts of hair tickled Dylan's ears and dusted the towel about his shoulders. She slipped into an old life, and he went with her into a world of chit-chat and gossip. She asked about girlfriends. He blushed and she teased Anila out of him. He noticed she avoided mentioning Chantel and the previous evening. He was glad of that.

'There,' Donna said with satisfaction, sweeping the stray hairs from Dylan's neck with a soft brush dusted with talcum powder. She produced a mirror to show him the results of her labour, preening the air around his head with an artisan's final touches. Handing Dylan the mirror, he looked at himself, inspecting the close shave over the ears, perfectly symmetrical on both sides and fading expertly into the longer hair above. Reflected in the mirror, he loved the way she gazed down at him.

It was a perfect moment. He wanted them to stay like that forever. Just him and her. But the moment was shattered. The whispers slithered back into his head, chilling his spine. Bad things could only be held off for a while before they clawed their way back.

A pounding came at the flat's front door.

23

BLUD LETTING

DYLAN AND DONNA'S new lives crumbled like a fantasy made from the ashes of dreams. A cold draft blew in the open door bringing Henry Grime and the rest of the senior members of the Blud Crew. They barged past Donna as if she wasn't even there holding the door open for them.

The looks on their faces said nothing but trouble had blown through the door with them. Dylan ducked back into the living room. Some, like Henry Grime, wore stares like hard masks; others fidgeted with their hands and blinked too much. As the Blud Crew piled into the living room, one or two made jokes with forced smiles and laughter that rang hollow with nerves.

Grime glowered around the room, taking in all the faces. He alighted on Donna. 'Why the fuck aren't you ready? Don't tell me your mobile's on, 'cos I know it ain't, bitch. I've been phoning you for the last hour, and if I've been calling, then punters definitely have.'

Holding herself tightly, Donna dropped her eyes and disappeared from the room.

'Right then, let's get down to business.' Henry Grime sucked his teeth and nodded approvingly at what he saw. 'You are bad men. I'm serious, fam. Every one of you has proved yourselves. You've earned your place in the Blud Crew.'

Grime walked among them, a general surveying his troops, and came to a stop next to Dylan. He threw an arm round the boy's neck and pulled him close.

'You know why we're here tonight.' Henry Grime squeezed Dylan as he spoke. 'We didn't start nothing. Duppy Crew been blotting at the edge of our patch too long. I'm a generous man: keep the peace; make money. Plenty of London to go around, nah? But Duppies be greedy lickle ghost. They done killed Annie Drew. Yeah, some of you didn't know that. Some of you probably think she was just some old prozzie-junkie what got whacked. No big deal. No loss, bruv. Why you give a shit?'

Grime tutted and shook his head. 'She's from Whitechapel, bruv, and she worked for the Bluds, worked these streets longer than most of your mum's been pullin' your dad's chain. They even tried to pin that shit on me. Feds dragged my ass in for questioning. But shit don't stick to Henry Grime, and I ain't fuckin' stupid enough to kill no revenue stream. How many times I tell you boys this is about respect and making paper? There ain't nothing else.'

Heads bobbed in agreement, and the group changed. The laughing had stopped. The nervous shuffling had turned into the rolling of shoulders, and hard faces darkened.

'And Duppies disrespected us and muscled in on our turf to take our cheddar. That shit can't stand.' Henry Grime shook his head. 'My boy, Little Dee, he's a bad man. I said, Little Dee, you go stick one 'dem Duppies, show 'em they nah come in our Ends.' Henry Grime let his Jamaican accent coloured the sentence. 'But Lee Dee, he's a gangsta and done ghost three of 'dem. Then today, they lift Isaac looking for our boy Dee, in broad fuckin' daylight in our Ends. Why don't you just finger my mum, bruv? Ah fuck it, while you're here, you might as well peg my half-sister bareback.'

A couple of the Bluds laughed.

'What the fuck are yous laughing at, dickheads? This ain't a fuckin' joke, fam. This shit can't stand, and we end this tonight. Right?'

'Yeah,' half the room muttered back.

'What? I can't fucking hear you pussies. I said, we end it tonight, right?'

'Yeah,' and 'damn right,' they all said louder.

'Nah, nah, nah. We're the Blud Crew. What you think that name means? You feel me? I said, do you feel me, fam?'

The room pulsed and surged like the flexing back of a dragon.

'Tool up, Bluds, and let's go ghost dem Duppies, *all a dem*.'

ABIGAIL SAT with Gemma Dobson next to her son Philip's bed, trying to be subtle about checking her watch. The sun set so early in England as autumn stretched on. It was as if when the rain came at the end of summer, it pulled a cloak of night around its shoulders. Philip would be okay, so the doctors said. There was talk of putting him in touch with addictions services, but the Registrar had managed Gemma's expectations by telling her their waiting list was over six months, adding the qualification that it was dependent on Philip wanting to engage.

'He will,' Gemma said, patting her son's hand while he slept.

For Abigail, the NHS was one of the great things about Britain. It, like the country, had its faults. The rain and waiting lists sprang to mind. But rolling green fields and almost biblical amounts of rain seemed to be a package deal, as was free health care for every citizen and waiting lists. Like the rain, British people did so love to moan about the NHS. But they'd moan even more at Nigeria's sun and the lack of healthcare for the poor. Abigail doubted that Philip wanted to face his demons, but regardless, the NHS would be there to pick up the pieces—cradle to grave, as the saying went, and she and her church would be there to pick up Gemma.

Drugs and crime were a festering wound in Whitechapel, just as they were in other parts of the city. Abigail checked her watch again, thinking of Dylan and Donna. That family needed help, both practical and spiritual. Her scars ached painfully at the reminder of what pure evil was capable of. The evil of man was bad enough, but pure evil, the type that was like God in that so many people fooled themselves into believing it didn't exist. Well, that type of evil was a different matter. The searing flames danced in Abigail's mind, their excruciating pain spiced with the malodorous incense of burnt hair; she heard screams that were indistinguishable from laughter. She slammed shut those memories when her phone buzzed in her pocket.

With a squeeze of Gemma's shoulder, Abigail hurried into the corridor outside the ward. 'Samuel, what is it? I'm at the hospital with Miss Dobson... I can't hear you... Tell me again.'

With her finger in her other ear to block out the noise of the hospital, she walked in search of a quieter spot. 'The signal is bad. Go to Mrs Gorski's for your dinner. I'll be home as soon as I can. Samuel? Samuel?'

The call cut out. Hospitals always had terrible reception. Did she detect an uncharacteristic note of concern in Samuel's voice? Possibly. It could have been from trying to make himself heard. Abigail's scars prickled. She needed to get back and she would, just as soon as she could pry Gemma away from her son's bedside and take her back to Renfield Tower for some sleep. Then those other matters could be attended to, matters of darkness.

SAMUEL HID behind a concrete pillar tagged with initials and crude drawings of genitalia. The Blud Crew left in small groups. They all seemed to have gone, and Samuel was about to leave his hiding place to call on Dylan and ferry him to his flat; there, they could wait it out until his mum came home.

Dylan stepped out onto the walkway. His name was forming in Samuel's mouth when Henry Grime came out of the flat and put an arm around Dylan's shoulders. Grime was speaking on his phone as they walked to the stairwell.

Samuel tried to think. He didn't like any of his options. His mother was too far away and tied up with pastoral duties. She could be at the hospital all night. The police wouldn't listen to a kid, and besides, what would he tell them? That he overheard three school children on a bus speaking in non-specific terms about a non-specific event, and all Samuel could say with any certainty about that event was that he had a bad feeling. They'd be more likely to send a police officer around to his flat to tell his mother he wasted police time with prank calls.

Instead, Samuel decided the only thing he could do was follow at a distance, keeping out of sight. What he would do if anything happened was a piece of the plan he'd rather not think about. With Henry Grime's voice fading down the stairwell, Samuel tightened the shoulder straps on his school bag and left the shadows.

THE WHISPERS CALLED in Dylan's mind, growing stronger as night covered the city. Yet again he was swept along. Every move made things worse. Just when there was a glimpse of light, it was snuffed out. No amount of counting, long division, or reciting of pi could ground him in a world in which he had control. Dylan looked behind. It was a foolish gesture driven from hope—that small word again, with the shyster small print.

'Don't worry, Little Dee, the feds are going to be too distracted for this. Tracks is taking care of a little diversion for us.' Henry Grime came to a stop next to a black Jaguar. 'Hang back,' he told Dylan.

Rain pattered down in a light drizzle, beading like black pearls on the Jaguar. The window rolled down, and Henry bowed. A man with white, waxy skin and dark rings under his eyes sat in the back of the car. He reminded Dylan of an undertaker, but then how many undertakers were chauffeured around in a top of the range Jag? The man's eyes alighted on Dylan for a moment. He felt the touch of a cold blade on the back of his neck and started up touching his thumb to the tips of his fingers in rounds of seven.

Someone else Dylan couldn't see was in the back of the car, because after a few words between Henry and the man, that other someone leant over. An arm appeared in the window and handed Henry an object wrapped up in a plastic bag. The man said more words Dylan couldn't hear, and Henry glanced around at him and winked. Waxy man's face was indecipherable. Maybe he was actually made of wax and no one else knew. Dylan sped up touching his thumb to his fingers—he knew there were things worse than Henry Grime in the world, and their whispers were growing louder, throwing off the stupor of daylight.

The black Jaguar slunk away. Henry Grime stuffed the package in the pocket of his puffer jacket and jerked his head for Dylan to follow.

Dylan jogged to catch up. 'Where are we going?'

'Gallows Court, of course. It made sense as it's at the edge of our territory.'

Dylan's stomach turned, and he wanted to puke. 'But it's too open.'

'Nah, bruv, the CCTV don't work there. We've always made sure of that. You scared?'

Of course he was, and there was no out. 'I lost my knife with those three Duppies.'

Henry Grime slowed a stride, sucked his teeth and carried on. 'No matter. No point bringing a knife to a gunfight. You stick close to me.'

'Gunfight?'

Yessh! The whispers tittered in excitement as the rain grew heavier.

SAMUEL WISHED he had time to change out of his school uniform. It made him stick out even more. He wished he wasn't so fat too, not for any vain reason (more than half the kids at school were overweight), but because he was getting out of breath. Being scared didn't help either. Hanging as far back as he could, he kept Dylan and Henry Grime in view, but when they rounded a corner, he would sprint to make sure he didn't lose them. As a police van screamed past, flashing blue against the buildings and kicking up spray from puddles, he realised where they were going. A police car followed the van, heading away from Gallows Court.

Samuel knew the area around Gallows Court well enough

because of his mother's soup kitchen and the other church activities. More than once, he had delivered care packages to those in need, mostly consisting of food and clothes. He'd even dropped off nappies and formula to a teenage girl only a few years older than himself. She nursed a little bundle of life in her arms when she answered the door, and if he hadn't already known, he would have taken her for the baby's older sister. Like a lot of boys used to ducking away from trouble, be it in the form of older children, teachers, or simply the many snapping twigs in the jungle that was life, Samuel knew the shortcuts and hideaways in his Ends, and that included Gallows Court.

From the corner of Blunderstone Street, Samuel could see the Blud Crew spreading out and pouring into the park at the centre of Gallows Court, where the streetlights had been vandalised so much the council didn't bother to maintain them anymore. The main road that ran along the bottom of Gallows Court was his best option. It was light and busy, and Samuel would have the cover of people and traffic, so he cut left and dodged between people until he came to rest by a fried chicken takeaway. They were doing a good trade, and the smell of bubbling flesh sweetened the air, but food was the last thing on Samuel's mind as he waited, the rain seeping through his school blazer. Moving his weight from foot to foot, he scanned the dark across the road, searching for his best friend. The wind and rain made swaying monsters of the trees in the park, crepuscular giants that dripped with the ink of night. They hung in the depths, while the smaller denizens lurked in their shadows or hid in still darker crevices of the park.

Another police car, an ambulance, and a fire truck raced one after the other, parting traffic and turning heads. Samuel watched them going the wrong way and followed their direction of travel, seeing smoke rise above the rooftops maybe a mile away. It was difficult to judge through the gloom of artificial light. Samuel pulled out his phone and started to write a text to Dylan.

Dude, what are you doing?

That wasn't helpful and he deleted it. His thumb hovered as he struggled to think what he could possibly say that could get his friend out of trouble. He was just coming to the conclusion that a handful of words on a screen the size of his hand could do what he wanted them to do, when there was a pop like a firecracker going off. His eyes darted to the park and he strained to see. Two more cracks, accompanied by tiny, orange flashes. People stopped and turned their heads towards the park. An icy cold feeling blew through Samuel; he caught a whiff of something fetid, as if the chicken bar had forgotten to put out its bins.

A series of pops with flashes came from opposite sides of the park, ping-ponging back and forth. A cry of pain went up. A woman on the other side of the street screamed 'Guns!' More screams and shouts went up. People ran and ducked for cover behind bins, parked cars, behind lampposts, shielding their heads as they crouched.

A young man in an LA Lakers baseball cap, carrying a heavy bike lock, the kind encased in tough plastic, bounded into the light. He stopped, looking left and right, panic squeezing his features, and made the decision to flee towards Spitalfields. But it was too late. Another loud, whip snap of gunfire rang out, and there was a flash of orange from the dark behind the Lakers fan. People screamed. The man dropped the bike chain, and his baseball cap was knocked off his head as he fell to his knees. His face screwed up, and he arched his back. From the shadows, a masked man emerged. Even with his face covered, Samuel knew it was Henry Grime. He raised his gun and shot the young man again, who fell face down. Henry Grime stood over him. Cars slowed. Pedestrians cowered. The man face down on the ground moved his legs, and Henry Grime shot him two more times, and he moved no more.

Samuel stood wide-eyed, unable to look away. Henry Grime looked up from the dead man and locked eyes with Samuel. Samuel tried to back away through the solid glass of the fried chicken shop. Another series of shots rang out. Henry Grime ducked, and the glass behind Samuel shattered. Instinctively, Samuel flinched into a ball and squeezed his eyes tight shut.

When he opened them again, crouching on the pavement, glass all round him, Henry Grime was gone. A police siren was heading their way, far, far too late.

People ran from the darkness of the park. Bystanders and gang members blended together in a maelstrom of movement and sound, but through it all, Samuel caught sight of Dylan at last. Dylan sprinted from under a tree onto the main road. He looked towards Samuel as though he was looking for him, but a teenager on a moped raced between the cars and cut him off, forcing Dylan to run the wrong direction, away from Whitechapel and into the Spitalfields territory of the Duppy Crew.

24

SLOW BLADE

It was supposed to be one-sided. It was supposed to be the Blud Crew teaching the Duppies who controlled Whitechapel. It turned out to be neither of those things.

Whispers hissing in his head louder and louder, Dylan stood by Henry Grime's side as they entered the park. Henry produced the guns from his pocket and gave one to Meathead. He had another knife for Dylan, only it wasn't *another* knife. It was the *same* one he'd dropped in the park the night he'd been sent to stab a Duppy. The night he'd run to Vieil's house for sanctuary and led those three boys to their deaths at the hand of the monster that lived there.

Dylan took the knife. Henry held onto it and looked him in the eye. 'We'll talk laters, yeah, little man? Don't leave my side. You feel me?'

Dylan said he understood, and he tried to stay close to Henry. Whatever Henry meant about talking later didn't matter right now. Dylan stuffed the switchblade in his coat and followed the men.

When the shooting started, their plans dissolved in the rain that had turned from a persistent drizzle to a heavy shower. Both sides had guns, blades, baseball bats and chains. They rushed through the dark. Dylan's whispers cackled with joy. He felt the pull to the old house. It would be a better place than this.

The grass was sodden and slick with blood. Henry Grime heaved Dylan up when he fell, popping off a round at a silhouette under a tree. A shot came back. They ducked out of the way. Two figures ran through the dark and came for Dylan. A man with a baseball cap hunted Henry Grime. Dylan heard a shot but didn't see what happened to Henry. Meathead rugby tackled one of Dylan's pursuers.

Dylan didn't look back; he ran, confused and lost. He zigzagged, tumbling through the melee until he found the light of the road. Number 25 Gallows Court called to him from across the street.

A boy on a moped hurtled through the traffic and cut him off. Maybe it was out of habit, maybe because gunfire and the boy on the moped lay between him and Whitechapel, but Dylan found himself heading the direction of the damn paper round which had landed him in this trouble.

A police siren was coming closer. He sprinted from the main road and down side streets. The moped was closing. No matter which way he turned, there was no losing it. Every muscle was on fire. Either blood or whispers or both crashed through his ears. He found an old, cobbled back alley, flung a wheelie bin from the wall so that it lay across the entrance, and slipped and tripped his way across the smooth, wet cobbles.

He was nearly there, nearly at the exit, when two boys ran past, just catching sight of him as they hurtled from view. They reappeared seconds later, slowing to a stalking walk, hoods pulled up, brandishing a baseball bat and knife. Dylan backed away.

The whine of a moped dropped an octave. Its engine idled at the other end of the alley. He was trapped.

They took their time closing in. Dylan moved to the middle of the alley, frantically searching for a way out. The alley was flanked by high, brick walls on either side, enclosing backyards. Some had doors. Dylan tried one and then another. Both were locked.

The moped pushed by the fallen bin and crept closer. The rider wore a red crash helmet with the visor pulled down.

Dylan remembered the knife. His hands shook as he hit the release button. The blade snapped out, tugging in his hand as if it were alive, a dog on a chain ready to bite.

The hooded youth with the baseball bat dragged it along the cobbles. 'Nowhere to run, blud.'

A rev came from the moped.

'No one to save you,' the hood with a knife said. But he was wrong. He was so terribly wrong.

It was foolhardy. It was beautifully brave. And it was stupid, like his naive ideas of becoming a lawyer or the Prime Minister or a comic book artist.

Samuel hit the youth on the moped with a brick. The youth fell off, and Samuel ran forward to grab Dylan by the arm. By the time he reached him, the moped rider was pulling himself off the floor and shook his helmeted head.

The two friends went back to back. Samuel hefted his brick. Dylan brandished his knife, deciding in wordless agreement that if they were going down, then he'd try to hurt them too. Henry Grime tried to teach him that painful lesson after the Duppies stole his drugs.

The three Duppies closed in. Dylan lunged with the knife, and the boy with the baseball bat hopped out of reach and then rammed the head of the bat into Dylan's stomach. Dylan doubled over unable to breath. Samuel was distracted, and the boy from the moped seized the moment, grabbing the wrist and headbutting Samuel. The impact of the helmet was dizzying.

Dylan was drowning in a vacuum, waiting for a knife in the back or a baseball bat to his skull. Neither came. They pulled him to his feet and spun him around to face his best friend, whose lips were split and his nose was pouring blood. Dazed, he was held in a chicken-wing arm lock behind his back by the boy in a helmet. Dylan couldn't understand what was happening until it was too late.

One of the Duppies held him in a choke-hold around the neck. The other gripped Dylan's knife hand in both of his. Dylan caught up with the situation and started to struggle and buck, but he was over-powered.

Like a boxer on the ropes, Samuel's eyes came back into focus. He saw the knife. He saw Dylan's ineffectual struggles, and Dylan saw the sadness and panic and hopelessness in his best friend's face as the Duppies made him slowly press the blade into Samuel's belly.

The knife resisted for a fraction of a second, teasing a childish fancy that Samuel had become a superhero from one of his comics. Then the instant was gone, and the blade slid into Samuel's flesh two inches deep. He gave a strangled squeal and seemed to take a long breath as they pushed the knife deeper until it could go no further.

They pulled out the blade. Samuel put his hands to the wound, and red began to trickle over his fingers. Dylan wanted to drop the knife, but his fist was clamped around the handle. The boy with the helmet let go, and Samuel fell to one knee.

Blood dripped from the switchblade onto the wet cobbles, and then the choke-hold tightened.

Dylan fought.

Samuel crumpled to the ground.

The world blotted into nothingness.

MEMENTO MORI

"Listen to them, the children of the night. What music they make!"
— **Bram Stoker,** *Dracula*

25

MELTED BUTTER

MISHA WAS SCREAMING; it was beautiful. Kenny sat at the kitchen breakfast bar ignoring his dinner plate of cold spaghetti bolognese, watching Misha crouched on the floor playing with Betty the Staffordshire Bull Terrier.

He and Roj had ended up at Judy Finch's place, looking for clues that didn't appear. What did turn up was the victim's menagerie of animals, including four dogs. The RSPCA were about to take them all for re-homing when, on the spur of the moment, Kenny found himself asking if he could have the black and tan Staffy with the white bib. He'd looked into her brown eyes as she gazed up at him with her thin tail whipping back and forth in a blur, appearing to smile from ear to ear. It wasn't just any smile.

Kenny thought of the homeless man from earlier that day, and the marshmallow mutt who accompanied him. Betty the Bull Terrier wasn't a marshmallow dog. Her smile was butter melting on warm toast—liquid gold—and the love she exuded coated everything around her, including Kenny. She had attached herself to him as soon as they came in and never left his side. Every room he investigated, Betty was right next to him, with a curious look mirroring his own. When he noticed her, the smile would burst on her face, and her eyes narrowed into slits. If he petted her, she revelled in it as if it were the most glorious thing in the world, so glorious, in fact, every time she would topple over, ending up with all four legs in the air for her tummy to be scratched.

The RSPCA officer, a friend of Judy's called Rose, came over all teary-eyed. 'It's not strictly protocol, but Judy would love to know Betty was in a good home.'

And so it was, Kenny spent the rest of the day with Betty on a lead. He drew some looks back at the station, every one of which disappeared as soon as Betty smiled and accepted each officer's fussing.

Kenny had arrived home with a bag of dog food under one arm and Betty's lead in his other hand. When Betty walked in the front door, it was love at first sight for Misha. Kenny knew how they both felt. Now, Misha slumped on the floor against the kitchen cabinets, with Betty curled up like an enormous bump of a baby in her arms, and regaled Kenny with staff room gossip, enthused about a mathematical prodigy she had in her class, and bemoaned Alan Bestwick. With Betty exuding affection and accepting it in equal measure, Misha couldn't help but talk of that dickhead Bestwick with a grin on her face. Kenny had met him at a staff party once and found multiple reasons to dislike him, not least the way his eyes wandered over Misha's breasts and backside when he thought no one would notice. There was something else too, a feeling Kenny didn't like the taste of, something slightly bitter and mouldering. It was from something down deep that he didn't fancy searching for if he didn't have to.

Belly exposed again, Misha rubbed Betty's tummy and spoke her monologue in babyish tones. Kenny nodded and made noises in the right pauses as he pushed the worms of pasta around with a fork. He hadn't been able to stomach anything all day.

Betty's tail whisked in a circle, her fat, doggy bottom sat on Misha's lap.

Even the echoes of the dead were a little quieter with Betty around. It had been a good impulse to bring her home. Misha seemed so happy with this big, furry baby. *Poor Judy*, Kenny thought, and his mind returned to the crime scene at the park.

The curved, sickle-like blade had a dull shine. Only, it couldn't be a sickle as they cut on the *inside* of the curve, and this one had sliced open Judy with the convex outer edge, more like a cutlass... But that wasn't quite right either.

Kenny remembered something else: the colour of the weapon. It wasn't the silver of steel; instead, it was muted, not gold... brass or copper? Bronze maybe. He'd not had time to scour images on the internet yet, but another sleepless night felt imminent.

Half-heartedly, Kenny lifted a forkful of spaghetti and even considered putting it into his mouth, until its similarity with poor Judy Finch's intestines struck him, along with the smells of death: blood, urine, feces, and the vinegar of terror. A wash of salty saliva filled his mouth, which he swallowed along with the instinct to gag.

'Not hungry?' Misha appeared at his shoulder and ran her hands around his neck.

'Not if you'd seen what I'd seen today.' Kenny welcomed the citrus-musk of Misha's perfume. He rested his head back against her chest, and she planted a kiss in his hair. He felt Betty pushing against his shins, both marking him with a love he'd never felt he deserved.

'The Jack the Ripper copycat? Was that yours?'

Kenny turned his head to look into her brown eyes. 'You know about that?'

'It's all over the news. Besides, I picked up the evening edition of *The Standard* on my way home. Do you want to talk about it?'

'I can't. Ongoing investigation and all that. Besides, you don't need to hear about things like that.' *God! No one should. And what if this is just the beginning?* How many more victims could there be, if all he and Roj had to go on was his extrasensory perception of a murder weapon and something to do with a dog? The latter point he kept to himself, for the moment, not telling even Roj. Either way, neither perception stood as anything like admissible evidence. They were little more than hunches, hunches that meant nothing as yet.

Misha ran her fingers through his dark brown hair, her nails sending sparks of electricity down Kenny's spine. 'Too late. *The Standard* had all the gory details. Should I be worried?'

'Not unless you start walking the streets late at night.' Kenny didn't want to say anymore. Command had got wind of Dominic

Priestley's story and were already pressuring them for results. It was their natural fear response at the coming hysteria. He and Roj had come up with a plan. Their boss mulled it over, with the Deputy Chief Inspector's flea still in his ear. Their idea wasn't without risk, and it might not work at all; in fact, even if it did work, there was a chance it could go sideways.

Misha leaned over and stole a piece of tepid spaghetti. 'I've no plans to go prowling around. Not around these streets anyway. Not unless...'

'Unless what?'

Misha's lips quirked mischievously. 'I'm no expert, but I'm pretty sure dogs need regular exercise. Has Betty had a walk?'

Betty's ears pricked up. She sat her bum down heavily on the tiles and licked her chops, her big, brown eyes shining expectantly.

'I guess I've got my orders.' Kenny got down from the breakfast bar and lifted his coat. Betty let out a bark and wagged her tail.

'I guess you have. But I'll come too.' As Kenny picked up his keys in the hall, she added, 'Where exactly did you get Betty from? Is it to do with the Jack the Ripper case?'

Kenny clipped on Betty's lead, and she bum-shuffled into him, knocking him back a step. 'Let's just say, at least someone got a happy ending today.'

Misha had put on her coat and fixed her hat so as not to ruin her hair. 'I guess you don't get many of those at work.'

'No, no I don't.'

Kenny locked the door behind the three of them. Misha took his hand as they descended the two flights of stairs to the ground floor, with Betty pulling the lead taut ahead of them. The siren of a police bike made Misha jump when they left the apartment block entrance, with Betty looking up at Kenny questioningly. The dog probably wanted reassurance after the loud noise, but Kenny had that uncanny feeling she felt the same thing he did. Her buttery happiness had hardened and she whimpered.

'It's okay.' Misha bent and petted Betty, and the dog made a show of wagging her tail. 'Isn't it, Kenny?' Misha straightened up and put up an umbrella for them to shelter under as they walked.

'Hmm?' Kenny's gaze followed the bike weaving in and out of traffic. 'Yeah, yeah, when is a siren *not* going off somewhere in London? Let's go this way.' As if it was nothing to worry about, he led them in the opposite direction from Whitechapel.

It was probably nothing, a stray echo of the dead, but he didn't like the tittering whispers he could hear. They were *new*, metallic in taste, and cut through the background psychic lament with the sharp edge of mirth.

The rain tick-tick-ticked on the umbrella as they walked. Betty sniffed the ground, her concerns having melted away. She was a compact ball of muscle, and Kenny had to hold tight to the lead; the bull terrier walked them more than the other way around. Misha threaded her free arm through Kenny's. It would have been a romantic walk in the rain if it wasn't for the hairs standing up on the back of Kenny's neck, as if something very, very bad was about to happen.

26

ULULATION

REVEREND ABIGAIL ADEKUGBE shepherded Gemma Dobson out of the hospital. Her son, Philip, had gone to sleep, and the Senior House Officer said he would phone if there were any problems and that Philip was stable and needed to rest. Reading between the lines, they were in the way.

The two women stepped out into the rain-drenched evening, buttoning up for the walk to the bus stop. Abigail's plan was to deposit Gemma with the Gorskis and head straight to the Savage's flat. But when she looked around to mention the tea to Gemma, she wasn't there.

Gemma had wandered back to the bright lights of the Accident and Emergency department. She was waiting for a lift, pulling anxiously at the sleeves of her coat. Abigail took a deep breath, heavy with sympathy, and headed back in. As the automatic doors parted, an ambulance sped into the parking bay at the front of Accident and Emergency. The driver's door opened and slammed closed. Abigail paid it no mind. Not at first.

Gemma was frowning at the light above the lift, blinking between floors too slowly for her liking. The automatic doors opened again, bringing with it an eddy of cold air from outside mixed with the oppressive heat of the hospital. A tingling ran over Abigail's skin as the two paramedics called for her to step aside. She did as she was told, giving them room to pass as she reached Gemma, and the lift doors opened. Gemma was ready to step in but stopped when she heard the whimper of anguish next to her.

Abigail clutched at her heart. 'Samuel?' She questioned the reality, unable to believe what she was seeing. 'Samuel!'

Now the questioning had gone, trampled under her running feet. She reached for the shoulder of one of the paramedics and pulled at him to get at her son, who lay unconscious on the gurney, bloody bandages being compressed onto his belly by the other paramedic. 'Samuel, no. What have they done? What have they done?'

'Miss, let us help him.' The paramedic tried to shake her off.

'Samuel!' His name had become an ululation of quavering fear.

Gemma stood dumbly, with the lift doors closing and opening on her. Strangers turned and stared. Nurses and doctors came. White coats and blue scrubs busied around the inert body of Abigail's son, like flies to a corpse. She had not lost a husband, crossed oceans, and literally walked through fire in service of God for him to now take her son, her loving, sweet boy who was as gentle and beautiful as a falling English snowflake.

'Let me take you to the family room,' a nurse said, trying to lead Abigail away from the bay in which they worked on Samuel. But she was unmoveable. Not even God himself would be able to take her away, though in that moment of rage and fear she wished he would show his face so that she could spit in it and castigate him for claiming another angel too soon. Then her fear multiplied at her blasphemy, and she prayed for forgiveness and for God's help in Samuel's time of need, hoping that it would be enough.

And dreading that it wasn't.

HENRY GRIME and Custard ducked into the alley and hid in the alcove of a side door. A police car wailed down the road, splashing blue light against the alley walls. Grime took the gun from his pocket, unzipped his puffer-jacket and wiped the gun down with the hem of his track-suit. A green dumpster-sized bin squatted halfway down the alley. Henry tried to lift the lid but it was locked. He swore and searched for an alternative.

'The grate.' Custard squatted and plunged his fingers between the bars of the drain and heaved. It wouldn't budge. Rain ran in brown rivulets down the alley and into the hole. Henry joined Custard, and with grunts of effort, they pulled the grate free. Careful not to put his prints back on the gun, Henry dropped it into the running water. Custard opened his folding knife and washed off the excess blood on the blade and handle in the brown stream and dropped the weapon in the hole. They fixed the grate back in place and hid behind the bin as a police van sped along the road, siren screaming.

'What happened?' Soaked to the skin, Custard shivered, teeth chattering. His hair matted to his face with rain. Drops of it were pink with someone else's blood sprayed under his chin.

'Double-cross,' Henry said, lacing his fingers together and resting his forehead to his hands. 'That wasn't a fight.'

'What was it, then?' Custard glanced around the bin and ducked back in again.

'A hunt.' Grime unlaced his fingers and scrunched his fists into balls.

'I don't get it, bruv. What were they after?'

Henry turned his face up to the falling rain. 'Little Dee.'

'Why, though?'

'Why'd you think?' Grime snapped and put his head back in his hands.

'What, revenge for those three Duppy boys? Why not just shank three of us?'

''Cos it was something else.'

'But what?'

Grime snapped and grabbed a handful of Custard's wet gilet-puffer jacket and pushed him over. 'I don't know, blud. Something we don't know, innit?'

Custard scrambled back for cover. 'Cool it, bruv. Why you so hyped over Little Dee? He's just a foot soldier. There's plenty more of him around.'

Henry Grime stood up in plain sight and glared down at Custard, fists clenched and ready for another fight. Custard cowed away and closed his eyes. When he opened them again, Henry was striding back out onto the street.

27

LOST BOY

DYLAN'S TEARS didn't help. They only dripped salt into the lacerations in the skin around his eyes, which had split open as they swelled. He couldn't see the thing he had become—a bloody pulp bound to a chair. They'd tied his hands behind his back and put a plastic bag over his head. A car pulled up, and they'd thrown him in the back, thrashing, constantly on the edge of suffocation.

On the drive, they grew tired of his struggling and landed a few blows in his stomach. The terror of asphyxiation was never-ending. Time shifted like desert dunes. As far as Dylan was concerned, the drive could have been five minutes or an eternity through purgatory. When it finally ended, they bundled him from the car, half carrying him under the arms, still thrashing for air. A door shut. A lock closed, and the bag was mercifully pulled from his head. Gasping, he tried to take in his surroundings. He was in a workshop in the arches under train tracks, with green wooden doors and a solitary chair in the middle of the floor. Soon, he found out that the chair would make removal of the plastic bag no mercy at all.

After being lashed to the chair, Dylan wished he was back in the car smothered in plastic. His ribs were broken. His nose had been smeared across his face. He'd spat teeth out with glutinous clots of blood. Each intake of breath caused a spike of pain, lung connecting to jagged rib, and the air wheezed from him in wet rasps. When he attempted to lose himself in numbers, counting on his fingertips, they had taken that away too. The digits on his hands jutted out at strange angles and dripped scarlet droplets onto the bare concrete floor, amid a litter of fingernails and a pair of discarded pliers they'd used to remove them.

They would kill him. He'd known that in the alley when they... The sad shock on Samuel's face added more salt to his open wounds. Dylan sobbed. With death looming, he fell back on the most useless of things: hope.

'Mummy,' he slurred.

Men laughed. 'They all call for their mummies.'

'His mummy's a whore.'

'Maybe we should invite her over?'

'What's your mummy's number, little big man?' Another punch to the stomach followed the words.

Dylan exhaled, involuntarily spraying his unseen tormentor with blood.

'You little wanker!'

The next punch whipped Dylan's head from left to right, and pain exploded through his ear. A high-pitched whine lingered afterwards and something he'd forgotten in the chaos, something which had been there since the sun started to set. Whispering. The voices of the room faded in and out, distorted and discordant. The whine spiked into Dylan's brain, and the whispers gave a high-pitched laugh and said what they always said, or at least the only word that Dylan could make out.

Yesshh?

The whine lessened, and a new voice entered the fray. 'Don't knock him out, you idiot.' It wasn't from London. Not English either. There was an accent, foreign, Eastern European maybe. It didn't matter. Dylan wanted it over.

Yessshh?

'Wake him up.' But he said it as 'Vake him up.'

Water splashed in Dylan's face. It stung and that bright burn made Dylan gasp and then whinny as his lungs inflated into his broken ribs.

'It is time for the tourniquet. Tie off his legs at zi knee and his arms at zi elbow. Ve vill cut him up like he did Demetry and post him back to his whore-mother. Except his head. Zat vill be a gift for my sister, for zis son he took.'

They tied thick rubber bands around Dylan's limbs. It hurt but less than his other injuries. Each breath was shallower now, as though his lungs had shrunk to the size of grapes.

Yessshhh?

'No, not zi power tool. Zi hand saw. Take your time.'

No one was coming for him. Not the Blud Crew, not the police, and definitely not his mother. She was at home in bed making money for Henry Grime, in her own kind of prison. A glimmer of anger flickered in Dylan. Metal clanked against metal. Steps moved closer. The anticipation of the saw was nearly as bad as its sharp teeth coming to rest on Dylan's flesh. Fanned by his fear, his anger grew.

The whispers giggled shrilly. *Yeeessssssh?*

Dylan had been falling for a long while. The world was a place beyond his control through which he hurtled; the adults, the ones supposed to guide and nurture him, only added to his speed, like gypsies at a carnival spinning the waltzer cars. Numbers had always been his only weapon. They made sense in a disordered world. They were abstract and ideal, fathomable, unlike the idea of God. But he realised now, just like God, just like his mother, just like Henry Grime and the Blud Crew, and even just like Samuel who'd come to save him in that alley, and that they'd made him stab, the numbers could not save him now. But maybe there was one thing that could.

'Yesh,' Dylan slurred with his head lolled.

The man with the saw stopped, the pressure of the steel teeth on Dylan's shin eased. 'What did he say?'

'Yesh,' Dylan said again.

The man with an accent barked. 'Ha, he mocks us. He has guts. I could like zis boy. Pity.'

'You stupid tosspot. You want me to cut even slower?' the man with the saw asked.

With blood and spit dribbling from his mouth, Dylan nodded, 'Yesh, yesh, yesh.' But he wasn't speaking to the man with the accent, or the one with the saw, or any of the other men in the room who participated in his torture. No, he spoke to the whispers because for the first time he understood them. Their susurrant affirmations weren't encouragement, they weren't praise. They were a question, Vieil's question. It was the only thing here when he needed it, and with everything to lose and all other choices gone, Dylan answered its call.

'Enough of zis. Take his leg slowly. Break him.'

The teeth of the saw dug into Dylan's skin, ready to chew through his flesh.

Loud and insistent, three bangs rapped at the green wooden door of the arches.

The teeth retracted. Dylan heard guns cock.

28

CURVED BLADE

ALL BECAUSE OF a pair of trainers. That's what brought Tibs here. His full name was James Tibbets, but everyone called him Tibs, except his mum. She mostly screamed at him and told him to stop being a useless little shit or a waste of space or, like yesterday, that she wished he'd never been born. They never got on well. She was a single mum, and in Tibs' most charitable of moments, he thought she probably had it hard, but she was still a bitch. Tried to snitch on him to the feds too, after he got his new trainers; she grew suspicious and started going through his things while he was out. Silly cow found two ounces of skunk and fifty mollies separated into little plastic bags of sellable shits-and-giggles.

She never brought him nothing. They never had the money for new clothes. Tibs found the trips to food banks and charity shops humiliating. There was always money for fags, though, wasn't there? And a rum and coke. But never for a new pair of trainers.

Tibs knew Drake, who knew Dimitri, who everyone called Dems. They were Duppies and owned their Ends, or at least Tibs thought they did. He knew now that was bollocks. They were street punks a little further up the shitpile than him. Above them was something much bigger, hidden from sight, pulling the strings, rolling their shit downhill.

Tibs curled his toes in his new trainers. They were pale grey and came straight out of the box yesterday. Brand new Nike Air Max Commands. The crepe-paper protecting them crackled how he imagined a Christmas fire would. They'd felt so good, like he could run faster, jump higher, and he definitely stood taller. After the rain and the mud from the park at Gallows Court, though, the trainers were dirty brown, and there were spots of blood sprayed on them, some from that fat boy in the alley, some from the boy in the chair they caught and brought here.

The night had spun out of control. The alley was okay, Tibs told himself. He'd shanked people before, cut them to get into the crew. He once smashed his mate Johnny unconscious to show allegiance. He'd set fire to a Chinese takeaway when they didn't pay their protection money, and the wife of the owner ended up in hospital with burns all over her body. Yeah, the alley wasn't bad. He was a bad man now. A Duppy, and Duppies be hard men.

Still, the Blud Crew boy screamed. Dylan Savage he was called. He was in the year below Tibs; they knew each other. Not mates or nothing. Dylan was a bit of a freak. Tibs was barely in school, but he knew enough that Dylan was a maths whizz or something. A teacher's pet. That Mrs Stokes thought he was special. Apart from being well fit, she was one of the good teachers, not like that prick Bestwick. The thing was, Tibs didn't get how Dylan could be the one they said killed Dimitri, Pugs, and Nutty, cutting them up into pieces and dropping them in the Thames. Then again, Tibs never thought he'd stab someone or commit arson. The things you'll do for your new family... and a pair of trainers.

This was it. They were actually going to chop Dylan up and do it good and slow. Saw off his legs and arms a piece at a time, keeping him alive, and take his head last of all like a Jihadi snuff video.

The beating had been bad. Bones snapped. Tibs had never heard that before. It made him feel sick. When they pulled out each nail and snapped his fingers one after the other, Tibs had puked in his mouth and gulped it back. He couldn't look weak, not in front of Mr Morozovo, the big boss man. He was stone cold, him and his henchman, Pavel, the guy with no neck guarding the street outside.

The saw came to rest on Dylan's leg. Mike Bridges was Tibs' immediate boss, running the Duppy Crew, king of the ghosts. Mr Morozovo, looking over Bridges' shoulder, had entrusted him with the torture, and Tibs was next to Mr Morozovo, wishing he'd picked another place to stand. Bridges braced on Dylan's leg, ready to saw through the flesh, when three hard bangs came at the green workshop doors.

Guns and knives were drawn. Tibs got out his own weapon, a bike chain. After that, the bad night got a whole lot worse.

With dull stupidity, Lardy Martin said, 'Who the hell is it?'

Mr Morozovo's no-neck henchman, Pavel, answered Lardy Martin's question, only it didn't sound right. It was his voice, with the same gravelly Russian accent, except it was whispery, as though he was breathless, or maybe had caught a sudden case of laryngitis.

Lardy hiked up his jeans to cover the crack of his fat ass, and adjusting his grip on his Glock pistol, he asked again who it was.

'Open zi door. It's Pavel.' The voice was breathier than before.

After a check with Mr Morozovo, Lardy shoved his pistol in the back of his jeans, exposing the cleft between his butt cheeks again, and unfastened the three heavy deadbolts on the top, bottom and, lastly, the middle of the door, pushing it ajar.

From that point on, the normal world, which had always had an unpredictable tilt for Tibs, spasmed on its axis.

What Tibs saw was impossible. In the few disconcerting seconds it took to make some sort of sense of it all, his mind ran through multiple, implausible options. Everything from it being a prank, through to him needing to get his eyes tested, and finally onto the possibility he was hallucinating or dreaming. Waking dreams, they were a thing, right? Night terrors or whatever, that's what they were called. That must have been it. That must be the explanation for why Pavel's boulder-like head was floating, without a body, through the door, blood dripping from the loose flaps of skin and the severed pipes that were once his neck. What little colour Pavel had in his face had drained to a sickening white. His eyes were wide, and the wrinkles on his forehead still moved, while his mouth opened and closed, saying something Tibs couldn't hear.

Whatever words Pavel might have been saying were lost amid the panic.

Lardy fell on his fat ass. His gun went off and shot his left heel clean off. Pavel's head kept floating forward, and then Tibs saw another strange thing. A hand clutched Pavel's head by a tuft of hair at the back of his skull. The arm held the head straight out at shoulder height and grew longer, extending into the arches. It was covered in a smart white shirt, with an old-fashioned garter around the bicep. The cuff was stained red like Tibs' new trainers. In this topsy-turvy world, for a millisecond, Tibs expected the arm to be as equally disembodied as Pavel's mawing head. But it wasn't. A man stepped into the room, dressed in brown checkered trousers and a matching waistcoat. He wore a bowler hat and had a handlebar moustache, like one of those hipster wankers found in Covent Garden or wanking on about modern art on the South Bank. They were always good to twat in the face when they visited the bog and, subsequently, to be relieved of their phone, wallet, and general smugness. But Tibs thought mugging this man would be a fatal mistake. Aside from the fact he held the head of a Russian gangster in one hand, in the other, he carried what Tibs could only imagine was the weapon he'd used to perform the decapitation. The weapon was big, something like a sword and an axe rolled into one, or like one of those old-fashioned things used to cut crops. Tibs couldn't remember what they were called. He really wanted to remember, because focusing on that meant not having to think about everything else that was going on, such as the disconcerting fact that Pavel was still speaking.

The man with the waistcoat and moustache was followed in by another man. In some ways, this second man reminded Tibs of Mr Morozovo. He was well dressed in a nice suit that would make the cost of Tibs' trainers seem like a lost penny in the gutter. He was pale too, but not in the same Eastern European way of Mr Morozovo. No, it was more like Pavel's new look. The second man also had grey eyes, at least grey was the closest colour Tibs could think of. And he had blood around his mouth, which he was dabbing at with a silk handkerchief.

A sickle! Tibs suddenly remembered. It didn't help. The man with the grey eyes—or were they actually silver?—and the thin, hawkish nose came to a stop next to the man in the bowler hat, a few feet inside the door. Lardy rolled around screaming and holding his lower leg behind them.

Everyone else, except Tibs and Mr Morozovo, were shouting, brandishing guns and knives, bats and hammers of varying sizes.

The man with the moustache and the sickle-like weapon threw Pavel's head across the room. It hit the concrete with a horrible thud and rolled over twice to come to a rest at Mr Morozovo's feet, eyes and mouth still working as if he'd forgotten how to die.

Mr Morozovo's stoney, almost bored face didn't change, not at first. With serpentine fluidity, he pulled a silver pistol with a mother of pearl handle from inside his suit jacket. This was the cue for everyone else with a gun, except Lardy, who was still screaming and holding his leg.

Bridges, who'd done most of the beating of Dylan, drew his revolver as the first of Mr Morozovo's bullets hit the moustache man in the chest. Then, Charlie 'Beefy' Botham levelled his shotgun, and Jax trained an antique six-shooter at the intruders and they let them rip.

Tibs put his hands to his ears as the percussion of bangs rang out. The two men made a herky-jerky dance of death, their limbs flailing, clothes punctured. When the second barrel of Beefy's shotgun took off half moustache man's face, knocking off his bowler hat, Tibs closed his eyes.

The gunfire stopped not long after that. Shells and cartridges tinkled on the concrete like windchimes in the growing quiet.

Tibs opened his eyes, but he wished he hadn't. He wished he'd never known Drake (who knew Dimitri) and fallen in with the Duppies. He wished that even his angry, shouting, crappy mother was there.

The man with the moustache moved. Mr Morozovo, the only one to reload immediately, pointed his silver revolver down at the man and fired three more rounds into him. The body went limp. Mr Morozovo gave a curt nod to himself, but a few seconds later the body moved again. The Russian took half a step forward, aimed and fired the rest of his clip into the body. It wasn't enough.

The body stirred. Mr Morozovo's implacable face furrowed at the brow. He reached for another clip hidden beneath his pinstripe jacket. By the time he'd released the empty clip and it hit the floor, the moustache man had, somehow, drawn up to his feet. Holes peppered his brown waistcoat and white shirt, but no blood. Tibs was shaking. The man had half a face, yet he stood, raising up his curved weapon of burnished yellow metal. His nightmare face of ruined gristle and bone was regrowing, in a spider's web of sinew, flesh knitting together as Mr Morozovo slapped in another clip. Everyone else was paralysed by what they were seeing.

There was a chuckle of mocking laughter from the second man, the one with the silver eyes. Yes, Tibs could see it now. They weren't grey at all but a glinting silver as poisonous as mercury. One second, the silver-eyed man was lying on the floor. The next he was face-to-face with Mr Morozovo, with Tibs just beside him. It wasn't possible. Tibs must be dreaming; this must be a nightmare, one of those night terrors for sure, where the laws of the natural world didn't apply, because what else could explain what happened next?

The man with the moustache moved through the room. He was a blur which reaped. There was barely time to scream. As the blur passed each man in the room, bellies opened, guts spilled out, legs were severed at the knee, hands dropped to the floor, and arms were lopped from the shoulder. Blood gouted and sprayed.

As each man was amputated and disemboweled by the blur of death, the man with the moustache would finish his dark dance by swinging his curved blade and relieve them of their heads. Tibs watched each of them fall, looks of incomprehension etched on their features.

Finally, it was Tibs' turn. He only became aware of his screaming when the man with the silver eyes placed a razor sharp talon to his lips. *Shh!* Tibs heard in his mind and obeyed as the man with silver eyes sunk a mouthful of fangs into his neck. It was excruciating, but he couldn't move. The man with silver eyes threw back his head and dropped Tibs, who, before he could collapse, lost his head to a blur of scything metal. The floor and ceiling waltzed around each other once, twice before his head hit the floor. The funny thing was, he saw it all, and was seeing it still.

Tibs' head had fallen in such a way that it came to rest facing the room, with the feet of his prone body partially obscuring the view. He could see his brand new trainers, soiled with mud and blood. As the pool of red grew around his body, he noticed several more terrible things, things that fueled his voiceless scream.

The other heads were inanimate, apart from his and Pavel's, whose eyes moved and mouth worked. The man with the silver eyes stood in front of Mr Morozovo, who seemed to be fighting an internal battle which he was losing, ending up on his knees, bowed beneath the power of the silver-eyed man's stare. The man with a moustache presented the silver-eyed man with Bridges; he took Bridges by the throat and looked from him to Dylan, slumped unconscious in the chair. The old man had a mouthful of fangs, all bunched together, crowding over each other and dripping with a pale ooze, like venom or pus. Tibs closed his eyes as the fangs bit into Bridges' neck. When he opened them again, Bridges' head was separated from his body and lay next to Tibs', confused and blinking.

The silver-eyed man stepped to Mr Morozovo, who opened his mouth. He reached inside the mobster's throat and, with a swift yank, tore out Mr Morozovo's tongue. Blood poured forth, but Mr Morozovo remained kneeling, arms by his side, until the silver-eyed man tossed away the tongue and walked towards Dylan's slumped body.

Tibs didn't see anything else, because the other man, if he was a man at all, bent down, picked up Tibs' head, inspected it and deposited it in a bag, the same bag that had once held the tools for Dylan's torture. Tibs glimpsed Pavel's round face facing his, eyes blinking and swivelling around, unable to get a better view. A zip closed his view on the bloody horror of the arches.

All this because he'd wanted something his mother couldn't give him: a stupid pair of trainers.

29

DARK GEOMETRY

LIGHTER THAN AIR. Was this a delirium brought on by pain? Was it the disintegration of reality during the transition to death? Dylan didn't know. He was weightless, speeding through the streets of London, floating above the buildings, glimpsed through fluttering eyelids. Below, tiny figures walked streets stained with electric light. A great dog bounded, tracing their progress, on Earth as in Heaven. Sleek, it wove unseen among them. Above, brooding clouds bled their tears, blotting out the moon's razored edge.

Dylan gave in to death. This was his final journey. He'd never thought there was anything else until he came across number 25 Gallows Court. Now, something else beyond this life was a possibility, not one he'd given much thought to. It was a logical conclusion, as much as a sum follows the addition of its parts.

He shivered. Perhaps the afterlife was a cold place, frigid and biting, and not the fiery furnace of the Bible. The sky lurched away from him as he fell down a shaft. The cold lessened though never left him. The clouds and rain were replaced with walls and ceilings, dimly lit and covered in opulent wallpaper, filigreed with plaster coving, gilded with paintings and crystal chandeliers, all coddled in the guttering light of candles and the pop and hiss of open fires.

Weightlessness went the way of the sky. Gravity imposed itself on

Dylan's body. He wheezed under its crushing force, crucifying him with nails of agony, hammered through his lungs, his broken fingers, and the swollen pulp of his face. Each breath was an agony he hoped only for an end to.

From somewhere a voice reached him.

'Drink. Drink, my boy. Drink to live.'

The cold liquid met Dylan's lips, dripped thickly into his mouth, a frigid ooze down his throat, and the pain of before magnified beyond endurance and ulcerated in a nebulous ferment of utter agony. Dylan felt his bones crack back into place. His broken vessels seared shut and wounds knitted together, just as the moth requires a chrysalis.

The pain was a blinding fog that swept away the rags of consciousness from Dylan's withering mind until he stood atop a mountainous black pyramid, adrift in an ocean of charcoal dunes. He teetered on its apex, its polished sides sheening dully and veined with red. Punctured with the light of countless meek stars, the infinite sky above swirled in a milky abyss, twirling and churning around and around and around, nauseating, drawing, inducing, abducting Dylan into the endless...

30

APOPHENIUM

SPREAD OUT THROUGH THE VASTNESS, the web reached into everything —it *was* everything. The fine threads of starlight knitted together the cosmos, and below that, or within and around it, Dylan realised there were parallel dimensions entangled in the silken fibres. The chaos and its knots of patterns clustered like spiders' eggs. He'd read about this, or rather, he'd read about three ideas in Mrs Stokes' textbook. Multiple types of infinity; order found in Chaos Theory; and the fractal spirals of the Fibonacci Sequence. One, one, two, three, five, eight, thirteen and on, never ending. Fibonacci squares were another among many infinities. One, one, four, nine, twenty-five:

Twenty-five!

The number arrested Dylan's train of thought. The fractal web stuttered, and an icy chill blushed across his body. Groping, he found the fractals again, in all their intricate beauty, like the refracted light of a snowflake. He now understood the concepts which before had been nothing more than marks on a page. They had been as confusing as the unfairness of the world, as irrational as a mother whose love wasn't strong enough to fight the booze, the pressures of money, and the desires of men.

Irrational! The word was a revelation, an epiphany, hitting Dylan in the epicentre of his mind. A shockwave rippled out in concentric circles, touching the stars and the web beneath, above, within, everywhere. Words failed the perfection of the mathematical relationships, which now he did not only perceive, but *embodied* as well, as if he was the sum of the whole universe. The fractals of the Fibonacci Sequence were made real. They were in the structure of plants, the spirals of tornadoes, the double helix of DNA. And if Dylan didn't only add them together but divide them, the next by the previous number in the sequence, one by one, two by one, three by two and so on until fifty-five was divided by thirty-four, there was the number, so perfect, so beautiful.

1.61803398875...

The Golden Ratio.

An *irrational* number, like pi, an endless series of numbers that didn't repeat. Irregular, yet predictable. Balance in instability. The symmetry in Anila's face; the ratio in a perfect spiral; the proportions of a prism, a pyramid. The calm eye in the centre of the spinning hurricane. Order in the infinite tumult. But tracking back, there it was, conspicuous in its banality, hidden in the code, easily skipped, one number among a never-ending sequence: twenty-five.

The icy chill flushed through Dylan once more. The universe of stars stuttered. Dylan tried to breathe, but frigid water filled his lungs. He couldn't understand where he was. Murkiness enveloped and smothered him. He wanted to scream and struggle, but his mouth and limbs were bound.

Was he hallucinating? Was what he was seeing nothing more than the addled phantoms of sleep? Or was he still in the torture chamber under the railway arches, and this was all just his mind reeling in the final throes of asphyxiation?

The connection with the celestial vision severed abruptly. Dylan thrashed, kicked his legs, twisted his body. He would die fighting.

The cold liquid swept across his skin. In the panic, Dylan's strength surged, and the bonds on his arm broke with a sudden release of tension. His free hand tore at the covering over his mouth. It was hard and coated with slime, and his fingers fumbled and slipped. He found purchase by clawing nails over his cheek, pushing the flesh out of the way. With a tenuous grip, he yanked at the gag. It was down his throat and dragged through his gullet. With a retch, he cleared the blockage, but air didn't rush into his lungs.

The cold water clung to him, and Dylan realised he *was* underwater. The Duppies, they were drowning him. A wild thing born of desperation, panic clambered over Dylan's rational mind. His flailing arm touched the edge of his prison. It was ribbed and as slimy as the gag, giving no grip.

Blind in the dark, unable to breathe, Dylan kicked and punched and struggled with everything he had. None of it worked. The sides were too slick. On and on he fought, drowning in lungfuls of dirty water, until finally he noticed he wasn't drowning, or dying. Liquid had long ago filled his lungs, yet he lived.

Dylan settled; swishing around in cold currents, the liquid calmed with him. He stopped. He couldn't breathe, and yet he wasn't dead. Wherever he was, it was dark but not lightless. Flecked with a filthy emulsion of particles, the surrounding water was more brown than black.

He let himself hang in the fluid. A faint, throbbing pulse hummed at regular intervals, quiet but perceptible, and synchronized with a red glow. The edges of his container were opaque but had a little translucency. Another timid flaring of colour shone through the murk.

Dylan reached for the next red palpitation of light. He took his time, feeling carefully along the slippery surface, probing, gathering information. When his fingertips found a crevice, like a seam, he tracked its length, located its ends, came back to its middle and pushed his fingers into it with a steady pressure.

At first, it felt impossible, but then the seam yielded a touch. He drove his hands in deeper until he could grab fistfuls of whatever encased him. Then, making sure he had the best grip he could, Dylan pulled. He felt strong, very strong. The seam moved. The stretching sound amplified in the liquid. The seam reached the limits of its expansion, and for a moment it tensed and resisted back. Dylan gritted his teeth and, with a drowned scream, yanked the seam apart.

With a sucking and tearing, suddenly the fluid gushed out of the opening. Dylan kept pulling until, with the absence of water, a new sensation informed him that he was upside down and that gravity was still very much the dominant force in his universe. The seam yawned wide as if giving up the fight.

Dylan lost his grip and pitched into the chasm below.

31

SECONDMENT

DEPUTY CHIEF CONSTABLE TERRY WILKINS sat straight-backed, scanning the file on his desk, flipping through the crime scene photographs, pausing occasionally for a sip of tea from his china cup.

Kenny, Roj, their Detective Inspector Celement Jackson, and the new secondment brought in from vice, Trinity Marshall, stood at attention on the opposite side of the desk. They hadn't been offered tea or coffee, and they hadn't been told to stand at ease. The Deputy Chief Constable of the London Metropolitan Police was a busy man, and yet he'd summoned them all. They wouldn't be staying long, though a clock ticked on the wall as if to remind them how much time they were taking. Pictures of Terry Wilkins lined the furniture, showing him smiling with politicians of the day. There was even one of him with Bob Geldof. They shook hands and beamed at the photographer. Terry Wilkins wasn't beaming now. His eyes scanned the file with cold precision, crisper than the way he turned each page with a sharp flick of his wrist.

Rain pattered against the seventh floor window of New Scotland Yard, blurring the waterfront view of the Thames and the London Eye, which revolved as slowly as the second hands of the office wall clock. The day's newspapers lay in a pile on the desk, their headlines blazed with the same thing: the Ripper.

Terry Wilkins closed the file, leaned back in his chair, and laced his fingers together. The clock's second hand carved off a handful more seconds before the Deputy Chief Constable took a measured breath. 'At ease.' The four police officers relaxed. 'The file is thorough. I see no operational mistakes. And you, DS Stokes, seem more than capable of leading this investigation. However, I do have one initial question. What evidence do we have that the Ripper copycat murders are related to the torso killings?'

'The evidence is circumstantial, sir,' Kenny said. 'It's based on the level of detail the copycat has of the original murders, which led us to believe the torso case could be related because of historical knowledge. However, we have nothing harder than that. It is one of many lines of enquiry.'

Wilkins gave a curt half-nod. 'Let's keep that hypothesis to ourselves. No point feeding the beast. There is enough of a media frenzy about this and that is without the derangement on social media. The cyber crime task force has seen a spike in everything from vigilante groups, women's rights activism, Far Right immigrant blaming, Muslim extremist propaganda and, my particular favourite, the conspiracy theory that the killings are blood sacrifices for the Illuminati lizard cabal of the patriarchal liberal elite. Of which, apparently, I'm the Chapter secretary. I'm not joking, Detective Dabral. I wish I were. Things are fragile at the moment.' Wilkins sighed. 'When are they not?'

The four officers waited for him to continue.

'I appreciate you coming here straight from the arches in Spitalfields, but I wanted to address your plan considering Jack is "out of the bag", so to speak.' He gestured at the papers on his desk.

Kenny interjected, 'Sir, we think there is a possibility the events at the arches are connected.'

Detective Inspector Celemant Jackson standing at the end of the line of his officers turned his head to Kenny. 'DS Stokes, not now.'

Wilkins held up a hand to silence the tall and broad Detective Inspector. 'Go on, DS Stokes.'

Kenny glanced sideways at DI Jackson, who nodded that it was okay to proceed, but the frown on his face said otherwise.

'The manner of the killings are similar to the torso murders, with dismemberment and decapitation. Add to that, all the heads were removed. The cuts might prove to be from the same or similar weapon. We are waiting for the pathologist's report.'

Wilkins interrupted. 'Doesn't that make it seem these are more likely to be connected with the torso murders? It has a gangland feel to it, does it not? And I understand from vice that there is a turf war going on in the East End.' His eyes alighted on Trinity Marshall, stood next to Roj, with her mane of dark and tight curls tied back.

'Yes, sir,' Kenny said, 'but the nature of the cuts suggests there is a possibility the same weapon was used in both sets of murders. Also, the bodies at the arches were all disemboweled, from groin to sternum, indicative of the Ripper's MO.' There were other things too, of course. But Kenny wasn't about to start going on about growling dogs or that he'd seen the same assailant with the same mystery weapon. Not that he could prove that in a court of law. Not yet. He and Roj had identified the type of weapon, and its odd origins didn't help matters one bit, even if they could talk about it.

Wilkins rested his index finger on his lips in thought, staring right through Kenny. Wind whipped up in sudden gusts, throwing rain against the windows in thick sheets that melted the city into a watery ooze, more glaucous than a Monet painting leached of its colour. Kenny heard Bob Geldof nasally opine his feelings about Mondays. Initially, he thought it was because he'd seen the photograph on the wall before he realised he was reading Wilkins. There was the bristle of nylon carpet under his hands, a faint taste of dandelion and burdock that had lost its fizz, the static of vinyl records and turning them up to block something out. Kenny didn't want to dig deeper. It would be invasive, and Kenny could identify with that echo of the young Wilkins. Besides, he'd barely got back on an even keel after the violent deaths in the arches. There were details in that wall of sound from the murder scene he needed to go back over. Maybe another trip there in a few days and the echoes would be less frenetic.

Finally, Wilkins removed his fingers from his lips, and his gaze came back to the room. 'The problem I see is that time is not on our side. Forensics will be the crux of some of these lines of inquiry. I'll see what I can do to expedite that for you. We are lacking hard evidence, and the community is clamming up, which as your report indicates, points to a gangland connection. In turn, I agree that teaming up with vice and attempting to get something out of surveillance and undercover might work. Homicide is reactive, whereas vice is more proactive. But, and this is a big but, you'll be on a short leash for this. We are walking a fine line between good policing and acting foolhardy because of public pressure. I'm uncomfortable about dropping female officers in the middle of a gangland bloodbath.'

Trinity bristled. 'Sir, I must—'

Wilkins cut her off with another raised finger. 'Don't presume it's misogyny, Detective, and watch your tone, unless you fancy pulling traffic duty in the back arse of Suffolk for the rest of your career. The proposed plan puts female officers at the sharpest end of this particular spear. Their gender is beside the point.'

'Sorry, sir, I apologise.'

Wilkins waved the apology aside. 'We need a result. Whether that is a solid lead, a confession, surveillance, anything. I don't care. We've a window here, a very small one, before the press links the two sets of murders. If you think the scrutiny is bad now, we won't be able to go to the bathroom without being noticed afterwards. And we'll be leakier than the Soho public toilets too. In short, I'm agreeing to the plan and the budget. But you've three days at the maximum before I review it again, and that's if circumstances don't force my hand before then. For everyone's sake, not least the next victim, let's hope that's not the case.'

32

DARK MATTERS

One arm took the brunt of the fall, and the rest of Dylan's body piled on the polished floor amid the puddle of dirty water. His forearm snapped, and the sound echoed in the vast chamber.

The concussive impact with the floor didn't wind him, but it helped him expel the fluid in his lungs in a gushing retch.

There was no satisfaction or relief in it, but he could breathe again. The air was hot and dry, and the act itself seemed inconsequential, a vestigial reflex.

He sat for the moment, swaying a little dumbly, taking in the peculiar sight of his forearm bent at an unnatural right angle in the middle. Waxy and pallid, the skin stretched with the break. Then, as inexplicable as the absence of pain, there was a grinding and squelching as the arm straightened of its own accord, finding its natural shape, though there was nothing natural about the process. With a final snap, Dylan's forearm healed. He flexed his fingers, turning the arm around, inspecting it with wonder. Through his splayed fingers, the rest of the chamber revealed itself.

Dylan put down his arm, and his mouth fell ajar at the size and shape of the chamber. The floor was square, with two intersecting paths of polished black crossing in the middle where Dylan sat. In the four spaces between the paths, each the size of a squared off football pitch, were pools of shimmering quicksilver reflecting the four sloping walls of the pyramid in the confusing oscillations of their rippling surfaces.

Craning his neck to take in the height of the chamber, Dylan saw pulses of red throb from the pyramid's apex, running in veins down the walls and through the floor. Slow thrums of light twinned with a hum. And to complete his strange awakening, there were two other things, side by side.

A pair of twisted cords dropped straight down, suspended from an indiscernible point in the blackness of the apex. At their ends, hanging six feet above the floor, were a pair of what Dylan first thought of as pods, then as cocoons. He had fallen from one, which hung agape. The other, slightly larger, hung intact, a knot of black and browns, ribbed with grey and sickly sinews.

Wet and naked, Dylan got to his feet and took a step closer to the second cocoon. The walls and floor thrummed, pulses of scarlet bleeding into the dark. A patch near the bottom of the cocoon was smooth and membranous. The red pulse shone through the translucent patch, and, shrouded in the dirty water, Vieil's sleeping face blinked into view. The light failed and took Vieil's image with it, and Dylan staggered away.

The memories of his torture came rushing back, but they made no sense. He held up his hands: perfect nails regrown, fingers straight and unbroken. His face wasn't swollen, his skin wasn't split and bleeding. His ribs weren't shattered. He was whole. Dylan re-examined his forearm, flexing the hand and muscles, which he'd broken only a moment ago.

A dream, it had to be a dream, but it didn't feel like one. There was a canniness, the palpable texture of reality. A strange reality, for sure, but reality nonetheless. So what? What was this? What had happened? Dylan searched his memories, back through the cocoon, through the entangled universe of numbers, back through flying over the city, to the workshop, the kidnap, the alleyway with Samuel. A pang of raw emotion at that last one: anger, love, hate, vengeance, all of it; and then back to himself standing on the floor of the pyramid.

Muzzled with knotted sinews, Vieil's face pulsed in and out of sight. Dylan heard the monster's voice as memory. 'Drink. Drink if you want to live.' He took the medicine. Then came his dissolution into pain, and it was all there.

These weren't pods or cocoons.

Vieil slept inverted, hanging entombed in his chrysalis from the apex of a polished black pyramid. They were sarcophagi. Not like the ones they studied at school in history, shaping clay models of them in art class, copying the hieroglyphs, and making displays about ancient Egyptians. These were the real things. Not coffins, but vessels to store and preserve the occupants on their journey into the afterlife.

Afterlife... It made sense now.

Dylan took another step back away from Vieil's inverted tomb. He stumbled away from the implications, staring at his hands as if they would hold the answer. In a way, they did. They stood for every other part of him which was smashed and broken in that workshop with the green door. They were fixed. There was no more pain. But how was that possible? Although Dylan didn't know the exact method, he knew how or at least why. And he reeled even further from the idea while the walls and floor of the black pyramid pulsed red, humming rhythmically. He was now whatever Vieil was. He could feel it. Strength. Power. Heightened perception too. He understood mathematical ideas that before now, even for Dylan with his felicity with numbers, lay years beyond his reach.

It was dark in the chamber, very dark. Even the red palpitations of light were muted. Yet, Dylan could see, with perfect acuity, the flecks hanging in the brown liquid around Vieil's face, the twisted veins running over the two hanging sarcophagi and, smaller than them, almost microscopic, silky, grey capillaries spreading out like the roots of a tree. Somehow, Vieil had turned Dylan into a monster like himself.

The Duppy called Dimitri appeared to Dylan. His mouth was open as Vieil fed from his neck, massaging the last drops of the boy's life out of his heart.

Dylan's heel met the end of the crossroad where the walkways intersected and between the lakes of quicksilver. He wobbled, about to fall from the path, but with his new life came agility and speed. He turned in the air, arresting his fall, and landed cat-like on all fours, his face inches from the undulating pool. Mouth ajar in a noiseless cry, another face sprang from the moving liquid, pulling against the silver surface. Dylan fell back. The face retreated, but others came forth, stretching the skin of the pool. Each failed to break through, sinking back beneath the restless ripples.

This was all wrong. Terribly wrong. Suddenly, the dry heat of the room was unbearably oppressive. The black walls were a mausoleum. Its pulsing red veins, were vestigial tendrils of the living world burrowing below the dirt, marbling the walls of his grave. His prison.

Naked and exposed, Dylan scrambled to his feet, slipping in the effluent of his hanging pod. Feet slapping along the icy floor, Dylan ran, choosing one of the four paths at random. He wanted to put Vieil behind him. The red veins pumped light across the path, each pulse outrunning him. Eyes glistening, Dylan had to beat them, he had to be quicker than the light. His body obeyed his whim, and he passed through space, from one place to the next, in a blur, only for the tapering walls of the chamber to block him, with the red light continuing to pulse rhythmically, unremittingly.

Dylan groped at the wall, pacing left and right, frantically searching for a way out. It was there, but he was panicking and too close to the wall to see it. A few more desperate paws later, and he found it. With an edge so defined it was almost sharp, the escape route was a simple square portal cut into the sloping wall. Without forethought, he threw himself into the black hole and tripped.

The floor sloped up with a steep incline, and Dylan didn't waste time. Using onto all fours, he crawled. Low and cramped, the tunnel consisted of the same polished black material as the chamber, with the arterial seams alternating between pitch black and gloaming scarlet.

Below, the entrance to the tunnel grew smaller and smaller. The polished surface ran out as the tunnel made a right-angled turn. Rough hewn rock, snaggled with roots and matted with cobwebs, closed around Dylan. The passage narrowed further. He'd made it to his feet but couldn't stand. Instead, in a crouch, he pulled aside the dangling roots, spraying his naked body with dust and dirt. As steep as ever, another right turn followed another and another. He ascended higher and higher, fighting thicker and thicker entanglements of roots and more netted veils of cobwebs. They closed in on him. Ensnared, he tore at them, ripping them asunder with ease, hardly breaking his harried progress up, up and up.

At last, there was a light. Through the miasma of dust, a meek glow above him. He inhaled it but didn't cough. Dylan's focus was to get out, and he put on a burst of effort and found himself back on all fours for extra speed, bounding along, lifting an arm higher only if a root needed ripping out of the way.

The light grew stronger and larger. A boulder had fallen from the roof of the tunnel. Dylan put a hand to the side and for three successive leaps ran along the wall until he cleared the obstacle. Fear propelled him on, but with the eerie chamber further and further behind him, he revelled in his own strength and gravity defying agility. It was new and strange and intoxicating, pushing him on toward the light that was already upon him. He bounded out of the dark, leaping up as if breaking the surface after holding his breath for a long time. The floor disappeared from under his feet, and he was flying.

33

TALKING HEADS

As HIS ARMS and legs scrabbled at thin air, the ceiling of the room rushed towards Dylan. While not strong, the sudden change exiting from the dark caused Dylan to wince. He put hands up to protect his eyes, saw the rusted iron beams and crumbling brick almost too late, and slammed into the roof.

When he opened his eyes, it took a moment to understand why the room was upside down. He was hanging from the ceiling, stuck there on his hands and feet.

'Where's the mutt? Mutt, mutt, mutt. He's coming, back, back, back.'

'Twenty-five bottles of beer on the wall, twenty-five bottles of beer. If one of those bottles of beer should fall, there'll be... there'll be... be... be. Twenty-five bottles of beer on the wall, twenty-five bottles of beer—'

'Don't, lose your head. Don't, lose your head. Don't, lose your head. Don't, lose your head—'

'There are worse things than death?'

'State the obvious, why don't you.'

'*Mon canard est orange. Votre chien est-il bleu?*'

'My days, this can't be happening.'

'Ha! Snot running out your nose; it's your brains. Brains. No

177

brains. Brains. No brains. Don't need brains. Snot, snot, blow your nose. Look no hands. No hands. Can't blow your nose. Can't blow your nose.'

'Fáte, fáte, fáte choíro. Fáte to prósopó sas.'

'No, no, no. You'll make the mutt angry. Very angry. His place. Our place. Place.'

Dylan hung by all fours on the ceiling, trying to take in the fact that he'd escaped an underground pyramid. Now he was in another bewildering room. This one was a windowless block, built of old, yellow, London bricks, with a furnace belching out heat in the corner. An oblong table sat in the middle of the room of dark brown wood, almost red with stains. It smelled of herbs and spiced oils, a heady mix in the heat that was cloying and masking, covering up another odour of sickly rot and earthy desiccation. Dylan was reminded of visiting his grandmother when she was still alive and he was tiny, how old, he couldn't remember now. He was small enough to hide his head behind his mother's hip, as much to cover his nose as from shyness. His grandmother's flat reeked of plug-in deodorisers, masking the not so faint smell of urine and the mustiness of the old and dying. But the smell wasn't the most arresting thing about this room Dylan now found himself in.

Around the room, wall to wall, floor to ceiling, were shelves, divided into cubby holes, with nearly every hole filled with another thing Dylan struggled to comprehend: severed heads, hundreds of them. Some were very old, dried and withered, with only a paper covering of skin still hanging from their skulls. Their eyes were closed and their jaws hung open, filling with dust. The other heads varied in their levels of decay, right up to the fresh ones lying on the table, one of which, with horror and disgust, Dylan recognised.

'Dylan, hey, Dylan. I'm sorry, blud, about the arches.' It was Tibs. Dylan knew him from school and couldn't remember him being at the arches. For that matter, he didn't know he was a Duppy.

'Oh, he's sorry now. Sorry, sorry, won't help now. You're the mutt's,' a severed head from one of the holes said. It was withered, with sunken eyes and greying skin that had flaked away to the bone on one cheek. Thin wisps of hair hung around its face, and it appeared to be attempting to blow the strands away from its nose to no effect. All their voices were like forced whispers, but this older head was coloured with a gravelly lisp.

Tibs blinked rapidly, and his cheeks twitched. His pleading expression twisted into a snarl, and his jaw snapped at the air, snarling, as if he wanted to bite Dylan.

The heads continued to chatter, and Dylan noticed how the ones that were awake switched between mad ramblings and contorted rage or vice versa. Some laughed maniacally or stared blankly at nothing, only blinking occasionally before an animalistic rage came over them.

'Oh my days! Oh my days! No, no, no!' This came from a head on the same table as Tibs, secured in a vice so that it was fixed, perched on edge looking at the floor.

'Yes, yes, yes,' chuckled a bald and very round head that had probably once belonged to a fat man, because its skin sagged in overlapping, loose folds that gathered around its base like melted wax. 'Oh, oh, oh, there she blows,' and it cheered insanely, breaking into a high-pitched titter of laughter.

There was a slurping and then a pop, and something slapped wetly out of sight under the head in the vice. Several of the heads cheered, others chuckled, and the head in the vice started to cry.

'Dylan, hey, Dylan.' Tibs had broken out of his rage just as quickly as it had come on him. 'Please, bruv. Will you take me with you?'

The other heads broke into peals of laughter.

'Don't steal from the Jackal,' said the head with sagging flesh.

Experimentally, Dylan took one foot followed by the next off the ceiling. He hung from his hands and pushed off to drop to the stone slabs a few feet below.

'What is this place?' Dylan said.

The heads laughed and screamed and rambled. One broke into song again, 'Twenty-five bottles of beer on the wall, twenty-five bottles of beer—'

'Anoup's lair,' said the head with grey wisps of hair and tittered.

'Better not let him catch you,' a head with mutton chops started to say, but the change came over him and he glared at Dylan, gnashing his brown teeth.

'*Le flocon de neige fait fondre les ténèbres,*' said another head, with a powdered wig and drooping eyes.

The head in the vice moaned, and out of the corner of his eye, Dylan noticed something drooping from it. He moved to get a better look.

'No, please no,' the head in the vice wailed. A long, gloopy tendril of snot-like matter was lolling from its nose. The weight of the gelatinous substance made it bounce, stretching before finally giving way. It tumbled from the head's nose and landed wetly in a pottery bowl beneath. Many of the heads cheered.

'Oh my days, this isn't happening. I want to go home,' the head in the vice said, and Dylan realised it was Bridges, the man who'd inflicted most of his torture. Suddenly, any sense of compassion he might have felt vanished into the mirth of the laughing heads.

'What is it?' Dylan wondered aloud, with a growing sense of unease, not only at the heads themselves but where they had come from and why they were here.

'Brains, brains, brains,' a bunch of the heads chanted. Others laughed, squealed or moaned.

On the table, a bloodied bronze rod, tipped with a hook, sat next to the vice. 'Why?' Dylan asked.

'Why do you think, bruv?'

Dylan stiffened at the voice he recognised. To his left sat three newer heads, the three Duppy boys he'd led into Vieil's parlour. A spider's egg of tangled starlight blinked into Dylan's mind, and behind it was the spectre of 25 Gallows Court. Its many-eyed arachnoid windows stared at Dylan, calling him. Dimitri glared out from a cubby hole, the downy tash on his upper lip quivering.

'Well then, bruv? Why do you think?'

'I want to go home,' the curly-haired, redheaded Duppy wailed and started to weep.

'Shut it, Nutty,' Dimitri snapped. 'You did this, blud. You brought us here, and then he...' Dimitri's cheek twitched. 'And then he...' His whole face contorted. The muscles in his jaw shook with the gritting of his teeth. He bared his teeth and opened his mouth, trying to reach Dylan, and growled.

A shrunken head beneath a lopsided powdered wig much farther down the wall began to shout. '*La neige. Neige blanche. Neige noire. L'arc-en-ciel de l'aube. L'arc-en-ciel du flocon de neige. La neige. La neige. La neige.*'

'The mutt is here. No, no, no,' cried a head on the wall behind Dylan.

Somewhere, a door closed. Dylan scanned his surroundings more thoroughly. There was a riveted iron door to the room on the opposite side of the passageway he'd entered by. He heard urgent footsteps knocking up the corridor beyond. The knocking grew louder and more insistent with each closing step.

A wave of shushing and hushing went around the room among the older heads that were awake and not possessed by the rage; the oldest, most desiccated heads remained with their eyes shut, some with quivering lips as though they were dreaming; others were slack-jawed.

'I want to go home,' the curly-haired Duppy cried.

'*Le flocon de neige fait fondre les ténèbres,*' the lopsided powdered wig said urgently.

'Take me with you, Dylan,' Tibs pleaded, back from his rabidity.

Dylan froze. The passageway seemed to repel him. But there was no other way out of the room apart from through the iron door.

Bridges started to gabber in his panic. 'No, no, no! Oh my days, no! Please God, no!'

Then the hinges screamed as the rusted door swung open.

34

KHOPESH

Roj put down the phone. 'You'll never guess what forensics say they've found.'

The office was manic with activity. Trinity Marshall had bunked in with Roj and Kenny and was going through the previous night's CCTV footage of the main shopping street running along the bottom of Gallows Court. Kenny was writing up his notes on the computer, selectively keeping back the less tangible insights he'd gleaned from their visit. No matter how much tea and coffee he drank, he could not get the taste of blood out of his mouth or the whiff of excrement out of his nostrils from the open guts and loosened bowels.

Kenny stopped typing. 'They found a signed confession written in blood?'

'Not exactly, Sarg. A metal fragment from a blade buried in a brick pillar. And that's not the best of it.'

Trinity paused the grainy black and white video and wrote the time on a pad. 'Don't keep us in suspense.'

'They think it's bronze and from a curved blade.'

'Bronze, right?' Kenny leafed through a pile of paper on the desk, trying to sound nonchalant.

'Bronze and curved.' The glint of satisfaction in Roj's face was unmistakable. 'Haven't we got something that matches that on the list we produced?' Roj knew they did, but couldn't let Trinity in on just how they had happened upon that specific blade.

Kenny found the printout with small square colour images of swords and long knives with descriptions printed next to them. 'The forensics on the first torso murders and the two Ripper victims suggested the use of a curved blade. We created a list of possible large knives and swords with curved edges. Here, this one.' Kenny tapped the picture and handed it to Trinity.

She raised one of her shaped, black eyebrows. 'A khopesh?' she said, trying out the new word. 'An Egyptian sickle sword that developed from battle axes. The inside curve can be used to trap and pull an opponent's weapon. The outside edge is sharpened and combines the cutting abilities of a sword and an axe. The earliest examples were made of bronze from 2500 BC...' She trailed off. 'That is very specific and a little weird.'

'Isn't it?' Roj was unable to contain his smile. 'That narrows the search down. I reckon we can hit the specialist antique dealers, any of your black market informants from our compadres in vice. That is one conspicuous weapon. If we've any touts, they're hardly going to forget something like that.'

'Well, boys, this is a day that just keeps on giving.' Trinity rocked back in her chair, legs splayed in her light grey trouser suit, tapping her pen on her teeth.

'The CCTV; you found something?' Roj shuffled his chair around on his wheels to get a better view.

Trinity cupped the mouse in her hand, tracked the video back and hit play. There was no sound on the footage. Terrified people crouched on the street trying to find cover. Cars slowed down and then sped away when they realised what they were in the middle of. A young man wearing an LA Lakers cap came from the dark of the park. He stopped and dropped the bike lock. The hat fell from his head as he crumpled to the floor. A masked man, wearing a padded body warmer, emerged from the park with a gun in his hand. He stood over the downed Lakers fan, and the muzzle of the gun flashed white twice more on the grainy CCTV. For a moment, he regarded his quarry. He was tall and broad of the shoulder, but too well covered up for a definite identification. On the silent video, something caught his attention. He whipped his head around and ran back into the blackness of the park.

'That's not all.' Trinity fast-forwarded the tape another thirty seconds.

This time, a boy ran out of the park. He looked to make a dash across the road towards the shops on the other side. This brought him to face the camera. It wasn't a great image, but it might be enough to get an identification. A moped sped down the centre of the road and cut off the boy's escape into the light of the shops. Instead, he turned toward Spitalfield, followed in short order by two more boys pursuing him from the park, along with the moped along the road.

Trinity rewound the video and paused and zoomed in on the boy's face. 'I'll make copies and start circulating it.'

'How old do you reckon he is?' Roj tilted his head to one side and then looked to his own writs.

'Younger teenager, probably. I'd guess around thirteen. Could be a year or so either way,' Trinity said.

'Are you thinking about those ties in the arches?' Kenny met Roj's gaze. There was a touch of horror there. Kenny felt a flash of anger in Roj like a white electric shock, but he tempered it, never letting it surface on his face.

'They were smallish, I thought a woman's because of the Ripper line of thinking, but then, that's not his MO with women, is it?' Roj now had the index finger and thumb of his other hand encircling his wrist.

'You're going to have to fill me in.' Trinity looked between the two of them.

'The chair we found in the arches had plastic ties, which were cut. Two for the wrists; two for the ankles, strapping whoever it was to the chair. We measured the ties, and they weren't very large. Roj is thinking they could have tied up this boy. Then there were the fingernails. I don't think they were a woman's. Certainly not a working girl's. There was no nail polish on them and they weren't shaped in any way.'

'Lots of women wear fake nails. You think these are real? I only put them on for tonight's work.' Trinity held up her hands, showing off brilliant scarlet nails that tapered into rounded off points. 'If it was a prostitute, she might not have been working that night. Besides, Judy Finch wasn't a prostitute. What I don't get, though, is why he or they took the body? I mean, they left all the other bodies apart from their heads.'

Roj shrugged. 'Maybe the survivor can tell us something. Me and Kenny are going to head over to the hospital soon.'

'Take your notepads. It's not as if he can speak without a tongue. Is he out of surgery?' Trinity got up and pulled on her suit jacket. She flicked her black hair out from the collar. She was in her early thirties and had a solid reputation, not least because she'd done an outstanding job on a big coke bust working undercover. Her dark, Eastern European looks and figure had opened doors for her in the criminal underworld in that case over in Bristol. Her face was known there now, so she'd moved to London six months ago.

Kenny looked at his watch. 'The constables watching him texted me thirty minutes ago to say he was in recovery and was stable. You're carrying tonight, right?'

Trinity hefted her satchel from under the desk. 'Going to brief the team and check out firearms after I get the picture of that boy and the shooter to patrol.'

'No risks and no heroics tonight, okay?' Kenny could feel the excitement coming off Trinity. It was like Roj's flash of electricity, except it came with a static fizz and the warm afterburn of tequila.

'You don't need to worry about me, Sarg. I've a good feeling about this. We're going to find something out tonight. And if not tonight, then tomorrow. If you want to uncover shit, you've got to go where people take a dump.'

'Thanks for that image.' Kenny winced and rolled his shoulder stiffly. 'We'll see you at the briefing.'

Trinity gave them a cocksure grin from one side of her mouth and swaggered out of the open plan office. The room was packed with the reinforcements transferred to the case, and they worried about computers like agitated flies.

As they packed up their own things a few minutes later, Kenny rolled his shoulder again, trying and failing to loosen the knotted muscles at the base of his neck. They pulled on their coats, ready for the rain that didn't want to let up, and an icy front was due in from the Baltic any time now.

'Sore shoulder, boss?' Roj was fishing in his coat.

'Turns out Betty the pit bull is not only strong as a tank, but she can't walk on a lead.'

'Ah well, I got you a gift.' Roj opened his hand.

Kenny took the two objects, smiled at one and puzzled at the other. 'She'll love this,' he said, holding up the bone-shaped dog biscuit. 'But what's this?'

'A dog whistle. Do you know Terry with the K9 unit? No? Well, he swears by them. It'll grab her attention when she's yanking your arm off.'

The whistle was about three inches long, steel and weighed next to nothing. Kenny gave it a prospective blow. His cheeks bulged a touch, as though he had gobstoppers wedged in each cheek. No sound came out, none that he could hear anyway, and guessed it was above his puny human range of hearing. He stuffed it, along with the dog biscuit, deep into his trench coat pocket.

Roj pushed the button for the lift down. 'What do you think the chances are of our Russian gangster spilling his guts?'

'I was wondering about that,' Kenny said, as they stepped inside the lift and the doors closed. 'Why take one body, kill and dismember six more, and leave one alive with his tongue ripped out?'

The growl that had followed them from crime scene to crime scene rumbled in Kenny's mind. It had been a thunderous roar at the arches, mixed with the screams and the smells of death and the dull glint of the khopesh as it sliced through the flesh, sinew, and bone. There were other things blending into the melee at the very limits of Kenny's perception, or at least partially obscured by the tumult of violence. A hiss of breathless voices. And numbers smashed and scattered around like pieces of broken glass. Try as he might, Kenny hadn't been able to read either of those things clearly.

The lift opened on the ground floor, and Roj held the door from closing on them. 'Looks like they wanted to send a message.'

Kenny turned his collar up ready for the rain. 'But about what and to whom?'

35

AFTER LIFE

THERE WAS NOWHERE to back away to. Behind Dylan stood more shelves of snapping, withered heads. He stood frozen to the spot as the door opened wide. The iron portal framed Mr Butcher, half in shadow, half in the furnace's glow. He still wore his bowler hat. In one hand, he held a bloody hunk of raw meat; its juices stained his chin. He stepped over the threshold, and the heads grew manic, their split personalities creating a demonic chorus of wails, cries for mercy, gnashing teeth, and animalistic snarls.

Dylan put his hands to his ears and edged behind the table, putting it between him and Mr Butcher. A cold draft followed Mr Butcher into the room. It chilled Dylan for the first time since the rain that soaked them in the park at Gallows Court, but he didn't shiver, his skin didn't gooseflesh. There was no bodily reaction to the change in temperature, only an acknowledgement of the difference.

Mr Butcher took a bite of raw meat, tearing it off with his teeth and a twist of his wrist. A smile twitched in his moustache as he chewed, open-mouthed.

Blood dripped to the floor, and Dylan's mouth watered involuntarily. He licked his lips. He could smell the meat and, more urgently, the blood.

Mr Butcher took another bite, squeezing the meat in his fist, so that, like a sponge, blood overflowed between his fingers. It ran down his wrist, staining his white shirt, and rained down on the stone slabs.

Dylan wanted it, the meat and the blood, especially the blood. His teeth tingled, and the hunger surged through his entire body. Mr Butcher gave a silent belly laugh with a mouthful of half-chewed meat and tossed his meal aside. Dylan watched it fly through the air and fall into the flames with a sizzle. The smell of it cooking was nauseating, and Dylan found himself hissing. Mr Butcher laughed again.

The hunger had bewitched Dylan for a moment, turning him into something other than himself, and now the hunger had faded, though not completely, Dylan noticed himself again, noticed his two sides and how the hunger had brushed his thinking self aside. He noticed his hands and felt his teeth. Taloned nails shrank back to normal, as did the multitude of fangs that had crowded his mouth. *No!* Dylan shook his head at the thing he had become and retreated further around the table.

Still grinning, though that smile could just as easily have been a snarl, Mr Butcher inspected the head locked in the vice. He unwound the grip's handle and lifted up the head by its hair. A string of brain matter hung from Bridges' nose.

'Please, no. What's happening?' Bridges started, but his panicked face changed. The eyes grew wide with rage, and he gnashed his teeth. Mr Butcher wiped away the snot-like excreta and flicked it with a snap of his wrist into the ceramic bowl on the floor. He patted Bridges' cheek patronisingly. Bridges bit and hissed to no effect, and Mr Butcher walked over to the section of shelves that already contained Dimitri and the other two Duppies and placed Bridges in an empty cubby hole. Other heads laughed psychotically, spat insults, or, worst of all for Dylan, hissed and snarled.

No! God, no! This can't be happening. But it was. This wasn't the dreaming visions of the connected universe, or pyramids in a charcoal desert.

'Please don't,' Tibs said as Mr Butcher picked his head from the table. 'Dylan, help, bruv. I'm sorry. Please, I don't want him to...' He didn't say what. Like Dylan, perhaps he didn't fully know what it was that was about to happen. He didn't have the words for it. Perhaps there were some things there shouldn't be words for. That way, it would be easier to live in ignorance of them.

Dylan circled around to the top of the table, buffeted by his growing dread. Mr Butcher spun Tibs' head to face the ceiling. Handling it with the skill of an artisan, Mr Butcher positioned Tibs within the vice and tightened it.

'What's happening?' Tibs said in a lungless cry. 'I'm going to wake up soon. It's a nightmare. Wait, what are you doing?'

Grinning at Dylan as he chewed, Mr Butcher picked up the metal rod with a hook from the table. As he pushed the hook into Tibs' nose, Dylan saw the open door.

There was a crunch when Mr Butcher put his weight behind the rod, after which it slid deeply into Tibs' skull. One foot stumbling over the other, Dylan was halfway to the door when Tibs screamed and Mr Butcher started to stir the rod.

Dylan ran, chased from the room by consequences of saying 'yes' to Vieil, while behind him Tibs pleaded, 'No, no, no.'

36

WINGS OF FIRE

DYLAN WAS LOST, speeding through cold tunnels made of brick, turning corners, doubling back, rattling locked doors. He ran always with one eye behind him. Finally, he found a set of bare concrete stairs leading up. It was colder here the further he went from the pyramid and Mr Butcher's chamber, not that the cold bothered him, even in his naked state. His exposure was the least of his worries, although finding some clothes was on his mind. As he reached the top of the stairs, it was only to find another locked door.

He waggled the handle to no effect. A bang echoed up the stairwell. Dylan pulled harder on the handle, growing more desperate. He growled with effort, and the handle tore off in his hand with a splintering of wood. A circle of light shone through the hole in the door. Dylan tossed the handle aside and peered through. There was an old carpet on the floor and a whitewashed wall. Everything else was out of sight.

Another metallic echo tolled from somewhere below, followed by the ghost of a scream. In a mix of fear and frustration, Dylan lashed out at the door, striking it with the pad of his fist, and was shocked by the effect. The wood cracked, splitting from the force of the impact. Dylan looked at his fist, clenched and white-knuckled, and then back at the door. He raised his fist over his shoulder, a sense of unbridled power surging through him, and struck the door. It splintered, breaking in two. He pushed through the shards of wood, sensing footsteps following in the tunnels behind.

The whitewashed room was crowded with large objects, all covered with dust sheets. A temporary fix occurred to Dylan, and he yanked off a sheet. A cloud of particles flew into the air as he wrapped the musty sheet around himself to cover his nakedness. Below it was, of all things, a headless mannequin, the kind used by a tailor. It wobbled as if chuntering a complaint.

There was another door ahead. Dylan readied himself to smash it down, but on trying the handle, he found it was unlocked. As he sprinted into the hall beyond, the footsteps were on the concrete stairwell. He slammed the door behind him, found a key in the lock on the other side and turned it. He had to hurry. Now he was at the foot of another stairwell leading up. How deep was he?

A tube train rattled past, like a stampede of steel horses, and Dylan noticed a passageway hiding in the angular shadow under the stairwell. It could be a way out; then again, so could the stairs. Curiosity drew him to the passage. He peered into the dark, but it didn't hinder his enhanced vision. A pair of rats followed the base of the wall, hopping over pieces of fallen masonry. A multitude of spiders lurked in webs. Dylan could see hundreds of shining black eyes regarding him, their mandibles pinching. A moth fluttered through the air, got itself tangled in a web, and a thousand little bells rang, calling a hunter for dinner. Dylan could even hear the worms and beetles churning in the dirt as the spider stepped onto its tickling web.

Another tube train rattled by, throwing a strobe of light into the passage through a hole in the brick wall only a few feet high and half as wide. The train receded as the spider busied itself preparing its guest for dinner, trussing it up in a cocoon after pumping it full of venom.

At the foot of the stairs, the handle waggled. With a quick calculation, Dylan decided the hole in the passage was too small and might drop him right into the path of a train. He took the stairs instead, leaping up them four and five at a time, his feet hardly touching down until he reached the midlanding. Springing off the wall, his white sheet flapping behind him, Dylan was at the top an instant later and flung open the next door. This one had deadbolts at the top and bottom, and he locked them both.

Now where was he? Yet another corridor rolled out in front of him, but this one was different. A plush carpet runner led down the centre of polished floorboards. The walls were covered in expensive wallpaper, patterned with ornate gilded flowers with thorny stems. Paintings stared down from gold frames. He was somewhere in 25 Gallows Court. Of course he was. That would make sense. Vieil and Mr Butcher hid belowground during the day. How they had built such an expansive network of tunnels and the great pyramidal chamber, Dylan didn't know. Perhaps it had already been there, something very old, hidden long ago. Or maybe Vieil's power created the structures? Dylan was curious to know, but more desperate to get away, and so put the thoughts to the back of his mind. One thing was for sure, things had changed since the last time Dylan had been in the house. It wasn't old and falling down anymore. Rotting floors were now solid. Decoration was plush where before it had been decaying. The plaster didn't flake from the walls like infected skin. It was as smooth and luxuriant as the brass handles on the doors and the crystal chandeliers overhead.

The door rattled in its frame behind Dylan, shocking him back into the present. His toes sank into the carpet as he ran, trying each door. Some were locked, others were not. He checked each open room for a way out as the door to the basement banged and shook in its frame. All were shuttered and drawn with heavy curtains, blocking out all the light. With his new vision, Dylan saw an empty ballroom, a library deep and high with books, a grand piano with a dust sheet half pulled away, another room with plants moving in the dark. He slammed the door shut on them as they began to creep toward him. Each room was too large for the house as seen from the outside, as if the rules of the physical world didn't apply in the same way here. With their many turns, the corridors seemed to never end, and the more Dylan ventured on, the more desperately he pulled at locked handles and frantically checked what rooms would give up their secrets.

At a set of grand double doors that towered over him, Dylan grabbed both brass knobs and pulled. The doors stayed fast, and from the far end of the corridor, a shape rounded the corner. Mr Butcher's white shirt seemed to glow in the gloom. Even from a distance, Dylan could smell the blood on the man's hands and staining his cuffs. Dylan's teeth grew as the craving surged.

No! He wouldn't be like them. Dylan pulled again at the doors to no effect. Mr Butcher started down the corridor at a relaxed stroll, his eyes fixed on Dylan, grinning his ivory smile.

Dylan dragged his eyes away and almost tripped on the hem of his sheet. Stumbling, he rounded yet another corner and another, when he saw the foot of a staircase and recognised it. He had seen it from the entrance hall of 25 Gallows Court, when it was a dilapidated and filthy skeleton of balustrades and splintered stairs. It was something more splendid now. The staircase wasn't far, which meant the front door wasn't either.

Dylan was there in the beat of a moth's wing, struggling in a spider's web. He undid the first bolt at the bottom of the door with a clang. With one hand holding his sheet around him, Dylan reached for the second bolt above his head. He threw it aside and, relaxing in its frame, the door gave a little.

Dylan didn't want to be as stupid as every dead character in a late night horror movie, but he couldn't stop himself from checking one last time to see if he would make it. Mr Butcher stood at the foot of the stairs. The smile had faded from his face, and for a moment, Dylan felt a rush of triumph. He was going to make it. The sides of his mouth quirked into their own smile. He was free, and Mr Butcher knew it and was shaking his head in one last futile gesture which, as far as Dylan was concerned, he could shove up his smug arse.

Dylan flung the front door to Gallows Court wide open. The daylight flooded in. It was raining outside, but the day still cut a searing shaft of light into the hall. Dylan only made it to the top step. Two strides, that was all, before he burst into flame. Spreading his arms wide, the sheet ignited into wings of fire.

MEMENTO MORI

"Our torments also may in length of time
Become our elements."
— John Milton, *Paradise Lost*

37

EMPTY SEATS

HOOKED UP to a drip on the children's ward, Samuel slept on and off. Abigail had sent a pair of uniformed officers away with a mother's fury in their ears. Her accent became so broad as she railed, she was sure the officers missed a good deal of the words she aimed at them, but the melodic tirade resulted in one officer swallowing down their reply, and the other closing her notebook. Once they left, Abigail dozed off, holding Samuel's hand while the monitors bleeped. She drifted down into sleep, cushioned by the doctor's words repeating in her head, 'Your son was very lucky. The knife didn't hit any major organs. His puppy fat probably saved his life.'

Her dreams were a scrapbook of memories. Times in their flat in London, Samuel growing bigger every day, not just physically into a young man, but the size of his heart too. He was like his father in that way. Older memories joined the ones in London. Samuel tidied the dinner plates away. Abigail followed him through the kitchen door and into their church in Nigeria. He was a toddler carrying the plates across the bare wooden floorboards towards the altar. The simple stained glass window they once had, depicting the crucifixion on the brown hill of Golgotha, wasn't there anymore. The dream replaced it with Samuel's chubby, radiant face on his most recent school photograph, while the younger version of himself climbed over his father on the front pew. Darkness fell and Samuel wasn't playing anymore. He cried inconsolably on his mother's shoulder, snot running from his nose. Torchlight flickered through the windows of the church, as three bangs came at the door amid the shrieking. The three of them were side by side as the smoke slithered under the door. Over the altar, the stained glass window that was Samuel's school photograph blistered. His face warped. The bubbles of chemicals popped and burnt black, and the paper ignited. The kiss of the flames chastened Abigail's skin, bathing her in their excruciating embrace.

She woke with a start.

'Hi, Mum. That hurts.' Samuel was looking down at her.

With the scars all over her body prickling, Abigail released Samuel's hand from her tight grip. She was overwhelmed with relief, both from the fiction of the dream and the truth of Samuel's awakening in the here and now. Taking his face in her hands, she smothered him with kisses.

'Mum, please. I'm alright. Can I get a drink?'

'A drink. Yes, a drink. Of course.' In a fluster, Abigail found the water jug and hurriedly poured a glass of water. A nurse had come over and raised Samuel's bed and checked his monitors as he sipped.

As the nurse fluffed up his pillows, she smiled. 'She hasn't left your side.'

'Was she any trouble?' Samuel said over the rim of the glass.

'Tons.' The nurse gave him a wink.

'Sorry about that.'

'Mums are supposed to be trouble,' the nurse said, fixing the sheets, and with a pat of the bed, left them to it.

Samuel handed his mum the glass and checked to see if anyone was listening. 'Is Dylan okay? We need to tell him it's not his fault.'

Abigail dropped the glass. It shattered, but she ignored it. 'Dylan? What has Dylan Savage got to do with this?'

MISHA COULD SENSE there was something wrong by the way the children filed into the classroom for second period. They didn't have their usual bounce. The boys weren't punching each other in the arm or larking around. The girls didn't gossip in their cliques. In fact, they all had the lonely air of acne afflicted, class pariah Kylie Johnston: quiet, unconfident, isolated. They had become solitary atoms jostling in each other's presence, never connecting. Misha was about to ask who had died, when the joke rotted unspoken in her mouth.

Two chairs sat empty. Misha's optimistic look to the door didn't find Samuel and Dylan rushing away from Alan Bestwick's detention patrol. Without her asking, the class had fallen silent. They fidgeted and Misha could tell they all avoided looking at empty chairs. A few of the girls had been crying.

Misha shut the classroom door and perched on her desk. She'd been so hopeful that the intervention of Reverend Adekugbe would have Dylan back in school. She'd even brought in a couple more of her university maths textbooks to inspire him. Now, her mouth was dry, and she had to fight to keep her voice positive.

'Okay, guys, I can tell something's wrong.' Misha tried not to look at the empty chairs. 'What's happened?'

One of the girls sniffed. The usually hyperactive Michael Groves in the back corner shuffled in his seat. Then Bobby Smith, street sharp but work shy, raised his hand.

'Yes, Bobby.' Misha lifted her eyebrows, but behind her teacherly demeanour a storm of foreboding was building.

Bobby's eyes darted around the room as if to see if anyone was going to stop him, but the rest of the class kept their heads bowed. 'Dylan stabbed Samuel last night.'

Misha's smile faltered. 'That's not funny, Bobby.'

Bobby hung his head and mumbled, 'I wasn't joking, miss.'

'But that's not... He would never...' A heavy tear tangled in Misha's eyelash.

Kylie Johnston spoke next. Kylie Johnston, who would never speak, partly because in the ruthless pecking order in secondary school, she wasn't permitted. But of all people, she was the messenger. 'It's true, miss. Samuel is in the hospital. And no one knows where Dylan is.'

Unbidden, more tears came, welling from both eyes and streaking down Misha's cheeks like the rain on the classroom windows. As if on cue, a knock came at the classroom door. Alan Bestwick, serious and hard, entered the classroom followed by two police officers.

38

CHAFFINCH

RUNNING out of the rain for the cover of the Royal London Hospital, Kenny answered his phone.

'What's up?' Happy to hear from Misha, he assumed it was lunchtime at school. 'Slow down, love. What's happened?... I'm at the hospital now... Right... I'll see if I can find him... Yes, I'll ask around. Wait.'

Kenny moved away from the patients and visitors smoking outside, shielding from the rain. 'Were they involved in the trouble last night in the park at Gallows Court?'

On hearing this, Roj cocked his head questioningly. Kenny's face told him there was something here for them.

Kenny went on, 'No, it's nothing. It's just news around the station at the moment. What does the missing boy look like?... Got it. I'll see what I can find out. Try not to worry. We'll find him...' Kenny's tone turned uncharacteristically stern. 'No, absolutely not. Promise me you won't go there... Promise me, Misha... Okay, good. Look, I'll be late home tonight... I know, I'm sorry but it's important. Don't wait up, but if you need to talk, phone me... I love you too... Yes, and Betty.'

In a failed attempt to avoid the clouds of cigarette smoke, Roj shuffled closer. 'Was that good or bad?'

Kenny wasn't lost in thought, as much as he was treading water.

Hospitals were noisy places for him, patinated with the full gamut of humanity's battles with life and death. And now Misha had dropped a possible lead into their lap in one of those rare intersecting coincidences the universe smushes together from time to time. 'You're not going to believe this.'

Roj rocked his head from side to side. 'I'm kind of re-evaluating what I do and don't believe in since I met you, Sarg.'

'Right enough. Two of Misha's students were involved in last night's turf war at Gallows Court.'

'It's not quite Newgate, but she teaches in an East End school. I'm not surprised some of the kids are tooled up. Sad, but true.'

'The thing is, one of them is recovering in there.' Kenny gestured through the smoke to the hospital beyond. 'And the other matches the description of our boy running from the park.'

'I guess we've got two witnesses to interview, then. Nice of them to congregate in one place for us, don't you think?'

They weaved their way through the wraiths lurking in the carcinogenic fog and shuffled along with one of those institutionally slow revolving doors. Kenny braced himself. The hospital was hot too and disconcertingly bright. It smelled of reluctant sanitisation, like those dissolving yellow cubes in public urinals.

They found themselves in reception, but Kenny missed what Roj said before he went to ask for directions at the desk.

Kenny was already sweating as the echo of the woman ran through him. Her fear was a rock rolling down a steep hill, and the further it descended, the bigger and more monstrous it became. The child she carried weighed heavily on Kenny's arms. His little body was limp and cold, and his lips were blue. The tragedy's echo was a desperate and futile scream, like trees snapping under a boulder tumbling inexorably towards an idyllic homestead. And yet, it came through Kenny as a murmured whisper. 'Help me, somebody help me,' Nothing could stop her personal landslide, and nothing would be left except a deep, unhealing scar gouged out of her world forever.

Kenny's lips mouthed the words, 'He's not breathing. Breathe, baby, breathe for mummy.' The little boy's head lolled side to side. She looked for a doctor, a nurse, anyone, please God anyone. There were thin ligature marks around the boy's neck. He couldn't have been more than two or three years old. Kenny saw the flash of a long, beaded pull for a widow's roller blind in front of a set of double glazed French doors, sticky with tiny hand prints. The boy drifted from the phantom woman's arms, away from Kenny, and she faded in his mind, but only momentarily, as the echo loop started over.

'Sarg... Kenny... *Kenny*. I got directions. Are you alright?' Roj looked around as if scanning for ghosts. Kenny brushed Roj off by changing the subject back to their need to hurry.

The hospital was a Byzantine network of corridors, floors, wings, departments, units and wards that swallowed them up to pass them through its tangled intestines. On the third double back, and second time of asking the way from someone with an NHS lanyard, Kenny finally spotted the two armed police officers through a set of double doors with a secured entry. 'I think this is it.'

Roj pushed the intercom. 'It's like stepping back to a time before Google Maps. You must remember what that was like, Sarg?'

'Just like this, but without the smart-arsed sidekick,' Kenny said, as the buzzer made an unhealthy sound, akin to a flatulent computer. A curt nurse with a Mancunian accent answered and told them to push the door. The buzzer broke wind more violently, and the door stayed shut. They tried the curt nurse again. She tutted and sighed. The buzzer prolapsed, and the door flung wide open on erratic automatic hinges.

A few flashes of their identification and they were entering the room of Nickolia Morozovo, former Spetsnaz captain, immigrant, multi-millionaire, and suspected head of the London franchise of the *Chernaya Ruka*—or better known locally, a Russian Mafia gang called the Black Arm. Nothing had ever stuck, of course. On the surface, he was a respected businessman. Last night's incident, however, confirmed what vice, MI5, MI6, Special Branch and any copper with half a brain knew but couldn't prove. He was as bent as a member of Parliament's expenses claim. But unlike the latter, his sleight of hand wasn't legal under Parliamentary Privilege, regardless of what his tax returns said. Nickolia Morozovo was a very naughty boy, and now they had him under police protection for his own safety and with a legitimate opportunity to talk to him without a bodyguard or an army of lawyers. The lawyers had been sent to the wrong hospital by what the MET was calling a bureaucratic mistake. And the bodyguard, well he was dead and his head was missing. That detail reminded Kenny of the line in Stephen King's *Pet Sematary*, about cats living and dying like gangstas. That story didn't end well for anyone involved. It's never good raising the dead. Kenny had heard enough of their laments to know that.

Roj leaned over the bed. 'Mr Morozovo, can you hear me?'

Drawn and pale, with shadowed and sunken pockets for eyes, Nickolia's lashes fluttered. Kenny hung back at the foot of the bed, concentrating. Nickolia's consciousness was like a block of ice, pitted with grit and stones, bobbing up through frigid, meltwater. His chest rose and he grimaced, waving a hand drunkenly towards his throat before it fell back. It was possibly an act.

Roj tried again. 'Mr Morozovo, are you awake? It's important. It's about your nephew, Dimitri.'

The forensics report had come back on the initial torso murders, identifying Dimitri Turgenev from fingerprints acquired after arrests for minor misdemeanors. None of which held up, because a £1,000 an hour solicitor would turn up and sledgehammer the walnut charges, that or witnesses would never want to take action, afflicted by sudden onset amnesia. One of Trinity's colleagues made the connection between Dimitri and his uncle. The Duppy Crew were the footsoldiers for the Black Arm, or as Trinity put it, 'They're like Amazon's logistics for drugs, but the delivery guys are children.'

Nickolia opened his eyes. Sharp and burning cold, Kenny felt the rocky ice block bob on the surface of awareness. Cordite and bleach fumes fogged things much deeper and hard to reach, secrets perhaps even from himself. Maybe that wasn't right. This was a man who'd executed his demons in sacrifice to far darker gods. His mind, soul, or whatever it was Kenny was poking around in, wasn't a nice place to hang out. He had the sense of a man used to being watched, observed through many mirrors through which he'd learned to reflect versions of himself, a babushka doll of identities. Even with tubes and wires attending his ills and the bandages around his neck, Nickolia's eyes moved from Roj to Kenny with precise cuts through the air, taking the calculated measure of his interrogators.

Kenny nodded for Roj to go on.

'We think whoever did this to you did the same to your nephew and his friends. Can you give us a description of your attacker? We can protect you.' Roj added the protection as a sweetener, but he and Kenny had already discussed it and concluded it was unlikely a man like this would countenance it.

Nickolia made a sound like a strangled growl and sneered in agony. He was laughing through the pain. It opened a gap in the fog of cordite and bleach, and Kenny stepped through.

Roj stood up from the bedside. 'We want to help. But if you don't help us, we can't do that.'

'Your sister,' Kenny said over Nickolia's mocking grunts. 'This man likes women. Have you seen what he does to them? It's not the same as the quick deaths in the arches. He thinks he's Jack the Ripper. Cuts them open with his bronze hook, takes their uteruses as souvenirs. Sometimes he slices off their breasts and has them wear their intestines as a shawl. We have a brilliant pathologist. She thinks the women were alive, at least for part of their mutilation. She's his type too, your sister, I mean. Petite. The red hair, like a chaffinch. *Zyablik*, that's the Russian, isn't it?'

Nickolia fixed the detective with a cold stare. Kenny knew the Russian was in a lot of discomfort, even with the cocktail of pain relief the hospital was pumping into him. Kenny could sense the agony. It was a living net of molten hot pins ensnaring Nickolia's throat. The man had shut a door on the pain in his mind. It raged and battered at the portal, while Nickolia calmly held it closed. Kenny had never seen someone do that before. But it showed him he had the Russian's attention. That detail about the chaffinch did it, making him suspicious about what the authorities actually knew. It was something Kenny found beyond the poisonous fog. It was as close as the man got to a warm core.

The memory was of his sister playing in the birch trees somewhere in Russia. She was young, on the cusp of puberty. Nickolia, her big brother, chased her playfully through the forest until they reached the lake. The sky was azure blue, but the day was crisp. They stripped and waded into the water laughing. She would only go into her knees, no matter how much he teased. When he splashed her, she retreated to the shore hugging her chest. The tips of her red hair darkened with water falling about her porcelain skin. Nickolia waded from the water, still poking fun, until he was holding her, saying he would warm her up, rubbing her cashmere soft skin, pressing their bodies together, and then their lips, and then... Yes, she was very special to him, his little chaffinch, his *Zyablik*.

Kenny sighed. 'It will be difficult to keep her out of the papers once it gets out that her son and brother have a connection with the Ripper copycat. The thing I can't work out is why keep you alive?'

'Mafia warning. Couldn't that be it, Sarg? Someone has to live to tell the tale?'

Nickolia's gaze slid from them to the rain drenched window.

'Help us catch whoever is doing this. Do it for Dimitri. Do it for your sister.'

The Russian seemed to not hear Kenny's words. His gaze remained fixed on the window framing a sky bruised with swollen, grey clouds. The sun had westered into heaven's nadir, promising to colour those bruises black soon enough. Kenny had taken a punt, and it hadn't paid off. A lifetime of conditioning prevented the Russian gangsta from talking to an English police officer. That, and he didn't have a tongue.

He might come around, but Kenny didn't think it likely and so nodded to Roj. 'Well, thank you for your time, Mr Morozovo. We'll leave you to recover. If you think of anything, you can text us on that number.'

Roj left a business card on the bedside unit, bare of any flowers or well wishing cards. Nickolia closed his eyes, and they moved to the door. Kenny knocked on the glass to let the armed officers know they were ready to leave.

A metallic tinging came from behind them. Kenny turned to see Nickolia staring at them, tapping the gold signet ring of his pinkie finger on the safety runner of his bed.

'Roj, have you got a pad and pen for Mr Morozovo?' Kenny

handed Nickolia the writing implements and watched him scratch three words in a drug-addled hand.

'YOU...'

'WILL...'

'DIE.'

39

HUNGER PANGS

THE STENCH WAS MADE WORSE by the knowledge that it was from his own burned flesh and hair. His skin was a mix of raw red and charred black, and smoke rose from Dylan's naked body. Candlelight guttered overhead from a circular, wrought iron chandelier. Wax oozed down the side of the tallow sticks like the thick unguent Mr Butcher applied to Dylan's skin with a flat wooden spatula. The ointment smelled of pungent herbs and spices, as if Dylan had been momentarily removed from the oven mid roast to be basted for a banquet.

Dylan complained through the pain, his superhuman immunity having abandoned him. Mr Butcher batted away his hands and finished coating the burns. Dylan watched the mute man work, noticing for the first time they were in what he supposed was the kitchen of Gallows Court. Around the walls, shelves contained jars full of organs suspended in yellowish liquids. On a countertop, a hunk of bloody, raw organ meat lay on a chopping board with a pile of finely minced flesh piled to one side. A cleaver was buried into the board at an angle, as if the chef had been interrupted during preparation of an offal tartare.

The more Mr Butcher applied the thick grease to Dylan's injuries, the more the pain became bearable. Still, each movement Dylan made was excruciating, especially at any joint or crease of skin, where coarse grains of salt seemed to sandpaper the edges of his raw wounds. He was hungry too, famished, with a watering mouth and a heartbeat throbbing in his head. A few feet away, the congealing blood on the cleaver's blade was deliciously metallic and sent tingles from Dylan's teeth to the tips of his toes and fingers.

Mr Butcher finished smothering Dylan's feet with balm and wiped the spatula and his hands on the cloth over his shoulder, impassively regarding Dylan on the kitchen table as he did so.

Dylan licked cracked and bubbled lips.

'Eat,' he croaked, shifting his eyes to the chopping board. With the merest inflection of his eyebrow, Mr Butcher picked up the hunk of raw meat and weighed it in his hand.

Believing with every fibre of his being that it was something he must have, Dylan croaked, 'Please.'

Mr Butcher shook his head.

'Please. So hungry.'

One of Mr Butcher's eyebrows raised. He looked at Dylan, then at the meat in his hand, and shrugged. Holding it over Dylan's mouth, he squeezed the flesh. Like bloody tributaries of a river, juices trickled between Mr Butcher's fingers. Gravity pulled them down to the base of his fist, forming a tenuous droplet that stretched until it fell through the air towards Dylan's open mouth. When it hit his tongue and splashed on his burned lips, the sweet and sour tang of spoiled meat diffused across his palate, absorbed through his taste buds to infect his blood stream. A cramp started in his stomach and spread to the muscles of his arms and legs. Dylan curled up in pain, folding over onto his side, and fell heavily on a chessboard of black and white tiles.

Dylan vomited bile streaked with blood and looked up at Mr Butcher mutely guffawing. Another convulsion hit him, and this time there was nothing to bring up so he retched. Without warning, Mr Butcher's face darkened, and he roughly pulled Dylan to his feet.

'*Quel est le sens de cela*, Anoup?' Vieil, angry and immaculately dressed, appeared at Dylan's side.

Mr Butcher gave a petulant shrug and wafted his hand, holding the organ meat in the direction of the hallway and the front door.

'And you are telling me, mighty Anoup, brother of Wepwawet, father of Kebechet, High Embalmer to the Celestial Masons of the Nile, Gatekeeper of Duat, fifth among all the Magicians of Khemia who solved the Eye of Horus, was bested by a hatchling? Bested?' Vieil spat the words, taking Dylan by the elbow.

Mr Butcher rolled his eyes and took a bite of raw meat.

Vieil led Dylan through to the parlour. 'He is jealous and will get used to you eventually.'

The cleaver slammed into the chopping board as Mr Butcher returned to dicing his meal. Risking the electrifying pain, Dylan peered over his shoulder and didn't think Mr Butcher looked jealous.

Vieil guided Dylan to a second winged chair opposite his in front of the fire. The two chairs resembled two thrones in the now opulent room, almost restored to its former glory. From the touch of leather on his raw skin, a whinny of pain left Dylan's throat when he sat down.

'You must never eat of the dead. Their flesh and blood must never pass your lips. They are Anoup's realm, not ours. Feed only while their hearts beat, for death is poison to immortals such as ourselves. You have much to learn, but...' and Vieil gave a small titter of amusement, 'you have all the time in the universe.'

The stomach cramps had passed, but Dylan's gnawing hunger returned along with the cold. Even though a fire roared in the hearth, he shivered and took in the horror of his burnt skin, a mottle of bright reds, weeping browns, and black scabs. He remembered the tragedy of the Grenfell Fire of a few years ago that claimed seventy-two souls because the council cut corners on the tower's cladding. They were all told to stay put and wait for a fire service who would never reach them. No one had invested in long enough ladders, and the cladding was an accelerant, which turned their block into a twenty-four-storey funeral pyre. With burns so extensive, Dylan knew he should be dead. Yet he wasn't. Or was he?

'What have you done to me?' Dylan's teeth chattered.

The amusement of Vieil's face dissolved as he took a seat in the other winged chair. 'Saved you and more. That is what you wanted.'

'Look at me.' Dylan's voice cracked. 'I didn't ask for this.' He held up his burnt arms.

'It is merely another lesson you have learned. Within certain parameters, we are immortal. But we can never stray into the sunlight. You were lucky Mr Butcher was there to pull you back, though he should never have let you get that far. You woke earlier than anticipated, and, well, his snout is out of joint. And besides, once you feed, you will regenerate fully. It is a bagatelle.'

'Feed, feed on what?' Dylan struggled to say. Vieil's calm tone was a sharp stick poking at Dylan's pain and hunger, distracting him, infuriating him, making it so hard to focus.

'Come now, Dylan. You are a clever boy. You know what. It is a small price to pay for all the gifts I have given you.'

'I can't.' Dylan shook his head at the idea; he saw the three paralysed Duppies on the parlour floor, the hundreds of heads in Mr Butcher's lair glaring endlessly. 'I can't.'

Vieil fixed Dylan with his silver eyes. Before, they had been hypnotic, but now they held no psychic sway over Dylan. Still, they were commanding. 'You will. You won't be able to resist. All things must eat: microbes, animals, humans, immortals, even gods.' A sardonic laugh sliced from his throat. 'Especially gods. They are the most gluttonous of all.'

Panic gripped Dylan, shocking him to his feet. 'I-I won't. I need to go. This can't be happening. I can't be...' He looked to escape through the parlour door as Mr Butcher appeared there with a pile of folded clothes, topped with a pair of trainers. Heavy curtains covered the windows, but even if they were boarded up, Dylan suspected that with his new abilities, he could burst through them onto the street. His mind was a maelstrom, struggling to think logically. No, he couldn't do that: the sun would burn him. Then again, perhaps that was for the best. He couldn't live like this, either burnt and in pain forever or an immortal killer.

'Not now, Anoup. Yes, I know the sun is nearly down. Of course, we are going out. *Mon dieu, mon chien de l'enfer!* Of course, you can play tonight, but only after Dylan and I feed.'

The words birled in Dylan's head along with that insistent throb, beating ever louder in the background, pulsing in the same way the red veins in the pyramid had. What clarity there was left in his mind was fading. *Gagung, gagung,* the throbbing beat pulsed. The hunger was as unbearable as the pain now. Dylan's teeth grew, forcing his jaws apart. *Gagung, gagung.* His fingernails lengthened into sharp talons. *Gagung, gagung.* The scurrying of rats under the floors. The scratching of insects in the walls. The roiling and churning of earthworms and a larva in the decaying matter of the earth. And most of all, the throbbing beat, *gagung, gagung.* It was the lifeforce of London, which now Dylan could discern not as one heartbeat, but the syncopation of all the heartbeats, millions of them, pounding beneath their chests, fluttering in the pulses of their tender necks. *Gagung.* Calling. *Gagung.*

Vieil laid a hand on Dylan's shoulder, causing a sharp pang of pain that brought Dylan back to the parlour, shoulders hunched, chest heaving.

'You see how easy it will be?' Vieil said with a small smile of satisfaction to show he was pleased with his protégé. 'And it will make what you saw in the Suhet, your...' he waved his hand in a circle as he searched for the right word, 'sleeping chamber, seem like a dusty scroll in a foreign tongue.'

That caught Dylan's attention. His breathing was slowing, and his hands and teeth were returning to normal as he looked wide-eyed at Vieil.

Vieil practically purred. 'Yes, the numbers, the universe. Why do you think we were drawn together? I had seen you in my long sleep, a recurring fibre out of place in the tangled web. The special boy with the right talents, one who would understand the gifts I have to give. The lost child whom the world is crushing with the heel of its boot without even noticing. I have so much to share with you. But first, you must feed to repair the damage, and then you will see wonders beyond imagining.'

With a click of Vieil's fingers, Mr Butcher presented Dylan with the pile of clothes to change into. Dylan took them. A pair of pale grey trainers sat on top. They looked new but for faint brown and red stains which remained after a thorough cleaning.

'Good boy, Dylan.' Vieil watched him dress. 'Soon the sun will set, and we shall own the night.'

40

MATERNAL GIFTS

'But it wasn't Dylan's fault, Mum. We've got to find him.' Samuel was trying to pull off the surgical tape keeping the cannula in place on his arm.

'You lie back down.' She sprang from her chair at Samuel's bedside and slapped his hands away. For a big lady with aching joints, Abigail still had swiftness when needed.

'But, Mum,' Samuel cried, 'he needs our help.'

From the doorway, Kenny coughed. Samuel and Abigail looked up with a start, freezing mid-battle.

'I think we've found the right place,' Kenny said, not fully intruding on the room yet. 'I also think you should listen to your mum.'

'It's true,' Roj joined in over Kenny's shoulder, 'Mums always know best.'

'Who are you?' Abigail's eyes narrowed on them.

Roj shifted under her glare. She smelled of the warmth of nutmeg and the savoury tang of thyme. There was the singing of hymns and the laughter of a small child. A sadness like an empty bed accompanied strong and comforting hands on her back, rough with callouses. And there was a light and a single note. It was hard to tell between the two because one was so bright and the other so loud that they blurred into one another because... Kenny's search was interrupted.

'We're police officers, madam, detectives actually,' Roj said with his usual disarming effervescence.

Kenny already knew the woman was called Reverend Abigail Adekugbe from constables who'd filed their report, and even though she now held his gaze, she wasn't really looking at his face. Through that damaged, glaucous eye of hers, *she* was reading *him*. Kenny very rarely felt himself under the microscope. He'd learned how to do it to others, and so, unlike average people, Kenny was aware of it when it was happening to him. It took him back, dragging him into the icier depths of his mind.

A door sat ajar over a sliver of old linoleum, a pool of water creeping over it towards the swirling patterns of the landing carpet. Taps ran. The door swung wide, and Kenny's mother stared through him with the glassy eyes of the dead, gazing into the beyond. Her arm hung limply over the edge of the bath, drip-dripping thick tears of blood into the overflowing water. The picture jumped back as the echo replayed. Naked and weeping, she lowered herself into the bath and slid the knife lengthways up each arm, gasping as the blade peeled open her veins. The bathwater turned red. She dropped the knife and ebbed away. The last echo of her life, the thing she left Kenny with on an infinite loop until he was taken away from that house and into care, was a sigh of relief as her heart stopped.

'That's enough,' Kenny said flatly. He wasn't angry, that would be hypocritical. But those emotions weren't going to help him now. Without words, they'd established who they were.

There were others like them, of course, though not many. Enough to know he and his mother weren't the only ones. Some were more gifted than others, and their gifts were never exactly the same. What they did share was a secret they kept largely hidden from the world. The gift was how Kenny developed his taste for horror. As a boy lost and in care up in Glasgow, a foster dad, trying to scare the shit out of him, had given him a battered copy of Stephen King's *The Shining*. Kenny had loved the writer ever since. King was the first person to make him feel he wasn't a freak, or rather that being a freak was okay. Teenage boys needed that. Everyone needed that, he supposed.

Every so often he would be in a movie theatre, or at a restaurant, or taking an elevator in a shopping mall and another soul like him would blow by. Occasionally, they'd look back, and their eyes would meet, and they'd each know, just like now.

Roj and Samuel looked between the Reverend and Kenny.

'We have already spoken to the police and told them everything we know.' Abigail remained standing protectively next to Samuel.

Kenny and Roj edged into the room.

'But that's not right, is it, Mum?' Samuel struggled to pull himself up from the half-reclined position the nurse had left him in. He winced as he did. 'I was asleep and you, well, you were probably you and gave them hellfire.'

Roj looked at his notebook and nodded sagely. 'Yep, that's what it says here. We'll have to talk to your mum about the smiting of two of the Queen's constables.'

Samuel laughed and Abigail ruffled like a mother hen and sucked her teeth, but she kept quiet, humouring her son. Kenny felt that note sing within her, and it reminded him of a sword being drawn. There was power there, not like his, something he'd not ever experienced before. The Reverend Adekugbe was watching him and Roj, watching and measuring.

Samuel grinned. 'I knew it. Don't mind her. She's just protective and worried about me and Dylan.'

'You're Dylan's mate, aren't you?' Kenny stepped forward. 'Could you tell me if this is Dylan?' Kenny brought up the blown-up image of the boy from the CCTV footage.

'Definitely, that's him for sure. Is that from Gallows Court?'

Kenny avoided the question. 'My wife is Misha Stokes, did you know that? She told me all about you two.'

'What? No way. Mrs Stokes is the best, isn't she, Mum? She even makes me good at maths, which is, like, nearly impossible. But Dylan, he's amazing at maths. He's like a genius or something.'

'Wait a second, Dylan is good at maths?' Kenny remembered the curiousness of those numbers scattered across the floor of the arches.

They made no sense at the time, glittering shards of starlight amongst the blood and gore, refracting all the colours of the rainbow. Now he knew they were because of Dylan. He was the one tied to the chair. But where was he?

'Yeah, dude, he's got mad skills with numbers.' Samuel beamed with pride. 'This one time Mr Bestwick came in—you know Mr Bestwick, Mum, he's head of year, but really he thinks he is the detention overlord or something—anyway, he comes in and is like "Dylan Savage, wake up!" right?' Samuel made an impression of Alan Bestwick lowering his voice and pulled a sour apple face. 'And Mrs Stokes was like, "Oh, Dylan wasn't sleeping," which he totally was because of home and getting up early for his paper round, well, until he got fired. Anyway, Mrs Stokes says, "Dylan was calculating pi to as many places as he could," which he totally wasn't, because I could hear him snoring. So Dylan is half asleep and just starts reciting pi. Bestwick was well annoyed. It was brilliant.'

'Misha, I mean Mrs Stokes, is pretty awesome,' Kenny agreed, taking a seat at the bottom of Samuel's bed. He liked this boy. Samuel reminded Kenny of Betty, only instead of liquid sunshine, his enthusiasm and kindness were more explosive, like multi-coloured fireworks. 'Dylan sounds pretty amazing too.'

'He *is*. He's the best, but he doesn't know it. His luck kinda sucks.' The brightness on Samuel's face darkened a little.

'Don't swear,' Abigail said, her good eye firmly on Roj, and Kenny could feel the other eye hovering over him.

'Sorry, Mum, but it does.'

'He's in a lot of trouble,' Kenny said.

Samuel looked horrified. 'Please help him. It's not his fault. None of it is. He was forced to deliver the drugs, and if Mr Chatterjee hadn't changed his route, he never would have had to go into the Duppy Crew's territory, and then—'

'Woah, woah, woah.' Kenny held up his hands, and Roj flicked to a clean page in his notebook. 'You are way ahead of us, Samuel. Start from the beginning. Who was making Dylan deliver drugs?'

'Henry Grime, of course.'

Kenny and Roj exchanged a look as Samuel went on, telling

them everything he knew about Dylan's paper round, about the rumours that Dylan killed three kids in the Duppy Crew, but that was ridiculous, because how could a kid like Dylan do that to three other kids? Something happened, but Samuel didn't know what. All he knew then was that Dylan was marked, and the Duppies wanted revenge, and there was a turf war going on between the Blud and Duppy Crews. He told them about Dylan's mum and her job, and how Abigail was about to help them, but it was too late and a big fight was organised; and how he heard about it on the bus. He spoke at a hundred miles an hour, desperate to get the information out. As he got to the last bit, he looked at his mum apologetically, but if anything she was proud, listening to how Samuel tried to find her and in the end went to Dylan's flat himself and followed them to the fight in the park at Gallows Court. He watched with growing dread at the margins, and when he saw Dylan run, he followed. This was a kid with some amount of courage, Kenny knew, staying close by while guns were being fired and knives were drawn. The story ended in the alleyway. It wasn't Dylan's fault, Samuel said. He had his hand on the knife, but they made him do it. They grabbed his hand, and the Duppies were the ones who forced his hand. As Samuel bled, Dylan was bundled into a car. It was only by luck an off-duty paramedic found Samuel in the alley and called an ambulance while he stemmed the bleeding.

Samuel looked at them earnestly. 'Will that help?'

'I think Detective Dabral will need a new pen,' Kenny said.

Roj shook his hand to complete the double act. 'You should think about being a police officer when you grow up.'

'Really? Thanks, but I want to be a comic book writer or maybe an illustrator if I'm good enough. No offense.'

Kenny tried not to laugh. 'None taken. Comic book writer sounds like a better choice.'

Samuel came over stern and serious. 'But you didn't answer my question. Will it help?'

'Maybe a lawyer would be a better choice of career, Sarg,' Roj said, but Samuel frowned.

Kenny stood up from the bed. 'It'll help plenty. You've given us a few good leads and descriptions to follow up.'

'But will you be able to find him? He's got to be alright. Those guys, the Duppies and the Bluds, they're bad, and Dylan, well, Dylan isn't. He's a good guy. He'd never hurt anyone. He—'

'Samuel.' Abigail put a hand on his arm to stop him. 'You have done everything you can. Let the police officers do their job. You need to rest.'

'But, Mum,' Samuel whined.

'That is enough, Samuel Adekugbe. You already got yourself stabbed. We will find Dylan,' the Reverend told her son.

'Mums do know best,' Roj said.

Samuel was surly. 'The nurse said that too.'

Roj fished a business card out of his pocket. 'It must be true, then. We've got to get cracking on this information, but if you think of anything else, you get in touch with us.' He gave Samuel the card, and the boy held it like a talisman. Kenny felt the prayer Samuel said in his head. A bare-chested offer to blunt the spear. *And the meek shall inherit the Earth*, Kenny thought. Abigail had closed her eyes and was nodding solemnly. Did Kenny get that phrase from her? He couldn't tell if she was agreeing with him or Samuel.

Kenny said they'd leave them alone, and he and Roj were halfway to getting lost on their way out of the hospital when the Reverend Adekugbe called after him.

'Detective Stokes.'

'Give me a minute,' Kenny told Roj, and walked back down the corridor to the imposing woman striding towards him.

Kenny was shocked when she caught him by the elbow and pirouetted them to the wall. She was smaller than him, and yet he felt as though she was the one looking down. She brought him close and spoke in hushed tones.

'Detective. Do not be reckless in this matter and believe you are dealing with the foolishness of man.'

'What else could I be dealing with?' Kenny tried one of Roj's disarming smiles.

'Do not play dumb with me, Kenneth Abraham Stokes.'

Kenny discarded the smile. 'Fine, what haven't you told me?'

'Dylan has got himself caught in the snare of evil.'

'I know that. Henry Grime is—'

'Stop being stupid. Henry Grime is a thug and a very bad man, but he is not *evil*, true evil, the kind the Bible teaches us of. Do not roll your eyes at me.'

'I didn't, Reverend,' Kenny protested.

'Not these eyes.' Abigail forked her fingers in front of her face. '*This* eye.' She pressed her index and middle finger into the middle of Kenny's forehead. 'You may have forsaken him, but you are still God's instrument, just as I am and your mother was.'

'I'm sorry,' was all Kenny felt able to say. She had cut him to the quick, peeling him back to his core with invocations of his mother, but she was impatiently waving off his apology.

'You have seen things, yes? Things that don't make sense. Things that do not have a rational explanation.'

Kenny nodded that he had.

'If you are looking for this evil, you will find it in one place.' The Reverend wet her lips, hesitating a moment and then came to her decision. 'You will find it at number 25 Gallows Court. But be warned. You cannot arrest what you will find there. You cannot shoot it with your guns. If you try, you will all die, and Dylan will be lost.'

That was the second time in an hour someone had said that to him. 'Then what should I do?'

The Reverend's face fell. She turned back towards Samuel's room. Troubles folded thickly on her brow, and all the forceful determination with which she had strode down the corridor had gone. She closed her eyes, whether in thought or prayer, Kenny couldn't tell— he was shut out behind double doors hewn from African oak and studded with iron. Finally, the Reverend shook her head and opened her eyes, already taking the first steps back towards her son. She waddled a little as if her knees were sore, moving farther and farther away as she spoke.

'Trust your gift and know this: you are dealing with things of the darkness. True evil can only be defeated by the light, but the price of the light is always...' She paused at the door, hesitating again. The strange conversation caught the attention of patients and staff wandering the corridor, but they shrugged off the conspicuous intrusion of religion into their lives on seeing the Reverend's dog-collar. They skirted the pair like late-night walkers stepping around a drunk tramp.

Kenny called down the corridor. 'But the price is always what, Reverend?'

The Reverend was now unable to meet Kenny with her double gaze, half dark, half light. 'Too high,' she said, and fled into her son's room, shutting the door on Kenny Stokes and his troubles.

41
———

UNIVERSAL TEACUP

THE TWO MATHEMATICS books made a squat plinth on Misha's desk. They were *The Universe in a Teacup* by K. C. Cole and *The Millennium Problems: The Seven Greatest Unsolved Mathematical Puzzles of Our Time* by Keith Devlin. She was going to mention them to the whole class, use them to inspire them, but really they were for Dylan. The children were gone now, and apart from the scratching of her pen, marking their papers, the classroom was silent. Rain pattered on the large, single glazed windows, thirty years beyond their use-by date. They managed to keep out the wet and the impending night but not the damp or the chill of early winter. The school governors and the local authority would say there was barely enough money for stationery and computers, so there certainly wasn't any money for renovations, or God forbid, a new school building. But what they really meant was that there was no money for children, not these children, not children like Dylan.

Samuel's and Dylan's workbooks were at the bottom of the pile. There were no marks to give for today's work. Misha flicked through Samuel's. It was a collage of Bs, Cs, and the occasional A. Whereas, except from the too many absent days, Dylan's was nothing but perfection. Misha would give him additional problems to solve, way beyond the level of the rest of the class, and let him occupy himself with these while the others wrestled with the basics of algebra and trigonometry. His equations decorated the space in the headers and footers of pages. She ran her fingers over these marks of such great potential, angry at how Dylan and his talent were being let down by everyone, by the police who couldn't find him, by social services for refusing to get involved, by the school for not advocating for him hard enough.

Misha grabbed her phone from her handbag. It wasn't just the school. Blaming it on institutions, expecting them to sort things out, as if they were actually people, was the problem. It was the individuals in the institutions that had to pull their bloody fingers out of their backsides and do something. Dylan's problems weren't someone else's problem, they were *her* problem. The buck stopped with every adult responsible for Dylan. She found the contact details she needed in the folder locked in the bottom drawer of her desk and punched in the contact number for Donna Savage. The number rang out and clicked to the answer phone.

Donna Savage delivered an upbeat script. 'Leave your number after the beep and I'll get back to you. I don't reply to text messages, Whatsapp messages, or private numbers. And no time-wasters, thanks. Here's the beep.'

Misha was about to say something but had a better idea. She hung up and made a decision. Once she'd finished the preparations for tomorrow's lessons, she would head straight over to Renfield Tower. It wouldn't take long. A quick check in at the Savage's flat to see if Dylan was there. Kenny said not to, but she couldn't be the reason Dylan fell through the cracks, and besides, she might pick up on something that could be useful to Kenny. Donna was more likely to talk to her than a police officer.

'Staying late again?'

Misha gave a start. 'Christ! Alan, you scared the crap out of me. Don't you knock?'

Alan Bestwick swanned into the room, 'Anyone would think you're avoiding going home.' He stopped in front of Misha's desk as if he was browsing in a store, but before he looked at the products, he took a glance at the cashier's breasts.

'We got a rescue dog yesterday called Betty, actually. I'm heading off in a second, so if you don't mind?'

'No, I don't mind,' Alan drawled and picked up *The Millenium Problems*, smirking as he leafed through it. 'I'm more of a cat man,' he said, 'but you do love your strays.' He tossed the book back on top of *The Universe in a Teacup*. 'Strays and lost causes.'

'Alan, I really don't have time for this today,' Misha said.

He glanced at the gathering gloom beyond the windows and shrugged. 'Time's up on the day and time's up on Dylan Savage. I told you he was trouble, but even I was a little surprised he stabbed his best friend. Surprised but not shocked...' He wandered back towards the corridor and stopped under a failing striplight. 'I'll be working late in my office if you get lonely. I've got a pot of good Guatemalan coffee on if you want a cup.'

A clammy, unclean feeling came over Misha, but she tried her hardest to be demure. 'No thanks, Alan. Like I said, I'm heading off soon.'

'Oh yes, to your stray,' he said, with a sickly smile. 'Well, you know where I am if you need me. I'll be sure to get Dylan Savage's expulsion paperwork finished in case they find the little scumbag.'

Before Misha could say anything in response, Bestwick sauntered off into the empty school, whistling as he went.

42

GRAVEN NIGHTS

PEOPLE RUSHED THROUGH THE DOWNPOUR, harried along by more than rain. The Ripper being plastered all over the newspapers and every app hadn't helped Chantel's anxiety. Down the streets of Whitechapel, she tapped out a fast clip in her boots, looking over her shoulder with a growing sense of unease. Where were the Old Bill when you wanted them around? She would have thought they'd be all over the place trying to catch the lunatic. But no, not in Whitechapel. It wouldn't be the first time people like her had been left to rot. Not the first, and not the last—*Except maybe for Dylan*, she thought. No one could find him, alive or dead.

The poor kid never stood a chance. News got around the Duppy Crew caught him, and he ended up at those arches in Spitalfields. The thing was, though, unlike the rest of the sliced and diced Duppies, who featured along with the Jack the Ripper fan club in the evening edition of *The Standard*, Dylan's body was nowhere to be seen. That's why Chantel had been dispatched to gather and report back what the word on the street was. No one thought much of her. She was a silly tart, was all. But that meant thugs, cops, and snitches paid her no mind and rolled their eyes at her dumb questions and gave up information for a quick tug on their wick. Anyway, she'd find out what she could as one last favour. Besides, it wasn't really for the dickhead who asked her.

The bloody rain wasn't helping her Good Samaritan routine. Water sluiced down drain pipes, overflowed guttering, and rushed away into drains as if it was fleeing for its life. She pulled down the hood of her raincoat, but the wet found its way in. Through the leather of ankle-high boots, her feet were getting cold and damp too. It seemed the downpour wouldn't stop until the whole of London was washed away.

She didn't want to be out in the downpour, but when was the last time Chantel did the right thing? Meathead would be angry, but even though he played the big man, he wasn't half the enforcer Henry Grime had been. The powers-that-be were quick to replace Henry when things went down the khazi at Gallows Court. Meathead was good at bashing the heads of ponces that didn't pay, but he was softer on the girls, and they were already taking the piss. A reckoning would be coming once the flow of money slowed, unlike the rain. But like the rain, shit only rolled one way from the top. For the time being, she had a little wiggle room. She checked she wasn't being watched again. The coast looked clear, and Chantel nervously shifted the bag biting into her neck, which carried the other things she'd been asked to bring. She cut into the narrow gap between two Victorian tenement buildings.

'That's right, you dappy bint, head off down a dark alley with a serial killer on the loose,' she muttered to herself.

Precariously, Chantel picked her way along the wet cobblestones and skidded. 'Pissing hell!' She steadied herself on the brick wall, slick with a cold sweat of running water, and checked behind again. The light of the street petered out, and Chantel tottered into the murk.

A little further on, down and down away from the light, she found the door. It was a slab of dented steel with a rubble of sodden cardboard boxes and torn, black bin bags piled in front of it. A rat hopped out of the debris of rotting fast food, and Chantel swallowed a yelp.

'Do us a favour, Chantel,' she mocked herself, her flesh crawling with an imagined tickle of rat's paws. 'Sure, why the bloody hell not? I like skulking down pitch black, rat infested alleys while a bollocking serial killer is slicing up prozzies.'

Calming herself with a long exhale and yet another reconnoitre of the alley's entrance, Chantel knocked on the steel slab with two pairs of quick raps separated by a pause and waited.

A cold trickle of rainwater cut slowly between her shoulder blades and she shivered. The blotches of darkness around her pressed closer, and Chantel wished she wasn't such a sucker. If it hadn't been for Dylan, she never would have agreed to this. Still, what use could it do the poor bugger now? He was probably chopped up into little pieces and floating in the Thames. Or maybe not. No one knew. Which was strange. Then she thought about the picture of that RSPCA lady, which was doing the rounds online, and inevitably her mind jumped to how it was going to be her next. She was about to give up and run back to the light of the main road and the company of strangers when a bolt behind the steel door unlocked.

Tentatively, the door opened ajar, and someone was hiding in the blackness within.

'You took your time.'

'Oh, you're welcome. Maybe I'll just bugger off and take what I've got with me.'

In answer, the door opened a few more inches. Chantel glanced back up the alley with a look that fell somewhere between longing and resignation. It was like peering up through the rain from the bottom of a deep, square hole cut into the earth, tunnelled down away from the living into the belly of the underworld. The downpour was growing heavier, drumming on the rooftops, feeding the puddles and potholes and turning them into dirty, swollen meres at the bottom of her hole. Maybe, once she was done here, Chantel could climb out of that hole? *Maybe*, she thought, shifting the awkward bag on her shoulder. *A girl's gotta dream.*

ON THE FINAL step down from Gallows Court, Dylan stood with his sweatshirt hood covering his disfigured face, hiding it from the world.

Mr Butcher shut the front door behind them, its brass number twenty-five gleamed dully by the light of the streetlamps. Vieil was at his side, dressed in a pinstriped three piece suit, tie in a perfect Windsor knot, and his hair slicked back.

Without a breath of wind to move it on, the rain fell straight down. Traffic ploughed through the water, racing it along the gutters. It was as if the turf war of a night ago had never happened. The blood was washed away so that the world could carry on as normal. But the world wasn't normal for Dylan anymore.

Vieil placed a hand on Dylan's shoulder. *Beautiful, isn't it?* The words weren't spoken. Instead, they appeared in Dylan's mind, another revelation in this new world.

Vieil was speaking of the intricate patterns that ran through everything. It was the skeleton of the universe. The red and brilliant pulsing thing had revealed itself to Dylan with that same insisting throb as in the pyramid beneath Gallows Court. It coursed through the rain and the vortex of the weather system above and the whirl of the galaxy beyond that, which, too, now was within Dylan's perception. And it was in everything else, an exciting and elegant equation expressed in the flow of traffic, the patterns of electricity running through cables, and the hustle of Londoners fleeing the weather. But more alluringly, the intricate patterns of the universe were in the pulse of life beating through the veins of the city's busy occupants. None of them had ever noticed Dylan before, but *he* noticed *them* now.

Vieil's silver eyes glimmered. *There is so much more. Shall we?* He gave a small gesture, turning over his hand to point at the street.

While the rain didn't fall on the steps of number twenty-five, as soon as Dylan walked back into the real world, he would be soaked in minutes. *But I don't have a coat.*

Vieil's thin lips quirked at the edges. *The rain will not presume to touch us. We will move between its intentions, blending from its purview. If you wish it to be so, it will be.*

Dylan put a hand to his burnt face.

And nor will they see us, until it is too late.

THE BACK of the van opened, and Roj hopped inside. He slammed the door shut and put down his umbrella.

'That's bad luck,' Trinity said, as she finished the safety check on her Glock 17 pistol and secreted it in the shoulder holster over a tight fitting T-shirt. With her black hair down, makeup and undercover clothes on, she looked every bit the modern incarnation of a gypsy harlot. Kenny noticed several of the firearms officers trying and failing to avert their eyes. At first, Roj was bemused, then caught on and grinned, quickly averting his eyes. For Kenny, it was like being back on the school bus with every other boys' Tourettes of involuntary yearning for Sarah Green and Tammy Saunders invading his thoughts through the miasma of Lynx deodorant. At least these guys weren't throwing spitballs into Trinity's hair—not if they wanted to keep their balls.

'Hardly recognised you,' Roj said, taking a seat next to his sergeant.

Kenny had already checked and secured his own pistol and moved on to fiddling an earpiece into place, passing one to Roj. 'Game faces,' Kenny said, with deadpan focus. They were in one of several undercover vehicles requisitioned for the night's undercover and surveillance op. This one was made up to look like a weather-beaten builder's van, nearly as ubiquitous as a Hackney cab and red buses in East London. They'd even put a parking ticket under the windscreen wipers to add an appropriate whiff of casual lawlessness.

'Is there any other kind of face?' Trinity snapped shut the compact mirror after one last check of her makeup.

Kenny tried not to frown. Trinity had a swagger. He liked that, because he knew she wouldn't take any crap, and they didn't have time for any of that. But it was where that swagger came from, the thing that fuelled it, that Kenny worried about. He hadn't gone prying, but it was there in the shadow of every sarcastic comment and every bullish move she made. It was the flutter and thrill of a jump that she might not be able to make. It was the moment before she'd bet everything on black, or made the decision to kiss a stranger in a bar. It was the "fuck it" Hail Mary of chaos before the first punch in a bar fight, because some strangers have girlfriends.

Kenny walked down the van and passed the armed response unit. They sat along one side of the van dressed in black combat fatigues, helmets, and jackboots with Heckler and Koch MP5s and G26 rifles slung. They were kitted out like the big brothers to Trinity's little black skirt. 'Is everyone else in position?' Kenny said, clapping Detective Ross Jeffery from vice on the shoulder, who sat at the communications terminal.

One ear covered with his headset listening, Ross began checking the wall of monitors bringing in feeds from CCTV and their other undercover operatives. 'Joe is moaning about wet feet, but everyone else is good to go.'

'It could be a long night. He should have worn his wellies.' Trinity was pulling on her raincoat, flicking her hair out from the collar. Suddenly, she changed her demeanour, taking on her new personality for the evening. ''Ello, darlin', don't suppose you'd let a girl borrow your brolly? You wouldn't want me getting all wet, would you?'

Roj gulped and handed her the umbrella. She gave him a wink and stopped at the door. 'Wish me luck, boys. Let's go fishing.' She hopped out into the rain and slammed the door.

'Trinity,' Ross asked from the comms terminal, 'how's the link? Good, you're coming through loud and clear.' He leaned back in his chair and stretched, letting out a long yawn. 'You ever gone fishing, Sarg? Real fishing, I mean.'

Kenny was hovering over Ross's shoulder, scanning the screens, which switched view intermittently. 'No, I haven't. Why?' The phone in his pocket started to ring. Misha's name was on the caller ID.

Ross adjusted one of the monitors. 'I do. I love it. My old man got me into it when I was a nipper. He would take me out on weekends. It's quiet, peaceful like.'

Kenny sent Misha to his answer phone. 'Sounds nice.' Kenny didn't care and hoped Roj would butt in and help with the chit-chat.

'Thing is, most of the time, it really is like police work. You sit around waiting, nothing much happening for hours on end, and you end up going home having not caught a thing. Not even a minnow.'

Kenny watched the image from Trinity's concealed camera jostle as she walked into the backstreets of Whitechapel. 'Maybe we'll get lucky tonight.'

'What bait did you use?' Roj chipped in to Kenny's relief.

'Ah, bait!' Ross said like an uncle on Boxing Day when his favourite topic gets brought up over the buffet. 'Now, having the right bait, that can change everything. You can pull in some real monsters if the worm is juicy enough.'

43

LOST AND FOUND

THERE WENT MISHA STOKES, with her red coat hugging those voluptuous curves, hips swinging from side to side as she walked towards the school gates. She had an umbrella to keep the relentless rain at bay and a phone in the other hand, probably talking to that socially awkward policeman she wasted herself on. Admiring the view from his office, Alan Bestwick sipped on a mug of his Guatemalan medium roast, black with just a soupçon of Madagascan brown sugar. She'd turned his coffee down, and he didn't offer it to just anyone, certainly not the torpid crew that manned this sinking ship of an educational establishment. 'Torpid,' he said out loud. It had a satisfying phonaesthetic quality, like phonetically spitting in someone's eye only for them to be too stupid to understand they'd been insulted. He'd slip that into a back hander to one of the impudent urchins tomorrow. It was the small victories that got Alan through the day.

The inmates on the prison barge hadn't yet worn Misha down. That was sort of remarkable. Alan wondered whether that was part of the attraction and smirked. Of course it wasn't. The only thing better than Misha's behind was her front. It would be fun watching the enthusiasm ebb out of her over the coming years, twisting her into something bitter—better. This business with Dylan Savage would help with stoking her disillusionment—Alan did so enjoy a pun. He would also enjoy doing what he could to exacerbate said disillusion-ment. Poke and cajole the inmates most affected. Speed up their degeneration. Save them all some time.

A bus pulled up, causing Misha to hop back from its bow wave. *Mmm, brown sugar getting all wet.* She mounted the red double decker. The doors closed, and Alan exhaled wistfully. Misha was carried away, leaving him to his Guatemalan medium roast and a pile of illit-erate drivel on Mary Shelley's promethean masterpiece. How could they butcher that exquisite tragedy tonight? Or more importantly, how could they ruin Alan Bestwick's life yet again?

OKAY, so maybe Chantel didn't quite have the wiggle room she thought. Meathead had turned nasty in his texts. She wasn't about to pick up his calls. Instead, she let the phone buzz angrily in her pocket, like a trapped and pissed off beetle. She messaged him to say she was coming, lying about doing an out-call for a punter. Luckily, she had a few Johns who really liked her and would agree to lie and pay a bit more next time for some 'special' extras Chantel normally didn't like to do.

'That's what you get for doing people favours,' she chided herself. She walked so fast it was almost a jog. The rain had pushed most but not all the people from the streets, especially on the main thorough-fares. She'd been down enough dark alleys for one night, but finding herself rushing against the clock, she needed a shortcut. If she nipped behind *The White Hart* pub down Gunthorpe Street, she'd be on Wentworth in no time, and Renfield Tower was only a few minutes from there. She wasn't far from *The White Hart* now. Fifteen minutes tops and Chantel would be back at her flat and could pull off her sodden clothes.

It was rush hour as she checked left and right for a space to cross in between the busy traffic. On the other side of the road, a little way further back, sat a dog. It caught her eye for a number of reasons. One, it was bloody enormous. It sat on his haunches and seemed to be watching her. And number two, he was beautiful, an absolutely magnificent beast, with a long snout and large, pointed ears. Chantel had always loved dogs. She would have got one if it wasn't for the smell and the hair. The former put some clients off, and the latter resulted in an allergic reaction from others. The last thing Chantel needed was her Johns sneezing all over her in the middle of their transactions. She crossed over the road, ignoring the cabbie blaring his horn at her for daring to come within ten feet of his precious black cab. When she looked for the dog again, it had vanished. She searched for it up and down the road, but with the angry beetle buzzing in her coat pocket, Chantel gave up and jogged on towards *The White Hart*.

Despite the deluge, a few patrons huddled under an awning, suckling on the teats of their vape pens and sending a thick pea-soup of vanilla and mint smoke out into the night air. It billowed around Chantel as she barged through it hurrying towards the entrance to the alley that was Gunthorpe Street. Head down against the rain, and wafting a hand to clear the fog, she made the turn into the cover of the alley. One of the vape pen smokers wolf-whistled.

Distracted, Chantel was nearly knocked off her feet. She gave a yell of surprise, but a strong pair of hands caught hold of her and helped her find her feet.

'Shit, sorry. Are you alright?' The handsome woman let Chantel go. She had curly, black hair, full lips, and was dressed like Chantel. Pulling out a packet of Marlboro Lights, the dark-haired woman popped one in her mouth.

'Want one?'

'Nah, thanks. I don't smoke,' Chantel said.

The woman laughed. 'I guess you don't have a light, then, either?'

'Nah, sorry.'

The woman put away her cigarette. 'Nevermind, they're gonna kill me in the end, aren't they?'

Chantel smiled thinly. 'That's what they say.'

The woman was standing right in front of Chantel, blocking her way down the alley. The only benefit to this was that the covered archway kept the rain off them. An umbrella was hooked over one of the woman's arms. Maybe it was that detail, Chantel couldn't be sure right away, but the first thing she thought was that this bird was Old Bill. If it wasn't for the perfume, she'd smell of bacon. Then that was it, Chantel realised, it *was* the perfume. This woman had dressed to the nines like a working girl—getting the look spot on. Chantel would bet her seizure EpiPen, this one even had on crotchless knickers. But the perfume was a dead giveaway. You can't have punters going back to their wives and girlfriends smelling of another woman. Chantel wasn't the only escort, as she preferred to be called, to opt for a quick Italian shower of men's body spray.

'Crappy weather, ain't it?' the woman said.

'The worst.'

'I had to get out of it. Where you heading?'

'Brick Lane,' Chantel lied.

'God, you're braver than me. I'm only keepin' dry. But you wouldn't catch me heading off down an alley like that with a psycho on the loose.'

'You should nip in the pub for a drink.'

The woman smiled as though they shared a secret. 'They don't like people like me in places like that.'

'Why? Don't they serve the police?'

The curve in the woman's full lip wavered. 'Whatchu mean?' She hardened, squaring up to Chantel, every bit the street urchin.

Chantel sidestepped but the woman blocked her way.

'Come on, love. I ain't the brightest, but you ain't what you're made up to be. You're good, don't get me wrong. The look's bang on, and if you fancied a change in career, I bet they'd be queuing up for a ride, darlin'. Fuck it! You should just be a cam-girl. No need for punters. Credit cards only, please.'

'Don't know what you mean,' the woman said, smoothing off her hard edges and stepping aside.

Chantel moved by. 'Course you don't, darlin'.'

As she walked away, Chantel heard the cop say, 'You really shouldn't head down dark alleys.'

To the echo of her boots and without looking back, Chantel asked, 'Why? Is it against the law?'

'WHAT WAS THAT ALL ABOUT?' Detective Sergeant Stokes said through Trinity's earpiece.

'Working the locals, Sarg.' She blew on her hands, warming them up and disguising their conversation.

There was a bit of interference on the line, and Stokes' accusation came through crackling. 'She made you.'

'No shit, Sherlock,' Trinity muttered to herself, watching as the woman became a stick thin silhouette, blending with the long, black vein of her shadow that stretched down the centre of the alley.

'What was that? The line is breaking up,' DS Stokes' voice fizzled. 'Crap, Ross, can you clear that up?'

'She was jumpy and defensive and got lucky. Wait a minute.' Trinity squinted down the narrow alley, which halfway along opened out into a small car park on one side.

'Say again, Trinity. Ross, come on.'

'I'm trying. It's the iron and lead in the old buildings. They interfere more than a priest at choir practice.'

Trinity reacted, throwing off her undercover character as she pulled the Glock from the shoulder holster under her coat. 'I think I see something.' The cold rush of adrenaline started to pump, and she snatched her police ID from her pocket.

'Trinity, say again.'

Eyes on the woman still tottering gingerly over the slick cobblestones, Trinity crept forward. The Glock was at her side, her finger off the trigger but ready. There it was again, a blur of moving shadows along the wall. The woman hadn't seen it, but Trinity had. It could have been a trick of the light, phantoms within the corona of the streetlamps. Her gut said different, as did the hairs on the back of her neck.

'I'm moving down Gunthorpe Street to get a clearer view.'

DS Stokes' voice was a judder of syllables amid the static. 'We don't have eyes and ears. Do not proceed. Repeat, do not proceed.' It was unclear enough for Trinity to ignore.

The woman stopped where Gunthorpe Street opened into the

small car park and turned towards the gap between the high buildings. Trinity wiped strands of wet hair from her eyes with her sleeve. Rain pattered on her coat and splashed on the cobbles. The woman looked to be talking with someone. She was craning her neck as though she couldn't quite make out who it was. Then she walked from the alley into the car park.

'Shit!' Trinity had a bad feeling about this. 'I'm moving in.'

Static fizzed painfully in her ear. She winced, shook it off and half-raised her Glock, index finger itching closer to the trigger. With the excitement making her legs and arms feel heavier than they were, she slowed her breathing as she'd been taught. Four on the in-breath, hold for two, out for six. Each exhale was a plume of faint white. She edged closer, oblivious to the rain soaking through her stockings, filling her high heels, trickling beneath the collar of her coat. The hairs on her arms stood on end. Every part of her felt alive, more than alive, electric.

A scream came from the car park, and Trinity broke into a run.

44

TANTALUS

VIEIL WAS RIGHT: the rain wouldn't touch them. As hard as it was coming down, they moved between the falling droplets. Mr Butcher trotted beside them as a huge, sleek hound, the sinuous muscles of his shoulders and back rippling. The oscillation of life was a continuous cascade of numerical perfections, patterns within patterns, shapes with shapes, constantly in flux, a ballet of life teetering on the apex, an exquisite imbalance always surfing the edge of confusion and chaos. Dylan gazed in wonder, but his pain and hunger gnawed at him.

They passed a couple, arm in arm, who were splashing through the rain towards them, only to inexplicably swerve out of their way at the last minute. Life radiated through the unctuous veins in their throats as they ran by. Dylan heard their minds, chattering with thoughts of what they would say next. Their plans for dinner. The man's desire for sex tonight. The woman's worry about whether she should phone her mother, was she putting on too much weight, would Jeff—that was the man's name it seemed—like her if she was chubby. She should start a diet next week. Had Zoe at work been a bitch on purpose? And deeper than that. Would Jeff ask her to marry him? He would not. Jeff still messaged his highschool sweetheart and masturbated over the pictures she put on Facebook. He thought Kelly

—that was the woman's name, Dylan found—was beneath him. She carried a little too much padding for Jeff's taste, which he believed made her try too hard in bed (which was good), and too hard in their relationship (which was smothering and needy). And so on to their most foundational memories and beliefs, every one as tedious and banal as a microwaveable dinner. All this in the instant of their passing.

Indeed, you can do better.

But it hurts.

I know. You must replenish yourself with life. Remember only to feed while the heart beats. You will not need to drink too deeply tonight. A little will be enough, and oh the things you will see through the membranous veil of these meat sacks, Vieil gestured to his body. *But there is another important rule. Mr Butcher must dispose of the bodies.*

The talking heads?

Vieil bowed his head to honour Dylan's insight. *My clever boy.*

They don't die.

Not exactly, Vieil's telepathy sounded in Dylan's head as more people and their verbose minds veered around them. *They most certainly aren't alive, in the biological sense. But they are not exactly dead either in the metaphysical sense.*

Metaphysical? What's that?

It is the word people use when they want to sound as if they know what they are talking about, particularly in matters of the soul.

So you don't know what happens to them?

My people discovered the mysteries of the universe and became immortal more than threescore and ten millennia ago, while the rest of humanity was still playing with fire and fornicating with lesser hominids, Vieil thought haughtily.

That's not an answer, Dylan told him, his agitation growing, and Mr Butcher let out a growl.

Assez, Anoup, Vieil tapped the dog on the nose with his index finger, and it let out a grumble and huffed. *You will learn many secrets, truths beyond the ken of these bipedal cattle. But you will also learn that there are always more questions to be answered, greater mysteries to be uncovered. And you will see that our search for them will be the greatest intoxicant of your life. We are masters of death. Their life is not only the fuel for our own vessels. They are our portals. Their life peels back the flesh of the universe so you may search its beguiling heart. Through them and our Suhet, we can travel beyond the physical realm, freed of our trivial shells.*

Dylan cried out in a spasm of agony, and rain smattered the raw burns on his face. A teenager smoking a joint at a bus stop saw Dylan appear and disappear in an instance, a screaming face of melted skin. In wan horror, the boy scanned the street. No one else seemed to see what he saw, and he dropped his spliff, grinding it under his shoe as he shook his head. In that long tortuous second, Vieil's mind centred Dylan.

Enough verbosity. Reach out now. Find one that interests you. They will all do the job, but some are better than others.

With the hunger and pain clawing at each other, the talons of their desperation shredding Dylan's ability to think clearly, he did as Vieil said. It was easy letting his new instincts take over, stalking the stream of patterns until he found the right one. It was beautiful— sweet and tender at her core, with hidden depths he wished to devour.

A GREAT, blundering red beast splashing through the shallows, the bus veered in and out of traffic. Its pressurised brakes hissed at every bus stop as it threw open its doors to regurgitate a cud of alighting passengers, only to swallow a handful more. Misha huddled next to a steamed up window, emblazoned with the ghostly outline of a cartoonish cock and balls. The man next to her read a crumpled up copy of *The Evening Standard* he'd found in the footwell when he sat down. 'Ripper Copycat Strikes Again,' the headline read. Misha paid it no mind. She was too busy texting Kenny. He must have switched off his phone as there was a long list of unanswered questions from Misha.

Any news?
How was Samuel?

Have you found Dylan?

Are you too busy?

What time do you think you'll be home?

I think I'm going to pop over to Gallows Court. Ok?

She'd do this one thing and go straight home to Betty. The poor girl would be busting for the loo, she was sure. But she had to try and wouldn't be able to forgive herself if she didn't. It would only take a minute, and she played out a little fantasy that Dylan would be there safe and sound. He'd be alright, and then they'd get the family the help they needed, and Dylan would be back in school and able to realise his talent. It was a good story, full of hope and with a ring of plausibility.

The bus pulled into a stop and lurched to a halt, unbalancing a few of the standing passengers, who acted as if this was as normal as breathing. The doors flung open. The brakes hissed, and with a juddering hack, the engine of the great, red beast died and the lights went out, throwing them into a half-lit silence.

CHANTEL WAS PLEASED with her final comment to the undercover cop. She stuffed her hands under her armpits, hoping to find a little warmth there, though it was a trade off for much needed balance on the slick cobblestones.

A little further down the alley, tarmac took over, right at the point her teeth started to chatter and she gave up on trying to find any heat. She came up to the car park, which simultaneously widened out the alley to her left and created a sense of a conspicuous void. The wire fence of the car park tessellated the solitary security light into feeble shafts. Chantel could see the other end of the alley and wanted to speed up. She wondered whether to cut left and go to the shop like she'd told the cop she was doing, or simply go to the right as she'd always intended. She could have kicked herself. It probably wouldn't matter; she was thinking of a way to check if she was still being watched when movement caught her attention from the car park.

The security light blinked as though someone had dropped

something from the rooftop. There was no sound of impact, however, and the oddness of that made her touch the collar of her coat nervously. She peered through the rain and dark along the roofline of the five-storey warehouse forming the back wall of the car park. She couldn't see anything there, but then a figure appeared between a white van and a beat up Volkswagen Passat. Their hood was pulled up. *Oh bugger*, she thought, *here we go. Some little scrot playing at being a hood. When Henry Grime finds... Meathead finds out*, she corrected herself, but never finished the thought because the little scrot spoke.

'*Chantel*,' he whispered. Even though they were on the other side of the car park, Chantel heard it plain as day. Not only did he know her name, there was also a familiarity to the voice. It took her a moment for her to place it.

'Dylan?' She strained to see the face of the hooded figure to confirm her blooming hope. 'Dylan, is that you?'

Yeah, it's me. I need to talk to you.

'Where you been? Everyone is looking for you! Your mum is...'

Come here.

Chantel found herself obeying the voice. She moved through the wire gate, its wet hinges squealing as it swung open. One foot followed the next, drawn to the voice.

Yesss, come here.

Chantel was aware of a strange disconnection between one part of her mind that did the reasoning and the part that moved her body. That awareness suddenly became an uncomfortable thing, like a game with a client that had gone too far; she wanted to say the safe word. But she didn't know what the safe word was for this game. Her unwilling feet carried her closer and closer.

'Dylan, what are you doing? What's happening?' She tried to keep the tremor out of her voice. There was a dreamlike quality to her compulsion, simultaneously aware of it, knowing it was something she didn't want to do, but also curious as to how the dream would turn and completely unable to resist.

Closer. I have to show you something.

'I don't like this, Dylan. Stop it.'

Whatever held her let go. Her body became her own again, and she stopped in the beam of the security light, rain splashing and reflecting the light like thousands of sizzling Bonfire Night sparklers. Her lump in her throat had gnarled into a rock she struggled to swallow.

Dylan spoke from the shadows. 'I'm sorry.'

He sounded in such pain, and her heart ached for him. 'Oh, darlin'. It's going to be okay.' She couldn't help it, and despite the moment of compulsion that drew her here, Chantel went to him.

Dylan shrunk away as she reached. 'No, don't. Stay away from me. Get away.'

It was too late. She took him in her arms. He tensed. 'It's alright, sweetheart.' With a tender hand, she reached for his hooded face and drew it to look at her. 'There ain't nothing...' Chantel's scream was an involuntary thing, a cry of revulsion and fear leaping from her throat before she could stop it.

45

QUICK DRAW

HIGH HEELS and wet cobblestones didn't make running easy, but Detective Trinity Marshall didn't let that slow her down. The woman's scream had stopped, and Trinity's mind ran wild with the possibilities of what that silence meant. Her heart playing a tattoo on her ribs, she paused, readying herself behind the cover of the wall just before the wire gates. Without line of sight, she called in the situation via the mic in her sleeve.

'I'm at the car park on Gunthorpe Street. Possible assault in progress. Requesting immediate backup.'

A fizzle of static fried words into disjointed syllables. The order that came through was indecipherable. She could detect the urgency, probably from DS Stokes telling her to hold her position. Holding fast was what she *should* do: follow procedure, be a good girl. Then again, there might not be time. If this was the wannabe Ripper in action, then like the original psychopath, he probably worked fast. And Trinity could be the one to stop him. If it was a regular sexual assault or mugging, well, in that case, she'd be the one to rip the scumbag a new arsehole. Either way, it would be a result and one less woman getting screwed over while waiting for the men to stop playing with themselves.

She took a deep breath and spun into the car park entrance,

checking the corners down the sights of her gun. Through the rain, she saw two people across the square patch of asphalt, between a white van and a Volkswagen.

'Police, let me see your hands!'

The woman half turned. 'It's alrigh'. I know him. He's just a kid.'

Trinity stalked forward. She'd dropped her umbrella at the head of the alley. The downpour had soaked her black hair. It clung in sodden strands around her face, and her mascara ran in streaking black tears. 'Good to know, but move away and let him come into the light.'

The boy, who had a hood pulled up covering his face, shrunk away into the shadows.

'Don't move,' Trinity shouted, now focusing all her attention on the boy with something to hide.

'Which is it, move or don't move?' the woman said in a voice full of sass, and then more scornfully, 'You're scaring him. Leave him alone.' She moved to block Trinity's sights.

'If he has nothing to hide, he can come where I can see him.'

The woman wouldn't move. She held her arms up to her sides to make her petite form bigger and more protective. 'You're scaring him, you muppet. He's hurt. Those Duppy bastards burnt his face or summit.'

Without a clear shot anyway, Trinity lowered her gun to the floor but kept herself primed. It occurred to her that this might be the boy they were looking for. With the rain coming down so hard she almost had to shout to be heard. 'I can help. You're not in any trouble, kid. What's your name?'

'His name is Dylan. How kind of you to ask, Detective Marshall,' a voice drawled from behind.

Trinity swiveled on the spot, snapping her pistol onto the new target. Down the end of her barrel was an impeccably dressed man, late forties to early fifties, greyish hair slicked back and a hawkish nose. He stood with his hands clasped in front of him, radiating an unsettling calmness and seemingly untouched by the rain. Trinity's pounding heart rate jumped, blood surging through her veins so forcefully she fought to keep her aim steady. She never heard him coming, and now she was caught between him and the boy. And how in hell did this toff know her name? Did he have a police scanner?

'Put your hands where I can see them.' She tensed on the trigger and stepped sideways so that the boy and woman weren't directly behind her, but the man with greying hair spoke over her.

'It's not *my* hands she needs to worry about, is it, Mr Butcher?'

A piggy in the middle, Trinity spun around again. She was about to back into a well-muscled man with a long face and handlebar moustache. He was close enough to grab her gun. How did she not see or hear him coming? He must have been hiding behind a vehicle.

You stupid bint, you missed him.

This second man was also dapperly dressed, but with a bowler hat and matching brown waistcoat, a gold chain pocket watch, and a white shirt with arm braces. Trinity pointed her gun right at the centre of his chest, and of all things, he smiled, showing white teeth. She retreated the way she came, searching for a place where her back wasn't exposed. Caught in the open, such a place didn't exist, so Trinity settled for the lesser of three evils and put the boy and woman behind her.

She still didn't know which target to focus on. *Fuck! Fuck! Fuck!*

'My dear Mr Butcher, she has a frightfully filthy mouth. Indeed, more your type than mine.'

Trinity jerked her aim between the two men. 'Both of you put your hands up. I'm not pissing around. Back up, I need backup.' More than a little panic had crept into her voice, and she found herself shouting into her sleeve for help, wishing she hadn't rushed in.

'Isn't that just the story of your life, Trinity? Rushing in where angels fear to tread. So much to prove. Can you see it, Dylan?'

'Leave him alone,' the woman with the boy warned.

Yes, the grey-haired gentleman said, but the word seemed to hiss like the falling rain: *yessh*, 'Chantel is an excellent choice. The proverbial good-hearted whore.'

'Fuck off, you old ponce,' the woman spat back. 'Gimme your hand, darlin,' she said to the boy.

'We're out of time. Dylan, if you please.'

'Nobody move.' Trinity was caught in a horrible game of eeniemeenie-miney-mo. Her gun panned from the hawkish man to the one in the bowler hat and back to the hawk; a frigid claw of dread raked down her spine. The man in the bowler hat produced a weapon. In a fraction of a second, she recognised it as the Eyptian blade Stokes and Dabral had shown her. This was the man, or these were the *men*, and she was trapped with them.

Trinity screamed, 'Drop your weapon.'

The man in the bowler hat smirked sardonically. They faced each other like gunslingers in the rain.

Alas, Trinity, you are precisely Anoup's type. The voice sounded in her head, as if whispered right in her ear. Trinity cast her eyes to the side, half expecting to see the hawkish man already there, breathing down her neck. In that moment of distraction, the bowler hatted man hefted his bronze sword. Snapping back to him, Trinity didn't hesitate and pulled the trigger.

But he wasn't there.

She tracked left and fired. Now, he was to the right and closer. The hawkish man chuckled, and the prostitute gave a shriek that seemed to ascend into the air with a ripple in the shadows.

Trinity went trigger happy, never able to hit her mark. The man with a bowler hat moved in a streak of preternatural speed. Each shot mirrored a jump in her own panic, until the Glock ran dry and the bowler hatted man's metallic breath kissed her lips.

There were so many things Trinity was going to do, starting with pistol-whipping this psycho into the dirt, and ending with making it to Detective Inspector in the Special Branch. They all became unfulfilled dreams.

Suddenly, she wasn't facing a man, but a great and terrible hellhound. It still had a man's face, but his wolfish grin and lifeless eyes betrayed his true self.

Life really did flash before her eyes. Trinity's grandmother was a Romani gypsy who married a plumber and gave up the travelling life. She told her granddaughter unsanitized stories from the old country. In her version of Red Riding Hood, the Woodcutter disemboweled the wolf at the end, and all the half-digested bits of Red and her

Granny spilled out. Trinity had always wanted to be the one with the axe.

The bowler hatted man jerked his shoulders in a swift motion from low to high and Trinity gasped. The gun slipped from her grip. She looked down at the curved sword buried beneath her ribs. Death glinted in the man's eyes, and he pulled out his hooked sword.

Crumpling to her knees, Trinity put her hands to her belly, trying to hold the bits of Red Riding Hood together. It was so hot, spilling over her hands like strings of sausages with lashings of gravy.

A shout came from the top of Gunthorpe Street. It sounded so far away.

The hawkish man sighed. *Don't pout, Anoup. The night is young. Now, come; we have to find our charge.*

Bewildered, Trinity looked up from the sausages in her hands. Bowler hat man wasn't smiling now. His moustache twitched irritably. Trinity thought she heard the growl of the Big Bad Wolf. With a flick of his arm, he whipped his sword laterally in a final *coup de grâce*. In an instant, he appeared by the side of the hawkish man at the car park gates. As ridiculous as it was, Trinity tried to say, "come back". Nothing came out except a gout of blood.

Another shout and the pounding of feet on cobbles were the last things Trinity heard. She pitched forward and rolled to her side, her intestines in her hands, and her glassy eyes fixed unseeing on the arrival of the Woodcutter. Too late.

46

HOMECOMING

WHEN THE GUNFIRE STARTED, Dylan grabbed Chantel and they leapt from the ground. They shot up into the rain, punching through the thin scaffolding of streetlights that held the burden of night, as if upon their tremulous shoulders. Chantel was flying and screaming, squawking and flapping her arms and legs.

They briefly touched down on the folded lead of a roof, surrounded by a low parapet of weather-worn bricks, only to bound away from the crack of the police officer's pistol. They sprang from the next roof, and a pair of slates slipped, pitching into the alley. Dylan cradled Chantel in his arms, and she knew he wouldn't let go. With London beneath them, laid out in a quilt of stars, she stopped screaming.

At first, she couldn't tell how far they'd travelled, or where they ended up, but there was no gunfire when they alighted on a flat roof. Dylan set her down, turning his head away.

She reached for him through the rain. 'Dylan, love.'

'Don't.' He cowered from her hand, backing into a drab green fire door.

Chantel approached with slow steps. 'You saved me. Let me see you.' She took the hem of his hood in her fingers.

248

'Please don't.' His words were slurred and afraid.

She pulled down his hood and could have screamed again, but she didn't, she wouldn't. But what had happened to him? What *was* he? Dylan had changed from the burnt boy in the car park.

'It wasn't the Duppies,' he slurred, a mouthful of fangs crowded his gums. All the hair having been burnt away, the skin of his head was a wretched mottle of browns and reds and sickly pinks. Eyes cast to the ground, Dylan's chest heaved up and down slowly, and he hid his hands in the pocket at the front of his hoodie.

Chantel's hand hovered in the air. 'Who?... What?' She spoke tenderly, moving closer, but he flinched again.

'A monster. They made me into a monster.'

'No, darlin'. You could never be that. You're one of the good guys.'

Dylan shook his head. 'Does a good guy look like this? Does a good guy get burnt by the sunlight?'

'I-I don't understand.' Chantel let her hand fall as she wrestled with the new world Dylan had carried her into, sweeping her away from danger, to spring across the rooftops of Whitechapel. 'The sunlight?' she said. *The fangs*, she thought, and shook her head, rejecting the conclusion.

Yeshh, came the reply whispered into her head.

He stepped towards her and she moved back, still trying to shake off the implications. Each step he made forward, she matched backward, retreating from his fangs, which beaded with a milky white venom. He drew his hands from his pocket, each finger a grotesquely long and curving talon.

'You could never be a monster. It doesn't matter what you look like. We'll figure it out. We'll...' Chantel spoke in rapid fire as she continued to give ground, her actions betraying her words until they trailed off.

'Figure what out?' Dylan spat angrily, strands of saliva and that opaque poison dripping from his lisping maw, his breathing heavier and growing more ragged. 'It mattered what we looked like before, didn't it? Tell me people didn't look at you and me and already make up their minds we were scum. Tell me they hadn't already decided we were less than them. We were already monsters in their eyes. Well, now I really am one, inside and out.'

'No, they didn't. You aren't. It's-it's not true.'

'Then why are you running away from me?'

Chantel didn't have an answer for that. She was afraid, terrified. She told herself she could see the old Dylan, the boy on the cusp of adulthood, the shy and sweet, clever school kid who dreamed of being an accountant and asked her about her own dreams. That thing stalking her was Dylan's height. It had his voice, near enough. It had a melted and scarred version of his face. But the more she fought to hold onto the vision of the boy as he was, the more he slipped away, like a monster shedding its skin, until she faced the new and terrible creature underneath.

Shtopp, the voice in her head commanded. Unable to resist, Chantel obeyed. She wanted to scream with everything she had, a cry from the depths of her childhood nightmares, a futile wail to prove she was alive in the face of certain death. But as in life, her body wasn't her own. She stood paralysed but utterly aware of the monster closing in.

It was Dylan who now held a hand to her face and finally lifted his gaze to hers. Silver eyes shone as two hunter's moons. He placed one talon on her chest. Heart drumming, she tilted her neck, involuntarily exposing the succulent artery pulsing there. A heavy droplet of white venom stretched from one of his fangs and broke free. More poison followed it, oozing down the crowded ivory blades. He opened his jaws wider than seemed possible. Somehow, Chantel closed her eyes. She told herself, *If this is what he needs, then he can have it.* If other men always took what they wanted, then why shouldn't he? His breath brushed the skin of her neck, and she made a prayer to a God she didn't have time for, because he never seemed to have time for her. The prayer wasn't for herself anyway.

The rain splattered Chantel's face. Her hands and knees trembled, and she noticed her teeth were chattering. In fact, these were all things that were uncomfortable realities, but they had only appeared along with the hiss of the downpour. Their strangeness lay in their previous absence just moments ago. Tentatively, Chantel opened her eyes. Droplets hung on the end of her lashes. She wiped them away, noticing her paralysis had waned, and looked for Dylan. The rooftop was empty. Only when she scanned around did she notice that she had backed right to the edge of the roof. One more move in retreat and she would have plunged down eight storeys. She drew herself back from the precipice. Had he stopped her from walking off the roof? She didn't know.

Overhead, black clouds clotted together as a tubercular thunder rattled the heavens. Searching the sky, Chantel couldn't find Dylan. Renfield Tower rose from the bric-a-brac of buildings, strewn between the streets of Whitechapel. It was a block away. He'd brought them home. If that's where he was going, Chantel hoped beyond hope he'd find a miracle there. Her heart broke at that thought, but the rain hid the tears.

ANILA CHATTERJEE STRUGGLED with the unwieldy pole, trying in vain to get the hook into the hole to pull down the steel shutters. Their family shop had a small overhang from the apartment block above, but the rain somehow found a way through and dripped on her head. It was cold and felt darker tonight. Passing through some impercep-tible transition, autumn had finally succumbed to winter. She thought the night hung over everything like a heavy sheet, and the people of the city were merely children huddled underneath it with their flashlights, failing not to think about the monsters that lurked under their beds and in their wardrobes. The idea made her skin tingle and the downy hairs on her neck bristle. She turned, putting her back to the glass of the shopfront, and scanned the square between her and Renfield Tower for the eyes she felt watching her.

The lifeless bing-bong of the shop bell made her squeak.

'What's the matter?' her father said. 'Still can't reach the shutters?'

'No, Pitā. Sorry.' Anila always used the Bengali word for father. She spoke English outside of the family home, but Pitā was always Pitā no matter where they were.

'Give me that and you get ready. We don't want to be late for the movie.' He took the pole from her and patted her shoulder as she left. 'What were you looking at?' He followed her gaze out across the square.

Anila paused in the doorway, rubbing the cold from her arms. 'Nothing, Pitā. What's showing tonight?'

Her father brandished the shutter pole like a rifle. 'Kakababur Protyaborton.' Mr Chatterjee was a sucker for an action adventure movie, and if it was a Bengali action adventure movie, then he was twice the sucker. More than once he had wished Bruce Willis was Bengali.

She rolled her eyes, but couldn't help but grin. 'How many times will that be?'

He frowned, a little crestfallen. 'Four, but you like adventures, no?'

'Not as much as you, Pitā. I'll get, Mā.' She let the door swing shut behind her.

'Your mother loves it too,' Mr Chatterjee called through the glass. Threading between the shelves of canned goods, Anila wobbled her head from side-to-side noncommittally.

Mr Chatterjee returned to the shutter and pulled it down three feet. It unrolled with a reassuring weight. Before he ducked under to shut up for their monthly early close and family night at the movies, he took the measure of Renfield Tower one more time and squinted. He could have sworn something was moving up the wall of the high-rise block, like a giant spider too fast to be seen with any certainty. That couldn't be right. He must have been on edge from all the recent news about this Jack the Ripper copycat and the gangland murders. He'd even heard the rumours that boy Dylan Savage was involved, and was glad he'd fired him. When Mr Chatterjee checked the tower again, normality had resumed. A figure with its hood up and head stooped, like all the little thugs on the estate, was walking along the twelfth floor walkway.

With a harumph, Mr Chatterjee ducked under the shutter and pulled it down to the floor with a rattle and clank. He locked it into the security frame set into the concrete and triple locked the door, turned off the lights, checked the security cameras were recording and turned on the alarm system.

IT HAD TAKEN every ounce of willpower Dylan had not to feed on Chantel. Her life had pulsed so seductively but was also forbidden. It was a taboo that, if crossed, there was no going back, and yet even its denial seemed to swell his hunger, which in turn fed his pain and his anger. The force of her life had tingled in his fangs, and he had sensed the deeper secrets it contained. The essence of her soul fluttered meekly in the darkness. It danced as playful and innocent as a child, twirling and giggling with the delight of life, despite all the leering bastards and bogeymen who haunted the upper layers of her existence. It was *his* to snuff out, until he heard her prayer. Her prayer for him, for the boy inside this thing he had become. No, whatever Vieil recommended, Dylan wouldn't take her, not when there were others far more deserving taking up space in the world.

He'd fled her and all her unpolished beauty, jumping through the sky and from roof to roof, and finally to Renfield Tower. With no need to find the comfort of numbers up the twelve flights of stairs, he scurried up the wall until the door to his home lay under his claw. It felt like an alien place. The filters of his world had changed, and he looked upon it with new eyes, seeing it for the blighted thing it had always been.

Tap, tap, tap—he let his talons rap softly, sensing the people inside.

Yeshh?

Yeeshh.

The door was locked, and he didn't have a key. No matter. Its handle a twisted tatter, the door flung open and banged shut again off the wall.

Dylan waited in the dark, standing on his old spot next to the lightswitch.

Yeeshh, for old time's sake. He clicked the light on and off. One.

A panicked voice in the other room asked who it was. A cautious voice replied that he'd sort it out, but that was a lie: he thought he'd die—which of course was true, but not how the man imagined. He had a little arsenal: a knife, a pair of brass knuckles and, how cute, a gun.

Dylan switched the light on and off again, flashing in and out of sight in the bleak hallway. Two.

Gun raised, Henry Grime shouted from the other room. 'Come on then, blud. Let's 'av it.' He sprung into the hall and opened fire. The gun flashed three times.

One bullet hit Dylan in the shoulder, another in the chest, but the third punctured the UPVC door at his head height. He saw each bullet coming and could have moved, but like a child playing with new toys, he wanted to see what would happen. Already in agony, the bullet was nothing, a hard pressure more akin to swallowing a piece of food with a dry throat.

Three.

Dylan flicked the switch, leaving the light on. It didn't make him feel safe. It never really had. And now, he didn't need it to.

'Dee?' Henry Grime croaked.

Hunched and panting, Dylan slowly lifted his head and pulled down his hood.

Donna was crying and whimpering in the other room. 'Who is it? Are they dead? Oh, my days!'

Henry Grime reeled away. 'Little Dee, is that you, bruv?'

Brothherr? Henry Grime winced at the mocking voice in his head.

'Henry, what's happening?' Donna sobbed.

'I thought you was dead, bruv. I've been trying to find out—'

Dylan covered the distance between them in an instant. His clawed hand wrapped around Henry's throat, lifting him off the floor. The pimp's eyes grew wide and wild, and he struck at Dylan's forearm. 'What happened to you?' he choked.

With a roar, baring his teeth, Dylan threw Henry Grime from the hall into the lounge. He struck the wall and fell onto the sofa and groaned, dazed. Plaster sprinkled on top of him from the man-sized indentation overhead.

Donna cried out, falling on top of Henry. 'Don't, please, don't.'

Dylan stood over them, and when Donna looked up into the face of her son, with tears streaking down her face, she didn't just scream, she shrieked a piercing ululation of utter terror.

Move, Dylan ordered, as he clenched and unclenched his talons. It was Henry who pushed Donna away and drowsily struggled to get up. He fell to his knees, finding the gun he dropped as he sailed through the air. Before he could grab it from the threadbare carpet, Dylan backhanded him, sending him sprawling to the floor at Donna's feet as she tried to scramble away over the arm of the sofa.

A huge haematoma was swelling on Henry's cheek, and he spat blood. 'Little Dee, please. I was looking for you.'

Dylan fell on him, straddling his chest. He seized Henry by the throat and pinned him to the floor. *Looking for me? What, so you could use me, like you used my mum, like you use everyone?* He pulled Grime's head aside exposing his throat, along with every seedy thing he'd ever done. All the back alley deals. All the beatings of his whores, Johns, and street punks. The crappy childhood. The beatings he'd taken as a kid. But he was strong, *yessh*, he was, and he wasn't stamped out. He would do nicely. A hot coal, fuming in the under-world amid a swirling vortex of heated currents. Those currents were so intricate but predictable in their oscillations, they would carry Dylan beyond the veil and into the deeper mysteries Vieil had promised and wash away his pain.

Dylan threw back his head and stretched open his jaws in antici-pation. His fangs inched forward, dripping venom. Something inef-fectual struck the arm pinning Henry's head to the side. When he looked down, his stupid, pathetic mother had thrown herself over her pimp protectively, who in turn was trying to push her away. What hold did this man have over her that she would come back to him time and time again, no matter how much he put her down and beat her? And there it was, the answer, a tumor nestled amid the calcified fractures and ugly scar tissue of a life in Whitechapel.

'No,' Dylan slurred and withdrew with a revulsion that mirrored his mother's.

A mess of snot and tears, Donna threw her arms around Henry

Grime. Dylan couldn't look at them. It was the size of the lie and the repugnance of the betrayal that saved them, in one sick way or another. Before Henry Grime could reach out a beseeching hand and call Dylan's name, he was gone, the broken door rattling in its frame.

47

HOUSE CALLS

THE BEAST WAS DEAD, or perhaps mortally wounded, and no matter how much the driver phoned for mechanical defibrillation, a roadside recovery unit wasn't coming to help. From the safety of his enclosed cabin, the driver informed the passengers that due to health and safety regulations, no one apart from the driver was allowed to stay on board. To much moaning and groaning, all the passengers alighted onto a rain drenched Whitechapel Road, the main artery running through the borough. The driver claimed another bus was due any minute, but there were over thirty passengers on the bus and space for less than half that number under the nearest bus shelter.

Nevermind, thought Misha Stokes. She was luckier than most and had an umbrella. Renfield Tower was close by. She would walk it and probably be back before the next bus came along. Police sirens wailed somewhere out of sight. An ambulance sped past the grumbling throng of commuters recently disgorged from their bus. Misha walked briskly through the puddles towards Renfield Tower, its lights hopscotching up out of the rooftops.

ONCE THE MONSTER WAS GONE, Donna finally heard her son's name. She seemed confused, punch-drunk even, or maybe just drunk, her consciousness swaying from the left-hook of shock and a guillotine choke of fear. 'What d'you mean, Dylan? No, not that thing. What was it? Oh, my days!'

'I'm tellin' you, it was Dylan.'

'Nah,' Donna said, still clinging to Henry Grime on the living room carpet.

Henry shook off her clutches and groped for the gun, stuffing it in the waistband of his jeans.

'What you doing? Oh, my days! What's happening?' She hugged her knees to her chest and rocked.

Donna was there in body, but nothing else. Henry knew whose fault that was. For the first time, it had been revealed to him. Not that he was oblivious to the fear he inspired. Violence and intimidation had always been necessities of his profession. It was a dog-eat-dog world and better to be top-dog than somebody's bitch. That was a convenient lie, though. What did the men in the black Jaguars make him, then? *A pussy*, he thought acridly. As a pimp, he knew very well what happened to pussies. He answered Donna's questions but knew he was the only one listening.

'I ain't never been a good man. Never had no need for it. Thought I was bringing him into the family business. Toughen him up. Turn him into a bad man. Earn him some respect.' Henry gave a half-hearted and hollow laugh at himself as he hefted the duffle bag.

Eyes glazed, Donna continued her self-soothing rock-a-bye, not realising the cradle had already fallen.

Henry looked down at her. 'You silly mare. You can't see it, can you?'

But Henry Grime had seen. At first he thought the Duppies had mutilated Dylan and jacked him up on PCP or crack. A junkie with enough juice in their veins, Henry knew, could be Hulk-strong. That wasn't the case here. When that thing pinned him as though he was nothing more than a baby, Henry felt it probe his mind. But, just as it could probe inside Henry, Henry glimpsed its inner-self. There was no mistaking it; Henry made it out for what and who it really was: Dylan.

Numbers patterned everything inside the boy, bright coloured equations and strings of figures, like fortifications built high around the things he wanted to protect. Henry saw other things too, things that should have been impossible, but seeing was believing. There were snatches of experiences from the moment Dylan left his side at the Gallows Court rumble. He saw Dylan being forced to stab his best friend. The Duppies torturing Dylan in the arches. The things which came to save the boy when no one else would. Henry saw the inside of a pyramid, sunlight burning Dylan alive, a room of talking heads, a man with a hook and another with liquid silver eyes. A black door with a polished brass number. Chantel, a gunfight, terrible hunger and terrible pain, and he saw himself under the monster's claw ready to satiate its hunger and cure its pain. He saw every bad deed as Dylan saw them. But then *it*, Dylan, found one important thing inside Henry: a lie among his many deceits, a betrayal among countless deceptions. In that moment, Dylan and Henry stared into each other's souls, but it was Henry who recoiled, seeing himself reflected back. Dylan wasn't the only monster in that room.

Huddled on the floor, the fight had gone out of Donna long ago. Tonight was just the final knee to the head.

Henry checked the contents of his duffle bag. 'If you're not coming, here.' He tossed her rolls of ten and twenty pound notes, all the money he had left. They scattered around Donna's feet, but she only buried her head into her knees. 'Get out of London. Start over, or buy all the vodka you want. It's up to you.'

He started to walk away.

'Stay,' Donna snivelled.

Henry didn't answer. He pulled up his hood and went hunting.

DONNA DIDN'T KNOW how long she'd been sitting on the living room floor. There was money scattered around her, tons of money, in fat rolls of tens and twenties. She picked a couple up, staring at them, trying to make sense of it. Henry had come back to her. He always did in the end. No matter how much he put her down, slapped her around, and put her to work on her back. He was never a generous man, but here was all the money he had left. It was supposed to be for him to make a break for it out of London. Donna didn't know why he'd come back to the flat. He hadn't gotten that far when that thing broke in.

Oh, my days! Donna shuddered. What crackhead had the Blud Crew sent around to finish Henry off? She never saw one so messed up. It looked burnt and deformed. Hardly human at all, and Henry, didn't he say it was Dylan? Nah, it couldn't have been. It was just another of the cruel bastard's manipulations.

Donna squeezed the rolls of money to her chest. *Why does he treat me so bad? Ain't I a good girl? I'm always there for him. Who waited while he did his stretch in Pentonville? Who was there at the front gate when he got out?*

The flat's door swung open and jangled softly off the hall wall. Donna scrambled to her feet.

'You're back. I knew you'd come. I...'

Donna stopped dead at the living room doorway. Two well dressed men stood in her hall. She retreated from them as they stepped into the room. Were they Old Bill, detectives maybe, come sniffing around again about Dylan? The first time, she'd told them everything she knew. But they wouldn't tell her anything about her beautiful boy. After that, she'd done the only thing she knew how to and dived headlong into a bottle of vodka.

Enchanté, Miss Savage, a man with a hawk's nose and salt and pepper hair said, as the other man with a brown bowler hat stepped out beside him and leered.

Donna stuffed the fists full of notes into her ears. The greying man didn't move his lips, but the words were like crashing waves in her mind. She tripped on one of the rolls of money and fell back onto the sofa.

The man with the bowler hat drew a long, curved sword from

thin air. Donna desperately wanted to scream, but the waves were smashing and foaming so loudly she was paralysed.

Don't worry about him. You are indeed to Mr Butcher's taste, but I think for the sake of Dylan, I shall have the honours.

48

BLOODY VALENTINE

KENNY HAD HEARD the snarling bark as soon as they'd entered Gunthorpe Street. The tactical unit was in the front, jackboots sprinting. Trinity's voice stuttered with interference in his earpiece, and a short snapping pop of gunfire came from down the alley. At the gate, the tactical guys rushed the space in formation. Kenny and Roj hung back, their own Glocks upholstered and pointed at the ground.

The call of 'Clear,' came too quickly, followed immediately by a shout of 'Officer down.' Kenny and Roj passed through the gate; Trinity lay on the ground. Kneeling in a pool of blood, two of the tactical unit were trying to administer first aid, but it was a futile gesture. Trinity's blank eyes stared through Kenny. But there was no time to reflect on the loss of a fellow officer, cut down in the line of duty and in the prime of her life.

The growl was louder here, fresher than at any of the crime scenes, and a thunder clap clattered petulantly off the surrounding buildings. Trinity's echo stood over her body, firing at a moving target. Kenny couldn't see what. Then, from groin to ribs, a terrible cleft like an obscene zipper opened up in Trinity's torso; her intestines bulged out. Two spectres walked through Kenny and Roj—a man in a bowler hat with his hooked sword, and a second unarmed figure dressed in an elegant pinstriped suit. Kenny couldn't make out their faces and turned on a sixpence to watch them walk out of the car park and turn left.

'We've just missed them,' Kenny muttered, as he ran for the alley. 'Sarg?'

'They headed to Old Montague Street,' Kenny shouted back, and Roj set off after him.

They burst onto the street next to Haajar's corner shop. With sirens screaming, marked and unmarked police cars were racing to join them. Scared pedestrians turned their heads and stepped aside seeing the two men holding guns. Kenny scoured the street for the two assailants.

'They could be anywhere,' Roj said, craning to see over the heads of pedestrians and the throng of umbrellas and traffic. 'Who are we looking for?'

'Two IC1 males, middle aged, I think. One wearing a bowler hat and holding the khopesh.' Kenny searched the other direction. Londoners gave him a wide berth, some raising their hands as they edged by. He flashed his ID and shouted, 'Police.'

'Can I call that description in, Sarg?

Kenny knew what he meant. He was asking if Kenny had actually seen them and not made them through one of his voodoo retrocognitions. 'Negative, don't call it in. We've got nothing. Damn it!'

The phone in Kenny's pocket vibrated. It would be Misha, and he didn't have time to speak and persuade her out of her Good Samaritan routine with the kid who was somehow mixed up in all this. Renfield Tower caught his eye, looming over the rooftops less than half a mile away, and his blood ran cold. He'd told her not to go there, but there was that feeling he got sometimes, not his reading of past echoes, but rather pulling things out of the ether, only for someone to do or say the exact thing he was thinking. That feeling developed into a fresco of mental images, feelings, and sensations.

Misha was wearing her red coat, huddled under an umbrella at the foot of a tower block, checking a note on her phone detailing the address. Floor twelve, flat thirteen. Her feet were wet. She went to the entrance, nervous of stepping into the dark, and silently chided herself when a man with a duffle bag slung across his shoulder burst out of the door. He neither met her eye nor said a word before bolting into the rain, his heels kicking up spray. The lift was out of order. The stairwell smelled like all stairwells in tenement blocks and multi-storey car parks the world over, a mix of stale piss and the damp fug of desperation. But she was determined. She was always so bloody determined.

Kenny grabbed his phone. Rain speckled the screen before he could answer. 'Misha, tell me you're not at Dylan Savage's flat... For Christ's sake, I told you not to. What are you doing?... Don't go in; it's not your job to check. Misha?'

Roj had walked over, seeing a look far beyond concern cast in Kenny's expression. 'Boss? Everything alright?'

'Get out, Misha. Get out.' Kenny shouted, drawing more stares and causing Londoners to give him an even wider berth, as if he was marked by some terrible hex. Kenny glared at Renfield Tower. 'No, please.' His voice had petered into a croak, and he screwed his eyes shut, clenching his jaw and shaking all over with tension.

Roj was at his ear, listening. Kenny didn't stop him. A short scream, as if it had been snatched out of the air before it could get away, came from the phone. Kenny's eyes snapped open, and without a word, he set off at a blistering clip. Shouting instructions into his Airwave radio, Roj followed his partner.

PAST CRIMES sometimes echo in the present.

Mary Jane Kelly was the last of the canonical five Jack the Ripper victims. Unlike the other four women, her murder took place indoors in the privacy of 13 Miller's Court, Spitalfields. It was a hovel, with a single candle to light the room because that was all Mary could afford. This was possibly why the Ripper burned Mary's clothes in the grate to adequately illuminate his dissection. Privacy provided time, affording the killer an opportunity to elaborate on his modus operandi. As such, Mary Jane Kelly, sometimes called "Black Mary", sometimes "Fair Emma", was more completely eviscerated. Her official post-mortem read as follows:

The body was lying naked in the middle of the bed, the shoulders flat but the axis of the body inclined to the left side of the bed. The head was turned on the left cheek. The left arm was close to the body with the forearm flexed at a right angle and lying across the abdomen. The right arm was slightly abducted from the body and rested on the mattress. The elbow was bent, the forearm supine with the fingers clenched. The legs were wide apart, the left thigh at right angles to the trunk and the right forming an obtuse angle with the pubis.

The whole of the surface of the abdomen and thighs was removed and the abdominal cavity emptied of its viscera. The breasts were cut off, the arms mutilated by several jagged wounds and the face hacked beyond recognition of the features. The tissues of the neck were severed all round down to the bone.

The viscera were found in various parts viz: the uterus and kidneys with one breast under the head, the other breast by the right foot, the liver between the feet, the intestines by the right side and the spleen by the left side of the body. The flaps removed from the abdomen and thighs were on a table.

The bed clothing at the right corner was saturated with blood, and on the floor beneath was a pool of blood covering about two feet square. The wall by the right side of the bed and in a line with the neck was marked by blood which had struck it in several places.

The face was gashed in all directions, the nose, cheeks, eyebrows, and ears being partly removed. The lips were blanched and cut by several incisions running obliquely down to the chin. There were also numerous cuts extending irregularly across all the features.

The neck was cut through the skin and other tissues right down to the vertebrae, the fifth and sixth being deeply notched. The skin cuts in the front of the neck showed distinct ecchymosis. The air passage was cut at the lower part of the larynx through the cricoid cartilage.

Both breasts were more or less removed by circular incisions, the muscle down to the ribs being attached to the breasts. The intercostals between the fourth, fifth, and sixth ribs were cut through and the contents of the thorax visible through the openings.

The skin and tissues of the abdomen from the costal arch to the pubes were removed in three large flaps. The right thigh was denuded in front to the bone, the flap of skin, including the external organs of generation, and part of the right buttock. The left thigh was stripped of skin fascia, and muscles as far as the knee.

The left calf showed a long gash through skin and tissues to the deep muscles and reaching from the knee to five inches above the ankle. Both arms and forearms had extensive jagged wounds [...]

On opening the thorax it was found that the right lung was minimally adherent by old firm adhesions. The lower part of the lung was broken and torn away. The left lung was intact. It was adherent at the apex and there were a few adhesions over the side[...]The pericardium was open below and the heart absent.

Roj knew these details well, having read them in several sources during the course of his investigation. He'd seen the crime scene images, one of the earliest such examples of forensic photography. They were an abstract thing, facts to be applied to their new case. They were filed away in his brain as he and Kenny ran pell-mell the half-mile to the tower block.

The lift was out of order, so they took the stairs two at a time. Roj had a stitch by the sixth floor, doubled over for a second on the mid-landing, and dug deep to catch up with DS Stokes. By the twelfth floor, adrenaline was the only thing keeping him going. DS Stokes was on the landing, shouting a warning into the flat. He didn't wait for a response or Roj, who barely had time or the breath to utter an expletive, or to remind DS Stokes how many protocols they were breaking. But when he dashed after his sergeant and entered the flat, he found Kenny slumped to his knees in the doorway. The noise coming from him didn't sound human.

When he was thirteen, Roj and his older brother Manni had found a cat in the yard around the back of their uncle's restaurant. It must have eaten the poison put down for the rats, or eaten the rats laced with the toxin, because it lay on its side making the most piteous sound that was a mix of excruciating agony and mournful lamentation. Roj put his hands to his ears while Manni, ever the more physical brother, hefted a spare paving slab propped against the back wall and used it to put the animal out of its misery. With a crunch, the sounds of agony stopped, and Roj had heard nothing like it again until now.

Both hands on his pistol, Roj raised it and crept towards Kenny. 'Sarg, can you tell me if the room is clear?' It was a blunt question, but he used it as much to appeal to the professional mind of his senior officer in hopes of calling him back from his despondent state.

Roj reached the door and kept the wall as cover. 'Sarg? Kenny?' There was no response except for his inconsolable keening. Speaking into his cuff, Roj called in their location and status as having entered the flat and that there were possible hostiles. With a quick dip of his head around the door frame, Roj caught a snapshot of the scene. He tried to understand what his eyes had taken in but couldn't be sure. With wan horror, he tried to pull apart the facts and images of the historic crime scene of Mary Jane Kelly's murder at 13 Miller's Court and this new murder scene in flat thirteen on the twelfth floor of Renfield Tower.

He needed to confirm what he'd seen, including that there was no threat. Roj pivoted into a firing stance behind Kenny, and after a second, lowered his gun and struggled to hold down his gorge.

Those old crime scene photographs were black and white. This one was similar in so many ways, with a female, legs splayed upon the sofa, and a mutilation just as malicious and extensive. But red was the colour here. It painted the walls, the ceiling, and the sofa. It sprayed ornaments and an ashtray, and it dappled the brown skin of the victim, whose face was, well, not a face at all anymore. Despite the impossible quantities of blood, Roj could tell, even the victim's coat was red. Like some hellacious marital bed, she lay cut open upon it with her legs of ragged sinew and bone spread apart, her own organs forming a pillow for her tortured repose.

MEMENTO MORI

"I am in blood
Stepped in so far that, should I wade no more,
Returning were as tedious as go o'er."
— William Shakespeare, *Macbeth*

49

TINDERBOX

KENNY KNEW the world carried on turning around him. They'd wrapped him in a foil blanket and sat him on the bumper of an ambulance with a cup of something hot in his hand. The full force of the London Metropolitan police force and emergency services were on display. Too little, too late. Like bag checks the week after a passenger jet explodes. Move along, everything is alright here. Control has been restored. There is nothing to worry about. Carry on with your lives. But Kenny had been sucked out of the fuselage and was in free fall. There was no longer any need for a seat belt. No need to take out his earphones so he could take part in the hymnal of safety exits, stowed tray tables, and an under chair life vest.

Roj remained with him until he was called away. 'I'll deal with everything,' he said. Kenny knew he wouldn't. How could he? Even Kenny had been playing catch-up. Even he had ignored what Reverend Adekugbe had tried to tell him, and now Trinity and Misha, his perfect Misha, were dead and defiled. The boy's house contained the same clue, twelfth floor, flat thirteen. The number twenty-five. What it meant exactly, Kenny hadn't worked out yet, but it wasn't a coincidence.

Even in the depths of grief, his detective's mind couldn't turn off.

The rain had let up to a fine drizzle and, as the night drew out, it grew bitter. Officers were going door to door asking questions, looking for witnesses. The estate was being cordoned off. Searches were being organised. Forensics had started processing the crime scene. Too little, too late.

An armed response BMW X5 was parked across from the ambulance. Its boot lay open. An officer Kenny didn't know, dressed in full fatigues and body armour, took off his HK G36 and began securing it when he was interrupted.

A shout came from another officer on the other side of the BMW. 'Kev, who've we got on patrol and who's running searches?'

Kev put down his machine gun and went to the front of the BMW. It was a break in protocol, but the area was in a tight lockdown, and he would only be away for half a minute at most.

Kenny left his foil blanket on the back of the ambulance with his paper cup and walked to the back of the armed response vehicle. He slid the machine gun under his trench coat, pocketed two extra thirty round magazines, and walked away through the bustle of activity. A couple of flashes of ID, and Renfield Town was far behind him, although he thought if he survived what lay ahead, the hell of that place would be with him forever.

VISITING hours had long since passed, but Abigail stood at the window of her son's hospital room, looking over her memories more than the city of twinkling lights. A nurse had recently come to the door. She was a Philipino girl named Mary who sent money home on the twenty-eighth of every month and wished she could bring her husband and two children to London. Mary held her hand over the door handle. She had the strangest of unshakeable notions that the handle was angry and hot, but before she could interrogate the queer feeling, she was overcome with a profound sense of guilt. Her youngest child, Adam, came from an affair back home with a doctor in Quezon City. It was a secret she had told to no one. Not even the doctor knew the child was his, and London was her penitence. Overdue a break, Mary hurried to the bathroom to dry her eyes.

In Samuel's room, Abigail stared at her open hand. In her palm danced a ball of flames, gliding over her skin and flickering with images she'd also fled to England to escape.

Charles walked away from her down the aisle of their church, a crucifix in one hand, a sword in the other. The abominations screeched and bayed outside, wearing down their holy walls. Samuel cried in her arms, and she rocked him harder than she should. At the door, Charles looked back at her with a wan smile. He turned away and flung open the church doors, and, crucifix held before him and sword raised, he stepped into the fray. Unable to hold herself back, Abigail placed Samuel on the floorboards with a prayer and ran to her husband, but the doors slammed shut before she could reach him.

'Mum?'

Abigail closed her hand on the flames, snuffing them out. She went to Samuel's bedside and fussed over his blankets.

'You're still here.' Samuel said the words brightly enough, but Abigail felt the weight of their accusation.

'I won't leave my boy.'

'What about Dylan?'

'I've told you, the police are dealing with it.'

'You're a terrible liar. Worse than me.' She would have admonished him for questioning his elders, but his words were gilded with truth.

'I don't know what you mean.'

With effort, Samuel shuffled into a sitting position. 'The only thing you're worse at than lying is keeping your voice down. I heard you in the corridor. Half the ward did. They probably think you're a lunatic.'

'Samuel!'

But his cheeky grin had already disarmed her. 'I know you think you are protecting me by not telling me stuff. I get it. I'm just a kid, but so is Dylan, and he doesn't have a mum like you.'

'Donna is a good woman. She only needs a little help.'

The look in his eyes made Abigail wonder if he had a gift like hers. She had never sensed it before and never spoken of her gifts, as Samuel said, to protect him. Gifts always came at a cost.

'That's not what I meant. You know I have dreams sometimes about Nigeria.' He took her hand in his, turning it over.

'Really? What do you dream about?'

Samuel didn't say anything; instead, he blew gently on the palm of his mother's hand. A tiny ember glowed like a beating heart, then it caught light, kindling into a flame and then a small crackling blaze. The fire was set.

50

GRAVE MAN

HEAD TILTED BACK, mouth agape, Alan Bestwick snorted and woke himself up. He blinked away sleep and found he was sitting in his office at school. It wasn't the first time. More than once he had slept the whole night and only roused when the caretakers opened the school before the inmates arrived.

Congealed spit lacquered his mouth and teeth. A good mug of freshly brewed coffee would wash away the funk—a nutty Italian affair for the morning, *Segafredo* or *Bei and Nannini*. Standing up, he realised it wasn't morning, not even close. A quick glance at the clock on the wall showed it was nearing midnight. Early enough to justify going home, but late enough that the bus ride would be a gamut of wastrels and ne'er-do-wells. Oh, how he'd like to slap their benighted faces with those words.

At the unmistakable sound of footsteps, Alan jolted his head to the corridor. Could someone else be working this late? There was a flutter in his belly with the thought that Misha Stokes had returned, perhaps after a fight with her husband, but he quickly drowned the notion in a cold bucket of reality. She was out of his league—for now. It was possible that another member of staff had come back to school, but highly unlikely. Teaching these—he corrected himself —*policing* these delinquents in preparation for their future roles as societal parasites—another most excellent choice of verbiage—did so take its pound of flesh. Mixed metaphors aside, did that cast Alan as Shylock in this whimsical self-badinage? In which case, who was playing Portia? Misha? He scoffed at himself. A Moor in Venice! This wasn't *Othello*. One shouldn't mix plays and metaphors. Alan doubted if there was a year ten pupil capable of mixing anything beyond drinks and bodily fluids.

A door closed, and the emptiness of the school magnified the sound. Alan sprung up, and for the briefest of moments, he was every bit a lonely sentry on a frontier outpost and chided himself for it. This was his school, and some spotty-oik with chlamydia and a swagger from listening to too much American hip-hop wasn't going to intimidate him.

All the same, he stepped gingerly into the hall. Left and right was nothing but a thoroughfare of educational grade vinyl tiling, so old it probably contained asbestos beneath the grimy patina formed from the downtrodden souls of countless teaching professionals. There was the unmistakable scrape of a chair across a classroom floor, and a Gilbert and Sullivan tune came to mind. Alan muttered it to himself while he soft-shoed his reconnoitre, trying to tell himself he was braver than he was.

'I am the very model of a modern Major-General,
I've information vegetable, animal, and mineral,
I know the kings of England, and I quote the fights historical
From Marathon to Waterloo, in order categorical.'

Viewed through the panopticon of paper thin glass, each class-room was the model of perfection. There were no children in them. Only chairs stood atop desks, all in neat rows of absolute silence.

'O Captain! My Captain,' Bestwick sniffed, not at Walt Whitman, but the movie that made so valorous the teacher's lot. Indeed, a thing of life and death. He replied to himself more darkly, 'My Captain does not answer, his lips are pale and still,' and rubbed the hackles from the back of his neck.

At the end of the corridor was the Mathematics Department—or "paint by numbers", as Alan liked to think of it. That would be finger painting, of course. Brushes were beyond them. They could barely oppose their thumbs, and if they did, it would be in a street fight over a pair of trainers or mating rights. As Fagin would a silk hanky, he mentally pocketed the pun.

Reaching the final two classrooms flanking the corridor, Alan was about to turn heel and check the other direction when he glimpsed something amiss through the legs of the desktopped chairs. At the head of the class, a figure sat in Misha's chair. He crept forward. Was it her sitting in the dark? He thought not, but had to be sure, crouching to see through to the teacher's desk. The sight was perhaps even better than if Misha had been there, though a different type of delectation to be sure.

So as not to be overheard, Alan retreated back up the corridor and pulled out his phone.

'Hello. Yes. Police, please. There is a break in at Mary-le Bow Comprehensive, and I think it's the boy the police are looking for.' Alan told them everything in hushed tones, and in turn they told him to lock himself in his office until they got there. He lied and said that he would, but he wasn't going to miss out on a front row seat.

Creeping back down to Misha's classroom, he made it all the way to the door. Dylan was rifling through the pages of a book, far too fast to be able to take anything in. Perhaps he was looking for something or idly passing the time before he set to vandalising the place. Alan thought he would record the vandal in the act and readied his phone. As he knew he would, Dylan then got up. But instead of ripping the book or flipping over the desk, the boy turned to the blackboard. Most schools had whiteboards, but the 21st century hadn't reached as far as Mary-le Bow. Pilfering a stubby piece of chalk, Dylan began to draw on the board. Alan was about to hit record, expecting to capture the classic teenage rendering of a phallus and testicles, no doubt replete with splurging ejaculate, when he held off. Dylan worked quickly, drawing overlapping circles in sweeping arcs of his arm before scribbling furiously, marking the board with equations. He looked back at the book in his hand, tilted his head, then shook it scornfully and returned to the board with more urgency. Next to the Venn-like diagrams, he wrote out a long equation of algebraic letters, mixed with other symbols.

Alan ground his teeth. This was even worse than vandalism, and he felt a spike of petty triumph when Dylan faltered, his chalk freckling the board with uncertain dots. The boy stepped away, tracing back through his work, trying to find his mistake.

This was Alan's moment. Over a long and arduous career, he had cultivated an acute sense of timing in these matters. Now was the perfect opportunity to undermine the boy, to pull him down so that he could accept his underachievement. What was the Bard's exact phrasing?

Alan yelped when a massive hand clamped his shoulder. The sardonic answer to his question sounded in Alan's head.

I must be cruel only to be kind. Thus bad begins and worse remains behind.

DYLAN DROPPED THE BOOK, and it slapped face down. Man-handled by the scruff of his sports jacket, Mr Bestwick stumbled in, followed by Mr Butcher, who held the teacher's collar. Lastly, Vieil glided into the room. Dylan could smell the blood on them. The sleeves of Mr Butcher's shirt were stained pink, and his face was smattered with red spots. Over his shoulder was a black bin bag bulging with awkward lumps. And while Vieil's face was clean, his herringbone shirt was as red as Mr Butcher's sleeves, and his normally perfect silk necktie was wrinkling as it dried.

'What's the meaning of this?' Mr Bestwick blustered, struggling ineffectually in Mr Butcher's grip. 'Are you the police? I'm a teacher at this school.'

'Let us not stretch the truth, Alan. You've barely taught anyone since your probationary year. Now do be quiet. Dylan, this... place,' Vieil said rubbing together his thumb and forefinger as if he had picked up something grubby, 'was a little predictable, if you were really trying to hide.'

'You know this boy?' Mr Bestwick spat.

Vieil sighed. 'Mr Butcher, if you will?'

Spun around by shovel-sized hands, Alan stiffened before Mr

Butcher's grinning face, who wasted no time in forcibly headbutting Mr Bestwick on the bridge of his nose. Blood pouring out, Bestwick fell back and landed at Dylan's feet. The smell was intoxicating. Dylan bit down on his growing fangs, wishing them to remain sheathed. His talons lengthened, cutting into the palms of his clenched fists, and he dropped the chalk.

Child-like, Alan wailed, 'You broke my nose!'

Vieil dismissed him with a wave of his hand. 'Shut up and bleed, little man. The end of your life will serve a loftier purpose.' Vieil stood over the bleeding teacher and assessed the blackboard. He took another piece of chalk from the dusty narrow shelf at the bottom of the board and made corrections, rubbing out letters and numbers and scribbling in new ones. He moved brackets and added additional ones populated with more equations. Mr Bestwick continued to bleed, tantalisingly. Finished off, Vieil amended the Venn-like diagrams of ovals and circles, replaced the chalk, and turned to Dylan.

Eyes dancing over the missing pieces of the puzzle, the proof appeared complete. The change Vieil had put him through had not only given him incredible physical gifts but mental ones too. He had come back to school looking for a shred of comfort and found the books Mrs Stokes had meant for him. They would have previously been only to inspire him, but now he could not only follow the mathematics but see the errors of their thinking. Even so, the P versus NP problem he had chosen to solve had seemed in his grasp, but in the end it had eluded him. Vieil had solved one of the seven millennium problems outlined in Mrs Stokes' book like it was as basic as multiplication.

'Don't feel bad. I see you did not partake of Chantel. He is a sentimental one, is he not, Mr Butcher?'

Mr Butcher glowered with a twitch of his moustache.

'If you had done as we suggested, this would have been a bagatelle. You would have seen so much more. Your talents will be so much greater, my boy.'

'I'm not your boy,' Dylan slurred.

Mr Butcher took a menacing stride forward, but Vieil stayed his attendant with a raised finger. 'Oh, but you are, Dylan. You are mine and I am yours. We are joined by forces far stronger than the circumstantial convenience of friendships or the coital accidents of family. Fate, the mathematics of the universe, the will of the Great Architect, these are what bind us together. It is stronger than atomic bonds, more pervasive than the field of dark matter, and more compelling than gravity. I know you can see that, and your will to fight it is why I chose you. It is why you chose Chantel. But now is the time to claim what is yours and become everything I know you can be. This,' he pointed at the blackboard, 'is nothing. It is beneath you.'

Vieil grabbed Mr Bestwick by his greasy hair and hoisted him effortlessly to his feet. Fear glistened in the teacher's eyes, but his usual sarcastic mouth hung open. 'I'll make it easy for you.' Vieil pointed his index finger. Its pale and slender form gnarled and lengthened, and he placed its sharpened tip on Mr Bestwick's neck. He drew this talon across the skin and opened up a neat slit, which turned into a bulging red globule that bulged and then trickled down the teacher's neck.

Dylan flinched away.

Vieil offered the teacher like a textbook to an obstinate child. 'Here, read him. See what he thinks of you, as if you didn't already know. Feast on his intricacies and know the mysteries of the universe.'

The blood dripped and Dylan hissed.

Yesh, you see. A smirk of satisfaction quirked on Vieil's thin lips. He let go of Mr Bestwick, but before he could hit the floor, Dylan caught him, his profusion of fangs bared, puncturing the teacher's neck.

The rush of hot blood nourished Dylan's injuries. The pain and hunger ebbed, and through the pulsing beats of Alan Bestwick's poisoned heart, Dylan was travelling without moving, surging along subatomic networks, dancing in the molten hearts of stars, diving through giant gas nebulas. Galaxy upon galaxy spun, each with a black hole at their dark heart, glistening pearls containing untold riches. Alluring, beguiling, irresistible. He let himself be drawn to one of those black hearts in a dying galaxy at the edge of the universe.

There was a thing lurking there, old beyond imagination, looking out from the neverwhere beyond space and time. A monster? A god? Another universe not of matter but pure intelligence, a place of infinite truth and knowledge? It was so close. He only needed to let himself be inhaled.

A tug came at Dylan's back. Wanting to stay and to know, he resisted. He was yanked back, as if on a rubber cord, speeding away from the black hole back through the universe, and snapping back into his own body. Vieil prised him from Bestwick's neck, the jugular vein spraying the blackboard. Beams of light danced across the corridor windows. Mr Butcher faced the door, black sack slung over one shoulder, and his bronze khopesh in the other hand.

No, Vieil ordered. *We've drawn enough attention, and the night grows short.*

ALAN BESTWICK WAS aware of a window smashing even though his head was woozy and his body felt numb. He was slumped against the wall under the blackboard as beams of light cut in different directions and converged on him. Voices shouted. Someone in a black mask fell upon him and seemed to be trying to choke him. A little sensation came back to one hand, and Alan tried to protect himself, but all he could manage was a limp wave. His lips and tongue were rubbery and disobedient.

'Don't worry, mate. I've got you. It's going to be alright. Hold on, okay?' the black masked man said while other men shouted orders.

He was a police officer, Alan realised, and tried to say, 'Ask for me tomorrow, and you shall find me a grave man.' Instead, like his career, it ended up being an inconsequential jumble that no one else seemed to understand.

51

PARK BENCH

THE COP SAT on the park bench. Henry watched him wandering around Gallows Court like one sketchy motherfucker. It was that DI Stokes, the fed who'd pulled him in over Annie Drew's murder. Stokes was looking for something and growing more and more frustrated as the night wore on. Not only that, but whenever the pigs were about to roll through in a patrol car, Stokes would magically disappear, until Henry realised he was listening to his Airway, the same way Henry monitored the police scanner in his duffle bag.

The scanner was how he'd found Dylan. The boy was in trouble so Henry doubted he would be able to stay off the filth's radar. When the call came in, Henry wasn't too far from the school and high-tailed it there, sneaking down back alleys and over walls. Panting to catch his breath, when he got there he hung back while the pigs piled in, all tooled up and in formation. He didn't need to wait for them to clear out. Skirting around the back and ducking behind an abandoned Ford Escort, with two flat tyres and a yellow clap, what he saw only confirmed the impossibility of what had happened in the flat.

A window shattered and three figures materialised, yeah that was the right word, the motherfuckers *appeared* out of thin air. Then in a blur they were gone. Henry set off after them with his best guess as to their direction. He caught one more glimpse of the trio before he lost them near Gallows Court, only to come across DI Stokes. It seemed like too much of a coincidence, and as Stokes was probably looking for Dylan too, Henry watched the watchman, and waited.

As the aching blue of dawn seeped through creases in the sullen clouds, Stokes seemed beaten and dog-tired. He pulled his sorry looking ass away from his strange frustration at the fried chicken shop and sat down on a bench, which squatted in the park's interior, overlooking the main road. Stokes was as soaked through as Henry was, crouched in the doorway. The cop sat there, shivering, never taking his eyes off the row of shops. All the Duppies and Bluds had gone to ground, presumably because of what went down at Renfield Tower. Henry had heard it on the scanner and knew it was Donna's flat, but whatever it was, he couldn't do any good going back there. There was no going back. Whatever it took, he'd see it through.

By the time the traffic thickened and the streetlights flickered off, Henry muttered 'Fuck it,' and came out of the shadows.

'What's a cop doing hiding from other cops?' Henry sat down on the other side of the bench.

Stokes didn't look surprised to see him, but he was tense. Henry already had his sawn-off pointing at the detective across his lap. Stokes half-smiled, half-sneered and tapped the machine gun pointing at Henry. 'I'm looking for something. Wondered how long it would take you to come over.'

Henry sucked his gold teeth and leaned back, splaying his legs. 'Ha! Nice one, bruv. Doesn't answer my question, though, does it?'

'Guess not.' Stokes kept his sights on the main road.

Henry looked that way too, though with one eye swollen to a slit, his depth perception was a little off, giving the world a flattened unreality. Seems like yous are looking for something. They do good fried chicken, bruv, if you want some breakfast. Local peelers always drop in for morning hot wings and an energy drink. You should go say hello.'

Stokes snorted something that might have been a laugh. 'After you.'

'Fuck sake, blud, are you dumb as shit or what?'

Henry's outburst managed to draw Stokes' attention, and he adjusted his grip on the machine gun. 'I'm not really in the mood. Piss off, will you?'

'Didn't it even cross your mind we might be after the same ting, bruv?'

'You couldn't fathom what I want.'

'Is that right, bruv? I wouldn't know anything about revenge, wouldn't know that mad dog stare you got going on, with your stolen police issue machine gun under your coat.'

Stokes ignored him and turned his attention back to the main road.

'Nah, mate, I wouldn't know anything about Dylan and his freaky powers. I wouldn't know anything about the two weird-as-fuck, Bell-gravier looking ponces. Smart suits. Bowler hat. Ah, got your attention now, bruv.'

With a whip of his head, Stokes brought up his machine gun, his face contorted with pure rage.

Henry reciprocated and cocked the second barrel of his shotgun. 'You wanna end it here, dickhead? Come on then, blud, let's do it.'

'You two will put those guns down this second.'

The sudden, unexpected interjection unsteadied both men's resolve. They twisted on the bench to see who was telling them off as if they were puffing themselves up prior to a playground scuffle. The Reverend Abigail Adekugbe, wrapped up in a heavy coat, woolly hat on head, and hands on hips, scowled down at them with her uneven stare. She strode around the bench and inserted her ample backside between the two men, who both hid their guns: Stokes under his coat; Henry in the duffle bag on his lap.

'We don't have time for petty nonsense. We are all here for the same reason. It is time to work together.'

Stokes bristled. 'You said I'd find the answers at number 25 Gallows Court.'

'And you will.'

'It doesn't bloody exist.' Stokes was shaking, and not just with the cold.

Abigail took his hand, and then, to Henry's surprise, she took his as well. Her grip radiated heat, and Henry nearly pulled away, but then found its warmth on that bitterly cold morning welcome. He couldn't remember the last time he'd held someone's hand.

'It very much exists. But I think by the time this is over, we will wish that it didn't.'

52

BLACK DOOR

THEY COVERED a lot of ground on that bench. Under the holy woman's touch, they found what led each of them there, locking together pieces of a puzzle previously scattered and lost in the clutter of their separate lives. Kenny wept, letting go of his vengeance, when Abigail asked him without speaking, *What would Misha have wanted you to do?* He'd wanted to kill Dylan for leading his wife to her death. But seeing what they had seen, he knew that the boy wasn't the one who did it. The true identity of the perpetrators, however, remained beyond any of their experiences or perceptions.

Shame was Abigail's mental confession. Kenny saw that she wanted to hide from the evil to protect her son, and that same son reminded her who she was supposed to be, showing her that the choice wasn't hers to make. There were many things he couldn't fathom about this woman, things that she didn't want him to know about her past. It would have to be enough. She understood the most, and her clairvoyant abilities were far beyond Kenny's. Finally, Henry Grime's sin within his many sins completed their trinity.

'Son?' Kenny said as they surfaced from the meeting of their minds, his voice still gruff with emotion.

Henry nodded curtly.

Abigail continued to hold their hands. 'Now look. There, between the charity shop and the takeaway. In plain sight.'

'I don't see nothing,' Henry said.

She squeezed their hands. 'It doesn't want you to see it, and a piece of you doesn't want to see either. Look again. Look for the thing trying to hide. Face it like you faced the worst part of yourself. It skulks in that same place.'

'Bugger me!' Henry murmured.

'Don't swear.'

'Sorry, but I see it.' Henry's eyes were wide in revelation.

Kenny could see it too. The Victorian townhouse nestled in the row of modern shops. Spread over three floors, the sash windows gave the house the appearance of a spider. Squatting behind a web of iron railings, it looked out over the park. Its door, shining with new paint, was a black mouth yawning wide, ready and waiting for unlucky flies.

'Detective?'

Kenny nodded, his face hard and unflinching. 'I hear it too. It's hissing and whispering.'

'So what's the plan? We've got a plan, right?' Henry turned to them. 'What are we talking about here? I think I know, but no one has said it. It's vampires, right?'

'I don't think one of them is a...' Kenny still found it hard to say but it was harder to deny, 'a vampire. What I've seen is a dog, and the killings were done with an ancient Egyptian bronze sword called a khopesh. I've never heard that in a vampire story.'

'Vampires can change into other animals, right?' Henry said, looking for confirmation from the other two.

'I don't know,' Abigail said.

'Great! I thought you were the expert? So, what are we dealing with, a vampire and his pet werewolf? And what kills them, because I didn't bring any silver or garlic.'

Kenny had to admit it, Grime had a good point. Events had brought them together and thrust them into the fray, but how prepared were they? 'I've got ninety-nine rounds for the machine gun, plus my sidearm, with two spare clips.'

'And I've got a knife, four cartridges for the sawn-off, a pair of knuckle dusters, and a mouthful of bad language.'

'Sticks and stones,' Kenny said.

'My point exactly,' Henry agreed.

Abigail let out a long, slow breath. 'There are many demons on this Earth. I have seen others, but never these. I have some holy water.' She produced a small bottle from her coat. 'But we have been brought together for a reason, and if we are to stand a chance, we must work together. *We* are all that we need. *We* are the Lord's weapons. "Blessed is he who, in the name of charity and good will, Shepherds the weak through the valley of darkness; For he is truly his brother's keeper and the finder of lost children; And I will strike down upon thee with great vengeance and furious anger those who attempt to poison and destroy my brothers; And you will know my name is the Lord when I lay my vengeance upon thee."'

'Did she just quote Tarantino?' Henry said.

Kenny nodded. 'Yep, she did.'

'What are you two talking about? The Lord has given us the tools we need to defeat these demons. We must trust in him and ourselves and enter the den of the beast. I don't know that Dylan can be saved, but we must try.' Abigail stood letting go of their hands, and they followed her up.

Henry slung his bag across his body. 'But I still don't f—' He corrected himself for the benefit of the vicar. 'I still don't get what they are. They looked like two rich geezas to me, or one rich geeza and his gnarly butler.'

'Shall we find out?' Abigail set off over the sodden grass of the park.

Henry gave Kenny a look. 'After you.'

'You're okay, I think I'll keep you in front of me.'

Henry flashed his gold teeth and started walking after Abigail and threw back, 'And there was me thinking yous was fam now.'

Kenny fell in behind and to the side. 'How was your last family Christmas?'

Henry's laugh had a tinge of genuine amusement. 'Good point, bruv. Nice to know we've got each other's backs.'

'You don't have to worry about me.'

'I ain't worried about you, bruv.'

The three of them crossed the road, and side by side, they looked up at the house. Drizzle beaded on Abigail's woolly hat, and their breath frosted, while early morning commuters on foot wove around them. Like clots in an artery, traffic stop-started along the road.

Henry looked down at his feet. 'Is it just me? I don't want to move.'

Kenny's legs felt as though they were growing roots. 'Same here.'

'Nothing will be easy from here on.' Abigail took their hands once more. A man in a beanie hat speaking on his phone rubbernecked at the odd sight. The three strange people stepped through the railings, and the man blinked, pausing his conversation mid-sentence. A mousy looking woman opened up the charity shop from the inside, and as if this explained what he saw, the man shrugged and continued with his day.

The hubbub of the city dampened down into a muffled chatter and hum. Kenny put a hand to his ear.

Abigail gently pulled down his hand. 'Try to focus on us.'

'The dead are so loud here. I looked up and down this street a hundred times and didn't hear them.'

'The viper only hisses when you step on his tail,' Abigail said.

Henry raised his eyebrows, but given everything else he'd seen and experienced in the last few hours, including some of what Kenny had let him see, he seemed to accept it as a part of his new reality. The veil had been pulled back, and Henry was a man apparently able to adapt to his new environment. Kenny guessed he had practice, living as he did in the cracks of civilised society.

Abigail approached the door up the short flight of steps. 'The living, the dead: we all make too much noise. Most people perceive less than they see or hear. Your mother is why you focus on one side of your gift more than the other. But you know how to read the living. Listen to us. Listen to the song of our lives.'

Kenny understood and steeled himself.

Abigail placed her palm on the black door, and the reaction was instantaneous. It started with a growl that was all too familiar to Kenny. Deep and rumbling, the growl blistered into savage barks, snapping against the back of the door. She began to murmur, and Kenny listened with both his ears and his mind. It was a psalm. He didn't recognise it, having given up on his mother's Catholic church after she had given up on life.

"The Lord is my light and my salvation—
whom shall I fear?
The Lord is the stronghold of my life—
of whom shall I be afraid?"

The dog struck the door, making it judder in its frame. The steps shook under their feet, and Kenny reached for the iron balustrade to steady himself. Abigail lifted her incantation to the level of her speaking voice.

"When the wicked advance against me
to devour me,
it is my enemies and my foes
who will stumble and fall."

The hound's rage grew into a tumult. It threw itself again and again against the door. Henry Grime looked around, and, seeing that they weren't drawing attention, pulled his sawn-off from his bag. Kenny did the same with his HK machine gun. Their eyes met, and Kenny gestured with his own gun for Henry to lower the barrel to the ground. Accidently shooting the Reverend probably wasn't the best way to start their misadventure. The gangsta understood and copied Kenny. The door seemed like it would splinter any second. Kenny readied to grab hold of Abigail should that happen. She raised her voice to a commanding call, not quite a shout.

"Though an army besiege me,
my heart will not fear;
though war break out against me,
even then I will be confident."

The assault of the dog ceased, but the rabid barking continued. Abigail shouted in the trembling timbre of a revivalist preacher:

"One thing I ask from the Lord,
this only do I seek:
that I may dwell in the house of the Lord
all the days of my life,

to gaze on the beauty of the Lord
and to seek him in his temple."

The barking tempered into a growl, and the tempest grumbled a sullen retreat. In the lull, Abigail seized the handle. The hiss of whispers flared in Kenny's mind. The door was locked and wouldn't budge. Abigail let go, and the whispers faded to a sussurant chatter.

'Mind if I have a go, Rev?' Henry holstered his shotgun in the duffle bag and got down on his knees before the door.

'Didn't have you pegged as the praying kind,' Kenny said.

'Never had a need for it.' Henry rummaged around the contents of his bag. 'God don't live in Whitechapel.' He gave Abigail an apologetic look. 'Sorry, Rev.'

She clucked her tongue. 'He's right; he doesn't.'

Henry produced a canvas roll and unfurled it, laying it out on the stone step. He inspected the lock quickly and unthreaded three long, thin tools from his kit. He put one in his mouth while he inserted the other two and felt around. When he positioned them to his satisfaction, he took the third lockpicking tool from his mouth and began to work the lock.

The whispers whipped up once more into great waves crashing on the shores of Kenny's mind. The door didn't bang and rattle this time, it trembled. Henry tightened his grip on his tools, sticking his tongue out as he tilted his head to the side feeling the lock. The trembling grew to a seizure, and the whole house shook. Masonry dust rained down.

'Shit!' Henry's grip slipped on one of the tools, and it tinkled on the stone step.

Abigail snached it up and handed it back. 'Hurry.'

'You can't rush a lock,' Henry said, reinserting the metal probe.

'You've really got to hurry.' Kenny felt the hackles bristle on his neck. 'Look out.' He pushed Abigail to the side, and they backed against the iron railing as a tile careened toward her, smashing where she'd just been standing.

It didn't phase Henry. He worked the lock even as the paint on the door started to melt and run in a black, hemorrhagic flow that oozed over his hands and dripped out of the brass letterbox, pooling like tar on the top step. Henry grunted in pain. 'Nearly got it. Be ready, Stokes.'

Kenny got behind Grime, secured the stock in his shoulder and flicked the rifle into semi-automatic. Thick, black liquid dripped onto the next step. Another tile fell and broke its back over the banister, showering Henry with ceramic shards.

'Fuck you,' Grime whispered. The lock clicked, the door relaxed in its frame, but it stayed shut.

The whispers were angrier than ever. More dust fell and the steps vibrated. Kenny felt for Abigail with his mind: the nutmeg and thyme and that same note he'd heard in the hospital that was like a bright light. Henry was tobacco smoke and vinegar and sandpaper, callous on the side everyone could see. 'What now?' Kenny shouted.

'Only mugs have one lock.' Henry grimaced as he hauled himself up and produced a length of thick wire from his bag that might once have been a coat hanger. He stood and inserted it into the door at shoulder level. In a swift series of movements, he lifted the wire, found what he was looking for, and waggled the wire some more. A bolt unlatched. Dropping back to his knees in the black tar, Henry did the same at the bottom of the door. 'Nearly there.'

Kenny noticed his shoes smoking in the tar. Abigail's were too. The tar was all over Henry's hands. 'The tar is burning.'

'Tell me about it,' Henry growled through gritted teeth. 'Nearly... got... it...'

Kenny aimed his machine gun at the door above Henry's head.

The second bolt gave way. The whispers receded to a disgruntled chunter, and the door cracked ajar.

53

AHAB'S WHALE

THE CORRIDOR WAS IMPOSSIBLY LONG, stretching out in a dark tunnel ahead of them. Kenny went first, gun raised. Henry grunted in pain and fell against the wall. Abigail came last, immediately tending to Henry while Kenny swung his sights across shadows, looking for the dog.

'Hold still,' Abigail said, producing a bottle from her pocket and sprinkling a few drops on the tar on Henry's hands. It sizzled, evaporating into an acrid smoke. 'Holy water,' Abigail said, by way of explanation. Baring his gold teeth, Henry turned over his hands, inspecting the raw, peeling skin. Swallowing hard, he made fists and screwed up his eyes. Abigail left him slumped against the wall. 'Inspector, wait.' She doused Kenny and her own shoes, as well as Henry's knees where the tar had already eaten through his jeans. By the time she'd finished, the small, plastic bottle of holy water was almost empty.

With shaking hands, Henry rearmed himself with the shotgun and pushed to his feet. 'Got any more of that?'

'No, I have not.' But Abigail produced a crucifix from her pocket.

Kenny backtracked to them and glanced from the dark corridor ahead of them down to Henry's ruined hands. 'Are you okay to go?'

Henry bounced Kenny's early comment back to him. 'You don't need to worry about me.'

Kenny crab-stepped down the corridor, with Henry Grime following behind. He didn't like having the gangster behind him, but Grime was the one who'd got them inside.

'Holy water and crosses: we're in a horror movie now,' Henry said.

The door slammed and Kenny stopped. Abigail was marching away from the door, woolly hat still on her head, armed with her crucifix and the last drops of holy water. The red runner down the middle of the hall was opulent and thick underfoot, enveloping Kenny's every step. Abigail helped Henry to his feet.

Behind the constant chatter of disembodied voices, just beyond Kenny's grasp, gas lamps hissed softly on the luxuriously wallpapered walls. The lamps lined the walls like torches in a tomb, jutting out between gilded paintings whose subjects were dark shapes trapped beneath centuries of dirt, almost black. They seemed to shuffle and follow Kenny through, tilting shadows cast by the gas flames. Ahead, several doors opened onto the corridor either side. At the end, there was perhaps a staircase, but it was too far away and too shrouded in gloom to tell. The corridor went on and on, impossibly so for a three-storey Victorian town house, luring them deeper.

The carpet began to squelch underfoot, infiltrating Kenny's shoes with a cold liquid. He froze, glancing down to see the carpet had changed. His feet were sinking into a stream of crimson, bubbling up between the floorboards as if they were stalking the deck of a floundering ship. Abigail supported Henry at the elbow as they splashed through the bloody stream, and mist began to slither its way down the walls, cloaking the ground around their feet. Henry battled with the pain of his hands, and their breath frosted on the air, fetid with a sweet copperiness. Kenny swung back around at the menacing rumble ahead of them.

From the nearest doorway, still some fifty or so yards away, padded the dog, huge and barrel-chested, yet sleek and sinuous at the waist and haunches. Its jowls pulled back from yellowed canines and pink gums in a mocking, menacing snarl. The hound lowered its head, glaring at Kenny with its empty black eyes.

Abigail was saying something, but Kenny couldn't hear it. His world narrowed to include only him and his monster, the beast he had been tracking, which had mocked him, always out of reach, and yet getting closer until it took his Misha. A blistering force, Kenny's anger roiled so hot it threatened to burn through the meagre fetters of self-control he had left. Where the dog went, its smirking master, with his khopesh and bowler hat, must go too. Kenny wanted revenge. Needed it. Misha was his everything, his solitude in a world of unquiet souls. The voices of the house chattered in excitement, waves slapping against the prow of a ship forging into the waiting storm. Ahab would have his whale. He would find and destroy whatever these men were and send them back to hell.

The massive hound, with a grace and speed that belied its size, turned amid the mist and bounded away. Kenny tracked and fired. The gun kicked. His aim was high and to the left. A plume of plaster dust exploded from the wall as the hind legs of the massive hound disappeared into eddies of fog.

'Wait,' Abigail called.

But Kenny was already at full clip, splashing through blood. The shape of the dog loomed in the mist ahead, only to dive deeper into the murk when Kenny loosed another volley. On and on the corridor went, until the foot of a grand, wooden staircase appeared out of the vapour. The dog, with its long snout and pointed ears, was sitting waiting for him on the first landing. Blood flowed down the steps. Kenny brought his eye to the sights, expecting the animal to leap at him. It didn't. Instead, it waited until it was in the crosshairs. In the time it took the tendons of Kenny's wrist to flex, the dog was gone, disappearing around the turn in the midlanding.

'Detective, wait.' The call was too far away to reach Kenny. The beast was getting away, probably heading to its master. Kenny would not be denied, and he leapt onto the stairs in pursuit.

54

FEED THE BIRDS

DYLAN HUNG UPSIDE DOWN in the dirty water of his cocoon, but his mind was elsewhere. Alan Bestwick had been the key to a door. A cypher unlocking deeper secrets. Dylan could have drunk until his malignant heart stopped beating, and it still wouldn't have been enough. Vieil had torn him away and back into the shell of his body. At least the blood had repaired him, taking away the pain, regrowing youthful skin and hair. He hated and loved Vieil for those things in equal measure.

Mr Butcher and Vieil had hurried them through the streets back to Gallows Court. Even when they shut the door behind them and they were in their inner sanctum, the coming sun was a stoking fire whose heat preceded the opening of dawn's furnace door. Many sunrises had accompanied Dylan's paper round, but he couldn't remember one of them. He'd taken them for granted, and now he would never see one again, and yet it was a small price to pay to be so close to the majestic intricacies of the universe. They fled the sun, travelling deep into the earth to their pyramid and to their Suhets. The sun was down. Their eyes were closed, and in his deep, blood-fuelled sleep, Dylan's mind was opened. He could travel further than ever before, deeper into the mathematical complexities of the universe. Now he knew what Vieil was looking for—that thing beyond complexity, mystery, and paradox. The thing that lay behind it all. The root, base, and propagator.

Vieil was a solitary hunter and an absent father in their psychonautic space. As they left their bodies, Vieil went his own way, his mind catapulting across the physical universe. Dylan didn't mind. The old man had delivered on his promise, and Dylan craved not only the answers but to find them for himself. He passed through gas giants and the fusion engines of stars' molten cores. Through twirling solar systems and galaxies, Dylan was drawn to one tinkling red light. Curious, he drew closer. It was a burgeoning galaxy, spilling out infrared light like a pulsing artery. He bathed in the crimson light, letting himself be seduced by the galaxy's dark heart. The gravidic forces pulled at him. He played with them, toying with resistance, as if swimming against an undertow before catching a wave's power to ride it to an inevitable and uncontrollable conclusion. Perhaps oblivion—but his adolescent mind thought not. The black hole seized hold of Dylan, and he surged toward its event horizon, where space and time compressed to an infinitesimal singularity. In that instant, that point of final existence, which was both ephemeral and eternal, Dylan realised his mistake. Vieil was never so foolish to look in such places. Whereas numbers governed the rest of the universe and were embodied in all energy and matter, because at the subatomic level there was no difference, at the event horizon the laws of the universe dissolved into paradox. A place without meaning. Without life. A dissolution...

DYLAN BLEW on his hands to warm them up and stuffed them in his pockets. Snow crunched under his feet. The distorted t-shaped pond that was the boating lake in Regent's Park had almost frozen over. Dylan could see it across the expanse of unblemished snowfall. Ducks paddled in a patch in the middle that must be shrinking imperceptibly smaller each second. The icy surface wore the puckering scars of geometric striations formed by the crystalline regularities of freezing water.

'I got the bread.' Samuel appeared at Dylan's side, carrying half a loaf in its plastic wrapper. His cherub face looked out from inside the fat hood of a puffer jacket, and with so many layers on, his arms could barely reach his sides.

'Shall we feed the ducks?' Chantel threaded her arm through Dylan's. In fingerless gloves and a short shirt, she didn't look warm enough. Her cheeks and the tip of her button nose were nipped pink by the cold. 'Your mum is meeting us down there.'

'I- okay.' Dylan felt lost. He had no memory of how he got there.

The snow wasn't that deep at first. They trudged through it, and Dylan's toes were soon numb. Samuel trotted along beside them. Chantel leaned into Dylan, pulling him along at the same time.

Samuel was struggling, as the snow he was trudging through now came up to his knees. 'I heard you're not supposed to feed the ducks. Makes their stomachs explode or something.'

'Is that right, Dylan?' Chantel asked.

'I don't know.'

'I thought you knew everything, darlin'? What's the square root of 7,391?'

Dylan answered reflexively. '85.970925.'

Chantel giggled. 'See? You do know everything.'

'But I don't know about ducks.'

As the snow crunched underfoot, Samuel huffed and puffed, wading through chest high powder, while Dylan and Chantel sank in no more than a few inches. 'Dylan, here. You better take the bread.'

Dylan stopped and crouched down, stretching out a hand to Samuel. 'I'll pull you out?'

'Why?' Samuel said. 'Take the bread.'

'But you're sinking.' Dylan looked to Chantel for help. She smiled down sweetly and shivered with her hands in her coat pockets.

'I'm not the one sinking, dude. I'm just walking in the snow with my best mate.' Samuel sunk up to his chin.

A crippling sense of guilt and loss washed over Dylan, and he shouted, 'Take my hand.'

'It's alright. The ducks are hungry,' Chantel said, as if nothing was wrong.

Samuel slipped below the snow. Dylan flung himself flat and reached for his friend down the hole. 'No!' he cried and caught hold of Samuel. But he was wrong. All he had was half a loaf of bread.

'There's your mum. Hey, Donna!' Chantel bounced on her tiptoes and waved enthusiastically.

Donna was sitting on a park bench in a cropped, faux-fur coat. She waved back with one hand and pulled on the cigarette she held in the other.

On his knees, cradling the loaf of bread, Dylan realised the hole in the snow had disappeared. 'I'm sorry,' he said to the patch of snow.

Chantel tapped him on the shoulder. 'Come on, silly. Your mum's waitin'.' She pulled him away, leading them over the snow-covered lawn. Quickly blowing out a lungful of smoke through the side of her mouth, Donna stood and threw her arms around Dylan and squeezed him tightly. It felt so good that it ached in Dylan's chest.

'Of course it feels good. Hugs are the best medicine,' Donna said as if she'd heard his thoughts. 'Oh, you brought the bread. You're a good boy.'

They sat down, Dylan between the two women. As he opened the bag and doled out three slices each, he felt guilty for not giving Samuel credit for bringing the bread. The pattern of three times three sparked a memory. Clicking on and off the hall light in search of something to hold on to, some piece of regularity in a chaotic world.

The ducks sensed the universe had provided them with a bonus meal, and five of them waddled over, quacking and fluffing their feathers. The three of them ripped off pieces and threw them to the birds, who quacked with excitement, pecked and gobbled. A few more ducks joined the party.

'This is nice, isn't it?' Donna said, looking happier than Dylan could ever remember.

Dylan grinned at two ducks arguing over a crumb. 'The best. I always wanted to do this.'

'Did you? You never said.'

Dylan didn't want to break the spell, so he said nothing about how Donna always had other things on her mind.

Chantel ran out of bread and brushed the crumbs off that had stuck to her fingerless gloves. She got up, causing some of the ducks to waddle away, bumping into the rest of the flock. 'You know,' she said looking to the sky, 'it looks like it's going to snow.'

'It's already snowed.' Dylan tossed another hunk of bread, and a plump mallard with lucent green plumage slipped and fell on its backside, quacking at the ignominy.

With an effervescent laugh, Chantel said, 'I told you, you know everything.'

Dylan was going to say that she was wrong and that he didn't know everything, but he wanted to. He wanted to know all the secrets of the universe like Vieil had promised, but with the memory of Vieil, Chantel was gone.

'This isn't real, is it?' Dylan stopped throwing bread to the ducks.

Donna juggled a slice of bread with her lighter and pack of fags as she lit another cigarette. 'Of course it's real.'

'You're not my mum.'

'Ah, well that's a different thing, innit, my darlin' boy?' Donna dropped the last of her bread at her feet so that the ducks waddled around her ankles.

'I'm not your boy either.'

Donna put an arm around Dylan and took a long, satisfying pull on her cigarette and blew a plume of smoke straight up in the air. 'I wouldn't say that; I wouldn't say that at all.'

'My mum would never do this with me.'

'Chantel was right: you must know everything.' Donna gave him a squeeze. 'Some people think that if the universe is infinite, and if it is, then it's a mathematical certainty that there are parallel universes where every possible alternative life is lived. Somewhere me and you feed the ducks all the time. Maybe we go for a big fry up beforehand, filling up on baked beans and sausages until we feel sick. Then we go window shopping on Regent Street and end up here with pieces of bread we wrapped up in napkins from the greasy spoon.'

Dylan sniffed back tears. 'That's a horrible thought.'

'Is it?' Thoughtfully, Donna blew out more smoke. 'Sounds nice to me. Hopeful. Like there's always a chance.'

'Not for me. It would be for some other version of me.' Dylan let the tears roll down his face, even though they stung as the streaks they left froze.

'You're right. I may not be your mum, but that doesn't mean she doesn't love you. And remember, Chantel was wrong: you don't know everything.' Donna planted a kiss on the top of Dylan's head. She smelled just like his mum, that mix of cigarettes and sweetish men's body spray. 'See, it's starting to snow.'

They looked up as plump snowflakes drifted lazily from the heavens. Donna held out her hand and caught a large, white flake. Its crystal structure refracted the sunlight into a billion pinprick sized rainbows. 'Here, this is for you.' Donna offered Dylan the snowflake. 'Come on, it's a present, for all the times I wasn't there for you.'

Dylan played along and opened his palm. She tipped the flake from her hand to his. 'Just remember that I do love you, and just because I wasn't there, doesn't mean I wasn't there.'

'That doesn't make any sense.' Dylan closed his hand around the snowflake.

Donna laughed as though Dylan had said something clever, and she was a proud mother. 'That's the funny thing about paradoxes, innit?'

55

EXSANGUINATED HUSKS

THE MACHINE GUN kicked into Kenny's shoulder. Bullets took chunks out of the wall, missing the hound once again as it darted around a corner at the end of another impossibly long corridor. The rifle ran dry, and Kenny slapped in the second of his three magazines and continued his pursuit.

Grecian statues lined the walls, hewn from marble or cast in bronze, tarnished a lustrous black with age. They gestured from their plinths, as if staying their silent warnings for a man who had no inclination to hear them. Instead, their shadows quivered in the fluttering gas light disturbed by Kenny's wake.

In case the giant dog was waiting to pounce when Kenny reached the turn, he ran wide to get a better angle and buy him a fraction of a second. Instead of finding the animal, there was another broad staircase, the fifth he'd encountered so far. The last two floors that should not have existed in a three-storey villa.

The dog had always been too far ahead, waiting for Kenny to catch up. He'd take aim and miss, and they'd be off again racing through corridors and room after room, most devoid of furniture, or, if they had any, they were draped in sheets forming a menagerie of ghosts. This new staircase descended towards more hissing gas lamps. He edged down the first rung, keeping the thick, polished banister close to his side. Each step peeled back only to show another of its kind, carpeted in the same lush red pile. Down and down he crept, tensing at the phantoms conjured by his mind from the darkness waiting between the lamps. At the foot of the stairs, nothing waited for him except towering oak panelled doors.

One lay ajar.

He reached for the brass knob as if it might be a poisonous snake, grasped it, and flung the door fully open. Slapping his hand back to the gunbarrel, he entered the room at speed, quickly panning left and right, and, disarmed by the size of the room, he panned up.

He was in a great library of three storeys, each double height. Balconies skirted the walls, every inch of which were packed with bound tomes and rolls of parchment, aromatic with the rich mustiness of paper, dust, and leather. Broad wooden tables, eight in all and each easily fifteen feet long, lay two by two between Kenny and the far end of the library. From the ceiling hung a spherical iron chandelier, more iron maiden than gilded cage. Wax dripped in heavy stalactites from its sputtering candles, and corresponding stalagmites piled on the floor and the central corners of the four middle tables.

Kenny caught a glimpse of movement along the one wall and didn't hesitate. Ancient books exploded in puffs of dust as the semi-automatic burst punctured them. The library ate the noise, sucking it into the pages of its endless rows of codices.

A section of shelving at the other end of the library swung into the room. Not wanting to expose both his flanks, Kenny ran down one side of the library. He was barely aware that his muscles burned and that he was panting. Sweat rolled from his brow. The metal of the gun rattled in quick time, bouncing against the buttons of his coat as he sprinted. Still two table-lengths away, the concealed door of books began to swing close.

'No!' He wasted a volley of bullets in frustration, which splintered into the frame of the closing bookcase. He darted for the end of the library and banged his thigh into the corner of the final table. Limping through the pain of a dead leg, Kenny lurched for the bookcase with both hands, letting his rifle swing on the tether over his shoulder. He was too late; the bookcase-door closed, and a lock clunked metallically into place.

Cursing, Kenny scoured the shelves looking for a lever, pulling at the books. He tossed aside copies of Homer's *Margites*, Aeschylus' *Achilleis*, Plato's *Hermocrates*, and *Ab Urbe Condita Libri* by Livy. Their spines broke and pages ripped, until Kenny yanked at Euclid's *Pseudaria*. It pitched on its end. The lock unlatched. Kenny hauled at the frame and, though heavy, the case started to shift.

Behind the bookcase was another corridor, but this one was different. Instead of being wide and opulently finished, it was a dank and narrow channel with smooth sandstone blocks forming the walls and ceiling. A single reed torch crackled ahead, casting a solitary orb of light in the dark. Cobwebs hung stickily, clouding the way. Kenny brushed them aside, but they clung to his arm in a tacky net, made him blink and clear his sweaty face as he tried to see beyond the torch light. A growl emanated from the dark.

At last, Kenny had it trapped, and he would have his revenge. He aimed for the centre of the black target that was the darkness ahead. In the hard and confined space, the rifle fire tattooed off the walls like overhead thunder and ended with a yelp. Kenny dropped to one knee at the returning echo, initially thinking someone was shooting back. The corridor fell silent but for the crackle of the torch. A faint breeze blew towards him and dried the sweat of his face. It was hot, with a faint mineral scent. That meant the tunnel had an exit. Kenny fired again. There was the fast rat-a-tat of bullets, the same echo, but no yelp. It could be lying dead or dying, or it could have escaped.

Kenny's chest heaved, and he suddenly became aware of his fatigue. Rising, he forced himself on. He waved his hand ahead of him, clearing the cobwebs, which started to hang from his arm in a feculent, grey beard. His other hand kept the rifle trained at the dark ahead. When he reached the torch, the cone of tightly woven reeds fluttered in the arid breeze and dripped cinders. As the light dimmed and the shadows pressed in, Kenny noticed something on the floor.

He crouched and dipped his fingers in the spots. Blood. A speckled trail leading into blackness. Kenny leaned into his rifle. All he could hear was his heavy, almost snorting breaths. Even the incessant whispering of the house had stopped, as if it held its breath, watching.

Total blackness enveloped him. The rifle trembled in his hands. With the tenuous grip of the grave, the unseen ghostly hands of cobwebs brushed Kenny, unable to pull him back. The torch disappeared. Spectral blotches of colour bloomed into the nothingness. Kenny's snorts quickened as he felt his way, creeping step by step. The tunnel grew hotter, though the breeze had faded away. Soaked with sweat, Kenny rubbed his face clear only to grind the webs and wetness into a grimy paste that got in his eyes. He winced and blinked to clear the dirt, but it only served to scratch at his eyeballs.

A wall appeared out of this confusion, colliding with the barrel of Kenny's gun. By some luck, he didn't pull the trigger and shoot himself with a ricochet, but he fumbled and dropped the rifle. Falling to his knees, Kenny groped around in the thick layer of dust. Something light and with many small legs scuttled over his knuckles. He snatched back his hand and rubbed away the indelible prickles of the insect's footprints. Drawn from every paperback from hell he'd ever read, a blanket of squirming bugs formed in Kenny's mind. Slugs from Shaun Hudson, oozing poisonous slime; cockroaches reeling from the mind of Gregory A. Douglas. James Herbert's flesh hungry rats beset Kenny's imagination from all sides, swarming around him. Those types of books had always been a joke. Light relief to pass the sleepless nights. Nothing compared to the horrors of his gift, and his day job. But now they tapped into a base fear located in the most primitive part of his brain stem, where the world of the prey animal was reduced to two choices: freeze or flee.

On the brink, Kenny caught hold of his panic and sucked in a deep, slow breath through his nose. He forced himself to remember what he was there for, and anger being the bedfellow of fear, Kenny ground his teeth together and plunged his hand into the dust. Another creature with a warm and furry body squeaked when his hand brushed it. He would have recoiled in revulsion, but he also felt something hard and colder. It moved away, scraping along the stone floor. Kenny groped and found it, blindly exploring until he located the stock and trigger.

Back on his feet, Kenny palmed for the walls. At first, he found more of the flimsy gauze of cobwebs, grainy with the exsanguinated husks of insect corpses. Then he stubbed his fingers on a wall, padded one way to a corner and back the other way to another. He double-checked, venturing further and back again until he was sure it was a dead end.

Where was the dog? Had it slipped by him in the dark? Had he stepped past it without realising? Was it dead nearby, or waiting for him? Kenny played through the options, feeling blind in more ways than one. He needed light and initially settled on a retreat to retrieve the reed torch but then laughed out loud. How stupid could he be? How blinded by his mission? The answer was "very" on both counts.

He fished in the inside breast pocket of his trench coat. The phone screen came to life in a glowing rectangle. He unlocked it, swiped down from the top of the screen and turned on the torch application.

A rat ran from the light back up the tunnel. Kenny slowly swung the phone around. He was right: it was a dead end. Just bare walls with a burnt-out torch hanging from its iron fixing.

An inspection of the floor revealed more skeletons of dead rats and beetles on their backs amid an inch or more of dust, and... a trail of blood weaving down the tunnel, as if the beast had staggered. That thought brought a dark quirk to one corner of Kenny's mouth. He followed the trail with his torch right up to the dead end, as if the hound could walk through walls. Maybe it could.

'But if it bleeds...' Kenny said to himself, taking hold of the unlit torch. With a firm pull down, like he was shifting gear, the torch arced a few inches away from the stones. As in the library, a metallic click followed, and sand began to pour from the gaps between the sand-stone blocks.

56

FORMALDEHYDE

THERE WAS no holding it back. Spouts of sand gushed from the walls either side of Kenny, hitting him in the body and legs with the force of a ruptured water main. He'd assumed the dead end was another concealed door, but the wall hadn't moved. The sand flooded the floor, piling over Kenny's shoes and covering the blood.

The blood, Kenny thought, holding the image in his mind. That was the clue, and like all the other clues through this entire case, it didn't add up. Nothing was as it seemed, least of all this house. But there were still clues pointing to something, something Kenny couldn't see. That didn't mean what he needed wasn't there.

The sand piled up to his knees, packing in and constraining his legs. With a futile look back down the way he came, Kenny knew he'd never make it. He would have to find the hidden switch.

If there was one.

There had to be one.

The hound didn't, it *couldn't* vanish into thin air. An icy wave flushed over Kenny's sweat drenched skin as he dove at the dead-end wall. Vanishing into thin air was exactly what the dog could do. Maybe that's what had happened on Gunthorpe Street. Maybe that's why they had no CCTV footage. The animal had led him into a trap, lured him there, let him waste his bullets, and disappeared like a phantom. For all Kenny knew, that was just what it was.

On his knees, groping at the wall, the sand rose up to his chest. He felt along the stone, feeling for anything out of place, pushing frantically at immovable walls. Kenny craned his chin away from the sand and gave up on the lower section. He easily could have missed it if there was something there. The sand made every movement a hundred times slower and draining. Kenny's knee buckled when he tried to stand, and he fell to the side, scrambling to find his feet. One foot found enough purchase on shifting ground to push him up; the other dug in nearer the top of the drift. When the jets of sand hit his body, grains sprayed in a backwash, almost blinding. Like a blind man, running his fingers down the straight edges of the rocks, Kenny felt his way. A nail ripped away, letting in sand through the thin wound. With a cry of annoyance as much as pain, Kenny fell back.

The tunnel was now filled two thirds of the way to the roof. Buoyed on the surface, Kenny was only partially submerged. He swam, a floundering man clawing ineffectually against a deadly undertow draining his energy. The wall was inches away from his touch, but the ceiling closed in too. It was about to press down, drowning him with lungfuls of sand.

Using one hand to hold off the roof, it gave him enough purchase to reach the end of the tunnel. He made manic sweeps of his arms. The hard stone above met the back of Kenny's skull and shoulders. He took one last gulp of air and was pushed down, cocooned in sand. It pressed in against his body, trying to force the life out. His body wracked with a convulsion to take a breath. His hands clawed at the stone wall. Fingertips caught a protruding edge, something out of place, a subtlety he hadn't seen. As the clue had promised, it *was* there. With the last piece of strength, Kenny pushed the stone. It gave way just an inch. He strained to the furthest reach of his fingers, hitching as he fought the urge to breathe.

There was a release of pressure from around his body. Stone moved roughly over stone, and Kenny slid forward and rolled down the heap, sluiced from the tunnel.

Exhausted and gasping for air, Kenny was deposited on the flagstones of a circular room. A growl emanated from somewhere in the meekly lit room. Kenny fumbled for his rifle and flipped to his back. He panned his barrel around the room, seeing nothing in the dim, silvery light. The room continued to exhibit the house's impossible geometry. The last staircase had headed down, the tunnel across, and yet Kenny appeared to be at the roof of the world. Overhead, the room wore a glass dome, as spectacular as St. Paul's Cathedral but transparent. A clear, starlit sky glinted down through the dome's golden ribs. Suspended from the apex, an enormous telescope of polished wood and brass speared through to the heavens, pointing at the misty reaches of the Milky Way. For a moment, it snatched away Kenny's attention, until the growl of the hound pulled him back.

Untrustworthy legs wobbled under him as he scanned the room again, searching the shadows. Instead of books, the walls of this room were covered in jars. Most were glass, but some were made of stone and clay and shaped like Russian dolls with varying heads of eagles, dogs, monkeys and humans.

Kenny cross-stepped away from the drift heaped from the tunnel, circling around the outer edge of the dome. Two pinpricks, like the stars above, glinted from across the room. A deep rumble accompanied them as they lowered. The rumble grew, and Kenny knocked into a jar. It tottered and fell, smashing at his feet, spilling its liquid. The smell it produced was a rank mustiness that burnt Kenny's nasal passages. He'd been a homicide detective long enough to know the smell of formaldehyde. The growl broke into a bark. The preserved organ from the jar lay bleached and slack next to Kenny's foot. He reflexively kicked away the dead meat. The hound let loose a string of rabid barks as its black form bounded through the starlight at Kenny.

Kenny fired, roaring in rage. The bullets pounded into the dog. It shook off the first volley from the semi-automatic with another bark that rent the air like the crack of a whip. Kenny loosed another volley. This one caught the massive dog in the shoulder; inky blood sprayed from the wound, and it stumbled off balance. A foreleg buckled. Kenny advanced, firing again. The dog yelped and fell heavily on its side. Kenny unleashed two more volleys into the heavy chest of the downed animal. The dog was a punching bag for

Kenny's hate, its body juddering. He was on top of it now, firing again and again until the magazine was spent. He kept pressing the trigger, the rifle clicking empty each time before he was done. Even then it didn't feel enough. Kenny quivered and screamed his throat raw until tears burst from his eyes. He walked away and crumpled to the ground.

Emotional and physical exhaustion drained Kenny; they sucked him dry in heavy sobs. He'd killed the monstrous hound, killed it for Misha. Kenny's tears slowed, and he wiped them away with his sleeve. He took a stuttered breath, and as he let it go, the weight of life wanted to drag him to the cold flagstone. He could have just laid down on them, like his mother lowering herself into that warm bath. His only regret was that the hound hadn't led him to its masters so that he could mete out the same justice to those sick bastards. That thought meant there would be no warm bath for Kenny or goodbye kiss from the pistol in his shoulder holster. No, no exit—not yet.

It was then Kenny noticed the faint pulses of light flashing along the cracks between the flagstone. He tracked their course, seeing them flowing from the dome, down the wall, connecting the many jars to its centre located beneath the inert body of the hound. The glow was like starlight, its ethereal silveriness channelled into the veins of the building. There was a hum too, a rhythmic heartbeat in time with the surging arteries of light. The whispers were back too. Kenny hadn't noticed them in the heat of vengeance. It was an unsettling thought that the only other time the voices of the dead left him was when he and Misha made love.

She wasn't avenged yet. Kenny released the spent magazine and slapped in his last. Thirty more rounds, plus his pistol and spare clips. Enough to finish the job. As he groaned and pushed himself to his knees, the light zagging between the flagstones caught Kenny's attention. It wasn't purely silver; the light gradually changed colour, tingeing pink as it approached the centre of the room. Kenny didn't know what it meant. Another strange detail in a strange house. But his eyes lingered on the pinker light weaving under the pool of blood around the hound.

Kenny stiffened. The massive barrel chest of the dog was moving up and down. Kenny brought the rifle up and fired. The safety was still on from changing the magazine.

He swore, turned the rifle over, located the safety by sight, and flicked it off. By the time he brought the machine gun up again and fired, the dog was on its feet and slipped from view. It had been playing dead, waiting, luring. That's what it did. It was toying with him then and now.

Kenny swung and fired. Missed. Swung, fired, and missed again. The hound circled, darting and weaving with preternatural speed. Kenny got lucky and tagged it a few times, but it threw off the shots as if they were nothing. The gun quickly emptied, and Kenny threw it aside, drawing his pistol. He dropped to one knee, tracked and fired, tracked and fired. The hound was closing now and presented a bigger target. Kenny hit its flank, but the lower calibre had even less effect. It was nearly on him. He got up and moved laterally, putting the wall to his back. The first pistol ran out. He changed out the clip, but by the time he'd reached for his belt inside his coat, the hound was leaping. Kenny ducked and rolled.

The clip went skidding away. Glass and pottery jars shattered, showering the beast in the stinking embalming fluid. Kenny found his last clip as the black dog shook off the liquid and then slowly stalked forward. Kenny opened fire, backing up with each shot, which barely affected the monster, even though blood still leaked from its wounds.

Kenny was almost out of bullets. Even if he could find the other clip, he wouldn't be able to change it out in time, but most of all: they weren't working. He wasn't afraid. Anger pumped through his veins. If he was going to die, then he'd meet the beast headlong.

The last bullet took off a chunk of the dog's ear. It flicked down and up as though nothing more than a horse fly had taken a bite. Kenny cocked his arm, ready to throw the pistol and set his feet to charge. The first fricative of a swear word fizzed on his lips.

'F—'

A ball of fire streaked across the room, struck the hound square in its flank, and knocked it off its feet. Kenny swung around to see Abigail marching forward with a look of thunder, both of her hands ablaze. Henry Grime, grimly set, circled from the other side of the room. Hair singed, the dog found its legs and snarled. Abigail pitched one arm forward and then the next, sending two balls of flames spinning across the room. The first hit the dog in the face, exploding in a shower of sparks and cuffing its head up like a stiff jab to the nose. The second ball powered into the chest. Off balance, the hound fell on its back. The sparks floated down and landed in the formaldehyde covering the flagstones. It ignited with a *whump* under the hound's paws. Kenny had no time to process the implication of Abigail's power and the way she and this house had opened up previously hidden realities. The hound wasn't dead yet.

As a yowl of pain from the dog transformed into a thundering growl, Abigail launched another fireball to hold the beast within its blazing lake. Kenny checked the floor and found the last clip. He snatched it up and reloaded. As if to try to shake loose the fire, the dog twisted and turned, snapping at the flames. Another fireball showed it no mercy, and Kenny followed suit, firing and closing the distance.

Henry Grime joined the fray. A glass jar hurtled in from the side and smashed over the writhing tangle of fire. In an explosive ignition, flames billowed out and up. The hound recoiled from the rising walls of mottled pink and black, twisting this way and that, every bit the hellhound trying to break free from its infernal chains.

Henry launched a second jar with its preserved specimen. The combined heat from the explosion staggered Kenny back, and he covered his face, smelling the stench of his own hairs singeing.

With a drunken step, the beast's front legs collapsed. Henry hefted another jar from the shelves. Kenny was out of bullets, but Abigail stood ready, a hand cocked back, a blazing torch held aloft. The dog seemed to forget where it was, and then remembering itself, fixed Kenny with a hateful stare before its eyes rolled and its forelegs gave way once more. The weight of its massive head and chest crashed to the stone floor. The fire licked hungrily over the corpse, stripping it of fur, boiling its flesh and blackening its hide until it cracked like the sun-baked mud of a dried riverbed. The beast fell still. The flames fed on sizzling fat.

'Shoot it,' Kenny said.

Henry put the jar down. 'I think it's dead, bruv.'

Kenny held out his hand, never taking his eyes from the beast. 'Your shotgun, give it to me. I already killed it once. Emptied my machine gun into it, and it still came back.'

Slung across his chest, Henry reached inside his duffle bag and passed Kenny the gun.

After checking and snapping the breach shut, Kenny aimed the sawn-off to the temple of the hound from as close as the flames would let him. The gums of the animal had pulled back into a rictus snarl, baring its fangs and twisting its grotesque features. Kenny thought of the victims, Annie Drew, Judy Finch, and Trinity Marshall. But most of all he thought of Misha. He gritted his teeth so hard they might have shattered and fired once, twice, until the skull of the hound was nothing more than a crater of shattered bone and leaking gore.

The beast was dead.

'One down,' Henry Grime said.

'Two more to go,' finished Kenny, handing Henry his shotgun back.

'Keep it. I can't hold it right with these.' He held up his burnt hands, which they'd wrapped in makeshift bandages of strips torn from a black T-shirt. 'Only two shots left anyway.' Henry handed them over and Kenny reloaded.

There was a crack as Kenny closed the breach, but it wasn't from his shotgun. All three of them flinched away from the sound, and Abigail extinguished her hands by clenching her fists together. The fire from their battle was spreading, licking up the wooden shelves nearest to the corpse of the hound. The embalming fluid was the fire's accelerant, and the more it burned, the more the other jars cracked, leaking fluid and igniting in a chain reaction that spread around the walls, beginning to encircle them.

They staggered back, momentarily hypnotised by the serpentine movement of the flames. Abigail was the first to snap out of it. 'This way,' she rasped, dragging them away from the inferno. Flames climbed high up the walls until the fire raged with such heat that jars exploded before the inferno reached them, igniting the embalming liquid in thin air: a galaxy of stars dying in a chain reaction of supernovas. Shards of glass and ceramic showered down. Abigail pulled up short, and Kenny could see why. They had found another way into the observatory, another of the hidden doors located across the rotunda. The jars in and around them burst into flame, cutting them off.

Abigail spun around, wild-eyed, her one good eye frantically searching for another way out. 'I could make it through, but you could not.'

The heat was intense and became heavy, like sucking a thick, acrid soup through a straw. Already two thirds around the room, the fire was spreading in both directions. For some reason, Kenny looked up. Heat rises but glass falls, and Kenny imagined the rain of razor sharp glass that would descend on them when the dome shattered. They'd be slashed and burned simultaneously. There was a titter from the ever present whispers, enjoying the unnecessary overkill and reveling in the chaos.

'There must be another door,' Henry shouted over the roar of the flames.

'But where?' Abigail called back.

It seemed a futile question. They set to searching, their eyes stung by the backlash of heat. Maybe because he was a detective and he had an eye for detail, or maybe because of his gift, Kenny looked down. The silvery light still pulsed along the gaps between the flagstones, turning pink as they flourished and faded; they had begun to grow even weaker. Kenny followed their path to the centre of the room near to where the hound had first fallen. The pool of blood was still there and something else too, something which the hulking body of the beast had obscured.

'There.' Kenny pointed and was already at a run, leading the way.

The final patch of wall erupted in a mushroom of fire that licked into the room, as if to push them back from their goal. Kenny stopped at the lip of a perfectly circular hole, dead centre in the room and immediately below the elaborate telescope above. The pinkish strands of light disappeared into the aphotic abyss but at least showed there was a curve to the hole; it didn't drop straight down.

'You gotta be kidding me, bruv?'

The entire room was a tube of flames, raging towards the heavens. Kenny slapped Henry on the shoulder and looked Abigail in the eye. 'Leap of faith,' he said. Abigail nodded and Kenny jumped.

57

HAIL MARY

HENRY WATCHED Kenny jump into the hole, arms folded across his chest like he was on a slide at the water park. The cop was absolutely radio rental—full on mental—but they were in a madhouse, so Stokes might be the right man for the job. Abigail was a little less gung-ho. She hurriedly sat on the rim and pushed off with a disconcerting squawk of shock. Henry had never been a fan of heights, which was funny in a kind of sick, laughing at a dead man's wake kind of way. He'd grown up and lived his entire worthless life in high rise tower blocks, hiding any sign of weakness, especially his phobia. Even with the heat of the flames burning his skin and the acrid smoke making him cough, he hesitated at the edge. A horrible crack issued from above. Henry saw a fissure fracture across the great glass dome just before it shattered, hurtling tons of glass down at him.

With the East End's version of a Hail Mary, Henry Grime jumped, shouting, 'Fuck it!'

The hole swallowed him. The temperature immediately cooled. Henry was in free fall for less than a couple of long seconds before his backside landed on the smooth side of a circular tunnel and he was sliding down. It was dark but not completely so. The fine threads of light from the observatory pulsed along the surface, growing darker until they turned red. Stomach lurching, Henry was flung around a bend. He could hear noises from Stokes and the Reverend below him, squeaking shoes, grunts and muffled cries. The sounds grew in volume and clarity, and he realised he was hurtling towards them. Using his hands and feet, Henry tried to find some purchase on the smooth chute. He dug in his heels, but the burns on his hand meant he couldn't steady himself, and he spun around on his back until he was sliding down head-first. Now, he did use his hands, regardless of the pain, flapping and gripping to no effect. The tunnel took a sharp bend, flattened out, and a red glow loomed ahead. Before he had time to do anything else, he was spat out—images flooding his mind of a furnace ready to devour him.

Hands shot out at him from the red glow. They missed. He rolled awkwardly, a tangle of arms, legs and his duffle bag. Clattering into a pointed object sticking out of the floor, Henry came to an abrupt and painful halt.

Stokes and the Reverend hurried over to him.

'My days!' Grimacing, Henry felt his back and rolled to his knees. 'What the hell was that?'

The Reverend let the blasphemy go. 'A pyramid.'

'A what?' Henry struggled to his feet. 'Could this place get any weirder?'

Sure enough, there *was* a pyramid, about five feet high, sitting in the middle of the room. Other chutes opened into this room, each channelling threads of red across the polished black floor, all coming together like the fibres of wool on a spinning wheel. The tip of the pyramid throbbed, both with light and sound, emitting a low hum and an aura which cast their features in scarlet shadows.

'You had to ask?' Stokes said. 'Somehow I think this is just the tip of the iceberg.'

Henry took in the room. It was a vaulted catacomb, with the black floor blending into a rough, unpolished veneer at the base of the walls. On top of this was an intricate layer of Victorian brickwork. Henry had once spent a night hiding in an old sewer after an armed robbery went sideways. He hid below ground and discovered the ornate tunnels and chambers constructed out of clay bricks. This room reminded him of that night. There were six other chutes, evenly spread around the four walls, and a riveted iron door, complete with a nautical wheel.

The tinkle and scrape of glass came from the tunnel they'd descended, and a drift of shards spilled out of the shaft.

The Reverend bustled towards the door. 'We must hurry. The fire is still burning.' She tried the door but wasn't strong enough.

'Let me,' Stokes said and leant himself to the wheel. It groaned, moved an inch, and wouldn't budge any further.

Henry reached into his duffle bag. 'Try this.' He produced a short crowbar, no more than eighteen inches.

Stokes took the metal rod. 'You came prepared.'

'Regular boy scout, me,' Henry said, his hands smarting.

The crowbar was long enough for Kenny to thread it between the axle and spokes and have just enough extra for leverage. 'Listen, I didn't have time to say,' Stokes began as he pushed his weight onto the cowbar, 'but thanks for coming,' he gritted his teeth with the effort, 'to get me.' The wheel gave with a sudden quarter turn. Stokes slipped off the rod, and it clattered to the ground. Righting himself, Stokes returned to the wheel and it moved stiffly, inching around. A crash came from above, shaking the room and raining down dust. Henry joined Stokes, ignoring his hands, and together they worked the wheel, gaining momentum until the unseen mechanism within the door released. They hauled it open, and Henry was about to run through when Stokes stopped him.

'Me first.' He tapped the shotgun in his palm.

The Reverend tutted and barged between them, opening her hands. They ignited and she walked through the door, lighting their way. The men followed and Henry found they were in yet another corridor, though this one was different to the others. It was as if the house had smashed together parts of many buildings from different cultures and times, and perhaps from some that had never truly existed.

'Which way?' the Reverend asked, moving her hands one way and the other to inspect the corridor. It was straight and windowless, made of the same characteristic yellow London brick as the room with the small pyramid. Rotting wooden doors led away from the corridor at irregular intervals; it smelled as rank as a smackhead's squat.

'Buggered if I know,' Henry said, and realised the question wasn't for him. The Reverend and Stokes were mixed up with some strange voodoo, which, until a few hours ago, Henry would have thought was bullshit, plain and simple. He was the third wheel, no mistake.

Stokes closed his eyes and tilted his head like he was listening carefully. 'Down there.' He pointed to the right.

The Reverend led the way, covering them in an globe of light that rolled along with them pushing back the blackness. Water dripped down the walls, tarnished with mould.

'Thanks for back there,' Stokes said. 'How did you find me?'

'Luck,' Abigail said without taking her eyes from the road ahead. 'You were foolish. We followed the sound of gunfire.'

Kenny stopped at a door and listened, then shook his head and they moved on. 'I know, I'm sorry. I—'

Abigail cut him off. 'We are not here for your vengeance, Detective.'

Henry checked behind. Only darkness followed them. He shifted his grip on the crowbar; he'd made sure not to leave it behind. It was a handy piece of kit. Not much of a weapon compared to the Reverend's fireballs and Stokes' shotgun, but it was the best Henry had, and better than the knife or the knuckle dusters in his bag. A crowbar was the Swiss Army-knife of any self-respecting petty criminal. What else could jimmy a lock for a bit of breaking and entering, pry the panelling from a car to get to the ten kilos of skunk stashed in the body work, and knock some ponce's head in if they got out of line? And someone was always getting out of line. The prospect of using it now didn't fill Henry with any of the usual bravado he'd used to get to be top dog in his Ends. If they found Dylan, would it be any use? How could a lump of metal help his son? For that matter, how could the voodoo hit squad in front of him help? Would they read Dylan's mind and then burn him to a crisp like that steroid junkie dog they just put down, burning the house around them?

Right on cue, the corridor shook. They didn't have time to waste, but Henry took the measure of his two companions against the weight of his crowbar. Dylan wasn't the soft boy from a rough estate anymore; he was a monster, and Henry knew all about those. The only problem was he'd only ever seen them end in one way. Stokes knew that, and he was a man with a hard-on for revenge. Henry got that too. Revenge was his business, it was the legal department ensuring the scales of profit and loss from a street hustle always fell in his favour. However the scales weighed up this last hustle, Henry made a promise to himself no one would touch a hair on his boy's head.

'This one,' Stokes finally said. He looked to the Reverend, and she nodded in agreement. 'Might need the crowbar,' Stokes told Henry as he tried the door, but it was unlocked, groaning on rusty hinges.

Stokes toted the shotgun. 'Ready?'

The Reverend cocked one arm, lighting her fist in a ball of flame. Henry twisted his bandaged hands around his crowbar and nodded.

Stokes kicked open the door, and they rushed in.

The room broke into a hysterical chatter of shocked voices, pleas, shrieks and guttural snarls.

What the fuck! Henry mouthed. The three of them stared wordlessly at the rows of severed heads lining the walls.

'*La neige, souviens-toi de la neige. Le flocon de neige fait fondre les ténèbres.*'

'Twenty-five bottles of beer on the wall, twenty-five bottles of beer. If one of those bottles of beer should fall, there'll be… there'll be… be… be. Twenty-five bottles of beer on the wall, twenty-five bottles of beer—'

'Mutt, mutt, mutt. Where's the mutt? No, no, no. This is his place. Not yours.'

They started to move through the room, checking for threats and clues. A furnace burnt in the corner keeping the room aridly hot, and it was rank with a blend of strong spices, sickly decay and the alkaline of mould. The house had shown them so many odd things, this was only another of them. Henry suspected some of these heads once belonged to the organs preserved in the observatory's jars. Stokes had pointed to an opening in the wall across the room. The brickwork around the entrance could have been the yellow and irregular teeth of a Bedlam patient, grinning through its bars. They worked their way around the butcher's slab of a table in the middle of the room, being careful not to go near the heads in the wall. Some of them jabbered incoherently, others snarled and raged, while a few called out pleas or tried to engage in conversation. It was when they reached the hole in the wall that Henry froze. They all did.

'Henry, is that you? Oh, my days! Please say it's you?'

Even though it was dry and breathless, he knew that voice. He turned around slowly, swallowing his dread.

Donna's head lay on its ear, blinking at him from the tabletop. 'It is you. What's happening?'

'We don't have time!' Stokes said, already climbing through the hole in the wall.

Henry walked up to the table. He felt drawn and repelled in almost equal measure. With a sense of being out of his body, he found himself putting down the crowbar and picking up Donna's head.

The other heads erupted.

'Don't steal from the Jackal.'

'Twenty-five bottles of beer on the wall. Twenty-five bottles of beer.'

'*La mère est la neige. La mère est la neige. La mère est la neige.*'

Henry held her in both hands like he might have in bed, and with no other words, he fell back on the absurdity of habit. 'Alright, babe. How's it going?'

Donna smiled weakly. 'I'm- I'm scared,' she whispered.

'I know, babe. I feel ya'.' Henry tried to wet his lips, but his mouth was as dry as an old whore's knickers.

'You came for me,' she said, and the note of surprise stabbed at Henry's heart in ways he'd armoured himself against for almost a life-time. Tonight, when he needed that armour most, he'd taken it off. He let her misunderstanding become a white lie.

''Course I did.'

'Where am I? Where's Dylan? How can I—' Her smokey voice was dissipating. 'How can I be alive after—' Donna's features spasmed as the room rumbled and dust showered down.

'We've got to move,' Stokes called urgently from down the tunnel.

Donna snarled and snapped her teeth, twisting her jaw in a futile attempt to bite Henry. He almost dropped her. The Reverend laid a gentle hand on Henry's shoulder.

'Henry, remember Dylan. It's time to go.'

'I'm on it. I'll be right behind you,' he said, eyes locked on Donna's as she glared and snarled at him.

He put her back on the table next to the crowbar, looking between the two of them, straining to make a decision. Finally, he took Donna by the hair and picked up the crowbar in the other.

'Sorry, babe,' he said, as she hissed and gnashed her teeth.

THE TUNNEL WAS dark and cramped. Crouched over, Kenny used his phone to light the way as the Reverend struggled behind. It led down steeply, turning through right angles like a mineshaft. Rock fallings littered the way, and at one point Kenny had to climb over a boulder. He stopped to help the Reverend through. Henry Grime had caught up and pushed until she fell through, and Kenny caught her on the other side. Down and down they went, hundreds of feet into the earth.

He'd thought the whispers of the house would have faded the deeper they went. When they came to the room with the heads, Kenny had assumed the whispers had belonged to them. At least some of them did, because Kenny had been able to track them: so many voices of the dead calling out. However, if anything, the farther they descended the louder the voices were getting, and they weren't just voices. What Kenny could hear was a screaming, wailing multitude, as if they were climbing down into the bowels of hell. He should have wanted to run away, but he didn't. He couldn't. Maybe this was his version of climbing into a warm bath to open his wrists. A deathwish dressed up as revenge. Either way, Kenny didn't run away. He hurried, calling back for the others to do the same as the tunnel shook and groaned as if it would collapse at any moment.

And then there it was. A throbbing red light signalling the end of their journey.

Kenny clambered out of the tunnel and straightened up, his heart lurching in his chest as if he'd just stepped off a cliff. The possibilities of reality had been rewritten for him once again today. Even the Reverend gasped as she emerged from the tunnel. Henry Grime swore, and all three of them looked in awe and terrified wonder at the cavernous black pyramid around them. Veins ran from the apex, lighting the interior with pulses of red, revealing the thin walkway between shimmering lakes of liquid silver to the centre of the pyramid. There, suspended from sinuous threads, hung two dark pods.

58

LAIR

STOKES WAS AGITATED MORE than usual, and that was saying something. He kept putting a hand to his ear as they hastened along the narrow path. Henry could only hear their footsteps on the polished black walkway and the hum of the red veins, but Stokes looked like someone was screaming in his head. *If he can hear the voices of the dead, this place must be like Piccadilly Circus for the poor bastard.*

The silver lakes on either side moved like mercury, undulating thick and slow whenever the pyramid shook, which was more and more often. Henry didn't like the look of them. There was something unnatural and otherworldly about how their surface shifted. Then again, there was something unnatural about this whole place. Eyes now used to the dark, Henry fixed on the two pods and could make out outlines. One was slightly smaller than the other. They were ribbed and striated, like muscles stripped of their skin and fat, dark brown as granulated scabs.

They reached the end of the walkway at the centre of the pyramid, and the pods loomed overhead, swaying almost imperceptibly. At first, Henry thought the pods' contents were hidden within their grotesque hides, but then he noticed near the bottom the skins thinned, filthy translucent windows to the things inside. Its end hanging at his eye level, he approached the smaller of the two pods.

'No!' he gasped. Dylan hung upside down, his eyes closed, in an emulsion of dirty water, a muzzle or mask over his nose and mouth. He had changed from the monster Henry had seen last night, the one that had looked into Henry's soul and seen him for the utter deadbeat tosspot he was. Dylan was healed. Henry could still save him, if he could only prise him out of the festering capsule that trapped him.

He hefted the crowbar and fixed it into the puckered seam running down the pod's middle.

'Wait.' The Reverend pulled at Henry's arm, but he shrugged her off.

'I'm getting him out,' Henry said, levering the bar back and forth. 'You two deal with whichever ponce is in that one.' The seam began to ooze as it creaked like stiff leather.

'We don't know what will happen if you open it!' the Reverend remonstrated.

'He's right,' Stokes said. 'This is what we came to do, so let's do it.' He levelled his shotgun at the face of the man inside the pod. 'Sleep tight, you murdering bastard.'

The man hanging upside down snapped open his eyes and focused on Stokes, who seemed to be fighting an internal battle with himself to pull the trigger.

The Reverend was now tugging at Stokes, shouting, 'Don't look at him. Don't look.'

It didn't make any sense to Henry at the time, and he was too busy to pay attention. Agony burned through his hands as he dug the crowbar a little deeper and pushed the seam apart. It creaked as it resisted. Then everything happened in a chaotic rush.

Both pods yawned open down their middles. Liquid spilled out, splashing on the shining black floor. Henry went to catch Dylan, but he wasn't quick enough and paled with a dreadful realisation.

Two forms crouched in the pool of fetid water between the open wounds of their pods. With looks of dark fury on their faces, they rose together, their forms glistening in the pulsing red light.

Henry staggered back, transfixed by the monster who looked like a younger version of himself. Stokes was still frozen, gun held straight ahead, arm quivering.

'Shoot, Stokes! Shoot!' Henry shouted, still backing up.

Dylan stepped forward, shoulders hunched and talons growing. *Why do you have to ruin everything?* Henry heard the boy roar in his mind.

The Reverend seemed to hear it too. She ignited both hands, but before she could unleash them, the hawk-nosed man had moved in on her in the blink of an eye and delivered a back-handed slap that knocked her off her feet and sent her sliding across the floor. Her limp body came to rest inches from the shimmering pool of quicksilver.

Is that for me? Dylan said of the crowbar. *You came to finish off your bastard, did you? Why couldn't you leave me alone? I was in a better place.*

Henry dropped the crowbar and teetered on the edge of the walkway.

Take your time, little Oedipus, the hawk-nosed ponce said. *Daddy has a lot to answer for. In the meantime, I can have some fun with this interesting Praetorian.*

Still rooted to the spot, Stokes started to move as the man cocked an eyebrow. With shaking hands, the detective turned the gun on himself and, with the same internal battle, opened his mouth.

Henry put up his hands. 'Dylan, wait. I came for you.'

Dylan's face mutated. His jaw prised apart with the overcrowded maw of dripping fangs. *Why?* his thoughts slurred. *So you could destroy everything like you've always done? Making my mum a whore wasn't enough for you? You had to make me your bitch too?*

'You're right, I know I'm a bad man. The worst. You shouldn't forgive me for what I've done. But this isn't you, Little Dee. You're not bad. You're not a monster like me.'

Dylan seized Henry by the throat, lifting him off his feet, and he dropped the iron bar. *Shut up, you worthless shit.*

Henry kicked and choked, turning red, pawing ineffectually at the talons around his throat, unable to breathe. The red nightmare of the pyramid throbbed and swam in and out of his vision, almost fading to black, when the pressure suddenly released, and he fell to his knees coughing and spluttering. He saw Stokes place the gun in his mouth and the Reverend laying still, maybe dead. The crowbar, such a faithful tool throughout Henry's life, was useless and out of reach. There was only him left. A punk from the gutter. A thug. A pimp. A hustler. A two-timing double-crosser. And without a doubt, a complete and utter bastard.

These few words were all he had to offer. One simple truth, as the monster closed in with its venomous fangs dripping.

'I love you, son.'

Dylan froze, hatred hardened in his face, the chiselled grooves of a gargoyle glaring down.

The hook-nosed ponce laughed, smug amusement playing on his thin lips. He left Stokes with the shotgun in his mouth, one moment casually taking a few steps towards them and the next appearing at Dylan's shoulder, travelling in an instant. How stupid they were. How foolish of them to think, even with the voodoo priestess and psychic cop, that they could do anything but come here to die.

Love? How delicious. 'Tis but the most delectable of things. Think what secrets his blood could show you? What mysteries he would solve. The ponce's voiceless lips stretched into a mocking smear. He seemed to be whispering wordlessly into Dylan's ear, gleeful eyes sparkling with the reflective shimmer of the pool at Henry's back.

Dylan arched his neck, looking every bit the smackhead about to chase the dragon, gone to that place beyond this world, to that fantasy that was a lie better than the bad dream of their life. Drugs, gambling, pussy: they were all fantasies that made good money, as irresistible as gravity. Henry knew the score and took no solace in his pathetic attempt to make amends.

Droplets of venom burned the skin on Henry's neck and then numbed the skin before the final bite.

'Henry, I don't like it in here. It's dark. Where are you?' Donna's breathless voice spoke.

Henry put a protective hand over the duffle bag slung over his shoulder. Dylan stared at the bag, eyes dancing, as if he was trying to do a difficult sum but couldn't work it out.

The ponce was still at Dylan's ear. *Vieil did it for you, Dylan. A gift to free you from your miserable life. And Mr Butcher was preparing her so she could be with us for eternity.*

'Show me,' Dylan slurred through his fangs.

Henry unzipped the bag. Eyes blinking in the red light, Donna looked up. At seeing Dylan, she smiled, her drained and gaunt face brightening.

See how happy she is, emancipated from laying on her back at your bastard father's behest? the ponce called Vieil leered.

The brightness flickered out of Donna's features, and they twisted into the snarl of a rabid animal. She snapped and hissed, eyes rolling back in their sockets.

Henry closed the bag over. 'I'm sorry, Little Dee. I couldn't leave her like that.'

Enough of this. Finish him and let us return to our Suhets.

Dylan closed his eyes. The ponce leered in the boy's ear. *Drink him until the moment his life stops, and you will fly beyond the stars to the edge of the known universe.*

When Dylan opened his eyes, his jaws yawned wider than seemed possible. His fangs pushed forward, slobbering and dripping.

Yessh! Yeeeshh! Vieil purred.

Dylan struck fast and hard, biting deep and tearing at Vieil's throat. He latched on, wrapping his legs and arms around the man, sinking his talons into the flesh of his victim's back. Locked together, they staggered, shock and bewilderment written all over Vieil's face.

Henry scrambled away.

Dylan and Vieil twirled. Dark blood poured from Vieil's neck, but he composed himself enough to seize Dylan by the shoulders. The boy wouldn't let go. He worried at the wound, snarling and ripping deeper as they spun clumsily to the edge of the silver pool, which rippled at their presence. With a cry of exasperation and anger, Vieil threw Dylan off him. A gout of blood, almost black, sprayed from his neck. Dylan flew in a high arc and clipped one of the pods and landed on all fours at the other side of the central platform. Blood coursed through Vieil's fingers which he'd pressed to his neck. He smiled darkly, blood flowing from his mouth, and his free hand lengthened into a deadly claw.

Do you think I can be so easily killed? I have lived for more than three-

score and ten millennia. From when the Sphynx hunted in the long grass and our kingdom beyond the Gates of Hercules...

Vieil jerked at the sudden tug and looked down. He had staggered to the very edge of the platform where solid black met liquid silver, and that liquid was alive. Hands of mercury had reached, clawing upwards from the pool, and seized Vieil by the ankles. Faces stretched from the surface too, as if to break free, hundreds maybe thousands over them, tortured and screaming. Vieil struggled, like a man in quicksand, trying to pull his legs free. More hands slithered from the depths, crawling over the backs of their brethren, wrapping farther up his legs, coiling around his waist. But still he struggled.

NO! he screamed, as he used his hands to pull off the quicksilver, only to have them caught and bound. *NO!* He strained with everything he had.

'Hey, dickhead!' Henry Grime said, appearing in front of the struggling man. 'Shut the fuck up!' Henry struck him with a two-handed blow across the face with the crowbar.

The ponce's head whipped around. The momentum pitched him off balance. For a moment, he teetered on the edge, flailing like a lunatic in a straitjacket. Then he pitched backwards and was pulled into the pool of silver.

59

RISING UP

HENRY HAD a spare T-shirt and boxer shorts in his duffle bag. Dylan had put them on as the lakes of quicksilver began to boil and geyser. Henry kept one eye on the pool where the ponce, vampire, or whatever he was had been dragged down. He never surfaced.

Stokes broke out of whatever trance he had been in and was smart enough to realise whatever beef he might still have with Dylan played a distant second to the immediate shit storm they were in. The pyramid was shaking and massive fissures were appearing in its walls.

With Dylan's help, Henry picked up the Reverend, taking her weight with her arms across their shoulders as they staggered down the walkway. She wasn't dead, but neither was she fully conscious yet. She moaned incoherently, and her legs moved but more as an afterthought.

Silver jets shot up from the lakes on either side. Masonry fell into its roiling depths and shattered on the walkway.

'Let me take her,' Dylan said, and he effortlessly hoisted the Reverend in a fireman's lift. 'Meet me at the tunnel as fast as you can.' Before Henry could say anything, they were gone.

'Time to leg it,' Henry shouted.

'Don't wait for me,' Stokes called back.

They ran pell-mell, dodging falling rubble and sprays of quick-

329

silver. They were nearing the end of the walkway when a quake knocked them off their feet. An enormous piece of black stone fell from the sky and broke its back on their escape route. Pieces of it sloughed into the boiling silver, but a piece ten feet tall and with a sheer, polished face blocked their way.

'No handholds,' Henry shouted over the tempest of frothing mercury.

'What about a boost?' Stokes yelled back.

'I ain't got anything better to do,' Henry called, putting his back to the wall and cupping his bandaged hands together forming a makeshift stirrup.

On a three count, Henry hoisted the detective as high as he could, but he fell several feet short of the top of the rock and jumped down awkwardly.

'Try from my shoulders!' Henry made the stirrup again.

Stokes clambered up from Henry's hands to his shoulders, but they were a couple of feet short.

'Any ideas?' Stokes shouted.

Henry shrugged looking around for something to help them. More masonry shattered on the walkway behind.

Henry pointed at the water. 'Fancy a swim?'

'After you.'

'Nah, you're alright,' Henry said. 'I'd rather— Dylan!' Henry pointed to the top of the giant slab. Dylan dropped down as if it was nothing and grabbed his father under the armpit and leapt. He deposited Henry next to the Reverend who was sitting woozily next to the tunnel entrance. Moments later, Dylan reappeared with Stokes.

There was an almighty crack; the pyramid juddered, and its apex fell. The two pods slumped, and their tethers coiled around them as the keystone plummeted to the ground.

'We need to go now,' Stokes shouted.

Henry went to pick up the Reverend.

'I'll take her,' Dylan said, getting there first. 'You just try to keep up.' He turned to the tunnel entrance, and Henry caught him by the wrist.

'Don't wait for us, Little Dee. Get her out.'

Dylan gave him half a nod, and then he was gone.

They scrambled up the pitch-black tunnel; it seemed it could collapse at any time. Dust filled the air. They clawed, coughing and hacking, with the desperation of someone trying to climb out of their grave. Over debris, around bends, up and up they struggled until finally they saw the light. Henry clambered into the room of severed heads first and reached back to give Stokes his hand, hoisting him clear.

Heads lay all around, shaken from their shelves by the collapsing building. They cried for help or snarled or gibbered insanely. Henry felt for Donna's head in his duffle bag. Which state she was in, sane and afraid or crazed and rabid, he didn't know. They hopscotched through the heads, careful not to be bitten, but in the windowless corridor outside they had a problem.

Stokes was looking left and right, shining his phone into the corridor and wincing.

'Which way?' Henry asked.

'Right—no, left.'

'Which one is it, bruv?'

'I don't know.'

'What do you hear?'

Stokes knuckled his fists into his eyes. 'Screaming. Everywhere, so much screaming.'

Henry put a hand on Stokes' shoulder and looked up and down the shaking corridor. 'No worries. We'll go right. What's the worst that could happen?'

Stokes unballed his hands and looked at Henry to see if he was serious.

Gold teeth flashed back. 'Fuck it, we've got to die sometime,' Henry said slapping the detective on the back and set off at a clip.

It was yet another long corridor. Henry had been jogging for a while, passed door after door, when a bang came from the darkness ahead.

Stokes caught up. 'What is it?'

'Don't know.'

They crept forward. A groaning crash came from behind, and

they spun around to see the roof caving in. A billowing cloud of dust blotted out the light from Stokes' phone. There was only one way to go, but they couldn't see it. They coughed and groped blindly. Henry felt Stokes back up against him, then the detective cried out, and the choking darkness swallowed him up. With the crowbar brandished in front of him, Henry turned this way and that, eyes stinging, hacking brick dust into his sleeve. He thought he heard a noise and spun around and swung the crowbar. It slapped into something soft and yet unyielding and was snatched from his grasp. Before he could retreat, he was yanked from his feet. Unable to see, he struck out, kicking and squirming.

Chill out.

The words rang clear in Henry's mind, and he stopped struggling. There was another bang, and Dylan deposited Henry on the floor of the room: hazed with dust and filled with furniture covered in white sheets. Stokes was spluttering on the floor next to Henry, and the Reverend was holding her head with her knees tucked under her.

'We've a problem,' Dylan said. 'The way out, up through the house, is blocked.'

'So what do we do, Little Dee?'

'There's another way. A hole in the wall comes out on the underground tracks. It's dangerous, though. Must be the District or Hammersmith line.'

'Sounds like we don't have any better choices,' Stokes coughed.

'Can you manage Rev Adekugbe? I'll need to make the hole bigger.'

They followed Dylan out to a landing at the foot of a dingy stairwell. The roof had fallen in at the top of the stairs, and it smelled of the acrid black smoke that was clouding menacingly above their heads. Henry and Stokes supported the Reverend, who was still mumbling incoherently, her head lolling, while Dylan disappeared under the stairs and into a narrow space between the walls. He only had his bare hands, but it sounded as though a sledgehammer was smashing the bricks. The smoke was getting thicker, and the two men carried the Reverend closer to their possible escape route.

Dylan reappeared. 'Detective, can you climb through first, and I'll pass you the Rev? Then...' —for a moment, Henry thought he was going to say dad— '...I'll help Grime through.'

Henry waited his turn, bouncing on his toes like he used to with nerves before a gang fight or a robbery. The Reverend was through, and it was Henry's turn, and he was about to leave when the rubble at the top of the stairs started to move. It wasn't from the house shaking. A few chunks of brickwork slid off in the smoke. Henry got a chill.

'Hurry,' Dylan said.

More masonry shifted, toppling down the heap, and then two hands burst through and ripped a larger hole. Henry shook his head, trying to deny his eyes, as through the gap climbed a man with a handlebar moustache and only one eye. Even as Henry stared, the cavernous space in the man's skull was regrowing.

Dylan joined Henry, saw what his father was looking at, and hauled him away.

At least out of the house, the screaming of the dead was quieter. When the vampire was dragged into the silvery pools in the pyramid, the wailing became cacophonous. With every laboured step away, the background chatter of London came nearer. Still, they were stumbling along live train tracks on a busy underground line. The District Line had a tube race through every two and half minutes. Kenny got it to work everyday. They'd timed their escape to right after the last train. Kenny was panting, trying to keep the Reverend moving. They needed to make it to a maintenance ingress and fast, or when the tube train came, they'd be hard to identify from their remains. Kenny thought he could see the opening up ahead, but even as he thought it, he felt the rumble of the train.

'Nearly there, Abigail. A bit faster.'

They limped quicker, the rumble of the train, like the tremors of a runaway stampede, vibrating up through Kenny's shoes. The train light lit up the tunnel. The driver must have thought he saw something because he sounded his horn. It clanged off the tunnel walls as Kenny swerved himself and Abigail into the ingress and pressed them hard against the wall. There was a brief screech of brakes, but then the driver must have thought he was seeing things. The train powered by and threatened to suck them from the wall with its slipstream.

It passed and the stampede faded away. Kenny breathed a sigh of relief. He noticed a telephone attached to the wall for maintenance and safety teams. He picked it up and, with only one purpose, the phone began to ring automatically. Someone picked up, and before they could speak, Kenny blurted out his name, rank, police ID number and that there were people on the track. The operator knew as much, as each phone had a unique identification code corresponding to its location. The lines were shut down, and the trains were called to an emergency stop. They were safe.

That was when Henry Grime came running up the tunnel, waving his arms, telling them to run. He held out his arms for Abigail. She tried to take a step but her legs would not obey, and she slumped back and slid down the wall. Panicked, Grime looked back for Dylan, but Dylan wasn't running. Kenny realised the boy had done the calculations. He was fast enough, but the rest of them weren't. He could maybe ferry one of them to safety but not all of them, but if he stood and fought, maybe there was a chance. Dylan's hands had grown into long curving blades, his shoulders rounded and tense, facing the man coming through the darkness. Kenny's rage surged at the glint from the hooked bronze sword carried in the man's right hand. The khopesh. The weapon that murdered and mutilated his wife, borne in the hands of the Ripper.

Kenny left Abigail where she was. He looked around for something to use, a brick, a rail spike, anything. Coming up short, Kenny began the futile gesture of checking his pockets for weapons he knew he didn't have.

Grime was shouting for Dylan to run, and when he didn't, he went to his son. The Ripper strode out up the tunnel, coming into view. A chunk of his skull was missing, a lump of pink matter showing through, and yet that wasn't the strangest thing. The man was changing before their eyes, growing, transforming. His skin turned almost black as his proportions grew, legs and arms longer and more muscular, tearing his clothes to ribbons. A long, pointed snout grew from his face; the triangular ears of a jackal pointed up from the sides of his head. His feet became paws with a raised ankle. His hands morphed into claws. The change was complete in a matter of seconds, and he stood a clear twelve feet tall. When he reached Dylan, the boy launched himself at the giant's neck. But the Jackal-man batted him aside with a sweep of his hand. Dylan slammed into the tunnel wall, cracking the concrete and dropping in a heap, down but not out.

As the last of its skull knitted back together, the Jackal loomed over Henry and pointed at the duffel bag slung over his shoulder. Henry half-retreated, holding onto the bag tightly, sidestepping toward his son who was shaking off the effects colliding with the wall. It gave what might have been a smile but developed as a snarl of massive, dripping jaws and pink teeth. Kenny remembered Misha playing with their rescue dog Betty on the kitchen floor the night he'd brought the dog home. They were so happy. Misha, with her beautiful face, and Betty, with a smile that was bigger than she was. These thoughts raced in the frantic moments while Kenny patted himself down in the futile search for a weapon. But now he remembered a small detail, a throwaway incident with a colleague and a friend helping him out with his new dog. Kenny stuffed his hands in his trench coat pockets, feeling through the keys, stubs of paper, his notebook, a dog biscuit, a paper clip, and...

The Jackal hefted its bronze khopesh, which had grown just as he had. The muscles under his black fur rippled with menacing power. Dylan staggered backward but set his feet to pounce. Henry tripped on a railway sleeper and fell on his back, clinging to the bag containing Donna's head.

Kenny blew the dog whistle Roj had given him. He blew it hard and he blew it long. It made no sound that he could hear. Dylan winced and covered his ears, but the Jackal dropped his heavy, curved weapon and clutched at its head, arching his back.

Kenny ran out of breath and sucked in another lungful and blew again.

The Jackal fell to its knees, roaring in agony. Kenny ran forward blowing his silent whistle, which could fell the giant who'd killed his wife and so many other women. The khopesh was almost as long as Kenny was tall, but when he picked it up, it was light and throbbed with power. The roars of pain from the Jackal bounced off the wall like the clatter of a coming train.

With one last blow of the whistle, Kenny pitched the sword over his shoulder and swung it: for Annie Drew and Judy Finch and Donna Savage and Detective Trinity Marshall. He even swung it for the gangsters killed under the railway arches. But most of all, he swung it for Misha and the boy she wanted to save.

The blade struck true, singing with a disconcerting feeling of joy in Kenny's hands as it tasted blood. It sliced through the Jackal's forearm, and then through the giant's enormous neck, severing its head from its body. On its final descent, the second hand was amputated.

The Jackal's head thudded to the ground and rolled to Kenny's feet, but there was no blood. Instead, as the head came to rest, Kenny heard the faint whisper of a desert wind and the blush of its arid kiss on his face.

The Jackal dissolved into a mound of sand.

60

LA NEIGE

BEFORE THE EMERGENCY services and London Underground safety teams reached them, Kenny had some decisions to make. He had a semi-plausible story brewing about wandering off in shock and not remembering where he was and finally ending up at the Reverend Adekugbe's. Her son had been a target of the Duppy Crew, so maybe they were after her as well? Still, he'd broken too many regulations over firearms for it not to affect his career. He'd be lucky to keep his job at all.

Maybe that wasn't such a bad thing. Time would tell.

He let Dylan, Henry, and he supposed Donna too, go. There was no way on earth he'd be able to explain away that modern day Addams Family. There was a service exit farther along. Now with time to think, they'd realised from the signage that they were on the Hammersmith Line and not District. Kenny remembered from an old case of a suicide on the tracks that this part of the network brought together the two underground lines with the Overground network. There was a service tunnel burrowing up under a bridge beyond Whitechapel Station.

The only other thing was the bronze sword. After the Jackal's death, it returned to its normal size. Kenny wrapped it in his coat and hid it among the overhead pipes in the service tunnel, planning to retrieve it at a later date. It was too powerful an object, and without the bodies of the men—Kenny snorted at the idea that they were *men* at all—there was no way to solve the Ripper case.

With most of the loose ends tied off, Kenny sat down next to Abigail and waited for help. She was badly concussed and needed a hospital, but she was tough, and he hoped for her son's sake that she'd pull through. He knew better than anyone how much a son needed his mother.

THEY HEARD the rescue team coming as they slipped through a door with a sign reading "London Overground" and "Staff Only" in red letters. From there, the stairs ascended steeply, the metal rungs tolling softly under their feet. When they reached the top, a ladder climbed straight up. At the top was a claustrophobic room of bare walls, conduits, exposed electrical cables, and another door with another sign. It read "Exit" and "Warning. Trains in operation."

'We should wait for dark,' Henry said.

Dylan had thought it through. It wasn't such a hard calculation, and every way he played it out, the equation never gave the answer he wanted. 'Nah, I can't live like this if it means I have to kill people.'

'Maybe there's another way. I could bring you blood somehow... animals or raid a blood bank?'

'It's got to be from a living person.'

'But there has to be a way, Little Dee.'

'There isn't,' Dylan said, giving his dad a weak smile. 'Let me say bye to my mum. You promise to take care of her?'

'Swear on my life, bruv.' Henry opened the duffle bag.

Donna was snarling and raging with whatever demons possessed her. In a way, Dylan thought the afterlife was not so different. She calmed, her eyes coming back to focus, her features softening.

'Dylan, oh Dylan. Henry found you. I—' Her eyes flicked around the bag, 'I don't know what's happening.'

'It's okay, Mum, Henry will explain everything. He's going to make sure you're safe. He promises.'

She smiled wanly, not sure of what to say.

'I love you, Mum.'

Her face lit up. 'I love you too, Dylan. I love you so much. You know that, right?'

'Yeah, Mum. I know.'

Donna's cheek twitched, and she gave a dry, breathless cough. 'I feel—' Her lips curled back from her teeth, and Henry closed the bag.

Tears ran down Henry's face. 'What I said back there, when you saved us...' He sniffed, embarrassed by the show of emotion. 'Well, I meant it, Son.'

Dylan said nothing for a moment, and then he wrapped his arms around Henry. 'Thanks, Dad.'

Henry was stunned and blushed, but finally he hugged his son, holding him tightly.

Far too soon, Dylan said, 'I've got to go.'

'I don't want you to.'

'I know, but it would just be later if not now. If you think about it, I'm already dead.' Dylan opened the door to the tunnel.

He squinted at the daylight. Snow whisked through the air. Sirens seemed to be wailing all over the city. Henry closed the door behind them and checked the track was clear. Dylan was already walking away, the snow frosted gravel crunching underfoot. When he reached the cusp of the bridge's shadow, he looked behind to see Henry following, his face wet with tears, his one eye still badly swollen and bruised from the night before. Dylan put up a hand in a static wave. His father did the same and stopped. His bandaged hands lowered, ringing around the strap of his bag as if to desperately hold on.

Dylan turned away. The snow was starting to lay, and it changed everything it touched, transforming the dirty world into something impossibly beautiful. To hold on to that image until the very end, he closed his eyes and stepped into the sunlight.

Henry shouted.

The daylight ignited Dylan's flesh. It hurt, but then life hurt, and he'd endured its slow pain year after year. This would be over in an instant.

He crumpled into a ball of flame.

The snow swirled around in fat flakes, coiling around Dylan as he burned. He clenched and shook, praying for it to be over soon. To hide from the pain, he went back to Regent's Park. Sat on a park bench with his mother, they fed the ducks, and she gave him a snowflake. It was a perfect little fractile of crystalline water that contained all the beauty of the universe. In these last few seconds, he mentally closed his hand around the snowflake and wished that the meeting beyond the stars was real. But it wasn't. Some things were impossible.

Like the absence of pain when burning alive.

Dylan unclenched. Maybe he was dead, really dead, and had passed over to whatever there was beyond this world? What was it supposed to feel like? Like passing through a black hole? Unimaginable pain and then...

He opened his eyes.

The snow was falling thickly, laying on the gravel by the train tracks, as he unfurled from his fetal position. Dylan straightened up. Henry Grime was running to him, calling his name.

Holding out his hands, Dylan inspected his arms in disbelief. The flames were out, as if every sin had been burnt away. The sense of the internal pulse and chatter of the city was gone, and with it his hunger had gone too. He was alive. Unharmed. Whole again.

He turned over his palms, and in the flurry of snow, a perfect snowflake landed in his palm, like the gift given to him in a dream beyond the stars.

MEMENTO MORI

"Everything that happens before Death is what counts."
— Ray Bradbury, *Something Wicked This Way Comes*

EPILOGUE

ONCE CHANTEL GOT off that bloody roof, she didn't go back to Renfield Tower. Instead, she contacted one of her regulars, for old time's sake, and with two hundred quid in her pocket, thumbed a ride up the M1 to Milton Keynes. She was hungry but saved her money and got a cup of coffee at the services and crossed her eyes at a little girl bored of eating with her family. The girl giggled and stuck out her tongue. Her mother caught her at it and was about to apologise, but the words piled up unspoken in her mouth, propping it ajar as she slammed on the brakes. She quickly herded her daughter back to her chicken nuggets.

In the toilets, Chantel tried to scrub off her makeup with paper towels and tied her hair back loosely. In the stalls, she pulled on a pair of trainers and jeans. She rolled up her thin faux-leather jacket and stuffed it in the bin along with her high heels. Then she bought a rain-mac two sizes too big from the shop selling everything from stale sandwiches to souvenir fridge magnets. "Straight Outta Milton Keynes" one read in typography aping the N.W.A. biopic movie, with irony as stale as the sandwiches.

The coat was too thin for how cold it was, but it came down to her knees. She had two cigarettes left and intended them to be her last. Taking one out, she lit it and blew out a plume of smoke as the first snowflakes started to fall. It was like breathing out all the filth and grime of London.

'Don't suppose you've got a spare fag? Left mine in the cab,' a woman in the twilight of middle age asked. Her hair was a nest of greying wire, and her face cracked into a thousand lines when she smiled.

'Sure.' Chantel offered the pack.

'It's your last one. I couldn't.'

'You'd be doing me a favour.'

'Quitting?'

'That's the plan.'

'In that case, it would be rude to say no.'

'Positively insulting.'

The woman with wiry hair took the pack and sparked the cigarette. 'Where you heading, love?'

Chantel took another drag, but this one held no satisfaction. 'Bit further north. Little town near Newark.'

'Which one?'

'Place called Southwell. But some of the locals say it like "Suvvell". You know it?'

'It's got a cathedral, hasn't it? Beautiful place. You don't sound like you're from there.'

Chantel stubbed out her cigarette half-smoked and put her hands in her armpits and attempted to stamp some warmth into her feet. 'My aunt runs a cleaning business there. Tidying up rich folk's houses. She said I should visit.'

The woman barked a phlegmy cough. 'It's not too much farther. You'll be there by lunch.'

'Yeah, maybe.'

'You're driving, right?' The older woman gave Chantel a firm look.

'Hitching. Started in London last night.'

The snow started to fall in larger flakes, and Chantel caught one on her palm. It transformed to a droplet of water.

'Hitching!' the woman said. 'A pretty young girl like you? No, no, no.'

Chantel shrugged and stamped her feet some more. 'No choice. Got to save my money.'

The woman nodded as if making up her mind and stuck out her hand. 'The name's Margery. But you can call me Marg. Everybody does, except my ex-husband, but he was a dickhead.'

'Chantel. Pleased to meet you.'

'Grab your bag. Your luck's in. I'm going to York. We'll drive right by Newark. I'll drop you off.'

'Really?'

'Call it payback for the fag.' Marge walked off, jerking her head for Chantel to catch up.

'I've only a few quid, but I can give you something.'

They rounded the side of the services away from the main car park. 'Keep your money, love. The company will be nice. Are you afraid of heights?'

Chantel thought of being in Dylan's arms leaping high over the rooftops of London. Her heart broke again. 'Nah, love 'em. Why?'

Snow whipped around the two women as Marge clicked her key fob, and an articulated lorry's lights flashed. 'Because we'll be cruising at altitude above the riff-raff.'

A smile, honest and broad as a long summer's day, broke across Chantel's face. The wind pulled strands of hair from her ponytail, making them dance around her head.

'What are you waiting for?' Marge said, hoisting herself up into the truck's cab.

Chantel ran through the swirls of snow and climbed up next to Marg, slamming the door shut against the snow, against Whitechapel, against the past. The cab was toasty and smelled of tobacco and a scented pine air-freshener hanging from a sun visor. With a rumble, the truck came to life. Chantel buckled her seat belt. On the radio, the presenter hoped everyone was having a good day. The brakes hissed, and Marge drove Chantel off into the future.

IT WAS NEARLY eight in the morning when the beeping on Alan Best-wick's monitor bottomed out into a sorrowful monotone. Snow flurried around the Royal London Hospital, and Londoners put their shoulders into the biting wind. The incessant rain had been bad enough, but snow meant traffic jams, train delays, and bloody cold toes.

For a while, it seemed as though Alan would pull through. He'd lost a lot of blood, but the police officer had done a good job in keeping pressure on the wound, and the paramedics transferred him swiftly to the Emergency Department. The jugular vein in Alan's neck was tied off by a skilful surgeon. The surgical team pumped blood back into him intravenously. Anaesthesia kept Alan blissfully unaware—although, in the deepest recesses of his mind, a little nightmare played out in which his form class ate him alive as he called out the morning register. They bit and worried into the flesh of his legs, stripping them to the bone, and feasted on his intestines and chewed off his fingers, crunching through the brittle digits. The skilful surgeon closed up and announced the operation a success. Alan was wheeled to intensive care and stabilized for a short time, but one by one his organs failed.

A porter wheeled the body from the ward with a sheet pulled over Alan's head. No family could be contacted as yet. They took the lift down into the basement of the hospital and navigated windowless corridors to the mortuary. Given that the death was involved in a police investigation, an autopsy would be carried out. For now, the body would be put into storage.

The strange thing was, Alan heard the alarm signalling his death. It was as annoying as his year nine double English lessons. He felt them pull the intubation pipe from his throat. It hurt but he couldn't cry out because the sedation they'd administered was still in Alan's system. His heart had stopped for a short time at least, enough time for them to confirm his time of death and turn off the monitors. But Alan's heart started to beat once more, this time to a different rhythm.

The trolley juddered over the threshold of the mortuary. Alan's arm fell out. The porter hailed a colleague.

'Any fights tonight?'

The mortician laughed, a female whose body was slackening into the third decade of life. Alan could hear the pulse of life pumping through her veins in a healthy, succulent dadum. 'Just the usual spitters and biters, Kariem.'

'This guy will fit right in. Someone took a chunk out of his neck earlier tonight.' Kariem had a heavier gagung to his life, which stuttered at a regular interval—g-gagung. Alan's finger twitched unseen.

'Ouch! Do you want to put him at the far end?' The mortician scribbled on a form.

'Will do. Don't you ever get scared down here?' Kariem started to wheel Alan off again.

'The dead never cause me any problems. It's the living you've got to watch out for.'

Alan heard her chair move as she stood up. *Dadum, dadum, dadum.* His mouth watered, and his stomach grumbled. In the half-light of semi-consciousness, he dipped back into the dream of cannibalistic morning registration. He really wanted to get to the end of the roll call, but the class were so ravenous they kept tugging him to and fro as they pulled off strips of flesh, lapped at squirting arteries, and slurped at the gelatinous marrow in his thigh bone they'd snapped in two.

'Is that fiancé of yours causing you problems?' The trolley jolted to a halt, and Kariem used his toe to snap on the brakes to each wheel.

The mortician pulled on rubber gloves. Alan's eyelids fluttered beneath his shroud. 'He's not my fiancé anymore.'

'Sorry to hear that. He must be an idiot.'

'That's sweet of you, Kariem. But it was me who was the idiot. Late shifts and dead bodies do not a wife make.'

'Like you said. There's nothing wrong with the dead.'

God help me! thought Alan. *She's not interested in you, you moronic, overweight dullard.* Misha Stokes came to mind, and with teeth-grinding rage surging through Alan, he realised that *he* was Kariem. Though his extremities still felt numb, prickling with pins and needles, Alan balled the fist of the hand hanging over the edge of his trolley.

346

'Are you making fun of me?' the mortician snapped tersely.

Kariem was horrified. 'No. What do you mean?'

'If you just want to ask me out, just do it. You don't have to pull a prank.'

Kariem's heavy heart pounded in his chest. 'Seriously. What are you talking about? I—'

The sheet slipped from Alan's head as he sat up on the hospital trolley behind Kariem. The mortician, a woman of Pakistani heritage, was pointing at Alan, who quivered with incandescent rage. Kariem slowly turned around. Alan snarled but it came out more like a hoarse growl as he lunged for Kariem and seized him by the shoulders. The anaesthesia hadn't fully worn off, so as Alan bit into Kariem's neck, his legs gave way drunkenly. Kariem's head struck the mortuary lab table on the way down. Alan tore and drank ravenously at the porter's throat, who moaned in a daze.

The mortician came to Kariem's aid. She pulled at Alan, but he only had on a hospital gown, and her attempts were little more than annoying. As poor, concussed Kariem flapped weakly, Alan snapped at the mortician's tugging hands. His jaws bit clean through the tip of her index finger and half of her middle finger. She cried out holding the squirting geyser of her severed digits. A tray of metal instruments clattered to the ground. She twisted her ankle, slipping on a pair of forceps. Alan threw himself at her, stumbling and veering from Kariem's twitching body.

The mortician screamed and cowered beneath her bloodied hands. Alan beat at her with fists and stamped and clawed and finally, when he saw an opening, he sunk his jaws into the fleshy part of her exposed flank. She howled in pain and flapped at Alan's head. Her legs kicked spasmodically on the mortuary floor. Finding a scalpel nearby from the spilled tray, she stabbed it repeatedly into Alan's shoulder and head to no effect. In agony, she dropped the weapon and passed out. Alan tore open her abdomen with his bare hands and feasted on the endless strings of pulpy intestines.

But for the wet snuffling sounds of mastication, the mortuary fell silent. After a while, Alan blinked, feeling the tepid raw meat half chewed in his mouth. He spat it out and stared wide-eyed at the sausage-like viscera in his hands. Revolted, he dropped them and flung himself away from the body of the woman. Another body lay nearby in a pool of blood, and Alan remembered the orderly named Kariem. Why he knew his name, Alan couldn't quite remember, just as he couldn't quite remember how he got here, wearing a hospital gown, covered in blood. A bricolage of disjointed images, including morning registration with the year nine cannibals, stood in for his memories.

Somewhere between drunk and drugged, Alan got to his feet. The horror before him turned his stomach and he vomited. Blood gouted out, splashing his bare feet with pieces of raw, half-chewed meat. Appalled, uncomprehending, Alan reeled away through the double doors and down corridors. Feet slapping the cold floor, he staggered this way and that, mumbling piteously, mentally and physically groping for some bearing to navigate by. The bowels of the hospital were a labyrinth. What other Medusal horror might he find? A twitch spasmed in his neck, and Alan made that same dry cough and blundered around another corner. Lights flickered on from a motion sensor. Knock-kneed, one arm twitching, Alan craned up at the phosphorus strips through bleary eyes. He hated those lights with an intense, irrational passion and snarled.

Down the other end of the hall, a man in blue scrubs and the disshevelled hair from the fag end of a fourteen-hour shift came to a halt. His trainers squeaked when he looked up from the chart he was inspecting. Out of the corner of his eye, he spotted Alan and turned his head to take him in. It took a moment to register that a patient was out of place down there, and another moment for him to decipher that the dark stains on Alan's hands, face, and gown were blood —by which time it was altogether too late.

Alan roared and sprinted in his ungainly, disjointed gait down the corridor.

BACK IN THE PATHOLOGY LAB, Kariem jerked and opened his eyes. He dragged himself to his knees and put a hand to his neck. The mortician he fancied, called Sharnaz, was in a worse state than him. The colour had drained from her rosebud mouth. He rushed to her, fearing the worst, but then her arm moved, and she opened her eyes. She sat up and lifted up the tangle of intestines falling out of her abdomen, trying to make sense of it.

A lift door tinged and, beyond the double doors, someone was whistling. It was a piercing tune, a taunting, hateful thing. Together Kariem and Sharnaz grimaced furiously and coughed a dry bark. The double doors swung open, and another orderly with a dead patient stopped whistling.

'What the f—'

THE END...

MORE BOOKS BY THE AUTHOR

NEOLITHICA

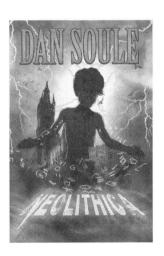

What happens when the archaeological find of a lifetime becomes a threat to life itself? After the death of her husband, Professor Mirin Hassan wants life to return to normal for her and her son. But when construction workers discover an ancient body in a Scottish peat bog, Mirin has no choice but to investigate the intricately tattooed Neolithic boy. Media attention and professional rivalries become the least of her worries because something other than cameras followed the corpse back to the university. Something beyond reason. Something evil. Something Mirin and the entire world will wish had stayed buried.

The must read horror of the year, Neolithica escalates to a shattering conclusion, in which the lives of a mother and son are intertwined with the fate of all humanity. A novel as epic in its vision as it is up close and personal with its frights. You won't want to miss this one.

WITCHOPPER

If you see her, then you're dead...

All Rob wanted to do was fit in at his new school after being torn from London so his parents could fix their marriage. But when Rob's journalist father dragged him along to investigate the legend of the Witchopper for the local paper, her curse became their reality.

She was priestess to the pagan god of the wild wood, hanged by a rabid mob for her unspeakable crimes. Now, something far worse than the hell of high school is after Rob and his dad...

In the vein of *The Wickerman* and *Midsommar*, *Witchopper* is an epic ordeal of a father and son relationship, where past sins echo in the present. Dan Soule delivers another terrifying Fright Night book, a story of love, lies and truth that will leave you sleeping with the light on. Available from Amazon.

THE ASH

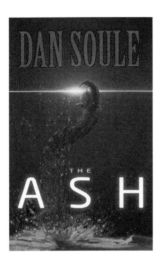

You know the drill: mushroom clouds, end of the world, only the clichés survive. This isn't that...

Even on the day of his divorce, Constable Jim Castle just wants to get back to his family, but no one can risk going outside. Not anymore. Worse still, when the fallout starts, Jim is hostage to a gang of armed thieves in a rundown farmhouse. Their plan is simple: wait it out as the radioactive ash piles higher and try not to kill each other. But they don't have to worry about any of that. Because all their assumptions about what caused the end of the world are about to be snatched away - like a body into the ash.

A blend of *The Road* meets *Alien* in the English countryside, *The Ash* is a breakneck horror ride. Another of Dan Soule's *Fright Night* tales, where even if one man can face his demons, it still might not be enough. So turn the page and get pulled screaming into... The Ash.

5 FREE BOOKS

NIGHT TERRORS

SWEET DREAMS AREN'T MADE OF THESE. If you love spine chilling horror, full of monsters and great characters, then Dan Soule's two anthologies of short fiction are the perfect introduction to one of the new talents in horror. Not only that but you also get three of the all time classics to keep you up at night.

Check out what some of the top editors of short horror fiction say about Dan. Paul Guernesy of The Ghost Story, said: "Dan is a cinematic writer... he steadily builds the mood of his narrative from a whisper of uneasiness to a crescendo of full-blown cosmic horror."

While Caitlin Marceau, editor Sanitarium Magazine commented, 'His stories aren't just guaranteed to scare you, they're guaranteed to devastate you.'

Join the growing horde of insomniacs who've said goodbye to sleep and hello to NIGHT TERRORS. Free from www.dansoule.com.

ACKNOWLEDGMENTS

This book was written during the global Covid-19 pandemic of 2020-21, amid the stresses of homeschooling and working from home. As such, this book wouldn't have been possibly without my wife, Jenny, and my children, Bronwyn and Owen, giving me the space and time to tap away at the keys. To them, as always, I owe the biggest thanks.

My editor Joe Sale was essential to bringing the story to publications. His guidance and feedback keeps me on track and makes me writing better. A big thanks also goes to Sherie O'Neil for her proofread. A number of beta-readers gave me invaluable feedback as well: Marie Murray, David Pearce, Billie Wichkan, and Doreen Fernandes, thank you one and all. You're the best. As a dyslexic writer, I am greatly indebted to all these wonderful folk.

COPYRIGHT